BROTHERS AND SISTERS OF BYLAND CRESCENT

An absolutely heartbreaking and unputdownable
historical family saga

BILL KITSON

The Cowgill Family Saga Book I

Originally published as *Requiem*

Revised edition 2021
Joffe Books, London
www.joffebooks.com

First published in Great Britain in 2018
as *Requiem*

Cover art by Jarmila Takač

ISBN: 978-1-80405-036-1

For Val
Wife, lover and best friend.

PART ONE: 1878–1898

'You may plant a field well;
But you know not who shall gather the fruits:
You may build a house well;
But you know not who shall dwell in it.'
Socrates
Memorabilia (Xenophon)

CHAPTER ONE

Albert Cowgill was in wool. Not only was he in wool, he was extremely successful in wool. By the tender age of twenty-three he had become a partner in one of the biggest wool merchants in Bradford; a major supplier to the West Riding woollen and worsted industries. Queen Victoria ruled an empire, and in Britain the industrial revolution was at its height. The textile industry was one of the powerhouses that fuelled the booming economy.

Ambition was Albert's spur, ambition which stemmed from fear. Fear of the poverty he had endured through childhood. Born to a weaver whose wife had produced eleven children in fifteen years, Albert had been one of only six who had lived to celebrate their second birthday.

His early experience had been of squalor in surroundings cramped beyond belief. Hovel is the best description of the cottage in which Albert was born. A rudimentary curtain, strung across the room in a vain attempt to create an illusion of privacy, divided the bedroom. Here, children were conceived, birthed, and, far too often, nursed through their final illness. Lacking proper medicines, diet, sanitation and living conditions, any number of highly contagious illnesses could prove fatal.

The downstairs room was as multi-functional as the bedroom, for in it, the daily tasks of cooking, eating, and living were conducted. There may have been no room to 'swing a cat' but that did not matter. If a weaver's pittance could not feed and house a family properly, a cat was a luxury they certainly could not afford.

Luck was with young Albert Cowgill. Luck, if it could be called thus, in that he was the eldest of the family. Luck, in that he grew and matured rapidly. Luck in that as he grew stronger he became determined to escape the environment that caused his younger siblings to die of one ailment or another.

Albert was a thinker and a planner. He was also very observant. Early on he saw that others did not live as he and his family lived. There was a better way. Albert resolved never to enter the weaving shed where his father toiled long and arduously for a pathetically small reward. This determination led to a confrontation with his father. Albert, at fourteen years old, calmly announced over the tea table that he had got a job.

'What sort of a job?' his father asked.

'I'm going to be a sorter,' Albert said quietly. There was an instant outcry. To Saul Cowgill it seemed dreadful that his son had taken this step. Weaving was a skilled job, but wool sorting was not only tedious, unskilled and backbreaking work, but it carried an element of risk into the bargain. Anthrax was not uncommon and, untreated, usually led to a painful and almost inevitable death.

Angrily the man and young boy faced each other, watched in fearful silence by Albert's mother, his brother, and sisters.

'Not bloody likely,' Saul roared. 'You'll go in t' shed same as me. Sortin's the worst job in Bradford, fit for nowt but scum.'

Albert withstood the attack calmly. 'I'm not going in that weaving shed, now or ever. And nowt you can say will make me.' His jaw jutted stubbornly as he spoke.

'And who's this outfit you're going sorting for?'

'Haigh and Ackroyd.' Albert named the biggest firm of importers and merchants in Bradford.

Saul was slightly mollified. 'They're about the best business in town. But it's nowt of a job, lad.'

'I know that,' Albert agreed. 'But I don't intend to stay a wool-sorter all my life. It's only a start. I mean to get to know every type of wool. That way, I'll be able to go for better jobs. Sorting will teach me enough to get those jobs, then I can move on.'

Saul realized the truth in what Albert had said. If he was to be any sort of success in the wool trade, and what else was there to do in Bradford, Albert would have to know the product better than those around him.

* * *

So, it proved to be. Day in, day out, he would touch and feel wool of all descriptions, along with fibres from other more exotic creatures. Mohair, cashmere, alpaca and the exquisitely silky vicuna all passed through Albert's hands, all added to his knowledge. He ate, drank, and slept wool. By the tender age of sixteen, he had risen to the rank of head sorter, his opinion sought by men three times his age.

Barely had his parents got used to him working as a sorter when, one Sunday afternoon, Albert shocked them once more. 'I'm quitting the sorting room.'

Saul glanced at the seventeen-year-old. 'What for?' he demanded suspiciously.

'I've been offered a job in the sample room as a snatcher.'

Saul spluttered with indignation. 'A sample-snatcher. That's no better than an errand boy.'

The argument that ensued made the row of three years ago seem like a minor skirmish.

* * *

Haigh and Ackroyd had been established twenty years ago. It was formed from the successful commercial union of two of the most respected figures in the industry. Each brought to the partnership a wealth of knowledge. Their talents complemented each other perfectly. If Edward Haigh was judged to be the best salesman ever to roll a sample, then Philip Ackroyd was deemed to be the shrewdest buyer in town. In addition, both had the ability to spot similar characteristics in others.

Thus, they gathered together the most formidable team of woolmen ever to grace the floor of the Bradford Wool Exchange, colloquially known as 'Change'; the imposing building where representatives from all sectors of the industry congregated twice weekly. Here, fortunes were made, doubled, trebled and sometimes lost on the strength of an agreed deal and that most binding of agreements, the handshake. As Edward Haigh often reminded his sales team, 'This is the best business in Bradford. That means it is the best in the world. It is your duty to ensure it remains so.'

The duties of sample-snatcher entailed collecting wool from warehouses in and around the city as each shipment arrived. These small sacks were taken back to the firm's offices and delivered to the head of the sample room for evaluation. Once he professed himself satisfied, the consignment would be allocated a type and lot number, then prepared for distribution to customers.

Brown paper was stamped and the impression completed with the company name, lot number, quantity, and price. A few ounces of wool were wrapped, sausage-shaped, and the ends tucked to secure it. Bundles of different lots would be put together ready for delivery, tied with a length of string secured with a slipknot and a loop fashioned into a carrying handle. Sometimes a sample-snatcher, leaving to deliver these, would have a dozen or more parcels, bearing the appearance of a badly trimmed Christmas tree.

Wool buyers all over the West Riding and further afield would receive samples in this manner. Without having to open them, they would simply be able to discard those that were of no interest by reading the description or the price. If interested, they would open the sample and check the contents for quality and fibre length. If the price was right, the following Monday or Thursday, on Change Day, when approached by a member of Haigh and Ackroyd's sales team, he would either accept or reject the lot, or alternatively, being a Yorkshireman, haggle over the price.

Albert had been snatching samples for over six months before his existence was noted by one of the partners. Edward Haigh was on Change talking to a buyer from a large worsted manufacturer. After exchanging a few titbits of trade gossip, the buyer made an odd comment.

'I'm not sure if you're desperate for business or adopting a new policy,' he stated.

Edward enquired as to the reason for the remark. The buyer laughed. 'We used to get our samples late on Wednesday or on Thursday. Recently they've arrived on Tuesday morning, or lunchtime at the latest.' He added that others had made similar comments.

Edward assured the buyer that there was nothing more sinister than a desire to offer the best level of service. Intrigued, he made other enquiries. The replies were of a similar vein. Everyone was getting samples earlier than previously. Edward left Change and strolled back up the hill towards their Manor Row offices with a smile on his face. Entering his office, he summoned the sample room head. He asked the man what had happened to bring about the improvement in their sample deliveries. That was when he learned about Albert. The man added that it was causing complications, as salesmen were complaining that they could have sold the same lots three or four times over. Masking his annoyance, Edward asked the man to compile a list of the lots in question and the customers they had been unable to satisfy.

The following morning, he met with Philip Ackroyd. 'The annoying part is we've missed the sale of more than three-thousand bales in the last four months.' He referred to the sample room head disparagingly, 'The man's an idiot. He told me this and even as he was talking, he failed to grasp the significance of what he was saying.'

Looking at the list, Ackroyd said thoughtfully, 'If I had known in time, I could have covered almost all these orders. We could have bought across town before the other merchants got off their backsides or even while the bales were still on the water. If they can sell the wool before the ship docks, they'll settle for a price that would give us a good margin. Now I know about it, I can get our agents to increase our purchasing on these lots. We could double our sales next season. You had better find out how that young man does it and make sure he continues doing it. If it's a fluke, we could end up with egg on our faces.'

* * *

Later that afternoon, Albert was summoned to Edward Haigh's office. He straightened his tie and smoothed his hair nervously before knocking on the oak door. On being bidden to enter, he did so with some trepidation.

Edward noted the boy's nervousness. 'Cowgill,' he said. 'I want to ask you a few questions.'

Half an hour later, Edward entered Ackroyd's office. 'Philip,' he told his partner, 'I think we have found a nugget.' He settled into one of the comfortable chairs and related the details of his interview with Cowgill. 'The boy followed instructions for the first few weeks until he had familiarized himself with the area and the customers. He soon noticed that he was delivering samples piece-meal, sometimes covering the same area three or four times, going back to mills that were virtually next door to one another. So, he ignored the old ways and used his own method. He calls it "territory planning".'

Philip Ackroyd looked puzzled. Edward continued, 'It's simple. He visits a different area each day, uses the tram as much as possible, and whereas it used to take the whole month to cover all our customers, he does it in less than two weeks. No wonder our sales are up. Because of young Cowgill, we're going to have to re-think our sales and purchasing strategy. Our salesmen have been surprised by clients asking for lot numbers they've never enquired about before. We didn't think they used them and they didn't think we stocked them, so they bought elsewhere.'

Before he turned eighteen Albert was no longer snatching samples; he was making them up as the sample-room junior. By the time he was able to cast his first vote he had progressed to the buying department; and from there to the sales staff. Albert showed great aptitude for all aspects of the business, but it was only when he went on the road that Edward Haigh and Philip Ackroyd began to appreciate the extent of his talent.

The successive promotions were reflected in the wages he received each Friday evening. The partners were liberal in their attitude to salaries. Believing they had the best employees, they paid the highest wages to retain them. Nowhere was the practice of poaching staff more prevalent than the textile industry, but other merchants were discouraged on learning how much it would cost to recruit someone from within the ranks of Haigh and Ackroyd.

So effective was this policy that Albert's first wage packet as a probationary salesman was five times greater than that earned from weaving by his father. Albert spent little of what he received, as determined in the matter of saving money as he was in earning it. The housekeeping money he gave to his mother apart, almost all went into Albert's bank account. His frugal lifestyle enabled him to present his parents with the money to buy a more comfortable home. The house was a large terraced property in a good area. Here they were surrounded by luxury beyond their wildest imaginings. Their neighbours too were of a different caste, mill managers, wool buyers, yarn agents, and the like. This move up the social scale had them dizzy with a strange mixture of excited apprehension.

To Albert the new home represented his first solid achievement, but it was merely the first rung on a long ladder. So single-minded was he that none of the usual attractions that lie in wait for young men with money in their pockets tempted him. To say that his social life was limited would be a wild exaggeration — it was non-existent. Not that Albert was disinterested in such matters, but they did not fit into his scheme of things.

All that was to change when Albert had been in Haigh and Ackroyd's salesroom for little more than six months.

* * *

The successful partners had invested in substantial properties to signal their position in West Riding society. Edward Haigh bought a huge house on the outskirts of Bingley. At about the same time Philip Ackroyd acquired an equally palatial home overlooking the River Aire at Rawdon. The extensive grounds kept two gardeners in fulltime employment.

From this luxurious home, Mrs Ellen Ackroyd would venture forth each Saturday into Bradford on a shopping expedition with her four daughters. Not for provisions, the respective tradesmen delivered these, but for those small luxuries Victorian ladies deemed essential. So exhausting were these forays that the ladies would seek refreshment at *Collinsons Cafe*. There a quartet of musicians serenaded the diners, to the accompaniment of the tinkle of fine china as cup was placed carefully on saucer, or knife positioned precisely on plate. Here, with the ambience enhanced by the aroma of freshly ground coffee, gossip would be exchanged such as to make the purchase of a newspaper redundant.

On one such outing however, matters did not run as smoothly as planned. Shopping had proved more expensive than Ellen Ackroyd anticipated. She surveyed the meagre contents of her purse ruefully. 'There's nothing for it,' she told her daughters, 'we shall have to go to Father's office to get some money. I only hope he hasn't gone out.'

It was lunchtime when they arrived and the empty chambers echoed to their footsteps. Mrs Ackroyd pressed the bell by the enquiry window and waited. After a few moments, the frosted glass screen was drawn aside, revealing a pleasant faced, serious young man.

'Is Mr Ackroyd available?' Ellen enquired.

'I'm very sorry, madam,' the young man replied hesitatingly. 'Mr Ackroyd is out.'

Ellen Ackroyd smiled knowingly. 'Then I expect that he's gone to watch cricket at Park Avenue.'

'Er, yes, I think he did mention something about cricket.'

'I'm Mrs Ackroyd, Mr Philip's wife, and these are my daughters.' She introduced the four girls and in turn the young man identified himself as Albert Cowgill. As he spoke, he saw Hannah Ackroyd for the first time. His eyes met those of Hannah, nineteen years old, the Ackroyd's eldest daughter. She was slim, pretty, and infinitely wholesome. Hannah blushed under Albert's gaze but returned it nonetheless. If love at first sight exists, they were both stricken on the spot.

'I'm afraid we've had a very expensive morning and wanted to get some money from Mr Ackroyd to complete our shopping, but as he is not here, we will have to await his return,' Ellen admitted.

'I'm sure that will not be necessary,' Albert replied, pink faced and stuttering under Hannah's close scrutiny.

He pulled out his wallet and completed the loan to Ellen, ignoring her protestations. After they left, he stood for a long time at the open enquiry window, his thoughts in a daze. Even when he returned to the salesroom, it was many minutes before he picked up his pen to complete the half-written order form. When he returned home that afternoon and for the rest of the weekend, Albert's mother found him listless, distracted, and inattentive. She worried that he might be sickening for something.

CHAPTER TWO

Monday saw Albert back to normal. A hectic day visiting clients resulted in several substantial orders. He returned to the office late in the afternoon to be greeted by the office boy, who had obviously been detailed to keep a watching brief for him. 'Mr Philip wants to see you in his office as soon as possible.'

Albert thanked the boy and put down his sample case in the corner of the room. He hurried through to the partner's suite at the end of the long, oak-panelled corridor.

Traditionally, the most junior salesman was given the least productive accounts, small manufacturers, whose requirement might be less than one hundred bales each year. Alternatively, they would have companies using the more esoteric fibres, where demand was lower, and one or two of the 'difficult' customers. The object of this was two-fold. It tested the mettle of the salesman giving him chance to prove his worth or otherwise, and it avoided the risk that an inexperienced salesman might lose the sales and goodwill of the more valued clients.

When the partners held their quarterly performance review it came as a surprise to find that Albert was keeping pace with his more experienced colleagues. It was time for action. Normally this would have fallen to Edward Haigh, but Ackroyd had other matters to discuss with Albert.

Albert knocked on the oak door and was beckoned, 'Enter.'

The partner motioned to him to take a seat and the younger man waited until Ackroyd looked up. 'Sorry to keep you waiting, Albert, but I had to get that finished.'

If the unaccustomed use of his Christian name surprised Cowgill, he concealed it well.

'I needed to speak to you on a few matters,' Ackroyd continued. 'Hopefully, I will not detain you too long. I expect you have lots of orders to write up?'

Albert cautiously admitted there were a few. Ackroyd smiled. In other industries the statement 'just a few' would have been taken at face value. In Bradford terminology however, Ackroyd interpreted it to convey that Cowgill had enjoyed a very successful day.

'I am glad about that,' — Ackroyd smiled — 'because that is one of the reasons I wanted this talk with you. We have been reviewing the last quarter's sales figures.' He paused for a second, watching Cowgill carefully. Although Albert's face was expressionless, Ackroyd noted that every line of his body had tautened. Ackroyd continued, 'Normally Mr Haigh would have conducted this interview, but I decided we should talk them through together.' He paused again, observing that Cowgill was, if anything, even more apprehensive. Although by no means a sadist, he could not resist the temptation to tease the junior salesman. 'One thing we found,' he went on, 'is that you seem to be causing quite a lot of additional expense to the firm.'

Albert's face took on a worried frown. Ackroyd grinned. 'Yes, we have had to increase our stationery budget to cope with the additional order forms, invoices, and statements you have generated. And that is to say nothing of the extra ledger sheets for the new clients you have gained.'

A nervous smile of relief crossed Cowgill's face before it resumed its habitually bland expression.

'In view of the level of sales you have achieved and the new accounts you have opened we have decided to suspend your probationary period. Normally, this would last twelve months, but we intend to ratify your appointment immediately.'

He saw Albert was about to speak and held up a hand to silence him. 'Before you start to think of this as some altruistic gesture I must tell you it is from pure self-interest. We appreciate you still have a lot to learn, but we consider you to have exhibited all the talents we require. Furthermore, we do not wish to invest more time, energy, and money training you only to have someone else reap the benefit of our investment.' Ackroyd paused and raised his eyebrows, inviting a response from Cowgill.

'Thank you, Mr Philip,' Albert replied bluntly. 'I will not let you down, sir, and I will not allow anyone to poach me either.'

Ackroyd gave a smile of satisfaction before resuming. 'From now on you will be placed on our intermediate sales staff pay grade. This will be reviewed every six months.' This was, in itself, sensational. Not only was Albert's probationary period being curtailed, but also his salary had been raised by not one, but two increments into the bargain.

'That suit you?' Ackroyd added dryly.

Albert's reply was a disjointed jumble of thanks.

'Now, to other matters.' Ackroyd reached into his coat pocket and tugged his notecase out. 'I am in your debt, both figuratively and literally. Thank you for assisting Mrs Ackroyd on Saturday. I gather you didn't give the game away as to my whereabouts.'

'She guessed before I had chance to lie,' he admitted.

'They always do,' Ackroyd said a trifle mordantly. 'Nevertheless, I know how grateful she is, as am I for that matter.'

Albert muttered that it was nothing, the least he could have done.

'Be that as it may, it was much appreciated. So much so, that we are holding a garden party at home next Saturday and Mrs Ackroyd and the girls have asked me to invite you, if you are free.'

As the import of his employer's words sank home, a vision of the delectable Hannah swam before Albert's eyes. He managed to stammer out enough to indicate that he was indeed free, that he would be delighted to attend, and to convey his gratitude for the invitation.

'Right. Three o'clock on Saturday afternoon.' Ackroyd signified the end of the meeting.

If Cowgill's footsteps were inaudible as he returned to the sales room, it was probably because he was floating rather than walking.

* * *

The following Saturday was bright, hot, and sunny. The garden party was a great success. For Albert, his escalating feelings for Hannah already consuming much of his thinking, the event and its surroundings were an eye-opener.

Late in the afternoon as he strolled through the more remote reaches of the grounds with Hannah, Albert confessed his ambition to her. 'One day,' he stated boldly, 'I mean to have something like this.' He gestured to the house and gardens.

'How will you go about acquiring it?' Hannah enquired shrewdly.

'I intend to become head of the biggest company in the wool trade and thus the most important man in the industry,' Albert told her. 'But what of you? What do you want from life?'

Hannah smiled. 'I want something like this too.'

'And how will you go about getting it?' Albert asked, half teasingly.

Hannah's smile deepened, sending shivers of excitement up and down Albert's spine. 'Oh, probably by marrying the most important man in the wool trade.'

They were ideally matched.

Philip and Ellen Ackroyd soon became aware that their eldest daughter had formed a distinct liking for his employee. The burgeoning relationship with Hannah did nothing to distract Albert from his work. If anything, it reinforced the energy with which he went about it. If he had been an able salesman beforehand, the broadening of his social horizons enabled him to talk to clients with a newfound confidence. This, albeit subconsciously, transferred itself to the buyers he encountered daily. Probably without realizing the gradual change in Albert, they were nonetheless aware that this was a young man approaching the peak of his profession.

* * *

A little less than a year later, Albert attended Philip and Ellen Ackroyd's anniversary party. Normally a quiet family affair, this occasion marked twenty years of marriage and was much grander. A string quartet had been hired to entertain guests and an area created for dancing. After several hectic excursions round the floor, Albert was a little breathless, aware that the dress shirt he was wearing was becoming a little tight. 'How about a breath of fresh air?' he suggested to Hannah.

Hannah laid her hand on Albert's arm and leaving the house through the French windows they strolled along the terrace, then veered down a small path leading through the shrubbery and sat on a bench in a secluded arbour. The night sky was clear, moonless, and the stars shone brightly. Albert took Hannah's hand in his and held it, feeling a throbbing pulse, unaware if it was his own or hers. 'Hannah,' he said gently.

She looked into his eyes. She guessed what was coming before he got down on one knee. 'Hannah, I want to ask you, er, I mean would you ever think of, er, that is, will you marry me?' The words were a disjointed jumble, the tone a strangled croak.

Albert, aghast at his own temerity, trembled on her response. Hannah gently pulled him on to the seat beside her, took his unresisting hand and placed it round her waist.

Albert's pulses raced as she lifted her face to his and they kissed. The kiss was long, gentle at first, increasingly fierce as their passion took control. Eventually they paused and Hannah whispered, 'Yes, Albert my dearest.'

After a certain amount of hesitation, the news of their engagement received the blessing of both sets of parents. Before adding her sanction, Ellen Ackroyd sought reassurance from her husband regarding her prospective son-in-law's prospects. Philip Ackroyd was equally protective of his daughter, but knew Cowgill to be a solid, worthy and reliable young man who was going to the very top of his profession.

In the case of Albert's parents, it was more like a non-swimmer floundering out of his depth. Wary of the enormous social divide between a weaver's family and that of a successful businessman, their first meeting with Hannah and her parents went a long way towards putting them at their ease.

* * *

It was a warm spring day in 1878 when Saul and Esther Cowgill entered Bradford Cathedral for the first time in their lives. An hour later they watched from their vantage point in a pew at the front of the magnificent building, as another Mr and Mrs Cowgill made their way down the aisle, followed by their retinue of bridesmaids, ushers, and pageboys. The feelings of the elder Mr and Mrs Cowgill were a mixture of pride, awe, and wonder. There were tears of course, tears of sorrow, pride, and happiness, from the female members of both families. Plus, some onlookers who cried merely because it was the done thing. But then it would have been a poor sort of a wedding if almost every female present didn't turn herself into a watering can to do justice to the occasion.

There were more tears at the ensuing reception. This time they were in Albert's eyes as he held the wedding present he had that moment been given by Edward Haigh and Philip Ackroyd. It was a deed of partnership, stating that henceforth the firm would be restyled Haigh, Ackroyd & Cowgill.

CHAPTER THREE

If Albert was ambitious, then so was Hannah. It was ambition that had seen them sell their house, in Ben Rhydding on the outskirts of Ilkley, to buy a newly built, luxurious property in Byland Crescent, Scarborough. Their intention; to take advantage of the clean, fresh sea air so much at contrast with the heavily polluted atmosphere of the mill towns of the West Riding. Albert would commute daily via the trains travelling to and from the West Riding from both Scarborough and the equally popular west coast resort of Morecambe. So full were these 'residents' trains, nicknamed 'the resi', of textile magnates that many business transactions were concluded in their well-appointed carriages, to the background music of the clatter of wheels over lines and points, as the powerful locomotives drew them towards the grimy, soot-blackened buildings of the mill towns.

The Cowgills took possession of the keys to Number 1, Byland Crescent and moved in two weeks before Easter of 1897, almost nineteen years to the day after their wedding in 1878.

As he journeyed to Bradford on the resi for the first time, Albert dwelt on all that had happened in the intervening years.

17

The death of Edward Haigh early in 1883, following a bout of pneumonia, had come as a great shock to the whole firm. So upset had Philip Ackroyd been by the death of his great friend and partner that he had asked Albert to take control of much of the legal and financial work, including the settlement to Edward's widow.

At the time of Haigh's death, Albert and Hannah had been living in a cottage located towards the centre of Idle village, on the outskirts of Bradford. Here they had taken up residence on their return from honeymoon in Scarborough. Their love for each other was complemented by their love of the seaside resort. Scarborough was at its fairest when they visited it; the weather was warm and sunny, with just the zephyr of a breeze to prevent it becoming uncomfortably hot.

It was in the main bedroom of the cottage, little more than a year after their marriage, that Albert and Hannah's first child was born. James Philip Cowgill made his entrance to the world at a satisfying 6lbs 12ozs and announced his happiness on arrival with a series of bloodcurdling screams. These made the attendant doctor and midwife smile with satisfaction at the obvious healthiness of the infant's lungs. None present at the birth paused to consider the likely discomfort the child's parents would endure from the same source during teething.

When James was approaching his third birthday, Constance Ellen arrived on the scene. Connie, as she was known from the moment her parents decided on her names, weighed only marginally less than her elder brother at birth. She was however, noticeably quieter.

Soon after Connie was born, and with the likelihood of further additions to their tally of offspring, Albert and Hannah decided to look for larger accommodation. A series of family outings ensued, by the end of which the Cowgills had decided on the area, if not the house, where they wished to continue and add to their family life.

The pretty little Wharfedale town of Ilkley and its even smaller near-suburb of Ben Rhydding stand four-square on the banks of the River Wharfe. One look up the dale towards Skipton and beyond to where the mighty Pennine hills stand watch against the coming of the enemy, those sporting the red rose of Lancashire, and Albert and Hannah were convinced that this was the place for them.

They completed the purchase of a fine house overlooking the Wharfe, on the edge of Ben Rhydding nearest to Burley and Otley. So protracted was the process that it was early in 1885 before the family swapped Airedale for Wharfedale.

Soon after the move, James and Connie were joined by their sister Ada Mary and later, Cissie Louise. After a short pause the family unit was completed by the birth of Mark Albert, known, for whatever obscure reason, as were so many youngest sons of West Riding families, as 'Sonny'.

By then, James, rising thirteen, was a boarder at Forest Manor Boys School, while Connie, three years his junior, was in her second term at Princess Caroline's School for Young Ladies, situated on the outskirts of Harrogate. That most exclusive of towns was Albert and Hannah's first experience of the North Riding of their home county.

The increasing size of their family meant they had again outgrown their accommodation, so Albert and Hannah decided to move once more.

The slowing of the train roused Albert from his reverie. He noticed they were pulling into Leeds New Station. He would need to alight and cross to Leeds Wellington to change trains. Once that operation was complete and he was settled in the comfort of his pre-booked first-class compartment, Albert returned to his reminiscences.

The years had been kind to the firm of Haigh, Ackroyd and Cowgill. The partnership, known almost universally as HAC, sometimes unkindly as 'Haggle & Cajole' had prospered. The sure touch and experience of Philip Ackroyd, coupled with the flair and enthusiasm of Albert Cowgill had ensured that prosperity. Whereas most merchants and manufacturers had been prepared for an anticipated glut of wool during the latter part of the 1880s, Philip and Albert had taken the opposite view. They had gambled heavily on their opinion, and it had paid off in a huge way. Shortages of supply had been coupled with increased demand, heightened by changes in fashion. Raw wool prices had doubled, even trebled for some types, within a space of two years. With warehouses across Bradford bulging at the seams and a dearth of alternative sources of supply, the firm had made immense profits. The effect did not stop there. As manufacturers were reaching the hair-tearing stage in the search for raw material, they soon learned the only place to turn with any hope of success was HAC. New clients were added to the ledger sheets in their Manor Row offices almost weekly.

As the firm went from strength to strength and the fortunes of their rivals dwindled, HAC's power in the marketplace became unassailable. Buying agents at wool sales in Geelong or Invercargill, Port Elizabeth or Buenos Aires would find theirs to be a hopeless task once HAC's representatives raised a finger to bid. With firm orders from across the West Riding, from Scotland and elsewhere to back them, it was by no means uncommon for HAC to take every lot in a sale catalogue, sometimes amounting to as many as 30,000 bales.

Following Edward Haigh's death, his son Michael joined the company. Blessed with his late father's business acumen and enough drive, determination and enthusiasm to rival Albert himself, Michael had served his apprenticeship in the Manor Row sample room. Watched over by both partners, neither of whom was prepared to grant him any leeway despite his family connections, he soon proved himself to be capable, quick, and accurate in his work.

They decided he would benefit from a tour of their supply sources. A five-year plan was implemented, with Michael spending a year in South America, then a year in South Africa, followed by eighteen months each in New Zealand and Australia. Following that the tacit understanding was that the young man would, on his return to Manor Row, start to learn the sales aspect of the business under the expert tutelage of Albert Cowgill. Planning had always played a major part in the firm's success. Leaving matters to chance, allowing events to take their natural course, was not a considered option.

Michael Haigh returned to England a week after Sonny was born. Before returning to work, he spent a quiet holiday with his mother and sisters at the holiday home purchased when her period of mourning had expired. The place chosen was select rather than fashionable at Grange-Over-Sands. Looking south from the Cumbrian peninsular across Morecambe Bay; a backwater, a haven of quiet in a busy world. An idyllic place for a restful break.

When he had settled in back at Manor Row, Michael soon demonstrated that the partners' opinion of him had not been misplaced.

Philip Ackroyd called Albert into his office one Monday afternoon, on their return from Change. He gestured his son-in-law to sit down and perched on the corner of the desk. 'Ellen and I have been thinking of taking life easier and we've made a decision. Actually, we've made a few decisions. We're going to sell the Rawdon house. Well, to be accurate we've already sold it. From now on I'm only coming to Bradford twice a week, on Change days. You and Michael are quite capable of running the business without me having to be here every day.'

'Where are you planning to live?' Albert asked him.

'We've bought a new property in Scarborough.' He reached into his desk drawer and pulled out a builder's prospectus.

Albert had read aloud from the brochure. '"An exclusive development of gentlemen's residences, close to the south cliff in Scarborough. Weaponness Park is the ideal retreat for those wishing to escape the rigours of town life and enjoy the many delights of this most elegant of seaside spa resorts.'"

He looked up at Philip, who grinned. 'It's also ten minutes from the cricket ground and although at present the nearest golf course is out at Ganton, there's a lot of talk about opening another one nearer to town.'

Albert smiled at the memory as the train slowed and Market Street station loomed large in the window. There was time for Albert to stretch, put on his hat and topcoat before alighting to walk up the steep slope of Cheapside towards Manor Row.

* * *

Over the past two months, Albert had learned that several of the most important woollen manufacturers in the West Riding had been negotiating with the French and Belgian governments for the supply of military uniform cloth. In addition, two of the major worsted manufacturers in Huddersfield had been bidding for export contracts to the United States of America, rapidly emerging as a major market force.

During the last few days these orders had been ratified. As a consequence, when HAC's salesmen had visited the clients involved, they appeared, in the local parlance, 'to have put their buying boots on'.

Leading the pack as far as sales figures were concerned was Michael Haigh, another fact that pleased Albert intensely. Earmarked for a partnership in the near future as much for his ability as any family influence it was, nevertheless, gratifying to have that judgement endorsed.

It was with a pleasant sense of wellbeing, brought about by one of the most successful days trading, even for HAC, that Albert had taken the opportunity to leave the office early. A brisk walk across John Street to the corner of White Abbey Road, thence onto Lumb Lane, soon brought him to Peel Square. His parents still lived at No. 56, the house he had bought for them over twenty years earlier.

Saul and Esther Cowgill were nearer seventy than sixty years old and the years of poverty, hardship and poor diet had taken their toll. Admittedly, they had been comfortable in the latter stages of life, due in no small measure to the ample monthly allowance from Albert. However, the earlier privations had taken an irredeemable toll. Both were bent with arthritis and Albert's mother's hands, from year upon year, day in, day out, were rarely dry from one minute to the next, would never be able to hold a teacup in the 'polite' manner again. So misshapen were her fingers, so gnarled the joints and knuckles that she could barely manage with her hands in the closed position.

Albert's father had legs so bowed he appeared to be permanently riding an invisible horse. To quote the local wisecrack, 'he couldn't stop a pig in a passage.' A lifetime spent in close proximity to fibres containing minute and invisible specks of dust had left him with a wheezy, asthmatic cough that, once started, never seemed to finish.

All that was behind him now, as was the need for Esther to launder anyone's clothing but their own. If 'taking in washing' had become some sort of music hall joke for some, to many poorer housewives it was part of that all too grim reality — daily life.

Despite their ailments, they greeted their eldest son with great good humour, mixed with admiration, almost reverence, generated by his continuing and increasing success. After enquiring about Hannah, they plied Albert with a host of questions about the health and progress of their beloved grandchildren. Their only regret, as Saul told his son, was that the move to Scarborough having been completed, they would be able to see the 'little 'uns' less frequently.

'Not so little now,' Albert had chuckled. 'As for you seeing less of them, Hannah has come up with a plan to take care of that.

'One of the houses close to us, at the other end of the crescent to be exact, has been opened as a guest house. That's a sort of hotel, but without all the fancy trimmings. Scarborough has become so popular and so many visitors want to take their holidays there that these establishments are springing up all over the place. Hannah has got to know the couple who are running the house and they seem very decent. Our idea is that you should come across during the summer when the children have finished school and spend a few weeks there. Unfortunately, the decorators will not have finished the guest rooms at number one by then; otherwise, you would be staying with us. And don't worry about the cost, I'll see to that.' Albert grinned. 'After a few more days like today I could book you into the Grand Hotel for a year.'

Saul was intrigued. 'Business going well then?' he enquired.

'Fair to middling,' Albert replied, his grin failing to dilute his answer. 'The orders are coming in nicely. We are hopeful for a successful year, but you know how uncertain things can be in the wool trade.'

Saul nodded. 'Any more surprises?' he asked; keen as ever to hear of his son's endeavours.

Albert grinned once more. 'Keep this one under your hat, but Philip and I have just signed a contract to buy one of the biggest scouring plants in Bradford. It will be renamed as A and C Scouring; otherwise, Ackroyd and Cowgill. We reckon that with the amount of commission we have been paying out to other scourers we'll get our money back in two years. The other advantage is that we won't have to wait to have our wool processed, because that has been a stumbling block. Sometimes we miss out on orders because we have to book time at the scouring plant, and if they have a big job on for someone else by the time, we get our work done it's too late. Obviously, other merchants will fight shy of sending their work to us, in case we find out who they are selling to. That doesn't worry us because we have more than enough work to keep the plant running day and night all year round, without accepting commissions, and if it is all being done in-house it protects our confidentiality. Also, our margins will be better, because all we have to do is protect the overheads; the rest will be clear profit. This will be useful when trade slackens and margins get tighter.'

Albert's father looked stunned as he tried to assimilate the news. 'Where is the plant?' was his first question.

'Preston Street. Between Thornton Road and Listerhills.'

Saul pondered. 'I know it. That's a bloody big outfit. From what I hear it isn't being managed very well though.'

'We know that,' Albert reassured him. 'The first thing we're going to do is clear out all the dead wood from the old management. Philip is going to take charge of it, to start with at any rate. I think this has done him the world of good. I can't remember him being so excited about anything for a long time. He is going to need a good deputy though, someone we can rely on to have our interests at heart, and someone we can trust to take complete control in the long term.' Albert paused and looked at his father, studiously.

'Have you anyone in mind for the job?'

'We were talking it over at the weekend and quite a few names came up, but Philip wondered if Ernest would be interested.'

'Our Ernest?' his father asked in surprise.

Albert nodded. 'He's got experience in processing and management. I know for a fact the top brass would be sorry to lose him.'

Albert's younger brother, Ernest Cowgill, possibly inspired by Albert's own success, had gone from weaver to day shift manager at a renowned manufacturing mill.

Saul eyed his son keenly. 'You want me to have a word with him, don't you?'

Albert confessed that the idea had crossed his mind. His father pondered the matter. 'I don't think he will take much persuading,' he confided. 'Apart from the challenge of the job and the chance to eventually take charge, he has always looked up to you. I think he would jump at the chance.'

'It isn't charity,' Albert hastened to explain. 'Ernest is doing very well for himself where he is. Philip and I are merchants, pure and simple. We have no experience in wool processing, or of running a mill day in, day out. We need Ernest, or someone like him. Someone with practical skills who can foresee problems before they arise and avoid them. If we tried to run it, sooner or later we would find ourselves chasing our own tails, mending fences as we go.'

The remainder of Albert's stay was spent updating the fond grandparents of the health and careers of their two grandsons and three granddaughters and enquiring into the wellbeing of Albert's four sisters.

CHAPTER FOUR

Almost before Albert realized it, the train had pulled into Leeds station and it was time for him to alight. There was a fifteen-minute delay during which he changed stations and spent time meandering through the concourse and out onto the chilly, wind-swept platform. He boarded the train as soon as it arrived, glad to be out of the cold draught. He settled into his seat and contemplated what would await him when he returned to Byland Crescent.

Albert's marriage to Hannah had done much to change his character. Her influence had enabled him to shake free from his inherent caution. Never indecisive, his was now a more rounded and mature character than would have seemed possible twenty years earlier. It reflected at work and also at home, where Albert had, without conscious effort, agreed the appointment of a large household staff. As the train galloped across the miles between York and Kirkham Abbey Gorge, Albert pondered what news Hannah might have to impart in respect of her day's endeavours. It would have been a full and busy one, of that Albert was already aware, for it was the day she had set aside for interviewing applicants chosen in response to their advertisement for domestic staff.

One role had already been filled, that of Hannah's own personal maid. How she would adapt to the change caused Albert a little amused speculation. Her duties revolved around the care and wellbeing of her mistress and in this she had, or considered herself to have, complete autonomy. In the new arrangement, this would change and she would be answerable to the butler as well as to her mistress.

Albert and Hannah had never come closer to a disagreement than over the decision to appoint a butler. 'We don't need one,' Hannah protested.

'You already have your maid; soon you will have a cook, two housemaids, a scullery maid, laundry maid and a general factotum. Your father has a butler, allow me one luxury,' he countered.

'Can we afford one?' Hannah wanted to know.

Albert grinned. 'I think so. A couple of weeks ago I did a few calculations. The firm's being doing very well these last few years, so I thought it would be useful to work out exactly what we are worth.' He quoted a figure.

Her genteel upbringing forbade Hannah from whistling in astonishment. There was no further argument.

* * *

Although Albert was anxious to discover how Hannah had fared recruiting servants, she was in no rush to share the details with her husband, opting to wait until their dinner was over.

'That was an excellent meal,' Albert remarked over their dessert. 'Truly remarkable given the hours you have spent interviewing staff. I must say you surpassed yourself.'

Hannah merely gave a secretive and slightly mischievous smile.

Once they had bidden the children goodnight, they retired to the sitting room for coffee. 'So, tell me,' Albert demanded. 'How did you get on?'

Hannah's initial response was a little oblique. 'I am so glad you enjoyed your dinner this evening, darling,' she told him. 'It puts the finishing touch to the day.'

She paused for a second, teasing him, watching the puzzled expression on his face before continuing. 'I would be more than happy to accept the plaudits, but the credit doesn't rest with me. You must thank Mrs Dallas for that.'

'Who,' Albert enquired in some astonishment, 'is Mrs Dallas?'

'Mrs Dallas' — Hannah replied, the smile broadening into a wicked grin — 'is our new cook.' She paused again to allow the import of her words to sink in. 'Well, you did request a trial before confirming her appointment so I thought it would be the ideal opportunity to try out her skills.'

It was some moments before Albert recovered from the shock. 'Well,' he confessed, 'you certainly struck gold there. If the rest of the staff you chose match up we shall be very comfortable.'

'Would you care to meet her?'

Mrs Olive Dallas was not a bit like the mental picture Albert had already formed of her. Whereas he had envisaged a plump, matronly woman in her late middle-age, Olive turned out to be only marginally the wrong side of forty and, although not slender her figure could certainly not be described as matronly. She looked, in fact, as if she would have been more at home in their drawing room than the kitchen, especially as she had discarded her apron for the interview. She was good-looking, with softly waving light brown hair framing an attractive face. During their brief conversation, Albert learned that she had been married, briefly, to a serving officer in the army, who had perished tragically in a training accident. Prior to her marriage, she had been educated in Paris, where her father had been a junior diplomat. She had excelled in domestic science and in particular the culinary art, a fact that, as she told Albert and Hannah, had amazed and intrigued her tutors whose opinion of English cookery was disparaging in the extreme. Both her parents were dead, and when she had been widowed, she was without income and had been forced to resort to the best skill she possessed in order to earn a living. Not, as she assured her new employers, that she considered cooking to be a chore, for her it was an enjoyable pastime and being paid for it was a bonus.

When she had returned to the kitchen Albert turned to Hannah, his expression one of awe. 'Did I say gold?' he enquired rhetorically. 'I should have said diamond.'

Hannah was seated on one of the large sofas in the drawing room. She reached behind her and picked up a small pile of papers from the oblong table adjacent to the sofa. 'Let me tell you the rest,' she said, arranging the sheets into order.

'I have hired a butler, two housemaids, and a laundry maid. Tomorrow I have to see three women who have applied for the post of scullery maid and Mrs Dallas is going to sit in on those interviews with me. There are also two young men who are seeking work as general factotum. I am hopeful our new butler will join me for those sessions.'

'Tell me about the butler,' Albert prompted.

'His name is Henry Burgess.' Hannah glanced at the top sheet of paper on her knee. 'He is forty-seven-years old and was butler to old Lord Hackness until six months ago.'

'Hackness, the one who . . . ?' Albert's voice trailed off.

'That's right, he's the one, or rather was the one. He lost all his money in a disastrous speculation in tin mines in South America and when bankruptcy threatened, he jumped from Valley Bridge. The estate was divided up and sold to meet his creditors and Henry found himself unemployed. As his previous employer was obviously unable to provide a reference, he has had difficulty securing another post. However, I found him to be open, pleasant and, I believe, honest. He is a church-going Methodist and a member of the Temperance Society.'

Albert winced.

'It's all right, he doesn't mind others drinking.' Hannah laughed. 'And at least you won't have to worry that he might attack your favourite port. I was very impressed with him. He has a quiet dignity about him and was by far the best of those I interviewed.'

Albert nodded his approval. 'I'm happy to go along with your instinct, Hannah. I've always known your judgement of people was excellent, like your father's.'

Hannah smiled and continued. 'Two of the girls I interviewed will do very nicely as housemaids.' She looked at the notes she had made. 'Sarah is a twenty-three-year-old local girl, from the Old Town and is engaged to a fisherman. She works as a chambermaid at the Grand Hotel but is anxious to improve herself. The other girl is an eighteen-year-old called Alice who is also a chambermaid at the Grand. She's an orphan and a foundling, from Harrogate of all places. When she was fourteen, she was sent to the Grand as a junior laundry maid, but has worked her way up to chambermaid. She's lively, quick and intelligent and very neat in her appearance. I've also hired a laundry maid.' Hannah consulted her notes once more.

'Don't tell me, she's another one from the Grand Hotel,' Albert laughed.

Hannah gave him a look of withering scorn. 'No,' she replied with some hauteur, 'she works at the St Nicholas Hotel. Of course,' she added, 'if you had wanted me to select only members of the Grand Hotel staff you should have informed me.'

'No, no, I'll be happy whoever you choose,' Albert hastened to reassure her.

'She comes from a farming family who live near Snainton and has worked at the St Nicholas for about three years. If her appearance is anything to go by, the family laundry will be in safe hands. As for the rest,' she ended, 'we will have to see what tomorrow brings.'

'That all seems to be most satisfactory,' Albert commented. 'I think you have done marvellously well.' He sighed with satisfaction. 'That roast beef really was delicious.'

* * *

The following evening, having made his way from the station, Albert was somewhat surprised as he climbed the steps to his home when the door swung open before him. A tall figure dressed in black held it open for Albert to enter the hall. 'Good evening, sir.' the man greeted him. 'I am Henry, your new butler.' he gave a slight inclination of his head, at the same time deftly removing Albert's hat from his hand. 'May I take your coat, sir?'

'Good evening, Henry,' Albert replied, recovering from his initial shock. 'I'm pleased to meet you. I hope you will be very happy here.'

The man beamed. 'I'm sure I shall, sir. Madam and the children are awaiting you in the drawing room. May I fetch you a drink before you change for dinner, sir, or would you prefer to wait until afterwards.'

Albert thanked Henry but declined the drink, then hurried across the hall to the drawing room. He paused on the threshold, looking with pleasure at the family scene before him. Hannah was seated on her favourite sofa, a magazine spread open on her lap. Ada and Cissie were on either side of her. The grouping emphasised the different appearances of his daughters. Ada was dark haired and slightly chubby, favouring her father in appearance, while Cissie had all her mother's blonde prettiness, her near-white hair framing her pale complexioned face, in stark contrast to the blush of colour in her cheeks, which gave her a fragile, almost doll-like appearance.

Sonny, who, like Ada and the absent James and Connie was dark haired and wore a permanently tanned complexion, was sitting in one of the large armchairs reading Mr Stevenson's excellent adventure story *Kidnapped*.

They all looked up as the door opened and the three children hurried across the large room to greet their father. Albert smiled over their heads at their mother, confessing the surprise he had got when Henry opened the front door and greeted him.

A further mild shock awaited him over dinner, which was served by the younger housemaid, Alice, in neat and proficient manner with only occasional prompting from the watchful Henry. Albert had leisure to study the girl, curious about the young foundling. He confessed later to Hannah that, although she had told him a little about her, she had failed to mention that she was stunningly attractive. Alice was small in stature, little more than five feet tall, Albert guessed. She was slender, as became her age, but with a burgeoning figure that promised much. Raven black hair framed her heart shaped face, her regular and well-proportioned features were pale and she possessed, rarely for one of her colouring, the most brilliant blue eyes. When she spoke, to enquire if she might serve more of anything, or to request permission to clear away, her voice was soft and gentle and pleasingly accent-less.

When they retired to the sitting room Henry served them both with coffee and a brandy for Albert.

'It is a shame to think,' Albert confided to Hannah, 'that we will be unable to keep Alice for long, as, with looks like that, she is sure to be snapped up by some lucky young man.' He smiled at his wife. 'And, my dear, last night's meal was no flash in the pan. It's not only me who thought so, judging by the way the children polished off their food.'

Hannah nodded her agreement. 'We've been busy today, Mrs Dallas and I, so it is especially gratifying that the meal was so good. Sarah, the other housemaid, will take up her duties tomorrow, as will the laundry maid. With the help of Mrs Dallas and Henry, I've selected a scullery maid and also a general factotum; George Mills. He will be ideal for the position. He is nineteen years old and sturdily built, able to cope with the heaviest of manual tasks. Like Sarah he's from the Old Town, the youngest son of a family of fishermen, but he is considered a disgrace within the family. Apparently, every time he goes near the sea, let alone on it, he gets violent attacks of mal de mar. He told me even the smell of sea air can turn him queasy.'

'Oh dear, not much good in a fisherman,' Albert commented dryly.

'As to the scullery maid, Mrs Dallas and I were in complete agreement. She's a married woman, but her husband is a long-term invalid so she needs the work. She has good references. Her present employers are moving house to Seamer and that would involve a lot of travelling. Being close to town is the main reason for her wanting to change jobs.'

'You know something,' Albert remarked with some satisfaction after Hannah had finished. 'I'm really looking forward to the Easter holiday. When James and Connie return from school, we will be together in our new home for the first time as a family and with the staff to look after us, it will be a new phase in our life together.'

CHAPTER FIVE

On the Tuesday before Easter, Albert commented, 'It is remarkable how quickly the servants have settled in. They have only been here a few days, yet the household is running smoothly.'

'I agree,' Hannah replied. 'There have been a few personality quirks to sort out. For example, Sarah's prone to gossiping, but Henry nips that in the bud. He's also got George out of the habit of whistling tunelessly while he works, which was most annoying. Apart from that they have fitted in effortlessly.'

Even Hannah's maid, who might have been expected to be resentful of the new regime, seemed to welcome the change. That might have been due to the lowered demand on her mistress, who now had time and energy to spare. This allowed Hannah to spend more time with the children and to accompany her mother, Ellen Ackroyd, on social outings.

If Henry had curtailed Sarah's predilection for gossip, he had certainly not eradicated it entirely. The habit must have gone into overdrive on the day Albert returned home with his eldest son and daughter for the Easter holiday. Sarah was passing through the entrance hall when Henry opened the front door to admit the travellers and so became the first member of the new household to catch a glimpse of James and Connie.

Albert had taken a detour, catching the Harrogate train from York rather than his usual connection for Bradford. After collecting Connie from school, he had taken her to his parents' house for the day, where James had joined them at lunchtime. Albert had finished work early and the three of them travelled back to Scarborough on the evening train.

The kitchen was a hive of activity when Sarah returned to impart her news. Everywhere was a flurry of bustle as preparation of the evening meal entered its final phase. The calm at the eye of this storm of work was Mrs Dallas herself, as she supervised all that went on around her.

'I've just seen Mr James and Miss Connie,' Sarah said as she entered the room, excitement lending a sparkle to her eyes.

'Sarah,' Mrs Dallas asked gently, 'could you please take over from Alice stirring the gravy? She will be needed in the dining room shortly and she ought to make herself presentable first.'

Sarah rolled her eyes, stepped across to the range and took the proffered spoon from Alice. 'You wait until you see that Mr James,' Sarah told Alice. 'He's a bit of all right I can tell you. He's tall, dark, and ever so handsome.'

Alice, busy replacing her apron with a clean one, merely raised her eyebrows in reply.

'What is Miss Connie like?' the laundry maid asked from the corner of the room, where she was busy folding starched napkins.

Sarah tore herself away from the vision of James Cowgill with an effort. 'Oh, she's a very pleasant-looking young lady, neat in appearance, what you would expect from one of Mr Cowgill and Madam's children.'

If Sarah had been favourably impressed by her first sight of James, he was equally captivated when he set eyes on her colleague for the first time. Alice entered the dining room preceded by Henry as the family were seated for dinner. It was with some difficulty that he bit back the whistle of appreciation her dark haired beauty prompted in him. Fortunately, neither of his parents noticed his confusion. Equally, they failed to see the look of open admiration that accompanied his words of thanks when Alice served his meal. She, however, did notice and there being no mistaking his expression, blushed slightly. The effect of the heightened colour, James thought, was to enhance her attractiveness even more.

* * *

Henry, the butler, requested permission to speak to Albert on Wednesday of Easter week. 'I wish to enquire, sir, if it will be in order for the domestic staff to attend religious services, according to their own beliefs, on Good Friday and Easter Sunday.'

'Of course, I would not dream of denying them the opportunity to worship,' Albert replied. 'Do you have any particular establishment in mind?'

'I cannot speak for the others, but I shall be worshipping at the St Sepulchre Street Chapel, as will Mrs Dallas.'

'The one they call *the Ranter Chapel,* locally?' Albert asked.

'I believe that is its nickname, because of the fiery sermons delivered there in the past.'

* * *

The Easter break passed in what seemed a blur of motion. For the Cowgill family it was all over almost before they had realized it had begun. On Good Friday, the family went to worship at St Mary's Church. In close proximity to Scarborough Castle, it stands in watchful vigilance over the twin bays of the resort. They made their way through the gate in the low railings close to the Hinderwell fountain, towards the solid yet beautiful grey stone church.

The remainder of the day was spent quietly. Following luncheon James and Connie escorted their younger siblings on a walk to the Italian Gardens and after a light supper, the household retired early to prepare themselves for the following day.

Easter Saturday was to all intents and purposes a house-warming party. In addition to the Cowgills themselves, Hannah's parents and her sisters, complete with their families, joined them. Michael Haigh had also been invited, together with his wife Charlotte, bringing the complement to twenty-one.

It was a rare pleasure for Philip and Ellen Ackroyd to see the whole of their family together at one time. James was a particular favourite, being the eldest grandchild, although the fond grandparents made no distinction between their growing list of descendants. Hannah's sister Florence and her husband Harry Binks travelled over from Bradford with their son. Susannah, the next eldest of the Ackroyd girls was also present with her husband Fred Lyons. They had been married seven years and had their young children with them. James referred to them as 'the pride' and the children had become known within the family as 'the Lyon cubs'. The youngest of Philip and Ellen's daughters, Hermione brought her husband with her. They had only been married a little over a year but were soon to add to the tally of grandchildren.

Michael Haigh was not considered family in the strictest sense of the word, but none would have considered omitting him from the invitation, despite the necessity to include his wife Charlotte, who was tolerated rather than liked. Both Albert and Hannah felt a tension between the Haighs throughout the time they spent at Byland Crescent. The party spread throughout the extensive ground floor and it seemed that whenever Michael entered a room Charlotte left it and vice versa. Michael spent the majority of his time with Connie, who, although fifteen years his junior was maturing rapidly into a highly attractive young woman. Connie certainly seemed to relish the company and attention paid to her by Michael rather than resent it, despite the disparity in their ages and his unsuitability as a companion.

The gathering warranted the attention of the full resources of the Cowgill household. Thus, Henry and Alice were reinforced in the dining room by Sarah, while below stairs Mrs Dallas enlisted the help of the rest of the servants to ensure the swift and efficient delivery of the succeeding courses.

Mrs Dallas had suited her catering to the needs of diners with a wide disparity in age and constitution, resulting in a succession of dishes of excellent quality and variety. If anything was needed to confirm the wisdom of their choice of cook and staff, it was the gratitude and appreciation with which their guests responded to the fare as they took their departure during the evening.

* * *

Following their attendance at St Mary's Church on the morning of Easter Sunday, the family were unanimous in voicing their approval of the suggestion that a brisk walk would be desirable. It was a warm, sunlit spring day as they paused at the gravestone of Anne Bronte, who had been lain to rest there almost fifty years earlier and made their way down Castle Hill through the Old Town towards the south shore, where they strolled along the harbour. Some of the more enterprising fishermen converted their small vessels to pleasure craft for the summer season, thereby earning greater rewards on busy days than could be obtained from fishing. Given that it was Easter Sunday however, the only movement made by these craft was to swing gently on their moorings.

By this time, it was early afternoon, but the hearty breakfast with which they had fortified themselves had been supplemented with some delicious ice creams. These had been purchased from a vendor who had positioned his cart close to the harbour. Advertised as 'Alfredo's Authentic and Delicious Italian Ices', the accent of the vendor himself, in spite of his luxuriant waxed black moustache, led Albert to ponder aloud if the man had ever been any closer to Italy than Ossett, or possibly Wakefield.

As can so often happen in Scarborough or for that matter any of the resorts on the Eastern coast of the British Isles, the sun disappeared behind a hazy cloud. The air took on moistness and with swift, yet imperceptible speed the bay was covered with a dense, cold mist, of the type known locally as a sea fret. It was a new, strange, and rather daunting experience for the family to be walking one moment in clear, bright sunshine, only a few minutes later to be in a thick cloud of damp, cold air containing enough moisture to be classed as a light drizzle.

So radical had been the change in weather conditions during the latter stages of their walk and so chilled had every member of the family been as a result, that the nourishing soup, in reality approaching a stew, provided by Mrs Dallas for their return was as manna from Heaven. They soon polished off the contents of the bowls placed before them by Alice, with several members of the family clamouring, Oliver Twist like, for more. Unlike Mr Bumble however, Alice, with the benign approval of Henry, duly served second helpings as required. Only Cissie among the younger Cowgills failed to do justice to a further bowl of soup. She had developed a slight cough since returning indoors and soon announced her intention of retiring to bed.

Her mother noticed the enhanced colour in her daughter's cheeks and the feverish brightness of her eyes. 'I think that's very sensible, Cissie dear. I'll come up with you and make sure you're comfortable.'

When she returned, Albert asked if anything was amiss. 'I'm not sure,' Hannah replied, 'it may be only a chill she's caught, but Cissie's so delicate she seems to be susceptible to anything. Unlike these two,' she added severely, gesturing at James and Sonny who were engaged in a tickling fight on the chaise longue. A one-sided affair as James was much taller and stronger than his brother.

On Easter Monday, Cissie was feeling somewhat better, although the cough persisted. So much improved was she that she agreed to join the rest of the family on their planned visit to a concert at the Spa Grand Hall. This was the venue for many of the town's best summer attractions and many artistes of current fame or future renown performed there. The concerts given four years earlier by Mr Charles Halle were still being spoken of admiringly by those who had attended. The Cowgills' enjoyment of the occasion was rounded off by a splendid meal taken in the luxuriously appointed Spa Restaurant adjacent to the concert hall.

* * *

The textile towns of the West Riding differed from most other regions in that the majority of woollen and worsted mills worked on Good Friday but remained closed on Easter Tuesday. There was a sound economic reason for this. It enabled mill owners to avoid disruption to production in two working weeks. When the mills closed for their Easter break the mighty steam engines that powered the looms were shut down, the furnaces cooled, so that engineers would be able to carry out essential maintenance work.

It was Wednesday therefore, before Albert, having spent a leisurely day at home with his family on the Tuesday, returned to the firm's offices. His was a state of contentment, brought about by his enjoyment of their first family holiday at Byland Crescent. He reflected with pride on the smooth running of the household under the direction of Henry and Mrs Dallas. Hosting social events, Albert felt, would hold no terrors for them with such attentive and efficient staff.

* * *

Michael Haigh was in the middle of briefing his sales team when Albert entered the sample room. 'I'd like to see you in my office when you've finished here,' he told Haigh, who nodded his agreement.

Once the salesmen had departed for their respective territories, Michael walked along the now-silent corridor to the large room at the end which had once been his father's domain. A portrait of the co-founder still hung in pride of place above the marble fireplace.

The two men spent a few moments discussing business matters, in particular their recently acquired subsidiary A & C Scouring. They examined consignment notes and forward orders to decide which lots could be diverted to the scouring plant. Michael promised to have a list ready for Philip Ackroyd when the senior partner returned to Bradford the following day.

There followed a slightly awkward pause, then Albert said, 'Hannah and I were very concerned to notice the strained relationship between you and Charlotte at the weekend.' He raised a querying eyebrow, inviting a response from the younger man.

Haigh's expression darkened at the mention of his wife's name. 'I suppose you would have had to be blind not to notice it,' he stated flatly.

'Was it a temporary difficulty, or are matters more serious than that?' Albert wanted to know.

'I'm afraid,' Haigh replied, choosing his words with care, 'that it is by no means temporary. In fact, things are about as bad between us as they could possibly be.'

'I'm very sorry to hear that. However, in view of what you have just said, I must make the following point. It was obvious that you spent most of your visit in company with my daughter Connie. Connie is barely sixteen years old, still at school and at a very impressionable age. I am sure you will agree that it is totally unacceptable for you to be paying attention to a young girl, especially in your position. I trust I make myself clear.'

'Abundantly so,' Haigh replied unable to keep the bitterness from his voice.

CHAPTER SIX

1897 marked the sixtieth year of the reign of Queen Victoria. The Diamond Jubilee was to be celebrated throughout the land and across the empire in lavish style. To pay homage to the landmark reached by Her Majesty, any number of statues, bandstands, assorted buildings, and clocks were to be erected. Special stamps were to be issued, commemorative mugs, plates, plaques and images of the Queen were to be struck.

Events in honour of the Jubilee would centre round the third week in June. Every city, town, village and hamlet was busy organizing, in whatever way best suited their own resources, some form of gathering that would involve as much of their population as possible.

In addition to churches of all denominations holding special services of thanksgiving, there were to be festivals and fetes, bonfires and beacons, parades and processions, games and gifts. Trees were to be planted, firework displays held, any number of band concerts were to take place, some in the brand-new bandstands, and every church throughout the land would ring a celebratory peal of bells. Mile upon mile of patriotic flags, streamers, and bunting had been manufactured. Every public building as well as many offices and shops would be decked out with these bright splashes of colour. Taking their cue from this, many homeowners, from the grandest of mansions to the humblest of cottages had followed suit.

Hannah Cowgill was discussing the proposed visit of Albert's parents Saul and Esther with the owner of the guest house in the crescent, when that lady mentioned the forthcoming event.

'Do you know, with all that has been occupying our attention, neither my husband nor I have given any thought as to how the family would mark Her Majesty's Jubilee,' Hannah stated. 'Perhaps,' she continued, 'we should look to organizing some gathering of our own, here in Byland Crescent, to mark the occasion. There are enough of us to hold a large party, with children and guests included. We could all contribute to the food and refreshments and we have enough domestic staff on hand to ensure a successful outcome.'

Her neighbour could see the sense in Hannah's remarks and so the idea was born. When they parted company, it was on the understanding that each would plant the seed in their respective husband's brain and leave it to germinate.

During May, the gentlemen residing in Byland Crescent, having been persuaded into this course of action by their wives, became acquainted with their neighbours.

Naturally enough, all that the gentlemen had leisure to involve themselves in was the master plan of the event. Organization and fine detail would have to be left to the ladies. This was only fair, as the men had work to do. Some, like Albert, had long distances to travel in order to get to their occupation.

Albert's immediate neighbour, Josiah Firth, was one such case in point. He headed a family business located in Leeds, textile engineers by trade. Admittedly, the owners of Number 3, Byland Crescent were locals, but as owners of a fishing fleet, theirs was a business that demanded their full attention and some extremely odd hours into the bargain.

The owners of Number 4 had only taken possession that week.

Doctor Steven Culleton and his family occupied 5 Byland Crescent; a combined home and surgery. Although he was locally based as a general practitioner, he had little in the way of leisure time.

Number 8, at the opposite end of the crescent, was the guest house.

Next door to them, was as yet unoccupied, although it had been earmarked for his own use by the managing director of the firm that had built Byland Crescent.

The only house whose occupants failed to respond to the invitation to join in the celebrations was Number 6. The couple who lived there were in their mid-thirties, childless and without domestic staff, which was in itself an oddity. When Albert had approached the husband, he had been met with a refusal that crossed the border from curtness to incivility with ease. Nothing much was known about the couple for they were seldom seen out and about nor did they solicit or encourage conversation with their neighbours.

By the end of May, arrangements were well in hand. The gardens at the heart of the crescent had been landscaped and planted out during the early part of construction work and were now maturing well. The centrepiece of the gardens was a large lawn. This area would prove ideal for summer picnics and was precisely right as a venue for this occasion. An awning had been erected in case of bad weather and some trestle tables laid out to cope with the food and other refreshments.

The Cowgill residence was the hub of the endeavour, with the combined planning and organizational skills of Albert and Hannah proving instrumental in ensuring the success of the venture. There was a constant buzz of activity enhanced by a stream of callers to the door. By the time Albert's parents arrived in mid-June, all was in readiness for the big day. Their first view of Byland Crescent was made even more appealing by the gaily fluttering lines of flags and bunting that had been secured, so it must have seemed, to every available projection along the thoroughfare. When Saul and Esther sat down for dinner with the rest of the family that evening it was such a merry gathering that it must have seemed to the newcomers as if the celebrations had already started.

It only lacked the presence of James and Connie to make the family party complete. They would be travelling home by train on the Friday afternoon of 18 June as they had been given special dispensation for the occasion by their respective head teachers. Such was the high-level of involvement demanded of him that Albert had entrusted Connie to the protection of her elder brother for the journey.

'So, tell me, Hannah love, who's coming to this party on Tuesday,' Saul enquired during the meal.

'Let me see,' Hannah enumerated. 'There will be my mother and father of course. My sisters, Florence and Susannah, with their husbands and children. Hermione, my youngest sister, is not well enough to travel. Her pregnancy is proving difficult, so the doctor thinks it inadvisable for her to risk the journey. Michael Haigh will be here, but as matters stand between he and Charlotte the invitation has not been extended to her.'

Hannah paused and leaned across the table to tell her father-in-law confidentially, 'A few days ago Michael told Albert that Charlotte has returned to live with her parents and solicitors' letters regarding a divorce have been exchanged. As for the rest, it will be the remaining families from the crescent, plus their guests.'

'Sounds as if it's going to be quite a gathering.'

On the Sunday of Diamond Jubilee week, the extended Cowgill family attended St Mary's Church for a service of thanksgiving. At the end of the memorable service, the choir had reduced many of the ladies in the congregation to tears with their rendition of *O Rest in the Lord* from Mendelssohn's *Elijah*. Following that, they had led the congregation in a rousing chorus of the *National Anthem*, followed by three cheers for Her Majesty. As the family walked home for luncheon, Albert remarked, 'If anything had been needed to give a fitting send off to the week of celebration — that was it.'

The day appointed for the Byland Crescent Jubilee Garden Party, Tuesday 22 June, dawned clear and hot, although a little humid. Albert and the other planners had arranged a series of none too competitive athletic races for the younger ones, including a sack race, egg-and-spoon race, a three-legged race, some vaulting and jumping competitions and a greasy pole to be climbed. A local entertainer had been enlisted to put on a Punch and Judy show. Several of the ladies, as befitted their station, were talented pianists, so a piano was brought out and placed under the awning. From there, with songs and instrumental pieces, members of the gathering would provide more adult entertainment. Chief amongst these would be Connie, whose clear, pure singing voice was much admired whenever she performed.

When the younger children had shown off their athletic prowess, then cooled off by watching the knockabout antics of Mr Punch, Mrs Judy, the hapless policeman and the scary crocodile, it was time for their refreshments. It was during the children's tea that the weather began to change. Heavy thunderheads could be seen in the far distance and the warm breeze had stiffened into a gusty wind. Out to sea, occasional flashes of lightning could be seen.

It was around that time that Hannah became concerned about Ada. She, of all the Cowgill family, had been the least interested in the celebrations. Indeed, as Hannah was well aware, her behaviour had been strange for some time. She was due to go to Connie's school, Princess Caroline's in Harrogate, in September, and at first Hannah had assumed that a reluctance to leave home might have been the root cause of the problem. When tackled on the subject however, Ada had been adamant that she was looking forward to her new school.

Subsequently, Hannah had wondered if Ada might have been jealous of the attention paid to her younger sister Cissie following her illness at Easter, but despite Cissie's recovery, Ada's strange behaviour continued. If Ada had been a few years older, Hannah might have suspected the normal heart pangs of a teenage girl, but at eleven years old, Hannah considered Ada too young for such to be the case. Hannah was an extremely good and caring mother, yet in this instance, her guesses had all been inaccurate.

The younger children were rounding off their feast with ice cream and ginger beer or lemonade, when Hannah noticed that Ada had gone missing. Her concern was not great enough to merit panic measures and even had it been there was little Hannah could have done. She glanced around and her eye fell on her elder son James, who was watching the feeding frenzy displayed by the younger guests. Hannah smiled briefly at the disdainful expression on James's face. She beckoned him over. 'James dear, do me a small favour will you? Ada has gone missing. She has been behaving a little oddly of late. See if she has gone to her room, or if you can find her in the house.'

'What and deprive myself of this fun?' James enquired ironically, gesturing at one of the smaller infants who was exhibiting symptoms of severe over-indulgence in cream cakes and other sickly products.

'I know,' Hannah said, matching his mood. 'It must be difficult to tear yourself away.'

James grinned and leaned across to kiss his mother's cheek. 'I shall sacrifice my own pleasure for your sake, Mama.'

By the time James reappeared the younger children had been herded into Number 3, where they were to watch a magician perform. They were unaware that the conjurer who baffled them with dazzling feats of sleight of hand had been the controlling influence behind the outrageous behaviour of Mr Punch and his troupe of artistes little more than an hour earlier.

James sought out his mother. 'Ada's not inside the house. I've looked everywhere, called out her name, but no response.'

'Really, she is the most vexatious child,' Hannah responded. 'I have enough to worry about. I have just got the little ones settled and now the adults are to have their meal.'

'If you wish I can continue looking elsewhere,' James offered.

'Would you, please? I will make sure some food is saved for you.'

As he set off to continue his search in and around the crescent, he noticed that the sky had darkened rapidly while he had been indoors, with angry-looking clouds that threatened a downpour. As he reached the end of Byland Crescent closest to Falsgrave Road, a sudden brilliant flash of forked lightening illuminated the sky before him. Repressing a momentary shudder, he noticed a small figure in the distance. Although the lowering clouds had by now rendered the scene too gloomy for a positive identification, he was fairly sure it was that of his errant sister. Almost as soon as he spotted her and before he could call out to her, the girl in front of him disappeared into the gloom, heading towards the town centre. Muttering a mild imprecation as he felt the first heavy splashes of rain on his hands and face, James hurried after her.

The rain had become heavier. James paused, staring down the deserted thoroughfare towards the railway station. There was no one in sight. A swift glance in the other direction assured him that Ada had not reversed her intention. The rising tempo of the rainfall was matched by the increase in James's temper. He hunched his shoulders into his jacket and set off grimly towards the town centre. He had only travelled a hundred yards before the rain changed from heavy to torrential. The power of the rain as it rattled on the cobbles caused large droplets to rebound in a series of miniature fountains. In an instant, James was soaked. Abandoning his search, he broke into a run, heading for the nearest cover, a shelter used by hansom cab drivers. As he neared it, he saw, through a curtain of rain, another figure dashing across the road, obviously intent on reaching the same shelter. It was a girl, but too tall to be Ada. As he got close to her, James, with no thought to his own comfort, pulled off his jacket and cast it over her head and shoulders. Together they ran the remaining fifty yards to their haven.

Once inside, James quickly removed his jacket and shook it to rid it of whatever he could of the rain on its surface. He cast a glance round their refuge. It was deserted, although evidence of recent occupation was provided by the litter of cigarette ends on the floor and the vague aroma of nicotine and stale urine in the atmosphere. Only when he had completed his cursory inspection did he turn his attention to his companion in adversity. His eyes widened in surprise as he discovered the identity of the girl who was regarding him with grave concern.

'Alice,' he stammered. 'I didn't realize it was you.'

'Thank you so much, Master James. It was extremely gallant of you protecting me with your coat but just look at you, you're soaking wet.'

It was the longest sentence she had ever spoken to him. Her closeness and their situation alone together set his pulse racing. Alice reached into the pocket of her coat and pulled out a tiny handkerchief. She started to dab the water from his face and hair, ineffectually, as the small square of linen was soon saturated. The touch was too much for James. He seized her slender wrist with his hand and pulled her close to him. He held her in a close embrace for a second, looking into her brilliant blue eyes, while circling her tiny waist with his other arm. Then, as his pent-up emotions overcame him, he kissed her, a long, savagely passionate kiss. For a brief moment it seemed to him as if Alice responded, before her struggles and muffled protests awoke him to the enormity of what he was doing.

He released her and swung away, his face brick red with shame and embarrassment. 'Alice, please forgive me? That was unpardonable. I don't know what came over me, it's just you are so beautiful, looked so attractive with the rain glistening on your hair. Please tell me I'm forgiven?'

There was a long silence before she answered him, her words and tone as gentle as ever, with no hint of reproof in her voice. 'Of course I forgive you, James. Look, the rain has ceased, perhaps we should go back?'

James looked outside the shelter, to discover that the rain had stopped as abruptly as it had started. He suddenly remembered his errand. 'I have to find Ada. The wretched girl's gone off somewhere and I promised Mother I would look for her.'

'Shall I help you search?' Alice volunteered.

The temptation to agree, to spend more time with Alice was almost too much for James, but he mastered it. 'It would be better if you go back first. People might think something was amiss if we returned together.'

Alice nodded her agreement, but her parting words lingered for a long time in his memory. 'Perhaps it would be best if we just tried to forget this happened, James.' With that, and the lightest of touches of her hand on his arm, she was gone.

It was only much later that James, with leisure to reflect on the incident and in complete disobedience of Alice's advice, remembered that she had called him James instead of Master James. He remembered also the touch of her hand before parting and, although he could not be sure, the more he thought about it the more convinced he became that, for one brief moment before realization came to her, she had responded to his kiss with equal fervour.

He discovered Ada as he strode back along Falsgrave Road. She was dry, in marked contrast to her brother. She told him she had got bored with the party and had gone for a walk. It had started to rain so she had taken shelter in a doorway. Her tone was surly, her manner sullen.

She did not tell him that the doorway she had chosen in which to take refuge was almost opposite the hansom cab shelter. Nor did she explain the reason for her attitude. While James and Alice had been inside, Ada had stared fixedly at the doorway through which her brother had taken the maid. Ada's expression had been contorted by an emotion totally new to the young girl, one she could not have begun to describe. She was, although very young and immature, aware of the shame attached to these new feelings. She knew she would never be able to confess the true reason for her unhappiness. The guilt of her secret admiration for Alice was something she would have to bear alone.

CHAPTER SEVEN

The rain on the day of the Byland Crescent Diamond Jubilee Garden Party, which returned in force overnight, marked the end of the long spell of glorious weather. For the rest of that week and for some considerable time thereafter, Scarborough suffered a succession of violent storms, with thunder and lightning accompanied by torrential, monsoon-like rain and occasional dramatic downpours of hailstones. It was also a summer of mounting concern for the Cowgill family and those close to them.

James and Connie had only been back in Scarborough for a week when their grandparents, Saul and Esther Cowgill, were forced to terminate their stay in Byland Crescent. The telegram arrived as the family were preparing for a picnic outing. Henry brought it to them in the sitting room. Instead of delivering it to Albert he took the silver tray to Saul. Saul ripped the envelope in his haste to open it. He scanned the contents, his face going pale.

'What is it, Saul?' Esther enquired fearfully.

'It's Ethel, she's been taken poorly. We must go home straight away. They don't say what the trouble is but it sounds serious.' The news cast a damper over the whole family, for Albert's sister was a favourite with the children, and it was not until they arrived back in the West Riding that Saul and Esther received more precise details.

Ethel, the headmistress of Great Horton Junior and Infants School, had spoken several times during the final week of term of feeling unwell. The symptoms displayed were continuing headaches, a feverish, flu-like condition, one minute burning, the next, shivering. These were accompanied by a sore, aching throat and occasional spells of dizziness. By the time Saul and Esther returned to Peel Square, the doctor, mystified by the ailment, had placed Ethel in an isolation hospital for the treatment of contagious diseases. Here, when they were eventually and with some reluctance on the part of the medical staff, allowed to see their daughter, Saul and Esther found Ethel to be slipping in and out of consciousness and even when awake she was at times far from lucid.

Albert's concern for his sister's health was added to and magnified by fresh worries at home; he summed these up one evening as he sat with Hannah. James had taken Sonny down to the sandy beach of the south shore for a game of cricket and the girls had retired to their rooms. 'It seems as if it's one thing after another at the moment,' Albert told his wife. First it was Ethel's health, now Cissie. She seemed so much improved during the early summer, when the days were bright and clear, but ever since the Jubilee she has declined. Then there's Ada, I don't for a minute begin to understand what's wrong with the girl. She mopes about the house, snaps people's heads off if they so much as speak to her. James might be here, but his mind's elsewhere most of the time. He's always daydreaming, except when Ada behaves so badly to him. She seems to be singling him out. Connie's the only one who appears to be normal at the moment, apart from young Sonny.'

'I know, but try as I might I cannot find out what this is all about,' Hannah agreed, 'and I think we ought to see a doctor about Cissie. She has been off-colour too long for it to be purely the weather.'

Hannah's burden was added to by the continuing ill health of her sister Hermione. Her baby was due, according to most calculations, sometime in early November, but the persistent difficulties she had undergone made it increasingly unlikely that Hermione would be able to carry her baby for the full-term.

In such circumstances, it might have been natural for Albert to regard work as a welcome relief from domestic cares, or even at worst a counterirritant, but that was not to be. Trading conditions were poor. A glut of wool, together with a lack of demand for cloth, combined to force raw material prices down. On one particularly disastrous week that summer, for the first time in the firm's history, there was not a single entry in their order book.

With Philip Ackroyd involved in the day-to-day management of A & C Scouring until such time as he could relinquish control to Ernest Cowgill, and Michael Haigh distracted by his increasingly messy and acrimonious divorce, Albert was left in almost total command of HAC during the summer of 1897. Although trade was poor and seemed likely to remain so for some considerable time, the reserves of Haigh, Ackroyd & Cowgill were immense. Nor were they overburdened with stock, for, in anticipation of the difficult times ahead, the buying orders sent out to wool sales throughout South America, South Africa, Australia and New Zealand had been minute in comparison to those of the halcyon days almost ten years earlier. These purchases merely replenished stocks to the minimum practical level or covered what few meagre orders the firm received from the bolder of their clients.

Some of Albert's worries had been resolved by September, when it was time for James and Connie to return to school and for Ada to go to her new school for the first time. Ethel, Albert's sister was definitely on the mend, her recovery, although less sudden than the onset of the ailment, was nonetheless satisfactorily rapid. Philip had relinquished part of the daily control of A & C Scouring to Ernest Cowgill and was thus freed to resume some of his executive duties at HAC.

In other areas, the news was less encouraging. Michael Haigh's divorce was turning more unpleasant by the week, with accusation and counteraccusation flying to and fro, no doubt to the delight of the solicitors whose charges would be mounting with each consultation or letter exchanged.

At home, however, Cissie's health continued its downward spiral. As Albert and Hannah waited on the platform of Scarborough station, ready to wave James, Connie and Ada off as they headed to school, the thoughts of both parents were back in Byland Crescent and their forthcoming appointment with their neighbour and new friend, Dr Culleton.

Once the train arrived and the passengers began to board the coaches according to the status of their tickets, Albert and Hannah said farewell to all three of their children in turn. As they did so, they were aware that it was a season of change. For James it was to be his last term. He would have left at the close of the summer term, but for the entreaty of his headmaster.

James had just played a leading part in the victory over one of their closest rivals and they were returning from the school cricket field. It was nearing the end of term, a fact mentioned by the head. 'Only a few more weeks and your time here will be over, James,' his tone matter of fact. 'I suppose you will be going into the family business?'

'My father wants me to go on to university, sir, but I'm not keen. To be honest, Headmaster, not wishing to offend, but I think I'm ready to be clear of the academic life.'

The headmaster was one of shrewdest teachers of his day, a sound choice for so prestigious an establishment as Forest Manor School. He thought over his head prefect's remarks for a few moments before replying. 'I think you're right, James. You have exceptional maturity and are ready to face the world. If you are not going to spend the next three years of your life in the cloistered environment of a university, I wonder if you could spare three months out of that time to do one last favour for the school?'

'For what purpose?'

'Well, the boy whom I have chosen to take over as head prefect has to take three examinations during the autumn term, examinations which will be vital to his chosen career. In order for him to give the fullest attention to these, he will be unable to fulfil his responsibilities as head boy properly. If you can continue for one more term, you would be doing me a great service.'

'I shall have to ask my father.'

The headmaster coughed apologetically. 'In view of the circumstances there would naturally be no fee for the additional term,' he added.

James grinned. 'That should sway him. He is a Yorkshireman, after all.'

* * *

Connie was also commencing her final year at Harrogate. Plans had been put forward for her to attend a finishing school once the year was over, although one had yet to be selected.

For Ada, in contrast, it was the start of a new adventure. She would be away from home for the first time, at a strange school and in the company of more than one hundred and fifty girls, all of them, with the exception of Connie, complete strangers. If this prospect was a daunting one, then it was certainly not apparent in her demeanour. She was, in marked contrast to her attitude over the past few months, animated to the point of excitement. Her normal cheerful and outgoing persona returned, replacing the sullen surliness that had become habitual. Even James, who had been a favourite target for her displeasure, was treated to the side of his sister's nature he had despaired of ever seeing again.

When the guards' van vanished round the bend on the first leg of their children's journey, Albert and Hannah turned to leave the station. Their hearts, heavy from the farewells, were further weighed down by the prospect of what awaited them in Byland Crescent.

* * *

The expression on Doctor Steven Culleton's face was grave and thoughtful as he faced Albert and Hannah across their drawing room. This was the worst task he had to perform amongst the many difficult aspects of his life as a doctor with a busy general practice.

He cleared his throat nervously. 'I'm afraid,' he told them gently, 'that Cissie's condition is more serious than anticipated. She has an advanced form of tuberculosis, what used to be known as consumption.' He paused, allowing the full horror of the diagnosis to sink home.

Albert held Hannah's hand tighter in response to her whimper of anguish. His jaw was rigid with stress, the pain visible in every line of his taut countenance, reflected in his dark eyes. There was a long, sad silence. Eventually Albert found his voice and asked the question that had to follow, dreading the answer. 'What are her chances, Steven?'

The young doctor was prepared for this, but preparation did not make the reply any easier. 'To be honest, her chances are slim at best. The disease has got too strong a hold and is too far advanced.'

He waited once more, although he knew the next question. This time it was Hannah, her hand still clasped tightly in Albert's, who asked it. 'You say her chances are slim, does that mean they are hopeless and if not, what must we do to improve them?'

'No one can say with any certainty whether they are hopeless or not. Although there is much research going on into the disease and we certainly know much more than we did fifty years ago, we have still not found a cure. However, there are certain measures that can be taken that would help to improve her chances. It would call for a radical course of action, I'm afraid.' Having prepared the ground for what he had to say he continued more confidently, 'There are certain establishments that specialize in the care and treatment of patients with tubercular infections and my colleagues have reported good rates of success. What we do not know is at what stage of the illness those patients were when they were sent for treatment. That is one part of the problem. The next is that they are highly expensive. Finally, and this might prove to be the biggest stumbling block, the location of the best of these sanatoria is in Switzerland.'

Steven Culleton waited once more before explaining, 'The reason they are in Switzerland is because of the climate. The Alpine air is clean, cold, and dry and it seems the disease cannot thrive in such conditions. I cannot say that Cissie will recover from the disease, for that would be highly irresponsible on my part. What I will say, is that if the expense and location do not present too great an obstacle, then taking Cissie there will improve her chances of survival. I will leave you to talk the matter over, but if you want any further information, details of the cost for example, I will gladly furnish you with them. Also, if you decide to go ahead with the treatment I have suggested, I will be more than happy to help with making the arrangements. I just wish it could have been otherwise.'

* * *

Almost as soon as their brother had delivered them to the school, Ada found herself separated from Connie. All the new arrivals were herded together to be directed to their appointed house. The house system was more than a way of dividing the pupils for dormitory purposes. It enabled the school authorities to foster a spirit of competition between pupils in academic performance, on the sports and athletic fields, and in extracurricular activities ranging from chess or bridge to debating and public speaking. It was felt that such competition represented a healthy challenge, enabling pupils to achieve their highest levels of performance. To encourage their charges, house tutors were appointed from within the teaching staff and it became a matter of pride to ensure their own house outperformed its competitors.

Amongst the pupils themselves, were the offices of head of house and house prefect, responsible to the house tutor, the school prefects, and ultimately the head teacher. Their duties gave them responsibility for discipline and order within their own house. It was a system that was open to abuse, but cases of bullying were not as common as might be supposed.

Ada lined up in the assembly hall with the other girls who had been allocated to Nightingale house. Their house tutor would be the first to address them, outlining their future within the school. She would be followed by the head of house, who would detail what was expected from them and would then hand them over to the house prefects.

Hilda Drummond, head of house, eyed the newcomers with interest. She was commencing her final year at Princess Caroline's and this would be the last intake she would have under her control. As the house tutor went through the customary speech of welcome, Hilda inspected each girl carefully. The position carried with it certain privileges. One of those was the choice of a first-year student to act as her general dogsbody. Hilda detested the term 'fag' so commonly used in boys' schools to denote this office, preferring to call them her 'Girl Friday'.

Looking along the line, she spotted a likely candidate, a dark haired, pretty girl with a ready smile and lively, dark eyes. She looked to be a good, biddable and eager girl, who would tackle the chores and errands Hilda set her. When Hilda took centre stage, she was pleased to see all the newcomers listening attentively to her little lecture. When she had finished her short speech, they waited to have their name called out by the prefects, who would then show them to their allotted dormitories. Before dismissing them, Hilda pointed to the girl she had selected. 'I want you to come with me. What is your name?'

'Ada Cowgill, miss,' the girl's reply was delivered in a voice tremulous from apprehension. She had only been in the school an hour and she was in trouble.

'Who has Ada Cowgill on their list?' Hilda called out.

One of the prefects signified with a wave of the hand. 'Very well, cross her off and adjust the lists. Ada is coming with me as my G.F.'

Ada followed Hilda Drummond from the assembly hall, past a crowd of first years from another house, waiting in the corridor for their turn. Once they had got clear of the mob, Hilda turned to Ada and smiled. 'Don't look so worried, Ada. You are not in any trouble.' She went on to explain. 'Your duties will be quite easy and will not interfere with your studies. You will be responsible for keeping my rooms clean and tidy, running errands, taking and receiving messages, answering my door, that sort of thing. You will have your own room, next to mine. Do you understand all that?'

Ada nodded, much relieved and cheered by the news.

'Good. First of all, I'll show you to your quarters, then we can go and find the porter to bring your bags and things up.' Hilda smiled at the young girl. 'I'm sure you and I will get along fine. I have the feeling you will be really happy here.'

Ada looked into the intelligent green eyes of her new mentor. It was a feeling she shared.

CHAPTER EIGHT

Michael Haigh looked bleakly at the solemn face of his solicitor. He reflected on the downward spiral of his marriage, of Charlotte's frequent and unexplained absences from the marital home, and of the lies and hypocrisy. He had been prepared to let matters rest, taking the line of least resistance and accepting responsibility but the latest communication from Charlotte's solicitor had changed all that. The letter had alleged mental and physical cruelty and made wild accusations of verbal and physical abuse. The solicitor's advice was to accept the terms contained in the letter, cut their losses, and settle. The sum proposed in settlement, although no more than Michael could afford, was far in excess of what had previously been suggested and a great deal more than he was prepared to pay.

He paused and took a deep breath before replying. 'No,' he said decisively. 'I do not; will not, accept those terms. If Charlotte wants that sort of money, she will have to go on the streets and earn it. That is pure blackmail, without foundation.'

He gestured contemptuously to the document lying on the desk before him. 'What you will do is to prepare a reply acknowledging receipt of the letter but refuting, line by line, word by word, every one of those allegations and rejecting the terms out of hand. In that letter you will also rescind all previous offers in settlement and finally you will add one or two insinuations that might give them food for thought.'

The solicitor pounced on the last part of Michael's instructions. 'On what grounds,' he enquired a trifle sarcastically, 'would I be able to level such allegations?'

Michael snorted with derision. 'By the time I have finished you will have all the grounds you need. Give me a month, six weeks at the outside and I will furnish you with all the required proof.'

With that, Michael rose, nodded to the solicitor, and left the room. He needed time to allow the white heat of his anger to cool before returning to his HAC office. As he walked through town, he remembered a sign he had noticed on a door in Ivegate. Changing direction, he climbed the steep, narrow street until he reached his destination. He read the small, discreet sign on the door and entered the building.

It was late afternoon when Michael returned to Manor Row. Immediately, he noticed something was amiss. The staff in both the sales and sample room would normally be working amongst a hubbub of chatter, gossip, badinage and the normal office skylarking. On this occasion, although they were certainly working, whatever conversation was taking place was being conducted in subdued, almost hushed tones. The firm's venerable cashier obviously deputed as a look-out, greeted Michael with the news that Mr Albert wanted to see him without delay.

Instead of his normal position seated behind the heavy oak desk, Albert was standing in front of the marble fireplace when Michael entered. His expression was grave and troubled. 'Michael, thank goodness you're back. I'm sorry to say I have some very bad news. Hannah's sister Hermione gave premature birth to a baby boy last night. Unfortunately, the baby was stillborn. Even worse, poor Hermione was unable to withstand the ordeal. She died a few hours later.'

Albert paused, giving Michael a moment to digest the shocking and tragic news, before continuing. 'Obviously, Philip is going to be absent for some time and with this on top of Cissie's illness I shall be needed at home. That means everything will devolve on you. Not only here, but also at A and C. Ernest is coming to grips with things, but still needs guidance and that means you will have to divide your time between here and Preston Street. Under normal circumstances I am sure you would be able to cope, but you already have enough to worry about.'

'Don't worry about me, I will manage.' Michael responded. 'Everyone here is well trained. We have the best team in the trade. That's what we pay them for. We have always tried to avoid crises, but there comes a time when all that planning and careful management will be needed.'

They spent a few minutes discussing practical matters such as cheque and document signing authority before Albert announced he was leaving to catch an early train. He paused at the office door and said reflectively, 'When I return, Hannah and I will have decided what we are going to do about Cissie's treatment. I think you may well be in charge for quite some time.'

* * *

Only two weeks following the start of the new school term, James escorted Connie and Ada on the short journey from Harrogate to Bradford where they joined up with their mother and father to attend Hermione's funeral. Only Cissie, who was too unwell to travel, and Sonny, held to be too young for such an ordeal, were absent. After the service, when the family returned to Hermione's former home for the funeral tea, Albert seized the opportunity to have a quiet word with James and Connie. 'I have to tell you that the news of Cissie is not good,' he began. He went on to explain the diagnosis and added, 'Your mother and I have not made a final decision yet, but I wanted you to be aware of how grave the situation is.'

A few days later, Albert and Hannah discussed the problem at length. 'As I see it,' Albert told his wife, 'we have no alternative, painful though it might be. James and Connie are aware of the situation, although I hesitated to tell them how critical it is. They are both old enough and mature enough to take care of themselves. Ada is at Connie's school, where Connie can look after her.'

'What about Sonny?' Hannah wanted to know.

'I have a suggestion. If you and I take Sonny to Switzerland, we can hire a house close enough to the sanatorium for Cissie to receive her treatment during the day and spend the evenings with us. To make things easier we could take Henry along. I can write to the headmistress of Connie and Ada's school and James's headmaster, requesting permission for all three to remain at their respective establishments over the Christmas holidays. We will close the house here in Byland Crescent, leaving Mrs Dallas in charge. With the family away, the rest of the servants can be sent home on leave of absence, reporting to Mrs Dallas once a week to ensure the house is kept in good order. Mrs Dallas and Alice will remain in Byland Crescent as they have no alternative accommodation.'

'What about the business?' Hannah was almost convinced but needed reassurance on every aspect.

'I've already touched on the possibility of this course of events with Michael Haigh. I have no doubt about Michael's capability. I also think more active involvement with the business will be a welcome distraction for Philip.'

'Above all else, we must think of Cissie,' Hannah agreed. Suddenly the strain of it proved more than she could bear. 'Albert,' she pleaded, her voice choked with emotion.

He put his arms around her as she wept, the tears pricking at his own eyes.

* * *

Albert requested Steven Culleton to put arrangements in hand and book the sanatorium. He also made travel reservations for the whole party, planning each step of their route with infinite care. He wrote the requisite letters to both schools, but delayed informing James, Connie, and Ada of their plans until he had received confirmation from their head teachers.

Hannah briefed the servants who were most cooperative. Cissie was a great favourite with all of them and each expressed their hope that the treatment would revive her. Dr Culleton confirmed the sanatorium had been booked from the beginning of November until the end of January. He suggested that if they were to return to England at that point, it might be advisable to take Cissie to the south coast, where the climate is more temperate, particularly during the winter months. He mentioned Bournemouth and the surrounding resorts as the most suitable places.

Albert received very quick replies from both schools, indicating that in the circumstances they would be more than happy to assist. With the older children's welfare taken care of, the last obstacle to their planned absence was removed. Albert and Hannah sat down to compose individual letters to James, Connie, and Ada.

* * *

Michael Haigh stared, grim faced, at the report on his desk. He looked up at the man seated opposite. 'You are in no doubt that everything in this document' — he indicated the two pages of foolscap paper — 'is able to be proved, if needs be, in a court of law.'

The enquiry agent nodded his assent. 'I have had considerable experience in such matters and it is as clear cut as any I have handled. There are reliable witnesses, copies of hotel bills and in here' — he produced an envelope from the inner pocket of his jacket — 'are some letters I managed to obtain. These are of a highly intimate and in some instances graphically explicit nature. There is no doubt that your wife has been conducting an affair for over two years.'

Michael's solicitor, normally the most cautious of men, was convinced by the private detective's statement and corroborative evidence. 'I am sure you are in a winning position they will not dare to challenge. I believe we can have you out of this marriage very quickly and at very little cost.' He smiled thinly, the first sign of humour Michael had noted in him. 'Apart from our account that is,' he added.

'Just do it,' Michael replied shortly. 'I'm sick and tired of the whole sordid business and want it over with.'

* * *

Although both Connie and James had been prepared by their father at their Aunt Hermione's funeral, this prior intimation did little to cushion the blow when they received his letters. He informed them, the house at Byland Crescent would be effectively closed down, and the travelling party would be en route for Switzerland. Their grandparents, Philip and Ellen Ackroyd, would be spending Christmas with Hannah's sister Florence and her family. Saul and Esther Cowgill, their other grandparents, were still nursing Albert's sister whose recovery from the mystery ailment was proving to be a long, slow process. In the circumstances, Albert wrote, he had made arrangements for them to remain in school over the Christmas period. He was sorry they would be unable to spend the first Christmas at Byland Crescent together in their new home, but he knew that they would understand. He added that Michael Haigh had suggested he might travel to Harrogate at some point to take Connie and Ada for an outing and Albert had written to their headmistress giving parental approval for such a visit.

However prepared James and Connie might have been for the tidings, they were nonetheless saddened by the content of the letter. For Ada, who had received no such prior warning, the news came as a dreadful shock. She was only just beginning to come to terms with the loss of her Aunt Hermione and now to hear of the severity of Cissie's plight brought upon her wave after wave of sadness, mixed with distress, loneliness and a degree of homesickness. She read the letter time and again in the privacy of Hilda Drummond's study that it was her privilege to share. Hilda found her there, her tear-stained face blotchy and red from crying. Gently she consoled and calmed the younger girl.

Late that same evening, when all was quiet, Hilda heard the muffled sounds of weeping from Ada's room. She slipped from her own bed, left her room, and crossed the study. She opened Ada's door quietly. The room was in semi-darkness. 'Ada,' she said softly, 'are you all right?'

A renewed burst of sobbing was the only response. Hilda found her way to the bed and sat on the edge. Ada was sitting bolt upright, the un-curtained window lending enough light from the waning moon to make her just visible. Hilda put her arm round Ada's shoulder and Ada turned to cling desperately to her. Hilda looked down at her young friend, sympathy for her unhappiness blending with admiration for her dark prettiness. 'If only,' Hilda thought with deep regret. Involuntarily, she tightened her grip on Ada at the thought, feeling herself stirred despite her best intentions. In some unfathomable manner Ada sensed the change. She looked up at Hilda with a watery smile.

CHAPTER NINE

It was the beginning of December and the school had a little over three weeks left before the Boars Head Feast signalled the break-up for the Christmas holiday. A small, rowdy, and hyperactive boy in the second year was the first to succumb. It was surprising that no one noticed how quiet he had become. His usual ruddy complexion vanished, to be replaced by a greyish pallor. This was accompanied by bouts of shivering and sweating followed by a weakness in his legs that made it difficult for him to stand.

The boy's removal to the sick bay was followed within three days by that of his three friends. Soon it became clear that the school was in the grip of an influenza epidemic. Within a week, the sick bay and four dormitories were filled to capacity with fresh cases being reported hourly. Over a hundred of the three hundred and seventy pupils were already afflicted. Nor was the teaching staff immune. The history, Latin and Greek, and mathematics teachers had already reported sick. Those who thought the chemistry and biology master would be rendered immune by the noxious gases he produced in the laboratory were proved to be sadly mistaken.

The headmaster of Forest Manor School stared at his senior prefect in dismay. 'Seventeen,' he repeated dully. 'You did say seventeen more cases, James?'

James Cowgill nodded. 'Mostly fourth form and lower fifth. The latest tally is one hundred and forty-seven. We can no longer isolate them. Someone has to feed them and members of the kitchen staff are reporting sick.'

The headmaster frowned. 'That is all we need. When the case count dropped yesterday, I began to think we were over the worst. It seems as if I was wrong.'

He reflected on the problem for a while. 'There's no alternative, James, I shall have to close the school, all the boys who are fit to travel will be sent home. The rest can go as, and when, they recover. With no staff the school cannot function. My senior master and two of the house tutors are unfit and it is only a matter of time before the other teachers are affected. Do you agree?'

James Cowgill nodded. 'I was going to suggest it.'

The headmaster sighed. 'You had better ask my secretary to come in. Tell her to bring all the telegram blanks she can find. Also ask her for a supply of railway warrants.'

The headmaster stared at the door that James had closed behind him. What an inglorious end, he thought, to Cowgill's time as one of the best head prefects in the history of Forest Manor.

Closing the school was a major logistics operation. Eventually, nine days before the scheduled end of term, James Cowgill reported that the final dozen boys and masters had been delivered to the station. The school was now empty.

'What about you, James?' the headmaster asked him. 'I quite forgot that I promised your parents you would remain here over Christmas. That is no longer possible.'

James Cowgill smiled. 'I shall go back to Scarborough, headmaster. Mrs Dallas, our cook, has been left in charge. She will look after me. I can catch a train tomorrow and be in Scarborough by late afternoon. All I need is one of your railway passes.'

The teacher smiled. 'I think we have one left. I want you to know how much I appreciate all you have done. It is far beyond the call of duty. I will find time before next term to write to your parents. It is the least I can do to let them know what the school owes to you.'

The headmaster rose to his feet and shook James warmly by the hand. 'It has been a privilege to teach you. You are a credit to the school. I shall look forward to hearing of your deeds in the world.'

With that valedictory message, James had to be content. He returned to his own study, his mind a jumble of emotions. He looked around the room, aware that when he left it the next morning his childhood would be gone forever. Slowly, almost reluctantly, he began to gather his belongings for packing, a mundane task with which to begin his adult life.

* * *

The solicitor's clerk waited nervously by Michael Haigh's desk. It was his first week in the post and almost the first task he had been given was to deliver these papers for signature. He had been instructed that he was to witness the document. Michael Haigh scanned the pages of the decree quickly, then reached for his pen and signed his name. With that, the slightest of physical actions, he effectively ended his marriage.

As the man left he almost collided with one of HAC's clerks, who entered Michael's office bearing a telegram. Michael took it and nodded dismissal. He watched the clerk depart then turned his attention to the paper. It was written in the Bentley code used throughout the wool trade. Quickly and accurately, he read and translated the encrypted message.

The telegram contained the text of an article from a Melbourne daily paper. 'Farmers are increasingly worried that the prolonged drought is going to have an adverse effect on their yields come shearing time. They are already concerned at the failure of the lambing season, which in the worst affected areas has resulted in a reduction of more than 50% in the number of surviving lambs.'

He laid the telegram on his desk, stood up and began to pace around the room. He was alone with this decision. He had no one to consult. Albert was in Switzerland and likely to remain there for some considerable time. The news of Cissie was not encouraging, as evidenced in the regular letters Michael received. Nor could he turn to Philip Ackroyd for advice. The senior partner had been hard hit by the death of his daughter, Hermione, and it was likely to be a long time before either Manor Row or Change saw Philip again.

Michael's quandary lay in the depressed state of the textile industry. There were signs that business was starting to pick up slightly. The difficulty was that these were only small signs and there had been previous instances when a mild recovery had proved to be a false dawn. Should Michael gamble or should he wait for further proof? If he chose the latter, he might miss the boat.

A knock at the door disturbed Michael's reverie. He looked up and bade the caller enter. James Cowgill appeared in the doorway, smiled slightly, and asked, 'Busy, Michael?'

Haigh smiled back. 'Never too busy to see you, James.'

When they were both seated, James explained that he was on the way to Scarborough but had decided to pop in and see how Michael was faring. He explained the crisis at school, then added, 'You looked to be deep in thought, how are you coping as the Great Panjandrum?'

Michael grinned and said he had been on the horns of a dilemma. He pointed to the telegram and outlined its contents, then explained the state of the industry. 'So the problem is whether to gamble on the strength of this telegram and buy a lot of stock, or whether to hold off and risk losing out as prices go up.'

'I can see the difficulty,' James agreed. 'Have you come to any decision?'

Michael shook his head. 'I was wondering how the others would have reacted. Do you have any idea what your father would do in this situation?'

James thought it over a moment before replying. 'I've no idea what Father or Grandfather would do, but I know what I would do.'

'Try me with it,' Michael prompted. 'I would be glad of any inspiration.'

'Well, I'd be tempted to buy on a limited basis. I would concentrate on the bestselling types and buy fifty per cent over and above what you need for stock. That way, you're covered. If the price goes up you will have a big profit on what you buy now. You can follow the market up and keep buying, maintaining a stock that averages below market price. If prices go down, they cannot fall very far, so you will not have lost more than you can afford.'

Michael stared at James. He could barely believe what he had heard. He knew James as a personable young man with a good brain and fine physique. He now knew that James also possessed a maturity far in advance of his years and had just exhibited business acumen many experienced merchants would have envied.

* * *

'Are you sure you will be all right on your own?' Mrs Dallas had asked for the tenth or eleventh time.

'I'll be fine,' Alice reassured her. 'Don't worry, everything will be quite safe.' She said farewell and locked the door behind the departing cook. With the freedom of the large house a spirit of adventure overcame her. She wandered through the rooms, her head held high, pretending for the moment that this was her home. She could do as she wished, she could even sleep in James's bed; perhaps even pretend he was there.

When the York train arrived in Scarborough, James alighted and crossed immediately to the exit. Had his carriage been at the rear of the platform he might possibly have seen Mrs Dallas in the station waiting to board the train for its return journey.

He was mildly surprised to find the front door of Byland Crescent locked. He let himself in, left his bags in the entrance hall, and went down into the basement. There was no sign of life in either the kitchen or adjoining rooms. He collected his bags then carried them upstairs to his room and decided he needed to freshen up following his journey. He took off his jacket, collar and tie, then removed his shirt, picked up a towel and headed for the bathroom.

In the first few seconds, it was difficult to judge which of the two was the more embarrassed. The slight rattle of the doorknob that preceded the opening of the bathroom door caused Alice to sit upright in the bath. James, expecting to find an empty room, stopped dead inside the threshold, as if he had walked into the door rather than through it. His brain cleared as he looked at Alice, her shoulders glistening from the array of tiny soap bubbles that had collected there, the creamy plunge of her neck towards her breasts and onward. She was mortified in that brief span, both at being discovered where she had no right to be, and from the embarrassment of her all too visible nakedness.

'Alice,' James said her name gently as he strode across the room towards her. He knelt beside the bath. 'Alice,' he repeated the word like a caress.

'James, oh, Master James, I shouldn't be in . . . I'm so sorry . . . I didn't know—'

'Alice,' he interrupted; his tone masterful. 'Shut up.'

He reached forward and lifted her from the bath. Cradled in his arms, soapy water cascading onto the marble tiling of the floor, she struggled, as much with herself as with James. Then he kissed her as he had in the shelter, only this time there was no struggle, no protest, merely a response that matched his own eager passion. He felt the blood pounding in his veins as his desire mounted.

Abruptly, or so it seemed, he turned and if he felt the burden of Alice in his arms it was unnoticeable. He carried her down the wide corridor to his room, shouldering the door closed behind them and laid her gently on the bed, following her there a second later. He saw the leap of matching passion in her face. He stood up briefly to remove the rest of his clothing, then once more took her in his arms. For a long moment they lay motionless, their bodies pressed close to one another, then he kissed her again. He moved his mouth from hers and kissed her neck, her shoulders, then her breasts, then back to her mouth once more. Moments later Alice felt a sharp, painful sensation as he entered her. Then they became lovers.

Several blissful hours later as they lay in each other's arms, James asked, 'What happened to Mrs Dallas?'

Alice turned, her hair tickling James's neck. 'She heard from a friend in York who is ill. She has gone to stay with her for three days.'

'Oh dear,' James said solemnly. 'What are we going to do for three whole days?' Alice's reply was suitably demonstrative.

* * *

During the swift passage of their stay in Switzerland, Albert and Hannah waited with dread for an appointment with the specialist in charge of Cissie's case. He would give them a report on their daughter's treatment and an appraisal of her chances of survival.

At the same time, in Hilda Drummond's rooms at Princess Caroline's School near Harrogate, Ada was settling to her new duties. She learned quickly and thoroughly, for Hilda's tutelage was adept and Ada was a willing and eager student.

Within the bounds of the same school, her sister Connie read and re-read the letter she had received from Michael Haigh, in which he proposed an outing to Harrogate over the Christmas holiday.

In Bradford, buoyed up by recent sales, Michael placed a big buying order for Australian fleece wool, in contrast to his major competitors, who, gambling on a fall in prices, were selling short.

During those days James and Alice never spoke of the future. Both were too terrified to think of it. Neither could contemplate a life without the other, so they blocked it from their minds. Instead they spoke of the past and their origins and it was then that James learned from Alice what little she knew of her background.

When she had been found on the doorstep of the hospital in Harrogate, there had been nothing to indicate her identity, or that of her parents. She had been named Alice after the nurse who had discovered the small bundle as she reported for work and the surname Fisher was derived from one of the patrons of the orphanage she subsequently entered. Alice's vivid and moving description of life in the orphanage, then the workhouse, held James's appalled attention. As Alice described the grim and often brutal daily routine of that upbringing, James knew that his feelings for Alice had gone far beyond that physical attraction so often mistaken for love.

In turn he told Alice something of the Cowgill family history. Alice was intrigued to realize how recent their prosperity had been. She was entranced by an account James gave of a visit he had made several years earlier to the tiny cottage where his father had been born. His detailed description of the appalling poverty and living conditions, the premature death of many children, the disease, poor food, and lack of sanitation, moved and horrified her.

Although they never spoke of it at the time, it was abundantly clear to both of them that, whatever the differences in their upbringing and station in life might have been and whatever difficulties lay before them, their future was to be spent together. An unbreakable bond had been formed. All too soon their idyll was ended by Mrs Dallas's return and the testing process began.

* * *

Christmas was a muted celebration in Byland Crescent. Christmas Day was spent in open fashion, due to James's insistence that Mrs Dallas and Alice join him to partake of the Christmas dinner.

A letter received from his father, in response to a note James had dashed off, provided a solemn background to the festive season. Albert informed him the doctors had indicated that Cissie's health was broken beyond repair and that the disease would, sooner or later, exact its final toll. What slim chance of recovery there might be would manifest itself within the next few weeks. Cissie herself, he reported, was remarkably composed and the letters she had received from James, Connie, and Ada had provided a welcome lift to her morale.

'She has been particularly amused by your description of the influenza epidemic, with pupils and staff "falling like ninepins". Sonny seems to have adopted the role of court jester, with the sole task of amusing Cissie. He entertains us all with his antics. Although I am sure he misses home, he is cheerful from rising in the morning until he is put to bed at night. Henry looks after our needs with speed and efficiency, so really we are most comfortable. I trust that Mrs Dallas and Alice are looking after you and you are getting all you want.'

The final sentence brought a wry smile to James's face when he read it.

CHAPTER TEN

Although Connie and Ada shared the same school they saw very little of one another. It was some days therefore before Connie was able to catch up with her sister to inform her of the proposed outing. Ada was pleased to be included in the invitation, for she was aware that it would be a lonely time. With her sister's approval, Connie sat down to compose her reply.

It was more than a week before Michael's response arrived. In it, he outlined his plans for the day, which included a visit to Harrogate shops, an art gallery, followed by afternoon tea taken at the Crown Hotel. He advised Connie that he had written to the headmistress with details of the excursion and expected no opposition from that quarter.

It was his final paragraph that brought colour to Connie's cheeks and set her heart fluttering.

Please accept my humble apologies, Connie, for the delay in replying, but I have been much occupied in business matters. Rest assured that I am striving to ensure that I prove worthy of the trust placed in me by your father and Philip. Even when I am so occupied, however, you are never far from my thoughts. Ever your friend,
Michael.

Connie read this paragraph time and again until she could quote from it verbatim. Not that she did, even when Ada asked her for details of the letter. Connie merely outlined the itinerary and told her the date. Of the existence or whereabouts of the original, neither Ada nor any other member of the Cowgill family was ever aware.

Michael had indeed been busy, for the influenza outbreak had robbed him of two of his senior salesmen and at the same time over at A & C Scouring, Ernest Cowgill had gone down with the same complaint. Fortunately demand was still slack and he had been able to pacify clients by talking to their representatives on Change. The problems at the scouring company were less easy to resolve and he was highly relieved when Ernest reported back to work.

On the Tuesday before Christmas, Michael's senior salesman came in with two large orders placed by two of the firm's biggest clients. Not only were these the two largest entries to go into the order book for over six months, but the price, quoted slightly tongue in cheek, was accepted without question. It represented tuppence per pound more than they had achieved for these types all that year. Still mindful of James's plan, but with the encouragement of these orders, Michael sent telegrams to the firm's agents in New Zealand and Australia, stepping up the buying programme by a further twenty-five per cent.

If the outing to Harrogate was the highlight of the Christmas holiday for Connie and Ada, it was no less so for Michael. Once they had escaped the restrictive ambience of the school, Michael turned to his two guests. 'Do you really want to go to an art gallery?' he asked. 'Would you prefer lunch at the Old Swan Hotel instead followed by a leisurely stroll through the Valley Gardens and a look round the shops, finishing with afternoon tea?'

The two girls needed no persuasion. The lunch was delicious. The Valley Gardens were picturesque, even in winter. Their stroll through them followed by an equally gentle saunter round Harrogate's shops set their appetites up for high-tea. The girls did an efficient demolition job on some delicious scones and appetizing cream cakes. On their return to Princess Caroline's, Michael bade them an affectionate farewell and if he lingered for a brief second while kissing Connie's hand, only she was aware of it. Equally, only Michael would have noticed the slight pressure of her hand on his in response.

* * *

Any opportunities for James and Alice to spend time in one another's company had been severely curtailed by the return of Mrs Dallas. Hastily snatched interludes when Mrs Dallas ventured into town were the best the lovers could manage. These few brief moments, added to a couple of 'accidental' meetings when Alice took a walk on the seafront of the North Bay were all they could contrive.

Partly to assuage his frustration, James occupied himself as best he could. He visited Michael in the Manor Row offices twice a week, cunningly purloining his father's first-class season ticket for the purpose. He ignored the warning printed by the railway company, threatening dire consequences for those who transgressed the 'not transferable' restriction. While in Bradford he visited his grandparents Saul and Esther Cowgill and spent several hours sitting with his Aunt Ethel, now well on the way to full recovery.

* * *

By mid-January it was already apparent to Michael that the suggestion James had made was beginning to pay off handsomely. It was impossible to estimate by how much the firm would profit but with significant increases in the price of raw wool at sales throughout Australia and New Zealand, the purchases Michael had made had already put HAC in a very advantageous position. James happened to be in the office one day in late January when a significant order was entered in the ledger from a worsted spinner in Huddersfield. The quantity ordered, fifty bales, was not immense, but the margin, after deduction of shipping and scouring charges, was. At ten pence per pound it represented the highest mark-up the firm had achieved for more than five years.

Michael's pleasure in seeing James was enhanced by the possibility that he might bring news of Connie. Although Michael realized the extreme improbability of a development in the friendship, he could not get her out of his mind. If James noticed Michael's eagerness for tidings of Connie, he was wise enough to refrain from commenting.

On the days when James remained in Scarborough he made a point of visiting his other grandparents, Philip and Ellen Ackroyd. James had always been their favourite grandchild. His visits cheered them enormously, for their grief at the loss of Hermione was compounded by loneliness.

* * *

No matter how well prepared Albert and Hannah had been, the verdict of the specialist was shocking in its finality. He offered no prospect of recovery, the brutality of this being heightened by the finite survival span. He was as gentle as could be expected with the distressed couple, but could not deliver the death sentence kindly.

When they returned from the clinic Henry had taken Sonny for a walk so they had chance to discuss the situation alone. 'There's no longer a reason for us to stay here,' Albert told Hannah. 'Why not return to England. I can take you to Eastbourne, see you installed there, then travel on to Scarborough. That way, when the crisis comes, the rest of the family will be only a train journey away. If matters don't worsen during the remainder of the winter, we can bring Cissie home to Scarborough in spring.'

They put the plan to Cissie, without mentioning the prognosis. Her face lit up with delight at the prospect. Albert smiled and told her he would write to the rest of the family to arrange visits, so that she would not be bored in Eastbourne. Her look of beaming gratitude convinced him of the wisdom of the plan.

* * *

On the last day of January, James travelled to Bradford. He visited the Manor Row offices briefly, for Michael was absent on a buying trip. From Manor Row, James walked briskly across town to Peel Square to visit his grandparents.

He walked in without knocking, to be greeted by a scene of domestic upheaval. His grandmother and Aunt Ethel were trying to tend his grandfather, who had suffered a fall. Saul was lying in the hallway at the foot of the staircase, barely conscious and bleeding profusely from a gash to the head. Neither woman had been able to lift him.

James took control. He lifted his grandfather gently onto a sofa in the sitting room and told the women to do no more than put a blanket over him and bathe the cut until his return. He then departed to summon a doctor from the nearby hospital.

* * *

On his return to Byland Crescent that evening, Alice knew something was amiss. Fortunately, Mrs Dallas was in the kitchen preparing dinner when James let himself in. 'James, what's wrong?' Alice asked, after one glance at his troubled face.

He explained then added, 'We got him to hospital; fortunately, it is directly across the road from their house. He woke up a few hours ago, but is very confused. I'm going back tomorrow morning and will stay as long as necessary. I only came home for some clothes and to write a quick note to my father. They think Grandfather has broken his skull, what they refer to as a fracture.'

Alice held him close for a few moments before they broke apart, guiltily aware that Mrs Dallas might appear at any second. After a hasty meal James wrote to his father outlining the facts, then penned quick notes to Cissie and Ada, plus one to Philip and Ellen Ackroyd. He packed a bag and retired early, intending to catch an early train.

Saul's condition was little better when James met his aunt and grandmother at the hospital the following morning. Brief spells of consciousness would be followed by long periods of coma. Not, as a doctor advised James, that this was necessarily a bad sign. Saul's brain, he explained, had been badly shaken by the fall and there would have been a lot of bruising at the very least. Neither should Saul's relatives be too concerned over the external bleeding. If the scalp had not been broken and the bleeding had been contained within the cranium, it could have led to far more serious consequences.

The following week was one of great anxiety for the family as they waited patiently at Saul's bedside. After a few days James began to notice a change, gradual at first, in his grandfather's condition. The periods of lucidity grew longer, the unconsciousness lessened.

Towards the end of his stay when the improvement had been marked enough to merit his absence, James travelled to Harrogate to see Connie and Ada and put their minds at rest about Saul. They greeted him with the news that they had been expecting his visit, having received a letter from their father informing them that James would be coming to see them. James was baffled by this statement. It was only on his return to Byland Crescent that the mystery was solved.

It was late afternoon when he reached Byland Crescent. He was tired after the stressful week, too much so to notice the troubled expression on Alice's face when she greeted him. Unaware that he was due back, Mrs Dallas had gone on an overnight visit to York, where her friend was still on the sick list. James paused only to collect the letters off the hall stand before he and Alice wandered through to the sitting room. He sat in one of the large armchairs, with Alice on his knee. 'James,' she said gently. 'I have to talk to you.'

'Very well, but first I must read this letter from my father. Do you mind?' He opened the letter and began to read. Alice saw the tortured expression on his face as he turned to her. 'Cissie is dying. The doctors have given her three months to live at most,' he said bleakly.

Alice took him in her arms and drew his head down to her breast. He started to cry and she knew that this grief must come first. Only when he had come to terms with the imminent loss of his beloved sister, on top of the stress concerning his grandfather, could Alice tell him that she was expecting his child.

When they went to bed that night James made love to her with an unexpected savagery quite at odds with his gentle, considerate nature. Alice acquiesced, aware that he was expiating his rage and grief. One small corner of her rejoiced that she was the one he had turned to in his need, no matter how he expressed it. Afterwards, as he lay exhausted in her arms, he remembered. 'You wanted to talk to me when I arrived and I forgot all about it. What did you want to tell me?'

Alice might have baulked had she been less confident in his love for her. That knowledge gave her the courage she needed. 'James, my love, I don't want to cause you any more worry now, when you have so much grief and anxiety, but I must tell you. I think I'm pregnant.'

'What!'

James sat up in bed. A long silence, an eternity for Alice, followed his startled exclamation. 'Oh, my goodness me,' he said at last. He turned and took her in his arms. 'We're going to have a baby. I can't believe it. That's wonderful.'

'I think so too, James. But what about your family?'

'How will they react, do you mean? Well, as I see it they can either accept it or not. Naturally I would prefer that they accept it, but if they don't we will have to manage alone. I love you, Alice and nothing will ever change that. Nothing that anyone could say or do will take me from you. Only you could do that.'

He kissed her long and tenderly then held her while she sobbed gently. Eventually exhaustion overtook them and they fell asleep.

So appalled had James been by the news of Cissie that he had failed to absorb the remaining content of his father's letter. The following morning he read it once more, relaying the contents to Alice. 'Mother is to stay with Cissie in Eastbourne, while Father returns here. He wants me to tell Ada and Connie the bad news and says he will be back in a week's time.' James looked up from the letter, his face, Alice noted with concern, haggard from strain. 'He has obviously not received my letter telling him about Grandfather's accident.' He looked at her with something akin to despair. 'So that is something else I will have to tell him.'

Three days later James travelled again to Harrogate for a distressing interview with Connie and Ada. After he had attempted to console them, without noticeable success, he went to Bradford where he called in at Manor Row. His conversation with Michael was sombre. When personal affairs had been dealt with James told him of Albert's imminent return. Michael said that he had suspected as much, as he had not heard from Albert for a couple of weeks adding that he had written to Switzerland informing Albert of the extensive buying programme he had instigated. 'I didn't tell him it was all your idea. I thought it would be a pleasant surprise for when he returns. The news is good, excellent in fact and getting better every day. Wool prices are on average over twenty-five per cent higher than they were before Christmas and we are stocked from cellar to rafters. Thanks to you, our margins are increasing all the time.'

James grinned. 'I'm so glad about that, for I have had an idea.' He pulled his chair closer to the desk and explained.

He continued on to Peel Square. Finding no one at home he went on to the hospital where he found his aunt and grandmother waiting in a corridor. Saul had recognized Esther and Ethel the previous day and although still far from lucid had seemed much brighter but had now suffered a slight relapse. The doctors had assured them there was no real cause for concern and were examining him at the moment. James joined them on the hard bench; all they could do was sit and wait.

CHAPTER ELEVEN

Albert saw his entourage safely installed in the house he had rented in Eastbourne. It was comfortable and well appointed, with large, airy rooms giving some splendid sea views. Cissie had withstood the journey well, so he was as content as could be expected when he began his journey north. The long hours on the train gave Albert time to reflect. Most of his thoughts were on Cissie, although from time to time he wondered and worried about how things would be at home and at work. Phillip and Ellen were still mourning Hermione, so Michael was still shouldering the burden at HAC. Concern over the state of the business added to Albert's worries. He had received Michael's letter informing him of the heavy buying orders he had sent out. Cut off from market news, Albert was beset by fear that the responsibility was proving too much for the younger man. The rash speculation in raw wool would, Albert feared, cost the firm dear.

Reaching Byland Crescent in the late afternoon, Albert dumped his bags in the hall. There was no one about, so after a brief spell of uncertainty he went into his study. A mound of correspondence lay on his desk. Each item had been opened and replied to. Copies of the replies were fixed to the originals and all were in James's handwriting. Albert was still standing behind the desk when he heard the door open. He looked up to see James and Alice standing in the doorway, hand in hand. Albert barely had time to register that his son was dressed in the deepest black before the significance of their pose struck home. A dull heaviness came over Albert's heart as he stared at the young couple and with it a rising tide of anger.

'Father, we must talk to you,' James said quietly.

Albert was incapable of holding back his rage. 'Just what is it you have to say that I have not already guessed?' he said with gritted teeth.

'Probably very little.' In contrast to his father, James was coolness personified. 'Alice and I are in love. We intend to marry, for Alice is carrying my child. That will happen, either with or without your blessing.'

Albert's scornful laugh rang round the room, making Alice flinch. James however, stood, unmoved by the sound.

'Blessing,' Albert repeated. 'Blessing, you have no chance of a blessing from me. You choose to amuse yourself with this trollop while your sister is dying, your mother and I are at our wits' end and you come along, calm as you please, asking for blessing because you have put the slut in the family way. No, you have not got my blessing, as you have chosen to disregard all the principles we tried to instil in you and have no sense of filial duty whatsoever. I want nothing more to do with you. Get out of my house now. Get out and take the whore with you, although how you will survive I dread to think.'

Without so much as the flicker of an eyelid did James acknowledge that his father's words had touched him. In cold, level tones, he delivered his reply. 'Alice is neither a trollop, a whore, nor a slut. She was a virgin until I seduced her. Now she is bearing my child, your grandchild, and she will do it with the protection of my name. Not because it is my duty, but because I love her as I hope she loves me. If you make us leave now, we will never return.'

James waited, but there was no response.

'Very well then, but before we go I must tell you one other thing,' James continued and now his voice contained a hard edge of steel. 'You spoke in high and mighty terms about filial duty. You never even stopped to wonder why I am wearing black. Very well, it is my painful duty to inform you that your father died two days ago.'

Albert sank into the chair. The room swam before his eyes. He neither saw nor heard James and Alice leave his study, nor, fifteen minutes later, when they had packed a few possessions, did he hear them leave the house. James paused in the entrance hall briefly before opening the front door. He fumbled in his pocket to check that his notecase was intact. Only when he was certain that the five-thousand-pound fee he had received from Michael Haigh was safely inside, did the couple step out into Byland Crescent.

* * *

It was too late for Albert to set off for Bradford that evening. He told Mrs Dallas brusquely what had occurred and declined the offer of dinner. The following morning as he was leaving the house, the postman thrust a letter into his hand. He put it into his overcoat pocket to read later.

It was to be a day of shocks for Albert. The first came when he opened the letter during the train journey. It was from the headmaster of Forest Manor School. It sang the praises of the former senior prefect for his exemplary conduct during the influenza epidemic. Albert was about to crumple the letter up when a phrase caught his eye. He spread the letter out and looked at it once more. Focusing, through misty eyes, he read,

> *I have only recently learned the extent of his self-sacrifice. James, with complete disregard for the danger to his own health, assisted both the medical team and catering staff in tending to the needs of afflicted pupils and teachers alike. Words can only touch on the selflessness and devotion demonstrated by your son.*

Albert's second shock came when he reached Peel Square. The time he spent with his mother and sister was a sad and difficult one. Grieving for his father was bad enough. He girded himself for the task ahead. 'Mother, Ethel,' he began gently, 'I'm afraid I have more dreadful news for you.'

Ethel laid a hand on her brother's arm. 'If it is about poor Cissie, don't torment yourself, Albert. James has already broken the sad news to us, on the same day as he told Connie and Ada. Mother and I could not have coped without James, from the moment of Father's accident, through the time in hospital to his death. James made all the funeral arrangements and sorted out the church, the vicar, and the undertaker. He even took care of the registration and obtaining the Death Certificate.'

Another shock came when Albert appeared at Manor Row. From the apologetic demeanour and comments of the staff he deduced that they were already aware of his loss. Michael Haigh's opening words confirmed this. 'Albert, I'm sorry to have heard about your father. James called in the day he died and told me.'

Later, when they got round to talking business, Albert received his final and probably greatest shock of the day. 'I guess with all you have had to endure you must be desperate for some good news. I know it is not much to counteract the terrible ordeal you are going through, but at least the business is prospering, beyond our wildest hopes.'

Albert looked up in surprise. Michael nodded. 'We have made some enormous profits while you have been away. What's more you have James to thank for it.'

'James?' Albert echoed dully. 'I don't understand?'

Michael told him of the coup, the result of which had been to catch their competitors unawares. 'According to the calculations I made, by yesterday morning we have already banked over seven hundred thousand pounds in clear profit. Forward orders already received will more than double that figure. I estimate we might clear three million pounds in the first quarter's trading alone.'

If Albert was stunned by these figures, the follow-up information came as a knock-out blow. 'Of course, none of this would have happened without James. He both thought up the plan and gave me the confidence to implement it. I would never have dared to do it on my own initiative.'

So jumbled were Albert's thoughts when he reached the station that evening, it was a minor miracle he reached the right train. Such was his emotional state he could equally well have finished up in Edinburgh or Aberystwyth. By the time he reached Byland Crescent however, Albert's mind was clear. After a swiftly taken meal he sat down to compose a letter to Hannah.

* * *

My Darling Hannah,
I have just done the most dreadful thing. I only hope that in time you can forgive me, for I have, in a moment of violent and ill-judged temper, cast adrift that which I hold dearest. To think that I, who have always been so proud of our eldest son, should have misjudged and belittled James's actions to such a degree.

He wrote on until he had filled six foolscap pages. Only when he had sealed and addressed the envelope did he begin, in the loneliness of his heartbreak, to weep.

* * *

The repercussions from Albert's quarrel with James were immediate, severe, and wide reaching. Albert felt the first of them four days later in the reply he received from Hannah. While sympathizing with Albert over the death of his father and apologizing for being unable to travel north for the funeral, the tone of the letter was cold to the point of iciness and Albert knew, from what was omitted as much as what was written, that Hannah held him completely responsible for James's departure.

The same day brought a visit from his father-in-law. It was clear that Philip knew of the quarrel. His knowledge extended to James's involvement in the firm's windfall prof-its. Philip told his son-in-law, in no uncertain terms, that not only had Albert parted company with his son, but he had also deprived Philip and Ellen of the chance to watch their eldest grandchild mature and develop. Into the bargain he had lost the opportunity to be a grandfather himself to Alice's unborn child. This last remark stung and hurt Albert deeply. He was unhappy that Hannah must have written to her parents to inform them of all that had happened. He asked if that had been the case and in turn received a stern rebuke from Philip.

'Of course not. Hannah would not be so disloyal. Whatever criticism she may have, she will make to you direct. It was James who told us what had occurred when he and Alice came to say farewell.'

'Farewell?' Albert echoed, looking around as if he expected to see James in the room.

'Yes, he came to introduce Alice to us before they left Scarborough, and both Ellen and I found her to be a pleasant and charming girl. She obviously loves James deeply, that is clear from the way she looks at him, nothing like the tart you made her out to be.'

'You say they have left Scarborough?' Albert asked. 'Do you know where they were going?'

'From what I could gather I would not be surprised if they chose to go abroad.'

'How will they survive without money?'

'Oh, they have money,' Philip re-joined. 'James charged HAC a five-thousand-pound consultancy fee.' Philip's voice took on a harder edge. 'So apart from the stupidity you have shown by quarrelling with your son, you have done the firm a grave disservice by depriving us of someone who would have proved indispensable.'

Never had Albert felt so alone. He knew he would have to heal the breach with Hannah and her father. He knew he would have to find James and Alice and attempt to repair the damage he had caused. He knew he would have to start immediately, even before his father's funeral. Gathering his wits, he mustered what meagre support he could in the attempt. The day following his painful interview with Philip he spent a long time in Manor Row explaining all that had happened to Michael Haigh. He did not attempt to excuse himself, merely presented the bald facts. He remembered the private enquiry agent Michael had employed during the course of his divorce proceedings and obtained the man's details.

Michael, who was shocked and saddened by the news of the rift, was unwilling to join in the general criticism of Albert's part in it. He sensed the older man's desperation and willingly provided the support Albert needed.

'Michael, I'm afraid I will have to rely on you for a little longer. I must return to Eastbourne immediately following Father's funeral. I must take Connie and Ada on a final visit to their sister. Will you continue your excellent stewardship of the firm? Philip has promised to return to work immediately to help out, given the high-level of business activity.'

* * *

Albert left to visit the enquiry agent, his frame of mind slightly improved. That evening he wrote to Connie and Ada and, in a separate letter to their headmistress, explained the need to remove the girls from school for a short while. A telegram from Hannah delivered to Byland Crescent on the evening before Saul's funeral heightened the urgency of this plan.

During the first part of the long journey to Eastbourne, Albert, to his consternation, found himself having to explain away James's absence to his daughters.

'James and I had a disagreement and I lost my temper with him,' he confessed. 'He has become romantically involved with Alice the housemaid and the two have run away together.'

More than that, he would not say, despite one or two searching questions from Ada, curious to elicit more detail.

Connie remained silent throughout. When their father eventually excused himself to visit the toilet, the girls were alone in their private first-class compartment. Ada turned to Connie for enlightenment. 'You knew about this beforehand.' It was a statement rather than a question. 'You were not at all surprised to find James missing at Grandfather's funeral and just now, you never bothered to ask Father any questions. So, tell me what you know and how you found out.'

Connie leaned forward in her seat, her face animated. 'James wrote to me. It wasn't a disagreement; it was a full blown quarrel. They did not run away, Father ordered them out of the house. James and Alice have been lovers for some time and now she is expecting his baby. When they faced Father with the news, he was extremely angry, calling Alice all sorts of vile names. He virtually accused her of seducing James in an attempt to trap him. James tried to get him to see reason, but he said there was no arguing with him, so when Father told James he wanted no more to do with him, they had no alternative but to leave. James has made quite a lot of money through some sort of scheme with Michael, so he and Alice are off to make a new life together. He thinks they will go abroad and, in the letter, he was talking about Canada.'

Ada was both thrilled and saddened by the news. 'It sounds just like a novel. We will see them again though, won't we?'

Connie was dubious. 'The way James put it, I think the break was final. He is very stubborn and determined, I realize that now, and once he has set his mind to something I don't think he would be easily swayed.'

There was no time for further confidences before their father returned.

* * *

Both Connie and Ada were shocked at the deterioration in Cissie's appearance since they had last seen her. Even Albert, who had seen her more recently, could not help but notice the change.

Albert was determined to attempt to put matters right with Hannah as soon as they arrived. Contrary to his expectation in view of the tone of her letter, her greeting was warm. He did not have long to wait for an explanation.

'James and Alice came to Eastbourne two days ago,' she told him. 'I think you were totally wrong in your opinion of Alice. She seemed to me a good, caring girl, the two of them very much in love. James told me,' she continued, 'that although you and he had quarrelled bitterly I must help you, both for your own sake and for the rest of the family. He knows how much you must be grieving for your father and how much you will suffer when Cissie dies. He wanted me to tell you,' Hannah's voice quavered and she was close to tears. 'He wants you to know that he still loves you, but that he and Alice are going away to make a new life for themselves.'

* * *

Connie wrote to Michael Haigh to tell him of how matters stood at Eastbourne.

Dear Michael,

We arrived here two days ago, after the saddest of journeys. So much has gone awry since our outing at Christmas that it seems a lifetime ago. Father is full of sorrow, quite different from the man you will know at work. Partly, I think this is due to remorse over what happened with James and Alice, but more because he, like the rest of us, feels so helpless about poor Cissie. Mother too is much distressed about James and blames Father for all that happened, but everything takes second place to Cissie. Our dear sister has become very emaciated, positively waif-like in appearance. Her limbs are now so thin; they are like those of a child half her age. She always had a doll-like appearance, but that is even more apparent now for there is a luminosity about her skin. Yesterday we went for a walk by the sea, but as the slightest exertion leaves her short of breath, she needed her

*wheelchair and blanket. I think on balance the excursion
did benefit Cissie, although she was much exhausted by it.*

*She is so weakened now that Father or Henry have to carry
her up or downstairs from her bedroom, as much for fear
of her falling as anything. This morning Father brought
her down in this fashion to join the rest of us for breakfast, which for her was a bowl of warmed milk, into which
she dipped a little bread, I suppose to make digestion more
comfortable. Ada and I felt quite guilty as we tucked into
our own, far more substantial meal, which the fresh air and
exercise had given us the appetite to eat.*

*Sonny contrives to keep all our spirits up. He will not be parted
from Cissie for long, even though Mother is terrified of him
catching the disease. He makes Cissie smile with his constant
antics, but despite her cheeriness, I fear that we are very close
to the end. I marvel constantly at Cissie's stoical acceptance of
her lot. She told me last night, as we sat alone together that she
knows her fate is now in other than human hands and that we
must not grieve for her when she has gone, but remember all the
happy times together. She spoke of James and Alice, how glad
she was for them and hoped the rift with Father will be mended
in time. I confess that after I left her I was in floods of tears.*

*I will finish now, for I am tired, as much from the emotion of
all we have been through than any physical cause. I wonder
how it can be that a family such as ours can rub along for
years, on an even tide of existence, with barely a ripple to
disturb our lives, and then suddenly be beset with storm upon
storm of upheaval.*

*I am grateful to have you there, for I need someone with
whom I can share my thoughts.*

Ever your friend,
Connie Cowgill.

* * *

Two days after Connie wrote to Michael, the morning
dawned sunny and warm. Cissie opted to stay in the lounge

and was positioned in the bay window where she could look out over the sea. The large sofa on which she lay was softened with a bank of pillows and cushions and she declared herself to be perfectly comfortable. After lunch Connie and Ada took Sonny for a walk along the sea front, leaving Albert and Hannah to sit with their daughter.

The warmth of the afternoon sun streaming in through the large expanse of windows made for a drowsy atmosphere in the room and Albert, emotionally weary, dozed off in an armchair. He was awakened by Hannah who was shaking his arm gently. She pointed across the room. Cissie was looking at her father, her arms outstretched.

Albert crossed the room and knelt by the sofa. Cissie put her wafer-thin arms around his neck and he held her close. A few minutes later, he felt a change come over her. Her limbs relaxed and she gave a long, weary sigh. Albert gently laid the lifeless body of his beloved daughter on the sofa.

* * *

They brought Cissie back to Scarborough, to be buried overlooking the town she had known for so short a time yet had come to love so dearly. As the funeral of his sister was taking place, James stood at the stern of a mighty liner, his arm around Alice. They watched as the shoreline of England slowly vanished into the distant haze, then, turning towards the bow of the ship, they looked forward towards their new horizon, their life together in a new land.

PART TWO: 1902–1913

'Alas, regardless of their doom,
The little victims play!
No sense have they of ills to come,
Nor care beyond today.
Yet see how all around 'em wait
The ministers of human fate,
And black Misfortune's baleful train!
Ah, show them where in ambush stand
To seize their prey the murtherous band!
Ah, tell them, they are men!'
'Ode on a Distant Prospect of Eton College'
Thomas Gray (1716–1771)

CHAPTER TWELVE

Connie stared at the envelope in surprise. She knew the handwriting at once and was glad her parents had left the house. Her father had departed for work more than an hour earlier. Her mother had announced over breakfast that she would walk to school with Connie's younger brother, following which she would go to visit their grandmother.

Sonny had looked far from pleased at this announcement. His grimace on receiving the news was so comical that Connie almost laughed aloud. At the age of ten, rising eleven, Sonny considered himself to be far too grown-up to require an escort. His new school was only a short distance from where Hannah's parents Philip and Ellen Ackroyd lived, so on this occasion he was overruled.

Ada was still at boarding school, so when Hannah and Sonny had left, Connie had the house to herself. She looked at the inscription on the envelope once more. *Miss Constance Cowgill*. She smiled, it was fortunate that the letter had arrived when it did, for in a month's time she would no longer be Miss Constance Cowgill and Byland Crescent would no longer be her home.

Connie's slit the envelope open and removed the contents. Inside the letter was a photograph of a family group comprising a young couple in their early twenties, a little boy of about three years and, cradled in the arms of the lovely young woman, a tiny baby. Connie recognized the proud parents at once. Her elder brother James stood next to Alice, who was seated on a chaise longue, with the little boy alongside her. It was the first communication any member of the family had received from the couple following their disappearance more than four years earlier. Since then, despite their father's frantic attempts to locate the young couple, there had been no word, no trace of them.

James had intimated that they would be leaving England and had mentioned Canada as a possible destination. The remorse felt by Albert had extended to making enquiries in Canada and North America, but to no avail. Given this background, Connie was more than a little startled to read the address on the letterhead. Hampstead, on the northern outskirts of London, was probably the last place the family would have considered looking for James. Nor, as Connie soon discovered on reading the text, would they have found him there, even had they searched every building in Hampstead.

Ralph French, an old school friend of James's had agreed to act as postman. James, it appeared, was not yet prepared to reveal his and Alice's whereabouts.

His news was good for the most part. Alice had given birth to their son, whom they had christened James Saul, but known to everyone as Saul. Three weeks before the photograph had been taken Alice had been safely delivered of their second child, a girl. Saul's baby sister was to be christened Cecilia Alice but he had no doubt that she would be known to one and all as Cissie.

James wrote that they had invested in a business, failing to reveal its nature. Although it was early days, he reported that the business was flourishing and three years hard work was beginning to pay dividends. He had thought long and hard before eventually deciding to make contact. It had been Alice who had persuaded him to recant 'his stubbornness' as she referred to it. He ended by begging Connie to write back with all the family news, directing her response to Ralph French.

* * *

The only discernible change to the Manor Row offices was the brass plaque attached to the stone wall outside the main entrance. The plate, which had only been in position a few months read: *Haigh, Ackroyd and Cowgill Limited, Wool Merchants and Importers.*

Albert Cowgill had suggested the protection of limited liability status for both the companies. The scouring plant also carried new signage. Philip Ackroyd was the major shareholder in both along with Albert and a smaller issue to Michael Haigh, newly appointed to the board. Ernest Cowgill, assigned the role of Managing Director at the renamed *HAC (Scouring) Ltd.* was also a shareholder.

The events of 1898 and 1899, when the firm had made enormous profits, had prompted the idea. Albert had been more than a little alarmed by the level of their success. Even as they were celebrating it, he had pointed out the dangers involved when wool prices fluctuated so wildly. The point Albert made was that it would be just as easy for the firm to be caught out by such changes.

Philip Ackroyd was Chairman of both companies; Michael Haigh became Company Secretary of both parent and subsidiary and was also Deputy Managing Director of the parent company. Albert held the Managing Directorship of HAC Ltd.

The Opening Statement of Affairs showed the company had a net worth, depending on the value of wool stocks, somewhere between six and eight million pounds — small wonder that HAC Ltd. was seen as the market leader. Not that the group was without competition. Although the vast majority of their rivals had suffered by comparison, one or two had been shrewd enough, or lucky enough to follow the market trends as accurately as HAC. One firm in particular had emerged at this time and was proving to be quite a thorn in their flesh. Formed by an alliance between three salesmen and a buyer from merchants in Bradford, the firm of Walker, Pearson, Foster and Dobson was in the process of following HAC's lead by becoming a limited company.

For a while, this entity was known by its initials WPF&D until someone asked what the initials stood for. Some wag, overhearing the question answered, War, Pestilence, Famine and Death. Ever after, they were known as The Four Horsemen.

The day following Connie's receipt of her brother's letter was earmarked for a board meeting of the directors of HAC Ltd. These meetings had been instigated by Philip Ackroyd and usually took place either at his home on Weaponness Park in Scarborough, or at Byland Crescent.

One director was particularly happy when it came time for a board meeting in Scarborough. For Michael Haigh it represented an all too infrequent opportunity to spend time with his fiancée, Connie. On the train journey to Scarborough, the evening before the meeting, business was not discussed, as the directors concentrated on lighter topics. Philip had announced that plans were afoot for the building of a golf course on the South Cliff at Scarborough, close to his home. Albert threw up his hands in mock horror at the idea. 'I suppose that means we will see even less of you next summer than we did last, which, as I remember, was spent on every cricket ground where Yorkshire were playing.'

Michael could not resist joining in the fun. 'Have you told Lord Hawke of your plans, to give him time to organize another twelfth man for the Yorkshire team?' he asked Ackroyd.

'I only went to a few games,' Philip protested mildly.

'Only because the others were rained off,' Albert retorted.

'Will you be able to switch role models easily?' Michael asked slyly. 'You know, one minute George Herbert Hirst, the next Harry Vardon.'

When the evening meal at Byland Crescent was over, Albert and Hannah took Sonny for a stroll down to the south bay. There, with Hannah acting as wicketkeeper, Sonny would be able to play on the flat, firm, sandy beach. Although Albert's bowling was not as testing as Grandfather Ackroyd's cunning leg breaks, to a young man with ambitions to play for Yorkshire, Sonny was nevertheless grateful for the practice.

Their departure gave Michael and Connie an hour or more to themselves. There were wedding plans to discuss, so it was at about the time when bad light curtailed play on the beach that Connie had chance to show Michael the letter and photograph she had received from James. Once Michael had expressed his admiration for the sturdy limbs and handsome features of Connie's nephew and voiced his hope for the young man's sister, he read James's letter with interest. Connie explained her predicament regarding whether or not to inform her parents about it, to which, Michael came up with a compromise solution.

'Why not write back to James, via this chap in Hampstead, telling him all the news. You can give him our new address in Heaton, for by the time he gets your letter we will be living there. You can ask James what he wants to do about telling the family.'

The following morning, Connie sat down to compose her reply to James.

Dear James and Alice, Saul and baby Cissie,
I really don't know where to start as there is so much to tell you. I was so excited to receive your letter that I have scarcely been able to concentrate on anything since.
Let me start with the family. Ada and I travelled down to Eastbourne shortly after your visit there. We were both shocked by Cissie's appearance, as I am sure you were. We managed to spend some time with her, but she died peacefully in Father's arms only two days later. We brought her back to Scarborough to be buried. Mother and I go to visit her grave at least once a month and I tell her all that is happening to those she knew and loved. I shall have much to relate on my next visit.

Grandfather and Grandmother Ackroyd are both well. Grandfather plays cricket on the beach with Sonny and bamboozles him with something he calls leg-spinners. Sonny vows he will master them soon. He is getting to be quite a young man now, he reminds me so much of you, James, especially now he has started going to Scarborough College.

Ada has one more year at Princess Caroline's before she leaves. I believe she is doing very well. She keeps her own counsel, but then she always did. She is very friendly with another girl in her year, called Eleanor, who came to visit us one holiday. She did a very good painting of Scarborough Castle and St Mary's Church while she was here and gave it to Mother and Father in appreciation of their hospitality. She is a fair, slender girl, not unlike poor Cissie, so perhaps Ada feels protective towards her.

Sadly, I have to tell you that Grandmamma Cowgill died last winter. She never really recovered from Grandpa's death. She was starting to wander in her mind and sometimes in a real sense too. Aunt Ethel had a hard time coping with her. Matters came to a head last November, when Grandma was found out in the garden late at night, clad only in her night attire. The sad but inevitable consequence of that escapade was that Grandmamma caught a chill, which turned into pneumonia. She died three weeks later. Aunt Ethel does not like living in that house alone. She has her eye on a little cottage in Clayton and has asked Father to sell Peel Square and buy the cottage out of the proceeds. Aunt Ethel is back to full health now. I think the relief from responsibility and worry has helped. She is back to terrorizing the infants at Great Horton School once more.

Father's sister, Aunt Bessie, who emigrated to America with her husband Maurice Barker, is back in Bradford. Maurice found it difficult to keep a job there and Bessie became homesick. They returned last year, together with their children, Clarence, the eldest, and the twins. Some things haven't changed though, as Maurice is still finding difficulty in getting work. Father jokes that it is because Maurice is a

103

shift worker. When anyone mentions work, Maurice shifts. I understand Father feels obliged to employ both him and his eldest son.

Mother and Father remain in the best of health, although much saddened and distressed by Cissie's death. Mother was very angry with Father for a long time over his quarrel with you. She blamed Father, and I am fairly sure deep down she still does, but the subject is not raised very often. I overheard her telling Father that anyone could tell at a glance what a nice girl Alice was. Father was so upset, he too blames himself and spent a lot of time and money trying to find you, to no avail. You must have covered your tracks really well.

As to my own news, by the time you receive this letter I will be married. I hope you approve of my choice, for he is Michael Haigh. Mother and Father are a little disappointed that, because Michael is divorced, we cannot marry in church but must have a civil ceremony. I do not mind, as long as I can be with my dear one all the time I shall be happy. We are to live in Bradford, in Heaton to be precise. I only hope the day will come soon when I can return the compliment and send you a Haigh family photograph.

The ceremony and reception are to be held in Scarborough. Michael and I will be going away on honeymoon, but provokingly, Michael will not tell me where, no matter how I try to wheedle the secret out of him. He says he wants to surprise me. In all other matters, he is attentive, kind, and considerate and I am the luckiest girl alive, so I must forgive this little foible.

Michael, Father, and Grandfather Ackroyd have been very busy at work and very successful too, although I know little about business. The latest thing they have done is turn the merchants and the scourers into something they call limited liability companies. I hope you understand a little better than I. They now have board meetings. These appear to be occasions when the three of them spend a lot of time gossiping, eating a large meal, and having far too much to drink. Father and Michael were both quite inebriated when they

returned from the last one and Grandfather complained of
a headache all the following day.
I am sure Grandpa Cowgill would have been proud that you
gave his name to your firstborn, Saul, and Mother, especially,
would be deeply moved to know that you have called your
daughter Cissie. I cannot close without asking if you will
allow me to pass news of you to the family. I was alone when
your letter arrived, which is perhaps a good thing, for Father
and Mother would have been sure to recognize your hand-
writing. I will respect your wishes in this, but I am certain
they would be happy to hear all I can tell them of you and to
know that you are well, happy, and prospering. They would
also wish to know about their grandchildren. Please let me
know, as I am bursting to tell someone. Michael knows, but
I have sworn him to secrecy.
Please give my dearest love to Alice, to little Saul and to
baby Cissie.
Your loving sister,
Connie.

She added her and Michael's new address, sealed the
envelope, slipped quietly from the house and headed for the
post office.

* * *

When Hilda Drummond left Princess Caroline's School,
Ada had been devastated. She felt bewildered, lost, and
lonely. Hilda, her friend, mentor, and eventually her lover,
had been a touchstone for Ada's early days at the school. Her
period as personal dogsbody to the head of house ended with
Hilda's departure and Ada was transferred to the less rarefied
atmosphere of a four-bed dormitory. She settled to the new
routine, keeping her own counsel before she made friends
with another girl in the same room. Eleanor Rhodes was a
slender, pretty, blonde girl, not unlike Ada's late sister and
with the same quiet ways as Cissie. Her shyness and timidity

made her much put upon by some girls. This formed the backbone for their early friendship. Ada, well able to look after herself in a physical sense, warned off the girls who were making Eleanor a target for their petty and hurtful bullying and thus a bond was formed.

Eleanor was an outstandingly talented painter, whose art teacher prophesied a great future for her. Her speciality was for landscape painting and the countryside around North Yorkshire provided ample scope for the expression of her ability. Eleanor's teachers gave dispensation for her to capture some of the local beauty spots on canvas. These involved field trips the teachers could not consent to being taken alone. Practically speaking it would not have been possible either, with all the impedimenta that had to be carried. Ada was co-opted as companion and porter combined. Fine summer days were spent on what were in effect elongated picnics with a little painting thrown in. Eleanor would select a scene she wanted to paint and Ada would unfold a blanket and sit reading until Eleanor tired of her work, or hunger called.

One hot summer afternoon the girls set up camp in a small clearing in a wood in upper Nidderdale. A small stream tumbled over stones nearby on its way to join the River Nidd and eventually the mighty Ouse. There was a small wooden footbridge over the stream, its timbers green from the continual damp. Ada lay down on the blanket to read, while Eleanor commenced painting. Soon, the warmth of the sun, the heavy, drowsy scent of the wildflowers and the lullaby of the stream as it ran gently by, combined to send Ada to sleep.

When she awoke, she had no idea how long she had been sleeping. She asked Eleanor, who laughed and replied, 'Hours, you were snoring so loudly you scared the birds away.'

Ada grimaced and sat up, straightening her dress. 'What luck with the masterpiece?' she asked.

'Come and see for yourself.'

Ada climbed to her feet, a little stiffly from the humps and hollows on which she had been resting. She stood alongside Eleanor and examined the painting. She blinked in surprise. It was a faithful representation of the scene before them, with the trees in full foliage, the many silvery hues of the stream as it splashed over boulders captured on the canvas, with the mossy wooden bridge faithfully depicted. What startled Ada was the foreground, in which was a blanket strewn with remnants of a picnic, a discarded book, and Ada herself, hair tumbled, skirt askew, lying fast asleep. 'Wow,' Ada said, impressed and pleased. 'That is brilliant, you got me wrong though, I just wish I was as pretty as you've made me out to be.'

'Nonsense,' Eleanor told her firmly. 'Of course you're pretty.'

Something in Eleanor's tone surprised Ada. She looked up at her friend. Eleanor blushed and smiled shyly. Ada stared at her for a long moment.

'Say it,' Eleanor breathed, as gentle as a whisper.

Astonishment had rendered Ada speechless. 'Do you want me to say it for you?' Eleanor asked.

Ada could do nothing but nod.

Eleanor cast a glance around at the deserted scene then gently laid her brush on the easel stand. Wordlessly she took hold of Ada's arm, pulled her close, then kissed her.

'How long have you known?' Ada asked. They were lying on the blanket, dreamily staring up at the few thin wispy clouds gently scudding across the blue sky.

'Oh, from the time you were protecting me against that gang of bullies. You took my hand once to guide to safety when they were all gathered round me. I could feel your wrist pressed tight against my arm and your pulse was throbbing like mine. That convinced me I was right, but I had suspected the year before, when you were with Hilda.'

Ada sat up in alarm, but Eleanor laughed. 'Don't worry I'm sure no one else noticed. It was just the way you looked at her sometimes.'

CHAPTER THIRTEEN

Three months later, Connie accompanied her husband Michael, first to London, then on to Paris and thence to Rome on their honeymoon.

Byland Crescent had been en-fete that day, much like Queen Victoria's Diamond Jubilee of five years earlier. The lawn in the centre of Byland Crescent was covered by a large marquee, where the guests sat in comfort to enjoy the sumptuous wedding feast prepared for them by the incomparable Mrs Dallas.

Thwarted by circumstances of his wish to see his daughter married in the splendid setting of St Mary's Church, Albert was determined that the reception should do the occasion the justice it deserved.

On such a day, business matters, if not forgotten entirely, were for most of the guests of subsidiary importance. All the members of the Cowgill, Haigh, and Ackroyd families that could be mustered were present, along with a host of friends and neighbours of both bride and groom's families.

Thus it was that Harry and Florence Binks, together with their son Charlie, found themselves in juxtaposition with Doctor Steven Culleton, his wife Elizabeth and their family. Charlie, much to his barely disguised delight, found he was seated next to the Culleton's daughter, Rebecca, alongside her was her much younger brother, Steven junior. At nineteen, Rebecca was two years younger than Charlie. She was tall and fair, with handsome rather than beautiful features, slim without being slender and with a roguish smile that masked a more serious, highly practical disposition. It was the smile that first captivated Charlie.

Harry Binks had been employed as a wool buyer for a large worsted manufacturer in Huddersfield for many years. Now, as he confided to his brother-in-law Albert, he was considering a change. Their conversation, although short, was to have far-reaching effects.

'Why are you thinking of leaving your employer?' Albert asked.

'It is for Charlie's benefit as much as mine,' Harry explained. 'He has gone about as far as he can with the chemical firm he works for. These are exciting times in the chemical side of the industry. New techniques and different compounds are making fabric dyeing a totally different process to what it was only a few years ago. Soon there will be ranges of cloth such as we have never seen before.'

Albert was intrigued and wanted to know more. 'So what are your plans in all this?'

'My idea is to use all Charlie's technical ability to benefit a company we have an interest in, rather than contributing to the profits of one where he is merely an employee. He has invented at least three really good dyes and all he has had to show for it is a pat on the back and that will not pay the coalman or the grocer.'

'How do you plan to go about it?' asked Albert, his interest seemingly casual.

'The problem is financial. We can find premises, we have suppliers lined up, and customers will be clamouring for all we can produce. But the equipment we need is expensive, so it would take a backer prepared to invest a large sum of money to turn it into a practical idea rather than a desirable dream.'

The conversation was interrupted by a chance remark from another guest and drifted into other channels.

Ada, from her vantage point on the head table, watched the assembled guests with interest, while wishing her dear friend Eleanor had been present to share the experience with her. As a surprise wedding gift for her sister and brother-in-law, Ada had commissioned a painting from Eleanor. The completed work, a large watercolour landscape, depicted a particularly spectacular and beautiful stretch of countryside close to the girls' school. Some months previously, during the Easter holiday, Ada had brought up the subject of her own favourite walks and had cleverly drawn Connie into the conversation and elicited the information she needed to furnish Eleanor with the right subject matter for the canvas.

The painting, proudly displayed at the centre of the long trestle table containing the wedding presents, was a view of Nidderdale, looking west from Harrogate towards Pateley Bridge and the distant Pennine hills. The contrasting shades created by sunshine and broken cloud were faithfully depicted on the sloping valley sides. The dale was dotted here and there with occasional grey stone farmsteads, and the fields lined with the dry-stone walls so much a feature of the Yorkshire landscape. In the lower right-hand corner was a tiny inscription, proclaiming the artist to be Eleanor Rhodes. Many guests, impressed by the beauty and grandeur of the tranquil scene had enquired about the young artist, which filled Ada with quiet pride. She had already been made aware that Connie and Michael were deeply touched by her choice of present. As Michael told Ada when thanking her for the gift, the landscape would have pride of place in their new home.

* * *

Hardly had Michael and Connie unpacked their suitcases upon returning from honeymoon, when Albert presented his plans at the next HAC board meeting. This time they had foregathered at Byland Crescent. Connie travelled over on the train with her husband, enabling her to visit her mother and grandmother while the meeting was taking place.

Albert opened the discussion. 'With the ending of the Victorian age, people will soon start to turn away from sober fashions. The new King and his consort Queen Alexandra will lead the move towards more colourful clothing. This will be helped by better quality, more colourful patterns of cloth soon to become available, made possible by the new generation of chemical-based dyes being invented, produced, and marketed. With these at their disposal, textile designers will be free to let their imagination soar. Mass production of chemical dyes will soon be here. Textile designers will have the freedom to conduct bold experiments with a wider range of fabric mixtures than previously. In addition, the most daring of new fabric styles will be capable of being mass-produced. Mass production means affordability. In the past only the very wealthy could afford such exotic creations. Soon they will be in the price range of the average buyer. With all this in mind I would like us to consider the following proposal,' Albert paused, 'to set up a chemical dyeing plant within the Group.'

Philip and Michael soon found evidence in plenty to backup Albert's proposal. Their meetings with Harry and Charlie Binks left them equally impressed. Six months later, The Outlane Chemical Dyeing and Finishing Company Limited, a further subsidiary of HAC Ltd, was born. Although fifty-five per cent of the shareholding was held by HAC Ltd, the remainder was evenly split between the new company's Managing Director, Mr Harry Binks and the Technical and Production Director, Mr Charlie Binks.

* * *

Connie had been mistress of the house in Heaton for three months when she received a further letter from her brother James. Although it added nothing to her knowledge of his and Alice's whereabouts he told his sister that the business he and Alice were running involved farming, mineral extraction and, as recently as the week before he wrote, the acquisition of a newspaper. James also confided to Connie that the reason he and Alice were able to act so aggressively in their business activities had come about as a result of a stroke of fortune. When they had reached their destination, they had seen a property for sale which had been on the market some time. As the previous owners had been unable to make it pay, there had been no takers for it. In two successive auction sales, the property had failed to elicit a single bid. The bank that had foreclosed on the previous owners had been obliged to remove the reserve. When the third auction was held, James and Alice found to their pleasure and surprise that they were able to acquire the property for less than half of what they had been prepared to pay. The bank, no doubt eager to recoup some of their losses, had offered them a mortgage. They had been more than a little put out by James's refusal. The real luck had come when they had discovered that there were significant mineral deposits on the land.

James ended his letter by adding that he and Alice had agreed that it would be in order to tell the family, provided, as he cautioned her, that no attempt at contact, other than through Connie herself, was made.

* * *

Connie's reply reached James and Alice in the first few days of 1903. She wrote that their news had been greeted with relief, pride, and pleasure in Byland Crescent and elsewhere. Mother had been greatly comforted by the reports of their wellbeing and had spent many hours reading the letters time and again or studying the photograph of her grandchildren. Father had, however, said very little.

Philip and Ellen Ackroyd were also much moved by hearing from James, albeit indirectly. Connie went on to report that Philip teased Sonny about James's ability to handle leg-spin bowling. Sonny was so aggravated by this that he had requested that she beg James to pass on any tips that would enable him to counter this weakness in his batting technique. Philip had asked her privately to request permission for him to write directly to James, or at least enclose a letter when next she wrote.

Connie ended with the news that next time she wrote, she hoped to be able to enclose a family group of her own, as she had been busy supervising the decoration of a nursery. The intended occupant was scheduled to make his or her arrival sometime during the latter part of June.

In his reply, James expressed his and Alice's delight at this news and added the hope that all would be well during the pregnancy. He also agreed to Philip's proposal for a direct letter, although he confessed to being a little mystified by its significance. He ended by asking his sister to pass the following message to Sonny. 'Watch Grandfather's fingers when he lets go of the ball, then play it off the pitch. Play back rather than forward whenever you can.'

* * *

It was early spring, the year 1908. The annual audit of HAC Group lay on the boardroom table. The financial year had not been easy. Wool prices had fluctuated unpredictably throughout the year. For once it was the youngest director, Michael Haigh, who led proceedings. 'We have lost money here, although those losses are balanced by profits in the chemicals division. That in itself is not disastrous, although demand is too low to make their results spectacular. What really concern me are the figures from the scouring plant. This never recorded a loss before Ernest Cowgill's retirement on health grounds.'

'It is only a result of the changeover,' Albert stated.

Michael Haigh disagreed. 'I do not think Clarence Barker is capable of managing the company properly. Mistakes have been made that would never have occurred while Ernest was at the helm. I know he is your nephew, Albert, but I am sorry, he just is not up to the job.'

'Well I say he is,' Albert countered stubbornly. 'Give the lad time and I am sure the position will turn round. It is a tricky business and when he gets to know it and becomes familiar with the work-force I know it will come right.'

'How long do we have to wait for that to happen?' Michael wanted to know. 'He has been in charge there almost two years and there is no sign of any improvement. Worse still, the losses seem to be growing rather than reducing. What is more,' Michael added grimly, 'the workers seem to be less than impressed with Barker's style of management. We have lost several good men recently; men who have been with the company for years. We cannot afford to lose good employees. HAC has always prided itself on paying the best wages to get the best staff and keeping them. Not losing men because of poor management.'

Albert banged the table with his fist. 'I don't need a lecture in how to run a company from you,' he shouted. 'I say give the lad a chance. When you can report some profit from your own division you can start criticizing other people. Or are you putting up a smokescreen to shield your own poor performance?'

This encounter led to several further, increasingly heated clashes between the two men. The rising hostility worried Michael, who was concerned at the way the Group was heading. Even Connie and Hannah, who were best placed to understand Albert's reasoning, were at a loss to understand his behaviour.

The problem was that Albert had lost much of his confidence, the very asset that had been the chief weapon in his armoury during his climb towards success. His ebullient manner and knowledge of both the industry and products had been the kingpins in his career. Albert felt threatened by Michael, whom he considered possessed greater talent than he. In this unhappy frame of mind, he preferred to surround himself with those of lesser ability. With James no longer able to take his place in the company, Albert needed someone to fill the gap until Sonny was able to take over, someone he could control, hence his championship of Clarence Barker.

Barker himself, although unaware of the cause of Albert's preference, nevertheless played on it for all he was worth. He lost no opportunity, with carefully weighted words, to give the impression that Michael was pursuing a vendetta against him. He also managed to imply that Michael was undermining Albert's own authority. These slyly delivered inferences served the dual purpose of arousing Albert's protective instincts towards Clarence, while at the same time fuelling his mounting distrust of his son-in-law.

CHAPTER FOURTEEN

James Fisher sat on the veranda contemplating the sheets of notepaper on the table before him. He was so used to the surname he rarely thought of himself as Cowgill. Normally, he would have picked up a pen and replied immediately, but the content of this letter was different. He would need to consider his response and talk it through with Alice before he took any action.

It was a warm, still evening. The last rays of a glorious sunset still illuminated the sky, but soon it would be pitch black. Even then, it would be warm, for at that time of the year the temperature never dropped low enough to warrant even a light coat. The silence was such that a mere whisper of sound signified Alice's arrival. James looked up at her and smiled. It was a smile that conveyed all the love and companionship that ten years had forged between them. Those ten years had barely changed her, at least in James's eyes. There was a little more maturity in her fine features, but that was all. The birth of their three children had not thickened her slender waistline or filled out her figure in the slightest.

She smiled back at her husband and when she spoke her voice still retained that gentle quietness that had first attracted him, 'Ellen's asleep now.' Their younger daughter was two years old. 'Cissie kept her awake for a while, wanting to play. Saul of course was just like his father, went straight off to sleep. So what has Aunt Connie to report from the Old Country?'

James smiled at Alice's ironic use of the term used throughout Australia to denote England. 'There has been a regular bust up,' he told her. 'Connie is very upset. It seems Michael and Father are having constant rows and from all accounts, they're getting worse all the time. Apparently, when not rowing, they hardly speak; just spend the time writing each other letters. Father refuses to see anyone else's point of view. Not that I have to tell you that, we both know how difficult he can be. Connie reckons Michael is almost on the point of walking out, but so far she has managed to persuade him not to do anything rash.'

'What are the rows about?'

'Clarence Barker,' James pulled a face at the mention of his cousin's name. 'Michael detests him and has never forgiven Father for employing Clarence. Now, with Uncle Ernest's retirement, Father has gone over Michael's head and appointed Clarence as Managing Director of the scouring plant. Connie says that Clarence is idle, sly, and devious, just like his father Maurice, and has got round father to wangle this promotion. There have been some mistakes that have cost a good deal of money and Michael is convinced they are all Clarence's fault. He cannot prove any of this, because Clarence is cunning enough to pin the blame elsewhere, so naturally Father will not entertain the slightest criticism of Clarence.'

'You don't like Clarence, but I thought you'd never met him?' Alice asked.

'I haven't but I remember his father from when I was tiny, before they went to America. He would come to visit us with Aunt Bessie and I once saw some bruises on her arms. She had been washing and I walked into the bathroom by mistake. I was only a five-year-old, too young to realize their significance, but he caught me and took me outside.

117

He was a cruel, unpleasant piece of work and made it very clear what he would do to me if I told anyone what I had seen. He reinforced his arguments with a few slaps and nips, delivered where they wouldn't show. That was dear Uncle Maurice for you. So I am quite prepared to detest his son and to believe what Connie writes about him, particularly as I trust Michael's judgement.'

'Why doesn't your grandfather, Philip, intervene?' Alice asked.

'He's semi-retired, Alice,' James reminded her. 'He only goes to the office twice a week and Connie says even that tires him out with the long journey. I think we tend to forget that in the ten years we've been out here, time has moved on back in England.'

'Has anyone heard from Ada since she left?' Alice wanted to know.

'Connie writes that she had a letter from her towards the end of last year. She and her friend Eleanor are living in Paris. Apparently, people there are much more understanding. Eleanor has a growing reputation as a painter, while Ada is writing articles on Parisian life for a magazine back in England, as well as taking students for English and doing some translation work. Of course, she is never mentioned in Byland Crescent. When she announced that she and Eleanor were going to live together it caused more upset than even you and I created.' James grinned at his wife.

They sat in silence for a while then James surprised Alice by announcing that he had an idea concerning Michael and Connie's problem. He outlined the suggestion briefly. Alice was dubious. 'James, you would never think of going back to England would you?'

James sensed the concern in her voice. 'Never, this is our home now. We have settled here and been successful too, far more than we could ever have expected. We have built up a business that is earning us a small fortune. That could never have happened in England. What's more, it is just the tip of the iceberg. Every sector of the business is going from strength to strength. The farming and minerals divisions still provide the bulk of the income, but the food processing and distribution company is already into profit, the newspapers are making good money. When these new-fangled motor cars become popular the oil and petroleum sector, which is still in its infancy, could prove the biggest money-spinner of all. Particularly if my other idea comes about.'

'And what idea is that?' Alice asked suspiciously.

'Well, given the size of Australia, people will want to move about and these motor cars will give them the opportunity to do that. However, they will need to refill the car with petrol and they will want toilets and places to have a rest and a meal. So I am planning to investigate the possibility of providing places with all these facilities.'

'I suppose I will get used to you eventually,' Alice remarked resignedly.

James shot her a sideways glance, his face solemn, then continued, 'Besides which, we have a lovely home in a beautiful part of the world. The climate is terrific, absolutely ideal for raising a family.' He reached out and took her hand, drawing her to her feet. 'And now, I think it's about time we thought about increasing the membership of our clan. After all we cannot allow my little sister to overtake us.'

* * *

Several weeks after this conversation, Ralph French was surprised to receive, along with the usual posting instructions from his friend James, details of work James wanted carrying out. Ralph's qualification as a solicitor made him ideally equipped for the task James had in mind. He read the instructions with interest and a certain degree of pleasure. It was clear that his friend was becoming highly successful. Not only was the course of action mapped out in detail, but also the procedures to be followed were carefully outlined and even the funds required to make the work possible had been made available. Ralph strode to his office door, summoned his clerk and gave him a string of commands. Only when he was completely satisfied that everything would be done according to James's requirements did he turn to the more mundane task of forwarding a letter to Connie.

* * *

It was Sonny Cowgill's opening game of the season for the school team and he was celebrating in style. The signalling of boundaries must have made the umpire's arm ache. The opposition had travelled from Hull, confident of notching another win against their Scarborough rivals. They had been victorious over the past few seasons and knew of no good reason why this should be any different. They had a strong bowling attack, with two good openers, fast enough to scare most school batsmen. To back them up they had a couple of medium pace bowlers, steady and accurate, added to which was their trump card, a leg-spin bowler whose talent was already interesting several county sides.

Sonny's innings put paid to all these aspirations. The young batting star cut, swept, pulled, and drove every guile-ful delivery to all areas of the ground. By the time his captain declared the innings, the visitors' hopes lay in ruins. Sonny's unbeaten personal tally of 179 had given the home side an unreachable total of 305 for three wickets. It was the highest individual score achieved in the history of the school.

There was a strong contingent of supporters for the tri-umphant Sonny, in addition to the boys from his school. His parents and grandparents watched with pride and admiration. His cousin Charlie had travelled across for the day, bringing his pretty young wife on one of their regular visits to her parents in Byland Crescent. On hearing of the match, Charlie and Rebecca had decided to come along with Rebecca's father and mother, Dr Steven Culleton and his wife Elizabeth.

Philip Ackroyd watched his grandson's innings with special pride and delight. Watching the cavalier treatment

Sonny meted out to the leg-spinner was particularly satisfying. Leg-spin had once been Sonny's weakness, but a combination of hour upon hour of relentless practice coupled with some sound advice from his elder brother had eventually cured it.

'Looks as if all that time spent on the south beach is beginning to pay off,' Albert remarked to his father-in-law.

At that moment, they were forced to duck as another fearsome blow sent the ball crashing amongst the foliage as it ricocheted between the trunks of a nearby copse of trees. Philip chuckled with delight.

Hannah shot a cautious glance at Albert before joining in the praise of her son. Her father's semi-retirement had left Albert as senior director of the group and the effect was a niggling source of anxiety to Hannah. She knew that he had argued fiercely with their son-in-law Michael. Although too loyal to admit the fact, Hannah had a lot of sympathy with her daughter and son-in-law, for she too was unimpressed by Clarence Barker's conniving ways.

Sonny had already shown interest in joining the family business and Hannah longed for the day when that happened, so that she could persuade Albert to take life easier. She was also aware how upset Albert had been over their daughter Ada's behaviour. Not that Albert had flown into a rage and thrown Ada out of the house as he had done with her brother James. But the sadness felt by both of them on learning of her intended lifestyle and sexual orientation had left deep scars. With Cissie dead, James and Ada out of the family circle and Connie at arm's length, so many of Albert's hopes centred on Sonny that it frightened Hannah.

* * *

Neither Sonny, nor any of the crowd was aware that Sonny's innings was being watched by one expert and far from disinterested spectator. News of Sonny's batting prowess had spread beyond Scarborough, where, in addition to his performances against other schools he had been impressing fellow players and opponents alike in club cricket. The first intimation of the regard placed on Sonny's ability was a letter postmarked Leeds that arrived a month after they had watched his record-breaking innings for the school. During the intervening period, Sonny had notched up a further three centuries against school opposition, plus two more in club cricket and an unbeaten 87 in a local representative match.

The letter, couched in formal terms, invited Mr Mark Cowgill to attend a session of net practice at the Headingley Cricket Ground, where his abilities would be tested against some renowned bowlers, for the purpose of assessing his suitability to play cricket at a higher level. The letter was signed by The Secretary, Yorkshire County Cricket Club. The date assigned for the session was checked against Sonny's copy of the First-Class Fixture List. Although the date was in the busiest part of the season, the County side, arguably the strongest in the Championship, had no fixture scheduled for that particular day. As a consequence, it seemed likely that Sonny was going to be tested by some of the finest bowlers in the country and his batting technique compared to that of the most accomplished batsmen. It is difficult to say whose pride, delight and excitement at the content of the letter was the greatest, Sonny, his parents, or his grandparents.

* * *

It was a searching examination, as it was intended to be. Sonny was in the net for over an hour, during which time he was subjected to lightning fast-pace bowling and highly accurate swingers. During it all, every movement of his feet, every arc of his bat and attitude of his head throughout each stroke was being carefully watched and critically analyzed. The assessors took their responsibilities seriously, that much was obvious. Grouped around the outside of the net, taking station alternatively on the off and leg side, they stared impassively at the young hopeful. No words of advice or encouragement were offered, neither was there any spoken criticism. They neither smiled approval at his strokes, struck cleanly and sweetly, nor frowned with displeasure when he played and missed, nor when he edged the ball. They simply watched.

Whether this lack of reaction was part of the testing procedure, Sonny was not sure, neither did he have the leisure to reflect on it, for he was far too busy trying to cope with the variety of problems posed by each delivery, between which there was little respite. When he was instructed to leave the net at the end of his examination, he was given no indication as to how he had fared. The watchers had formed themselves into a group, their backs firmly turned towards him. The only encouragement Sonny received as he left the arena sweating and breathless was a nod and the words, 'well done, young man,' from the batsman replacing him in the crucible.

It was much later, when Sonny had retired to the dressing room and was sitting trying to recover his composure that he realized the identity of the world-renowned cricketer who had uttered those encouraging words. After he had attended the secretary's office to collect his travelling expenses, payable even to one of his amateur status, he boarded a tram bound for Leeds City Square. From there it was a short walk to the station to board a train for the return journey to Scarborough. He was still unaware if he had covered himself in glory in the eyes of those critics, or disgraced himself.

The offer contained within the second letter he received was cautious. It had been decided to offer him the chance to play some games during the following season with the Yorkshire County Cricket Club's second XI, better known as the Yorkshire Colts. This would enable him to gain valuable experience at a higher level and offer the county's selectors the opportunity to evaluate his talent and performances. The tacit promise was that if he proved himself worthy during those trial games, an opportunity might be forthcoming for him to play in the full County XI. Naturally, the letter continued, he would be expected to play as an amateur cricketer. This distinction, of the utmost importance in the social structure at that time, hardly merited discussion in the Cowgill household. For weeks after receipt of the letter there was a general air of euphoria about the household. This was ended, with brutal savagery, by some distressing news from Bradford.

CHAPTER FIFTEEN

Connie and Michael had needed to call for a doctor to attend the elder of their two daughters, Nancy, who had been diagnosed with whooping cough and was seriously ill. This was worrying in itself, but of even greater concern was the highly contagious nature of the disease. Marguerite, Connie's younger daughter, was only two years old and the fear that she might contract the ailment from her sister and the potential consequences for the infant paralyzed them all.

Hannah's brain cleared quickly as she planned a decisive course of action. Losing no hesitation, she travelled to Bradford with Albert as soon as they received the news. When she reached Connie's house Hannah put the situation to Connie in clear, unambiguous terms. Nancy's condition was worsening and Marguerite was also in danger; far better to remove Marguerite from the potential source of infection. Although at first Connie was naturally reluctant to be parted from her child, the logic of entrusting the toddler to her grandmother soon swept such doubts aside. Besides the benefit to Marguerite, as Hannah told Connie, she would be able to devote herself fulltime to looking after Nancy. When Albert and Michael returned to the house that evening, the matter had been decided. All that remained was for Albert to escort two ladies back to Scarborough rather than one, as soon as the much younger of these had said goodbye to her mama and papa.

If Albert and Hannah lavished care and attention on their little charge, it was Sonny who entertained her and brightened the long days when the infant was homesick for her parents and big sister. Sonny would spend hours joining in Marguerite's favourite games, or giving her piggyback rides up and down the staircase at Byland Crescent. If the weather was fine enough he was first to offer to escort his tiny niece on walks to the nearby beaches. For these services, he received his mother's gratitude, for it relieved her of a considerable burden of stress. It also meant that Marguerite was happiest when in Sonny's company. If she were unable to locate him in the large Byland Crescent house she would call out for him and although she had not quite mastered his full title, her cry of 'Ukelson' was unmistakeable in its meaning.

Ten days after Marguerite's arrival in Byland Crescent, Henry admitted Albert into the house on his return from Bradford. One look at his master's face told Henry all he needed to know. Suddenly Albert Cowgill looked an old man. Henry took Albert's coat and hat in silence then gestured towards the living room. Albert acknowledged the gesture with a nod of the head. As he crossed the hall towards the living room Albert bit back his tears and squared his shoulders before opening the door.

He stood for a moment in the doorway. He smiled weakly as Hannah, Sonny and Marguerite looked up. 'Ukelson,' Albert asked Sonny quietly. 'Would you mind taking Marguerite into the library for a short while, I need to speak with your mother.'

Of the three, only Marguerite was unaware that there was anything amiss. When she left the room with her uncle, Albert turned to Hannah. The distress in his face was mirrored in her own, for she had guessed the news he had to impart. 'It was a wise precaution bringing the little one here,'

Albert said quietly. He took Hannah in his arms. 'I'm sorry, my love. Nancy died this afternoon.'

* * *

The differences between Albert and Michael were put aside as they mourned the death of Nancy. Byland Crescent was a sad house as the family came to terms with the loss.

However, the earlier divisions re-surfaced at the next board meeting. Michael Haigh brought matters to a head. 'This year the Group results are the worst in our history. I for one am not prepared to stand by while all our hard work is frittered away. The root of the trouble is the scouring plant. I've been examining some of the yields and they are so poor they are dragging HAC results down with them. That's why the merchants' operation is showing losses. It's all very well grouping the figures together and writing it off as a bad year, but without Outlane Chemicals the Group would have made an enormous loss. We cannot expect one part of the business to continue to shore up the rest due to the mismanagement of one man. Barker is not fit to be in charge and the sooner we get rid of him the better. Apart from the fact that he doesn't know what he is doing, he's idle, devious, and divisive. He will go to any lengths to cover up his own inadequacies and I for one am not prepared to put up with it any longer.'

Albert rose to his feet. 'That's slanderous,' he thundered. 'Clarence is doing his best. You have never given him a chance. It couldn't be that you are using him as an excuse to cover up your own deficiencies could it? Or is it that you are jealous, frightened of the competition?'

Michael stood, facing Albert across the table, fury showing in his eyes. 'The day I'm frightened of competition from that worm is the day I give up,' he snarled.

Angry exchanges continued as their tempers mounted. Eventually, after considerable difficulty, Philip Ackroyd managed to restore some level of calm by adjourning the proceedings to allow his co-directors to cool off.

Although this solution was less than wholly satisfactory to either Albert or Michael, both of them realized that they had no alternative but to accept the decision. Philip, unhappily aware that matters between his two co-directors were coming to a head, was forced to use his majority shareholding as a lever.

The worsening relationship between her husband and son-in-law was an increasing source of concern to Hannah. She was conscious that the ever more acrimonious nature of the exchanges was affecting the whole of the family and worried that Albert and Michael were either unaware of the effects of their quarrel, or did not care. After some consideration, Hannah consulted the only person she thought might reverse the worsening situation between the two men.

She arranged for Sonny to accompany her on a walk to Scarborough Castle one afternoon. It was a bright, warm day as they strolled amongst the ancient stone fortifications that overlooked the town and its twin bays. Hannah opened the conversation by referring to Sonny's successes on the cricket field. 'Have you come to any decision over the offer from Yorkshire County Cricket Club,' she asked.

'Not yet, Mother,' Sonny replied. 'To be honest I'm in two minds about it. I would love to play cricket for a living and I know Grandfather would be proud if I got into the County team, but it's a gamble. For one thing if I was injured, that could end my career at any point. Secondly there's no guarantee I would be considered good enough to be offered a professional contract.'

'Have you any alternatives in mind?'

Sonny eyed her shrewdly. He had some idea where the conversation was leading. 'Such as the family business for instance?'

Hannah nodded. 'I know your father would be pleased if you decided to join the firm.' She cast a glance about her, as if fearing Albert would be following them. 'Especially so,' she continued, 'after he was so disappointed by James.'

In the end, Sonny agreed to defer any decision until the following spring, when he promised he would take all his mother's concerns into account before he made his final choice.

* * *

In another boardroom, at their suite of offices in Bradford, the four directors, founders of WPF&D, were also meeting. The company that had been formed in a spirit of enthusiasm fifteen years earlier had made great progress. The problem they now faced stemmed from the fact that they were all of a similar age. The Four Horsemen had galloped through the trade with enormous zest and success followed them in their ride, until they were in a position to challenge even such giants as HAC Ltd. Like their greatest rivals, The Four Horsemen had diversified buying up a firm of wool-combers and a yarn spinning business along the way.

Now, age was against them. The Horsemen were ready to be put out to pasture but had no one to whom they could entrust the stables. George Dobson and Henry Pearson had sons, but both had elected to stay clear of the textile industry. One was a captain in the Royal Marines, the other a solicitor. None of the directors' daughters had married into the trade so there was no likelihood of a chain of succession via the distaff side.

The directors' dilemma was to find an exit strategy. To close the businesses down seemed an admission of failure. To sell out to a competitor such as HAC represented an equally ignominious end. Martin Foster had been the first to raise the subject almost a year earlier. Despite their best endeavours no acceptable solution had presented itself.

Only ten days ago, each of the directors had received an identical letter by registered post from a firm of solicitors based in the City of London. Their clients, the solicitors wrote, were desirous of purchasing an established business in the textile industry based in the West Riding of Yorkshire. The buyer was an overseas based conglomerate involved in many different industries, including textiles. The letter contained an offer for the whole of the issued share capital of WPF&D. The price tendered was adequate rather than generous, but worthy of consideration. The letter stressed that no changes would be made in either the style of operation or the company name.

There was never any doubt about the directors' ultimate decision. Being Yorkshire men and wool merchants at that, they haggled, but this was only to be expected. Negotiation had become part of their nature. In this instance however, the process was neither as easy nor successful as they imagined. They were attempting to bargain with a buyer they had never met, of whose persona they were unaware, whose reaction was impossible to gauge. To add to this handicap they were negotiating through a third party.

Eventually, terms were agreed. Although they had achieved some success by obtaining a small increase in the purchase price for their shareholdings, this was at the expense of their promise to remain in office during the transition period. This would mean that their retirement would be postponed for up to two years following the takeover, unless suitable replacements had been recruited in the meantime. During that interim period, one of the solicitors from the practice in London would sit on the board to safeguard his clients' interests. It appeared as if The Four Horsemen's ride off into the sunset would have to be deferred.

On several occasions during the negotiations, the directors requested information about the unknown and unusually secretive buyer, but all they were told, was that the information they sought was confidential and could not be divulged.

CHAPTER SIXTEEN

In the first few days of 1909, James drafted two letters. The first was to his solicitor and friend in London, Ralph French, the second to his sister Connie. The letter to French contained, not for the first time, a string of highly specific instructions culminating in the draft of a communication that surprised even Ralph.

James started his letter to Connie by congratulating her on the news that she was pregnant once more and sympathizing with her over the trouble between Michael and their father. He suggested that if matters between the two of them became too difficult, she should advise Michael to leave, as his services would be readily snapped up by any number of other companies.

The secret of James's continuing and growing success was a business philosophy light years ahead of his time. He believed that men worked best when they worked for themselves so he bought the services of the more talented executives by offering them a stake in the enterprise. All his managers owned shares in the companies for whom they worked. To enable those shares to pay dividends the companies needed to make good profits. To ensure those profits, men worked harder than they would have as employees. They took great pride in the dividends they earned.

The two directors of the parent company, James and Alice, took the profits and the dividends and ploughed almost all of them back into the group to fund further expansion. By these simple methods, they had created one of the richest groups of companies in Australia, but neither was satisfied with that. Australia was growing, and growing rapidly. They wanted to share in that growth and what is more, they wanted to lead it. If James and Alice's relationship was a love match, their business partnership was a merger of two ambitious and far-sighted brains.

As James told Alice of his letter writing activities, he confessed that he had been thrilled to finalize the purchase of the English company, although he was by no means certain that the plans he had for it would come to fruition.

'If they do, will you ever reveal your true identity?' Alice asked him.

James grinned. 'No, I don't think so. When we left England, there was a sound reason for the decision we took. Father could have caused us all sorts of trouble if he had been able to find us, so James Cowgill had to disappear altogether. It was something of a gamble using your name, but James Fisher would have meant nothing to searchers, so it worked and we were left unmolested. It would be far too much trouble to revert, besides which I quite like being Mr Fisher. It suits the group identity as well as my own. Fisher Springs Pty. Has quite a ring to it.'

'I'm glad you don't want to change your name back to Cowgill,' Alice said. 'For one thing it would be very confusing for the children. They are used to being called Fisher and to change their names back to Cowgill would risk upsetting Saul, Cissie, Ellen etcetera.'

James was nodding his agreement when the import of her final words struck him. 'How do you mean, etcetera?' he demanded.

'Well, we can't choose a name until we know whether it is going to be a boy or girl can we?'

Alice's grin stretched from ear to ear.

* * *

The day after James's letter arrived at Ralph French's City office the directors of HAC met once more. Michael was determined to force the issue. He told his fellow directors that the time had come for a decision to be made regarding Clarence Barker. He reiterated that he considered Barker to be divisive and warned them that his ambition was limitless. He concluded by delivering an ultimatum. He said that he could no longer work with Barker and that they must make a choice. Either they accepted his viewpoint and dismissed Barker, or, as previously stated, he would resign in protest. Albert replied that he had no intention of dismissing Barker, even at Michael's insistence. With great reluctance, Philip Ackroyd cast his vote with Albert.

Michael rose to his feet, a great feeling of weariness over him. 'Very well, gentlemen,' he said, his voice cold and formal. 'You leave me no alternative. You will receive my resignation tomorrow morning.'

Neither Philip nor Albert had believed Michael's threat until that moment. They sat in shocked silence long after he had left the boardroom. True to his word, the following morning his letter of resignation arrived at the Manor Row offices.

* * *

Four days after Michael Haigh's resignation, those closest to the Cowgill and Ackroyd families and the HAC group were rocked by even more traumatic news. Ellen Ackroyd woke early that dark February morning to a loud knocking at the bedroom door. The housekeeper hurried in pleading with her to come quickly to the kitchen. She looked to find Phillip's side of the bed empty. Nor had Philip dressed, for his clothes were still hanging as he had set them out the previous evening. Ellen rose quickly and donned her slippers and dressing gown. As she reached for the gown from the hook on the back of the door, she noticed that Philip's was missing.

She hurried downstairs and into the hallway glancing to left and right as she made her way towards the rear of the building. All the living rooms were empty and unlit. She followed the housekeeper into the kitchen where the maid was kneeling on the floor, tears streaming down her face as she frantically tried to revive Philip. Shock held Ellen rigid for a long moment, temporarily trapping her scream of fear and distress.

The massive heart attack that had hammered through Philip Ackroyd's chest had hit as he made his way into the kitchen, as he often did, for an early morning cup of tea. He was probably dead before his crumpled body reached the white marble tiles of the kitchen floor.

* * *

St Mary's Church was packed for the funeral. Philip Ackroyd was respected throughout the textile industry for both his shrewd business brain and his strong sense of ethics, and was held in great regard for the business empire he had created. His open and cheerful personality left many friends mourning his loss and few enemies rejoicing.

For those closest to him there was an air of unreality about the funeral ceremony and the gathering that followed it. Hannah, deeply distressed at the loss of her father, and Albert occupied one corner of the sitting room in Weaponness Park, while Michael and Connie sat almost directly opposite them. Such conversation as took place had a stilted and unnatural tone to it. Ellen and the rest of the family shuttled uneasily between the two factions.

Two days after the funeral Ellen and her daughters gathered again for the reading of Philip's will. If anyone believed that Philip had lost his capacity to surprise them, the terms of the will, delivered in the dry, formal tones of his solicitor soon put an end to such complacency.

The lawyer began.

"To my beloved wife Ellen Ackroyd, I hereby bequeath the house at Weaponness Park with an annuity of twenty-five thousand pounds for the rest of her life, together with the residue of my estate after all other bequests. A single bequest of two hundred thousand pounds to each of my daughters, Hannah, Susannah and Florence and a further one hundred thousand pounds in trust for each of my grandchildren."'

The solicitor looked up, the pause adding emphasis to his next words, *"with the exception of James Philip and Mark Albert Cowgill."'*

There followed various smaller bequests to members of the household staff. The solicitor adjusted his half-rimmed glasses before continuing to read.

"Finally to my grandsons James Philip Cowgill and Mark Albert Cowgill, I leave the sum of five hundred thousand pounds each, together with all my shareholding in HAC group companies to be divided equally between them. Until such time as Mark Albert Cowgill attains his majority those shares and monies to be held in trust for him. The administrator of that trust to be the said James Philip Cowgill."'

To Albert, the news of that distribution came when his vulnerability was at its height. Having lost both of his fellow directors within a week, he now found himself beholden to both his sons to ensure a majority in any shareholder vote. Even more galling, with Sonny's shares being held in trust, the policy of HAC, even his own position on the board, could be dictated by his son James. Following Albert's fruit-less search for James, the anger that had caused him to cast adrift his eldest son had fermented. He had not spoken to James since that day; indeed, he had no idea where James was. Even if Albert came to regret his actions of that fateful day, he could not be certain that James would forgive him.

Now that Albert was not on speaking terms with either Connie or her husband Michael, he felt certain that any reports she sent to James would paint their father in the worst possible light.

* * *

For Connie, the year 1909 had started in the shadow of grief and uncertainty, but ended in the sunlight of joy and renewed happiness. The shadows created by the deaths of her daughter and grandfather were deepened by the uncertainty consequent on Michael's resignation of his directorship of HAC. Added to this was the gloom cast by their continuing rift with her father.

The worry over Michael's future was the first to be lifted. Only two weeks after Philip Ackroyd was laid to rest, Michael received a letter by registered post from a firm of London solicitors. Freed from the standard legal phraseology the letter invited Michael to attend an interview, at which, subject to mutually agreeable conditions, he would be offered the post of Managing Director of WPF&D.

The appointment had been duly ratified and Michael had taken up his duties when Connie's shadows were finally lifted by the birth of her son. Edward Michael Haigh weighed a satisfying 7lbs 6oz and was pronounced sound in wind and limb. So much had happened that Connie found difficulty in keeping pace with events and relating all the news from England to James. When eventually, she wrote to inform him of the birth of Edward, her letter crossed with one from James. In it, he told her that Alice had successfully presented him with their second son; to be named Philip Mark.

* * *

Several years earlier James's grandfather had requested permission via Connie to write to his grandson. James had acceded to this request and a long correspondence had commenced, using the same indirect route via Ralph French. Philip Ackroyd was an excellent judge of character and, with the possible exception of Connie, knew his eldest grandson better than anyone else in the family.

Philip had talked to James and Alice prior to their departure for Australia and was convinced of their ability and determination to succeed in their life together. Subsequent events had proved him to be right in no uncertain terms. When James had mentioned some of his plans for business expansion Philip had written to ask if he needed any financial assistance to put them into practice. In his reply, James had thanked his grandfather for the offer but refused, quoting in that refusal his own bank balance. The sum mentioned had made Philip whistle aloud with surprise, pride, and pleasure.

In recent times, as Philip had become more and more concerned by Albert's intractable and erratic behaviour, he had confided his worries to James. As matters developed, he mentioned his plans for the disposal of his estate. Philip's assessment of his grandson's character, untainted by the paranoia governing Albert's fears, led Philip to the belief that James was the right person to be entrusted with the stewardship of the affairs of HAC at least until such time as his younger brother was able to assume control.

James had readily agreed to the plan on the proviso that he would merely hold a watching brief via his legal representative in England. It would be impossible, as he pointed out to his grandfather, to expect a more direct and active commitment given the extent of his other business interests.

All of this had been conducted without Albert's knowledge, so when Hannah revealed the contents of Philip Ackroyd's will to Albert, the news did little to reduce his fears. His confidence level was already at a low ebb, so a further jolt such as the details of the will was the last thing he needed.

A month later however, Albert received the most welcome boost imaginable. It resulted from a conversation between Sonny and his mother. Sonny had already come to the conclusion that his future lay in the textile industry rather than on the cricket field and merely required convincing that he was making the right decision. Hannah was only too glad and relieved to supply this. The news that Sonny had decided to join the family business pleased Albert and for a while, he returned to the figure of old.

Clarence Barker, now Group Managing Director and heir apparent to Albert's throne was less than pleased by the news. Albert had promoted Clarence to fill the void left by Philip's death and Michael's resignation. There had been objections to the appointment from Harry and Charlie Binks but Albert had soon dealt with these. Once the furore over the will had died down and business life returned to normal those in charge of the daily running of the group began to relax. James Cowgill was a shadowy figure, unknown to most of them, over whose very existence there was room for speculation. Even had it been deemed necessary to inform him of any actions or appointments, they would have been at a loss to know where to reach him.

What Albert failed to recall and neither Clarence nor Sonny fully grasped was that overall control of HAC group had passed out of their hands. With the inheritance he had received from his grandfather added to the shares he controlled as Sonny's trustee, James Cowgill was now the sole author of the destiny of the group. The voting power he was capable of exercising, should he choose to do so, ensured he could veto any of their actions from the appointment of a Managing Director to the purchase of a paper clip.

As time passed without any indication of interest in the affairs of the companies being shown by James, it was convenient to forget his existence. That way they felt sure that until Sonny came of age and was able to take control of his own affairs, matters would continue as previously. Four years was not long to wait and as ten had already passed with no direct word from James, there seemed little likelihood of interference. So when it came time for the next set of annual results to be published, notification of the holding of a shareholders meeting was not deemed necessary.

CHAPTER SEVENTEEN

When Michael Haigh accepted the post of Managing Director at WPF&D, he had a host of excellent reasons to do so. His prime need, that to support his wife and family was balanced by the fact that he both knew and respected his new employers for their reputation and achievements. Aware that The Four Horsemen wished to relinquish the reins of control as swiftly as possible, he was confident of his ability to attract executives of a calibre fit to replace the founders.

There had been only one stumbling block to the smooth hand over of control, caused by Michael's request to know the identity of the ultimate owners of the company he was to run. The solicitors representing the owners had refused to divulge the information but Michael had argued convincingly that he would need to be satisfied on that point before agreeing to take up his new duties. That he would need to have confidence that the owners were of the right stature and were not involved in activities of an unsavoury nature.

The solicitor's reply, couched in the briefest of terms, merely stated that the parent company was named Fisher Springs (Pty) Ltd, a company registered in Australia. The name meant absolutely nothing to Michael.

Satisfied on this point, Michael assumed control at WPF&D. Once there, he had little leisure to dwell on the matter any further. If he had, he might have speculated as to the reason he had been approached at so apposite a moment, but even that is open to doubt. His main preoccupation was the recruitment of the best sales force in the trade. That had once been the prerogative of HAC but there were many fine salesmen in the town and the package Michael was in a position to offer made the selection process a simple one. The major difficulty was which men to offer jobs to from the list of fine applicants.

During the course of the next few years, Michael was aided in his task by the acquisition policy adopted by his parent company. Fisher Springs had opened offices in New Zealand and South Africa and had appointed an agent in Boston, USA. This had all been achieved following the opening of their own exporting subsidiary to which Michael now reported. Day after day, he received cables from all these sources and from the group headquarters. The market information contained in them was second to none, with the result that by the start of 1913, despite a period of poor trading conditions, WPF&D had achieved the position Michael had wanted for them — that of market leaders.

Spring of 1913 proved to be an exciting time. In early March, Michael was advised that the export director of Fisher Springs would be visiting the Bradford office. Michael's curiosity regarding the identity of the owners of the business re-surfaced and he resolved to pump the visitor for all he was worth.

In the event, although Michael learned much about the size and scope of Fisher Springs' activities, he was thwarted in his quest for information regarding the identity of the owners themselves. The export director proved to be an affable and extremely competent executive. He told Michael that the group operated in strict compartments and although each knew of the existence of all the component members, their activities were run entirely separately. In response to

Michael's request, he was able to tell him that the full range of activities encompassed sheep and cattle stations, meat processing and distribution, minerals extraction including mining, fuel distribution, regional newspapers, and most recently, construction. The international trading division had been set up four years earlier, which was the point when he had joined. His division was not restricted to textiles, as they also had minerals and metals trading arms.

The information comforted Michael in that he now knew the owners to be a massive and solidly based undertaking. The visitor had told him that, according to rumour, the ultimate head of the organization was young and dynamic, but was also said to be something of a reclusive and mysterious figure. Even the heads of some of the operating divisions had never met him. In this, the man was not telling the strict truth. Admittedly, not all the group executives had met the founder, but the export director knew much more about him than he imparted to Michael. Prior to leaving Australia, he had been told in no uncertain terms that he was to reveal absolutely nothing, no matter how hard pressed he might be.

* * *

The success achieved by Michael at WPF&D was not totally at the expense of HAC. Although they were no longer the dominant force in the trade of a few years previously, HAC was still a powerful group, despite Clarence Barker who was proving as ineffectual as Group Managing Director as he had been while in charge of the scouring plant.

Sonny had entered like a blast of fresh air, taking control of the scouring plant. Although young and inexperienced, he had revived the fortunes of the ailing company through an efficiency and economy drive that had left the employees breathless with excitement.

As quickly as he had entered, Sonny moved on, having first promoted the production manager in his stead. He left behind a legacy of goodwill and good business practice in an organization that had merely lacked sound management, to thrive once more. He went from there to join the staff at Manor Row as junior salesman, where his dynamic and forceful personality proved an irresistible asset. His charming and easy-going manner impressed his clients, who tended to overlook the early deficiencies in his product knowledge. Not that these were apparent for long, as Sonny was a quick and avid learner. Sonny, as anyone who had watched him batting could have testified, refused to accept anything short of complete domination of the opposition. In his first full year on the road, following a performance that uncannily mirrored that of Albert many years earlier, Sonny achieved the accolade of HAC's leading salesman. With the scouring plant returned to profitability and good contributions from Outlane Chemicals, where Charlie Binks had taken control following his father's death, HAC Group was back to something resembling its former glory, challenging WPF&D for supremacy in the industry.

* * *

During this time, Hannah had become very concerned about Albert's behaviour. Over the years of isolation from James and the increasingly acrimonious dispute with his son-in-law, Albert had taken to indulging himself with the odd drink or two taken in the bar at the station, or from his hipflask on the train to Scarborough. On arrival at Byland Crescent, he would often continue drinking throughout the evening. At first, this appeared to have little effect, but slowly, insidiously, his manner and demeanour changed. His mood swings became more pronounced and after a particularly heavy session, the following morning would be a time of trial for family and servants alike. Both those at Byland Crescent and at Manor Row learned to recognize the symptoms. Avoiding Albert while he was drying out became something of an art.

An additional cause for Albert's drinking had been the performance at HAC. The year following Philip Ackroyd's death had seen the group post its first ever loss. It had also come as an unpleasant surprise when he received a letter from a firm of London solicitors. The solicitors pointed out that they had been instructed to act on behalf of James Cowgill, in his own right and acting as trustee for his brother. They pointed out that the failure to hold a shareholders' meeting was in contravention of company law and requested that one be called immediately.

The hastily arranged shareholders' meeting was a slightly farcical affair, as only Albert and a solicitor turned up. Although he was still a shareholder, Michael allowed Connie to persuade him to stay away. The solicitor, reading from a prepared list, asked several searching and highly pertinent questions, noting down Albert's response to each one. At the end of the meeting, he told Albert that the information would be passed on to his client, following which any suggestions would be transmitted to Albert by letter.

The ignominy of having to report to his own son on the performance of his own company coupled with the thought that James would be telling him how to run his business made Albert incandescent with rage. Six weeks later, when a further letter arrived from the solicitors, Albert crumpled it up and threw it, unread, into the waste-paper basket. Not that it remained unread, for Clarence Barker, who paid the cleaner a small retainer to sift through the bins and remove anything interesting, examined his cousin James's ideas for improving the running of the company closely. Clarence was particularly interested by the suggestion that the most immediate and beneficially effective step would be his own dismissal. Forewarned, Clarence began taking defensive steps to safeguard his own future.

Hannah attempted to remonstrate with Albert regarding his drinking, but to no avail. Conversely, it increased Albert's feeling of isolation, to combat which he stepped up his alcohol intake. When Clarence Barker took it upon himself to install a drinks cabinet in the boardroom at Manor Row the temptation was difficult to avoid. So Albert didn't avoid it. The downward spiral accelerated.

Fortunately for Albert rescue came in time, in the form of Sonny who accompanied his father daily on the train. This pleased Hannah, as Sonny's presence limited the scope and desire for heavy drinking by Albert. Sonny also took the opportunity to remove the drinks cabinet and its contents from the boardroom. Small measures these, but they distracted Albert's attention from alcohol. Soon the adverse effects began to be reversed. Albert seemed to be on the road to recovery.

CHAPTER EIGHTEEN

Michael Haigh's ex-wife, Charlotte, was bored. Although the general expectation had been that she would marry the lover whose affair had ended her marriage, this had not happened. Instead, Charlotte had married Isaac Tunnicliffe, an accountant. It was a disastrous mistake. She found out all too soon that he was dull. Extremely, mind-numbingly dull.

Charlotte, who was still a highly attractive and desirable woman, craved for the social scene, with dinner parties, trips to the theatre, race meetings, anything in short, containing a little excitement. She was also highly sexed and yearned for the stimulation provided by the flirtatious attentions of handsome and charming men. Instead, she got Isaac. Night after night, she got Isaac. She would sit over the dinner table listening to the minutiae of his office routine while inside she longed to scream out with frustration and tell him what a dreadful, crashing bore he was.

It was in this dangerous state of mind that Charlotte met Jesse Barker, Clarence Barker's younger brother. Charlotte had been shopping in the new department store that had opened in Bradford and was laden down with boxes and parcels. As she was coming out of the entrance she collided with someone hurrying in; the packages slid to the floor. She was instantly furious with the young man who had occasioned her discomfort. While Charlotte's tirade raged about his ears, Jesse was all apologies, grovelling around on the floor to retrieve the errant parcels. Eventually, he looked up. There was no doubt that Charlotte was a most desirable woman. Jesse, who, from the moment his voice had deepened, had made a vocation of pursuing every attractive and available female he could, was instantly smitten. 'Gosh, you look lovely when you're angry,' he exclaimed.

He got a witheringly disdainful look in return for the compliment.

Jesse grinned. 'I know. I am an incompetent, inconsiderate lout, who should know better and am not fit to lick the soles of your shoes. I should look where I am going. Please forgive me?' The look with which he accompanied his request for forgiveness was so pathetically appealing that Charlotte smiled slightly, albeit stiffly.

'Allow me to attempt to make amends by summoning a cab for you,' Jesse continued.

Jesse secured the services of a hansom cab and when the driver had brought the horse drawn vehicle to a halt, assisted Charlotte inside, together with her parcels. Then, somewhat to Charlotte's surprise, he climbed in alongside her.

'You do not have to escort me home,' Charlotte told him stiffly.

'The very least I could do. Now, my name is Jesse Barker,' he continued, then paused, awaiting a response.

'Charlotte Tunnicliffe,' she responded, weakened by a look of eager anticipation as droll as the earlier one of appeal. '*Mrs* Charlotte Tunnicliffe,' she emphasised severely.

If Jesse was perturbed by this distinction, he did not allow it to show. When they reached her home, Jesse, despite Charlotte's protests, insisted on carrying her parcels into the house. 'I suppose you had better stay for tea.' Even as she spoke, Charlotte could not believe she had said it.

As an invitation, it was well on the lukewarm side of gushing, but Jesse was by no means abashed. 'I was beginning to wonder how I could go about wangling an invitation,' he remarked.

'Why? Are you so desperate for tea?' Charlotte asked, her tone one of mild sarcasm.

'No, not tea,' Jesse replied, giving Charlotte the full benefit of his disarming smile. 'I just did not want to leave, not when I have only just met you.'

Charlotte felt a slight flutter as her pulse raised momentarily.

* * *

A week had passed since Jesse Barker had introduced himself in such a novel manner, yet Charlotte found herself unable to forget the encounter. Although he had behaved with punctilious correctness during the tea she had provided, he had made it abundantly clear that he admired her. At forty, she was twelve years older than Jesse and a married woman into the bargain. But she kept remembering his flashing smile and the dancing imp of mischief in his deep blue eyes. Time and again, Charlotte told herself to forget him and their chance meeting for nothing had come of it, nothing would come of it. No matter how often she told herself this, the thought kept returning to her. She was daydreaming along these lines when she heard the front door knocker. She opened the door and almost gasped aloud with surprise to find Jesse Barker standing outside. He gave her an apologetic grin.

'What do you want?' Charlotte asked, her tone more abrupt than she had intended.

'May I come in for a moment?' As he spoke Jesse moved forward slightly, and, hesitantly, Charlotte opened the door wider to allow him to pass. Instead of preceding her down the hall, Jesse turned and closed the door firmly behind him. He looked at Charlotte. 'I came back because I had to see you. I tried to stay away but I couldn't get you out of my thoughts.'

Before Charlotte could react, even to protest — if that had been her intention — Jesse took her in his arms and kissed her, gently at first, until her brief struggles subsided and the passion in his kiss touched a response from her. His tongue caressed the inside of her mouth until it entwined with hers. As she returned his kiss with equal fervour an alarm bell should have been ringing somewhere in the recesses of Charlotte's mind. If she heard it, she ignored it. Silently she led Jesse across the hall and together they mounted the wide staircase to the upper floor. Reaching the landing, she pushed open the first door. Jesse looked into the bedroom and grinned. 'Are we going to desecrate the marital bed?' he asked.

Despite the word 'marital', the alarm still failed to ring. 'Oh I do hope so,' she murmured.

Even as she was speaking, Jesse slid his hand up inside her dress, his sure and accurate touch locating the place he sought. With his other hand, he guided her to his trousers and deftly undid two buttons. He directed her hand inside and as she felt the hot firm flesh between her fingers Charlotte moaned with anticipatory pleasure. She knew there was no going back even had she wanted to.

* * *

Although classified as boring by his wife, Isaac Tunnicliffe was not stupid. He had suspected for over a year that his wife was having an affair. Her attitude and behaviour had changed significantly enough for even her husband to notice. Isaac resolved to try and catch the guilty parties in the act. This would make for a nice juicy divorce case, with plenty of scandalous headlines. These would ruin Charlotte's social pretensions. Added to which, Isaac, as the wronged husband would be able to exact substantial damages from the co-re-spondent. An accountant's revenge is a mean and far from pretty thing.

When the crisis occurred, it happened almost by acci-dent. Isaac had purchased a small and underpowered motor car in which to visit some of his more remote clients. He was leaving for the office one morning when he noticed a car travelling slowly down the road in front of his house. There was something furtive in the manner of the driver, who, despite a voluminous motoring coat, hat and goggles, could be seen peering cautiously from side to side, in front and behind.

Isaac, watching the street all the time, had succeeded in firing the engine of his own car, by cranking the starting handle, when the other vehicle came past once more, slowly and with similar suspicious manoeuvres from the driver. Isaac was convinced that the man must be Charlotte's lover. He determined to attempt to find out the identity of the cuckold. He swung his car onto the road, took up station some fifty yards to the rear of the other vehicle, and followed it at an equally sedate pace. Four times the vehicle travelled the full-length of the road at speeds never exceeding fifteen miles per hour, with Isaac some distance astern, creeping along at an equally gentle rate. Each time they reached the road end they swung right, then right once more onto the next street, where the pace increased until they were flying along at speeds almost reaching twenty miles an hour, until they returned to Isaac's street. Once they did, the lead vehicle slowed and the whole rigmarole began again.

On each occasion the lady who lived three doors away from the Tunnicliffe's home, saw her gentleman friend drive slowly past at the head of a convoy of two vehicles. Four times her lover attempted to shake off his pursuer, whom he was convinced was a detective in the employ of his lover's jealous husband. On the fourth drive past, by which time the lover was becoming desperate with fear, Isaac noticed out of the corner of his eye someone strolling nonchalantly up his own drive. He pulled his car to a halt some fifty yards passed the house and watched as Charlotte, still clad in her dressing gown, admitted the stranger.

Isaac stopped his car, climbed out of the vehicle, discarded his motoring coat and crept cautiously back to the house. He peered in through each of the ground floor windows, but to no avail. He went to the back of the house and down the garden to get the ladder he used for pruning his fruit trees. He carried it to the front of the house and set it up against the wall outside the main bedroom window.

He checked the stability and stealthily started to climb up towards the bedroom. He reached the sill and cautiously peeped in through the window. The shock of what he saw made him step back involuntarily, not the wisest of manoeuvres in Isaac's situation. Attempting to rectify matters only made bad worse, there was a momentary pause as the ladder, with Isaac clinging on desperately, gyrated wildly in front of the bedroom window. Then they separated. The ladder departed to the left, where it landed noiselessly, its fall cushioned by a clump of rhododendron bushes. Isaac went in the opposite direction where his fall was broken by the stone path surrounding the house. Not only was his fall broken, but so too was his neck. Isaac died instantly.

As in life, so it often is in death. Isaac, who had spent much of his life being unnoticed and overlooked, lay on the path for several hours, unnoticed and overlooked. When his body was eventually discovered several hours later, Charlotte was sad for a short while, for she did not actively hate her husband, especially now he was dead. Charlotte's neighbour and her gentleman friend were also sad, as their morning had been quite ruined.

Charlotte told the enquiring police officer that her husband must have taken the opportunity to clear a blocked gutter. The young and impressionable policeman taking her statement did not think to question the fact that Isaac had donned his business suit to carry out this maintenance work. Nor did he think to query the timing of such an act, when there had been no rain for over two months, but then he was young and impressionable and Charlotte was undoubtedly very glamorous.

* * *

In spite of the passage of years, there was an improbability about Christmas in Australia. For James and Alice this feeling persisted throughout their lives, enhanced possibly by the high temperatures at that time of the year. Nevertheless, Christmas 1913 was a happy time for the Fisher household. The presence of children made the season more special and although Saul, at fifteen years old and Cissie, approaching twelve, might have been expected to treat the festivities with lessening enthusiasm, Ellen, only seven years and Philip who had just celebrated his fourth birthday made up for any shortfall in enjoyment.

Alice was pregnant again and both she and James were looking forward to the birth of their fifth child, which would they thought, make 1914 a special year for the family. Added contentment was provided by the progress of the Fisher Springs business empire. The financial year reported on shortly before Christmas 1913 had been another record one, which made the signing of the bonus cheques a pleasant duty.

The group's overseas branches were treated differently, but in no lesser way. Their cheques were sent out earlier to ensure safe delivery before Christmas. It was important to James and Alice that everyone representing the group got their reward in time for the festive season. One of the highlights of this year's reports had been the performance of WPF&D in England. That part of the group, although under new ownership for some time was still referred to in the West Riding as The Four Horsemen. Michael Haigh's stewardship and the excellent efforts put in by his employees ensured that the English arm of Fisher Springs (Pty.) Ltd remained a major contributor to the group.

Several thousand miles away, Michael and Connie Haigh, unaware that the large bonus cheque Michael had received a fortnight before Christmas had been signed by Alice Fisher, also celebrated the festive season in style, albeit at much lower temperatures. Their seven-year-old daughter Marguerite and three-year-old son Edward had been joined by baby George only a year ago. Despite a certain residual sadness occasioned by the loss of their eldest daughter Nancy, Christmas was always a jolly time. It would have been merrier still had it not been for the hostility that remained between Michael and Connie's father. Apart from occasional conversations between mother and daughter when they could get a decent telephone connection, the only contact between the two households was by letter, or messages passed by Connie's brother Sonny.

For Sonny himself, Christmas of 1913 was a particularly happy one. He had reached his majority, was now a company shareholder and at the tender age of twenty-one, just recorded the best sales figures ever achieved by a salesman at HAC. They used the only true measure of success available in the trade, where prices of wool and other fibres fluctuated so wildly, that measure being the number of bales sold as a first guide and the actual tonnage invoiced as a more accurate and fairer count. Sonny's performance in 1913 had outstripped even the figures reached in the heady days of the late 1880s and 1890s when trade was in such an ebullient mood. 1913 was different however, with trade being so poor generally. Apart from HAC and WPF&D, the other Bradford merchants were bemoaning their lot at Christmas 1913. As they complained, Sonny rejoiced.

When January of 1914 arrived, it seemed to Sonny and his colleagues that the Christmas season had been extended into the New Year. Not only were the provisional trading figures for the group, buoyed up by Sonny and his colleagues in the sales room, one of the best sets of results for many years, but Charlie Binks at Outlane Chemicals had announced that a new dye they had recently patented promised to be a great money-spinner for the group.

Albert congratulated Sonny, Charlie Binks, and Clarence Barker, his co-directors on the figures at their January board meeting then delivered his bombshell. 'I have decided that the time is right to reduce my commitment to the day-to-day running of the group. Much as Philip Ackroyd did years ago. I am almost sixty now and I feel ready to take life at a more leisurely pace. I want to spend more time with Hannah, and intend to play more golf,' he told them.

His decision was partly influenced by his new addiction to the game of golf, played for the most part in the company of two of his neighbours, at South Cliff Golf Club. Their love for the game seemed to involve as much time in the nineteenth hole as the previous eighteen put together. Here they could analyze their game shot-by-shot, hole-by-hole, green-by-green, and bunker-by-bunker. Such in-depth analysis, conducted in the comfort of the easy chairs provided, was assisted by regular supplies of liquid refreshment delivered to their table by an attentive steward. Thus, the intrepid golfers often returned home much the worse for wear long after darkness had rendered the playing of outdoor games impractical.

In the weeks prior to the board meeting Albert had been preoccupied with the making of his will. The terms of this document caused Albert much heart-searching and several drafts found their way into his waste-paper basket before he made his final decision. The provisions of the final draft made interesting reading, for Albert, ignoring his other surviving children, James, Connie and Ada, left the residue of his estate, after a generous allowance to Hannah, to Sonny. Albert further stipulated that should Sonny predecease him and die without issue, that portion that would have fallen to him should pass in entirety to Albert's nephew, Clarence Barker.

Retrieval of a copy of this final draft from Albert's waste-paper basket by his trusty henchman gave Clarence considerable food for thought.

CHAPTER NINETEEN

If the change in Charlotte Tunnicliffe's status from a highly desirable married woman to that of a widow altered Jesse's feelings towards her it was only to intensify his passion. Although his visits were still irregular, he explained his absences as business travel. Quite what that business entailed Charlotte was never sure. When questioned, Jesse merely grinned and told her he was a trader in various commodities. Although this vague statement merely raised her curiosity level rather than satisfying it, she was unable to get any more detailed explanation. If pressed on the subject Jesse merely smiled enigmatically and changed the subject. Usually he changed it to one that was more immediate, interesting and mutually exciting.

Charlotte had not seen or heard from Jesse in over four months when he arrived on her doorstep early on Christmas Eve of 1913. Having had no word from her lover, Charlotte had resigned herself to a Christmas spent alone, until the familiar rat-a-tat of the doorknocker signalled his arrival. The festive season passed in a blur for them both, with little respite between their bouts of passion. It seemed to Charlotte that the prolonged absence had heightened Jesse's prowess and the strength of his ardour.

Then, as suddenly as he had appeared, Jesse was gone. Nor was there any indication of when he would return. When he left her, two days after Boxing Day, she tried to remember the last time she had eaten a normal meal. Hastily prepared snacks taken in the kitchen before returning for another bout of carnal delight were all she was able to recall.

By the end of February, Charlotte was aware that something was amiss. To be one week late was surprising, two weeks startling, six weeks unheard of. With the onset of morning sickness, all lingering doubts were removed. Charlotte Tunnicliffe, a respectable lady, widowed just over a year, had to come to terms with the fact that she was bearing her lover's child. Not a situation that would be easily explainable at the Bridge Club.

* * *

As Bradford based its prosperity on the textile industry, so Sheffield, fifty miles further south, owed its wealth to steel. Steel, as with textiles takes many forms, from the heaviest of products used in the construction industry, in shipbuilding and in other forms of transport, to the lighter, more delicate steel that went into decorative homewares such as cutlery. The growing popularity of motor transport, especially the motor car, was adding to the use of steel thus increasing Sheffield's prosperity. The mighty steel mills spread from Sheffield along the banks of the rivers Rother and Don, providing lucrative sources of business for South Yorkshire's other mighty industry, coal mining.

Within that belt of industrial conglomerates lay the factory of Edwin Graham. Edwin was fifty-three years old and master of more than one hundred men producing light steel. His products were finding homes in an ever-widening number of market places, his order books were full to overflowing, and his factory worked twenty-four hours a day, seven days a week.

With the wealth he had acquired since he had started in business, Edwin and his wife Lena had moved to the select

Sheffield suburb of Abbeydale, which housed most of the city's wealthiest inhabitants. Their large mansion, standing in extensive grounds was a far cry from the back-to-back terraced house they had occupied when *Edwin Graham Steelmaker* had first opened its doors.

The move to Abbeydale was partly to accommodate their extensive family, for it was not only in the factory that Edwin Graham practiced productivity. In order to provide space and comfort for themselves, their five sons and three daughters they needed a big house. Then there was the additional space required to house the servants essential to maintaining that comfort which amounted to luxury.

By the spring of 1914, the eldest of their daughters had already left home, following her marriage to the son of a local coalmine owner. The middle daughter was shortly to follow her elder sister's example by treading the matrimonial aisle. The two older boys, now young men, were working in the family business, the eldest being a foreman, while the other was in the drawing office. The two youngest boys were still at school.

This was a source of quiet satisfaction to Edwin and Lena. Less predictable, comforting, and satisfying was the decision of their youngest daughter to follow her own path. Rachael Graham was accounted to be one of the most beautiful girls in the area. Fired by tales of the deeds of Florence Nightingale and with a burning desire to help those in need, Rachael had chosen to follow the nursing profession on leaving school. This decision, although not quite unheard of, was to say the least unusual.

Edwin might have chosen to play the Victorian father in accordance with his upbringing, and remonstrate with Rachael over her actions had not Lena intervened. Lena, aware of her daughter's strong will and stubborn nature, counselled her husband against such a course, which would be counter-productive. If Rachael entered the nursing profession without her parents' blessing, at least she did so without their overt censure.

Any romantic notions Rachael might have entertained about the glamour of her calling were soon swept away by the drudgery and unpleasant minutiae of the daily routine. Doggedly she stuck to her task, while her heart craved for adventure and freedom. As her training progressed, the cheerful and light-hearted way she tackled the most menial or repelling of jobs made her popular with patients and staff alike. Improvement in the condition of some of the sickest of her charges caused comment amongst the medical staff. More than once her superiors were advised to give a recalcitrant patient a dose of 'Nurse Graham's tonic' in the hope that it would speed their recovery.

* * *

With his father semi-retired, Sonny found he was answerable to Clarence Barker. Sonny soon discovered that life under the new regime was far different. Although technically Sonny and his father controlled the Group, in practical terms there was no such alliance.

Sonny was in a quandary over his father's attitude. What governed Albert's preference for Clarence puzzled and hurt Sonny deeply.

Whenever Sonny tried to implement a change in the group's strategy, Clarence went out of his way to be as obstructive as possible. Sonny, unlike Michael before him, was unprepared for a long drawn out struggle. He was younger and far more impetuous than Michael. He was also in a stronger position. By the end of March 1914, when Sonny found himself barely able to restrain himself from violent action against his cousin Clarence, he decided on a desperate gamble.

Sonny needed an ally; moreover, he needed one with power. With this in mind, Sonny went to visit his sister and brother-in-law. Michael and Connie were on the point of moving to Baildon. This pretty village, perched on a hillside that marked the edge of Rombalds Moor, better known as

Ilkley Moor, fitted their ideal precisely. Sonny wanted an address, that of the solicitor via whom all correspondence with their brother James was channelled. Having obtained that, Sonny lost no time in writing to James to enlist his support.

* * *

Ada Cowgill and Eleanor Rhodes had taken to Parisian life with delight. In the more tolerant and relaxed atmosphere of the great cosmopolitan city they soon learned to enjoy the easy-going lifestyle. Success added to their happiness. Eleanor's paintings were much sought after, while Ada's column in an English language paper, with its incisive commentary on Parisian life was eagerly awaited by an ever-increasing readership. It came as a bitter blow to the young couple when, in May of 1914, Eleanor received word from England that put an end to their idyll.

Eleanor's mother had been taken ill. She was a widow, having lost her husband several years earlier. Eleanor was their only child. She had no alternative but to return home. As neither Eleanor nor Ada had any idea how long she would be required in England, Ada decided to remain in Paris. The hope they shared was that they could resume their comfortable routine in the very near future.

* * *

As Eleanor Rhodes was returning to England, Jesse Barker was leaving. His route led him ever eastward, until he stopped in Vienna. The capital of Austria-Hungary was the most elegant of European cities at that time. The many attractions of the ancient city were gripping enough for most travellers, but Jesse had a particular reason for hurrying there. Or to be more precise, two reasons.

The first concerned business. Business for Jesse was a matter of supply and demand. Jesse knew how to obtain what other men needed. If someone had a quarrel with their neighbour and lacked the means to press home their own point of view, Jesse could provide it. Similarly with a government that wished to reinforce their policies. Alternatively, his supply chain was open to those wishing to overthrow governments. Jesse, in short, was an arms dealer.

Vienna was a gateway to the east of Europe and the Balkans. In those areas there was perennial unrest amounting at times to upheaval, which made it fertile ground for Jesse. Amongst his many and interesting clients was an organization known, somewhat dramatically, as the Black Hand.

Jesse had come to know the organization by that most Viennese of channels, an acquaintance of an acquaintance. After the initial contact, the agent sent to meet and treat with Jesse was a stunning blonde girl, half-Austrian and half-Serbian, by the name, or so Jesse was led to believe, of Hildegard Cabrinova. Within weeks of their first meeting, they had become lovers. The Black Hand, a collection of fervent Serbian nationalists, was committed to the overthrow of the Austro-Hungarian Empire that had subjugated the tiny Serbian nation for centuries. The members of the Black Hand were sworn to end that repressive tyranny. Dangerous beyond measure in the extremity of their fanaticism, they lacked merely the widespread support to foment such an uprising, or the hardware to implement a revolt. Gaining support from discontented Serbian nationals was a task they could perform for themselves, but to affect an uprising they needed to obtain arms and ammunition. Their only recourse was to men who could supply the required weaponry, men like Jesse Barker.

Their initial contact with Jesse had been through recommendation. England was far away, a land so remote from Serbia as to make any clash of political interest or ideology improbable. The leaders of the Black Hand argued that dealing with an Englishman represented a lesser risk.

It had been no part of Hildegard's orders to seduce Jesse, or to become his mistress. That came about through mutual attraction. What little she knew of Englishmen was that they had the reputation of being cold, aloof and arrogant, with a passion for playing games, that they ruled an enormous empire and cared more for their animals than their women.

When she met the handsome young Englishman with the ready smile and eyes alive with mischief, Hildegard was captivated. Jesse, for his part, saw in Hildegard another challenge. She was beautiful, sensual, and young. She had a wicked smile that hinted at wanton delight. Within minutes of their first meeting, Jesse set about providing as much encouragement as he could. That had been almost a year ago, but both Jesse's other commitments and the fear of discovery kept them apart for much of the time.

Jesse's reunion with Hildegard that May was all that he had hoped it would be and more. For over two weeks, they were together in her Viennese apartment and their passion, far from cooling after four months of separation, had increased to a point when they were unable to satisfy their hunger for one another. Their time together passed so quickly that all too soon the message they were expecting arrived. It was time for Jesse to move on, his destination still further eastward. First, he was to travel to Zagreb, capital of Croatia, thence to Belgrade and eventually to Kosovo, where he was to supervise the safe delivery of the required munitions. Only when he reached Zagreb would he be told of the place in Belgrade where he would rendezvous with leaders of the Black Hand. From there they would direct him to the required meeting point in Kosovo. The armaments, which would travel by an altogether different route, would be handed over, at which time Jesse would be paid.

Late one morning towards the end of May 1914, Jesse took his leave of a tearful Hildegard and set off on the first leg of his journey.

Three days later, in line with the instructions given to him in Zagreb, Jesse sat in a small, cheaply decorated café in Belgrade. The café, which went by the name *Zlatana Moruna*, was of the type used by artisans and students. It was dimly lit by flickering gas mantles and had a seedy, depressing air to it. As he sat at one of the small, rickety tables covered with worn and grubby oilcloth drinking barely palatable coffee, he was joined, one by one by a series of grave-faced young men, leaders of the Black Hand. Jesse was aware that they were planning some desperate act, although he had no idea what that act was to be, or against whom it was to be directed. Furthermore, he had absolutely no desire to know.

He was introduced to the four men who would rendezvous with him in Kosovo, given detailed instructions as to time and place, then how to depart on the final leg of his journey. When doing so, all his movements from that point on would be observed. He was given bloodcurdling threats as to the consequences of his straying, however minutely, from the detail of his orders, especially with regard to the delivery of the arms. Jesse was to leave the café via the kitchen entrance. Once outside he would be guided by one of their waiting members to the railway station and put safely on board his train. Others would be on hand but hidden to ensure that neither Jesse nor their co-conspirators had been detected.

When Jesse arrived in Kosovo, he would have a little less than two weeks to ensure the safe delivery of the arms. Time, he was told repeatedly, was critical, so there had to be no question of delay. Later that evening, having dined on a barely edible type of meat stew, partaken of principally to ward off potentially suspicious onlookers, Jesse left the building as directed.

* * *

Alice leaned over James's shoulder, her arms about his neck as they read Sonny's letter together. It was mid-May of 1914, a calm and pleasantly warm evening following a hot day. They were comfortable in each other's company, in a way many couples do not achieve until much later in life. Consideration of the letter gave the couple cause for much speculation.

Most of this centred on the actions of James's father and the reason for them. Alice, who had much less insight into Albert's character, sought enlightenment from her husband. James, although unable to answer her questions with entire accuracy, recalled for her something he had read recently.

'There is a theory that has no foundation in scientific knowledge. It is that as one gets older, changes occur in the brain that can cause attitudes and perspectives to alter. Thus a decision made by a man our age would be totally at variance with what the same person would opt to do at Father's age. It is only a theory and to be fair, when it comes to the workings of the brain, even the most distinguished specialists recognize they are still working in the dark most of the time.'

'Do you mean your father is mentally ill?' Alice asked in some alarm.

'I wouldn't class it as an illness as such,' James reassured her. 'If that theory is correct what happens is a gradual process of decay. There is a condition amongst the elderly called senility. It doesn't affect all old people, but those who get it behave very oddly. The article I read cited some examples of things that elderly patients had done and, if it wasn't sad it would have been funny. Now I'm not suggesting that is happening to Father, but part of the theory is that these changes in the brain happen so slowly that it can be many years before they become apparent. In Father's case we have already seen examples of odd behaviour in his attitude to Michael and Connie.'

'Might it also explain his behaviour towards you and me?' Alice asked.

'Oh I don't know.' James grinned. 'I think that was quite in character. Father is an autocrat, a snob and a social climber, so when he was faced with the news that his eldest son had got their housemaid pregnant and intended to marry her, his reaction was understandable. He probably had ambitions for me to go into the family business and marry an Earl's daughter.'

Alice frowned. 'Do you think you married beneath yourself?'

'No fear.' James kissed her. 'Anyway,' he chuckled, 'for all we know you could be an Earl's daughter.'

'So what do you intend to do about Sonny?' Alice wanted to know.

'I shall write to Ralph instructing him to request a shareholders' meeting at which he is to put the power of our vote alongside Sonny's holding. I've held off so far to avoid antagonizing Father, especially as the business is performing better, but I cannot stand by any longer. I have no intention of allowing Sonny's future to be spoilt as Michael's so nearly was by Clarence Barker's scheming and conniving ways.'

'What do you think the future holds?' It was a question Alice had often asked during their life together. Experience of his forecasts had taught her to respect his grasp of events. His predictions were disturbingly accurate.

'I'm more than a little troubled. At the moment everything appears settled, there are no major trouble spots in the world, but there is a restless air about that I don't care for. Minor unrest it may be, but we are only fourteen years into this century and already there have been wars in Africa, Asia, and the Americas. Added to that there has been civil unrest in any number of countries, in particular an attempted revolution in Russia. I reckon Europe is a powder keg waiting for the fuse to be lit. If Russia goes up too, it will be like the whole magazine exploding. It may well be quiet at the moment, but that might be the calm that comes before a storm.'

* * *

June 28th was a calm, bright sun-filled morning as the postman turned into Byland Crescent. He dropped a small bundle of envelopes through the letterbox of Number 1 then went on his way. Among the letters collected from Henry by Sonny was one for himself. It was in a strange hand, the envelope bearing a London postmark. He opened it to find a further envelope inside. In it was the letter he had been waiting for, the promised support from his brother James.

As Sonny was reading the letter, across the continent of Europe, in a town called Sarajevo, capital of Bosnia and Herzegovina, the Archduke Franz Ferdinand, heir to the throne of Austro-Hungary, arrived with his wife Sophie to direct army movements in the surrounding mountains. It was the anniversary of the battle of Kosovo in 1389, when the defeat of the Serbian army by the forces of the Ottoman Empire had ended Serbia's independence as a nation. The radical Serbian terrorists feared the Archduke's accession to the throne would lead to further persecution of Serbs. The choice of this day of shame for such a visit was the final humiliation.

As the Archduke's car was proceeding along the route it slowed and Gavrilo Princip, one of the Black Hand's trained assassins, calmly stepped up to the vehicle and fired two pistol shots. Both Franz Ferdinand and Sophie died within minutes.

Exactly one month later, without much attempt at conciliation, Austro-Hungary, backed by Kaiser Wilhelm, declared war on Serbia.

* * *

It was 28 July 1914. World War One had begun.

PART THREE: 1914–1918

What passing-bells for these who die as cattle?
Only the monstrous anger of the guns.
Only the stuttering rifles' rapid rattle
Can patter out their hasty orisons.
No mockeries for them from prayers or bells,
Nor any voice of mourning save the choirs,-
The shrill, demented choirs of wailing shells;
And bugles calling for them from sad shires.
What candles may be held to speed them all?
Not in the hands of boys, but in their eyes
Shall shine the holy glimmers of good-byes.
The pallor of girls' brows shall be their pall;
Their flowers the tenderness of silent maids,
And each slow dusk a drawing-down of blinds.
Anthem For A Doomed Youth
Wilfred Owen (1893–1918)

CHAPTER TWENTY

For several months Hannah had been preoccupied with her mother's failing health. Since Philip's death Ellen had been in a gradual spiral of decline. In spring of 1914 a bout of influenza, amounting almost to pneumonia had accelerated her frailty. She was far from senile, but from time to time would get confused. She occasionally referred to Sonny as James, and Hannah herself had been called Hermione more than once. Distressing as this was, worse was to follow.

Late in April, Ellen, having barely recuperated from the influenza attack, suffered a fall. It was not serious in itself, but following it her confusion grew steadily worse. This caused her to retreat within the walls of her home. A glorious summer such as that of 1914 would have been ideal for Ellen to have pursued her favourite hobby with vigour. Day after day would have been spent supervising the care and maintenance of the grounds to the house she loved so dearly. The carefully manicured lawns, well stocked flower beds, shrubberies and fruit trees that surrounded the house were Ellen's pride and joy. Her self-imposed exile from her beloved gardens was so out of character that Hannah feared her mother's condition was far worse than any of the family realized.

Hannah visited her mother each morning after breakfast. This gave time for Ellen's personal maid to help her mistress bathe and dress. When the maid telephoned Byland Crescent early one morning in mid-July Hannah knew something was amiss. The maid informed Hannah that Ellen was too ill to get out of bed. She was unable to describe any specific symptoms, but had merely told her maid that she felt a great weariness.

Steven Culleton was a family friend as well as being both their neighbour and doctor. In all three capacities, he knew a great deal about his patient. Although he was unable to define the cause of Ellen's illness, he was in no doubt that the problem was serious. This led him to a conclusion that both alarmed and saddened Hannah.

'The problem is, I believe Mrs Ackroyd is not concerned whether she recovers or not. Since the death of her husband she has been going through the motions of living, somewhat like a disinterested spectator. It is a curious thing to say,' he concluded, 'as there is no such medical condition, but I truly believe that your mother is dying because she does not want to live any longer without Philip.'

Hannah made urgent phone calls to her sisters to inform them of their mother's condition. They travelled to Scarborough immediately. Despite the constant attention of all three of her daughters, Ellen continued to weaken. On 27 July, the day before the outbreak of war, Ellen Ackroyd slipped peacefully from the life she had lived with such gentleness and grace.

* * *

The consequences of events in Sarajevo were immediate and far-reaching. Although no one could have predicted how cataclysmic the fall-out from the assassination of the Archduke would turn out to be, the short-term effects were severe enough in themselves. Few could have guessed, in those ever-darkening days of a hot, bright summer, what horrors lay in store for the world over the next four years.

Tension was high in Vienna, the secret police were everywhere, rooting out Serbian nationals and suspected sympathizers. Their actions, vindicated by a need to protect national security, cloaked a desire for revenge and reprisal. It was an attitude of mind that was to be magnified a million-fold as it crossed all European borders and spread even further.

Within days of the Archduke's murder, Hildegard realized she would have to leave the city. Her anxiety for her own welfare was heightened by concern over Jesse. No word had come following his departure for Zagreb. Hildegard had no way of knowing if her lover was alive or dead.

A visit by one of her colleagues from the Black Hand did little to reassure her. 'All those who took part in the Sarajevo execution, plus many of our leaders have been detained. There is no doubt they will be tortured to reveal the identity of their co-conspirators and collaborators,' he told her. 'Nobody, no matter how tenuous their connection, will be safe. You should leave Vienna as speedily as possible.'

'Do you know what has happened to Jesse, the Englishman?' Hildegard asked.

He shook his head. 'He delivered the arms as promised then he was put across the Albanian border. After that . . .' the man shrugged his shoulders. Hildegard was left with the impression that he had little interest in Jesse, who was of no further use to the Black Hand.

Hildegard prepared to leave, but was uncertain where to go. Austria, Hungary, and their ally Germany were clearly to be avoided; neither would the Balkans provide a safe haven. Russia, Serbia's ally, was taking a keen interest in affairs, so the only route offering the slightest hope was to the west. Westward lay France, not yet committed to any action, and beyond, England. Hildegard knew that England represented the best chance of being reunited with her lover. If Jesse had survived the bloody aftermath of the Sarajevo assassination he would surely make for his homeland. When Hildegard had been chosen to act as Jesse's agent, one of the reasons had been her command of English. This would stand her in good stead if she succeeded.

In the midst of her anxieties, another cause for concern had been overlooked. Hildegard was forcibly reminded of this when she started to experience bouts of nausea. At first, she put these down to worry and the stress of her situation. After some calculations, Hildegard looked at the calendar in numb surprise. There was now an added spur to her urgency to leave Vienna, another valid reason to head for England.

* * *

What Jesse Barker had failed to take into consideration was the desperation of the leaders of the Black Hand, or the scale of the atrocity they were planning. Such was the atmosphere of suspicion, deceit, and betrayal within the nationalist movement that it proved a breeding ground for paranoia.

The first inkling he had came immediately after the handover of the arms. Once the weapons had been carefully checked over, the money was counted out. Jesse placed the cash into the small bag he had brought along then stood up to leave the rendezvous.

The meeting had taken place in the kitchen of a remote farmhouse close to the Kosovo border, high in the hills. As he made to depart, Jesse was disconcerted to find his path to the door blocked by two of the Black Hand members. Any confusion as to their motives for this action was erased by the pistols they had levelled at him. Ironically these were two of the batch for which he had just been paid.

The leader of the group, the only one with a command of English, announced their intentions in chilling terms. 'I regret that we cannot allow you to leave, sir,' he told Jesse. 'Not until our mission is complete. We cannot allow any chance of discovery. Therefore, until we have achieved our goal you must remain here. You will not find the accommodation comfortable, but that is a sacrifice you will have to make. You can console yourself by counting your money. Once our task is accomplished you will be escorted to a border of our choice. When you have crossed that border our involvement with you will cease.

'I must warn you not to attempt to escape. The men who will remain with you will act as your guards as well as your hosts. They have instructions that if you attempt to escape, they are to shoot you dead.' He did not add, 'do I make myself clear'; there was no need.

The hours and days that followed proved unutterably tedious for Jesse. The small room in which he was kept prisoner lacked a window or any means of illumination, so the brief excursions for food or to answer a call of nature were the only breaks in the monotony of his existence.

His imprisonment came to an end as suddenly as it had begun. He had been held captive a little more than two weeks by his calculations when the door to his makeshift cell was thrust open. Both guards stood framed in the entrance. For once their stern demeanour was replaced with broad triumphal smiles. They spoke and from his sketchy knowledge of their language Jesse adjudged them to be telling him: 'It is done. The enemy is brought down. You are free to leave.'

They gestured to him to collect his belongings. These consisted of a small suitcase containing his clothing and toiletries in addition to his cash bag. Jesse needed little encouragement to comply with their orders. Two days later they left him, having watched him cross the border in safety. Contrary to Jesse's worst fears, they made no attempt to confiscate his money. Although he was now a free man, Jesse was faced with one enormous problem. He had absolutely no idea where he was.

* * *

There was a sinister and frightening velocity in the way Europe rushed headlong into the conflict that would engulf the whole continent and spread far beyond, implicating men from all corners of the world. In the process it would kill more than nine-million soldiers, sailors and for the first time, airmen, besides countless civilians, and leave many more mutilated, bereaved or homeless.

There was no pause for thought, mediation, or conciliation in this eager and indecent haste. No phoney war to provide respite for clearer heads to attempt wise counsel before hostilities began. Hildegard made her escape from Vienna on 25 July, three days before Emperor Franz Joseph made his fatal declaration and the borders were sealed. She went with a false passport, prepared for her at great speed by one of the Black Hand's few remaining contacts in the capital. The forger had only escaped detection following an administrative mix up. Two hours after Hildegard left the printer's shop with the documents she needed, he was arrested. As she boarded her train out of the country, secret police officials broke down the door of her deserted apartment.

Her headlong flight preceded closing borders in the wake of her passage. Using her new identity, that of an Englishwoman calling herself Naomi Fleming, she reached Paris. As she arrived in the French capital, the newspapers carried news of Russia's decision to mobilize her troops. She managed to change what money she had for unfamiliar British sterling in the French capital one day before the banks ceased trading in Austro-Hungarian currency. The following day she left Paris, bound for the coast as Germany mobilized her troops and declared war on Russia.

Hildegard, or as she kept reminding herself, Naomi, reached London on 3 August She struggled to read the announcement on the newsvendors' placards that Germany had declared war on France. She was puzzled by the accompanying headline, 'Cabinet in Crisis Talks'. Her recollection of English vocabulary told her that a cabinet was a piece of furniture. Her unfamiliar accent caused a few sideways glances in the English capital, which fuelled her insecurity. Desperate to be out of London she sought information at

King's Cross Station. She knew she must head for Yorkshire. The railway official was baffled by her request for information on trains running to Yorkshire, as well as by her accent. Eventually she told him she wanted to reach a place called Bradford and the misunderstanding was cleared up.

When Hildegard reached the West Riding textile town, she had travelled through country after country that was becoming embroiled in the ensuing conflict, only to find herself adrift in a strange land that was itself at war. By now Hildegard was certain she was pregnant. The small amount of money she had was dwindling fast. If the future looked bleak for the continent of Europe, it was an equally chilling prospect for Hildegard.

As the crisis in Europe escalated, anyone suspected of being connected with the Black Hand would be in the gravest of danger. Although she spoke good English she knew it would not stand up to close examination. She knew few of the colloquialisms and some of the accents were equally baffling. In the West Riding the latter was less of a problem as most of the voices resembled that of her lover. Neither was she too worried by her own accent. When Jesse had teased her about it she had asked if the English would know where she was from. She remembered him laughing as he told her that most English people would be unable to distinguish an Austrian accent from an Australian one. Hildegard clung to that thought for comfort. If asked, she would tell the enquirer that Naomi Fleming had been born and raised in Australia.

CHAPTER TWENTY-ONE

In the closing days of August 1914, when France was reeling at the loss of 27,000 troops during one day of the ill-fated Battle of the Frontiers, Sonny visited his solicitors in Bradford. As he walked from Manor Row to the lawyer's office, preparations for war were already visible. Windows carried patriotic posters and flags and queues of serious-faced young men signalled the opening of recruiting centres, each of the eager applicants keen to 'do their bit'. Many of them had been seduced into the conviction that this would be the shortest of campaigns. The generally held and much publicized expert opinion being that it would 'all be over by Christmas'.

Sonny deposed that his estate should be divided between his father and brother equally, in the event that he predeceased them, unmarried and childless. He added the proviso that in the event of his marriage subsequent to the making of the will the estate should then devolve to his widow and any legitimate offspring of that marriage. The solicitor had given him a sidelong enquiring glance on hearing this provision, on seeing which Sonny had grinned and explained that, as matters stood it was a purely hypothetical clause.

* * *

In Paris, general consternation abounded. Most Parisians were at a loss to understand, let alone explain how they found themselves at war. To an Englishwoman such as Ada, short of informed opinion as to the possible outcome, confusion was all the more extreme. A visit to the British Embassy proved fruitless as the building was besieged, both by fellow nationals seeking similar reassurance and hordes of others keener still to escape to what they saw as the last refuge of security on the continent. Neither set of petitioners seemed likely to gain much in the way of satisfaction, so Ada retreated to her apartment to take stock. She missed Eleanor whose wise counsel she trusted in such matters. Equally, Ada longed to be back in the comfort and safety of her own family surroundings, for so long forbidden to her. Suddenly, Paris was a lonely and frightening place and Byland Crescent seemed a long distance away.

* * *

Nor was it only in Europe that events were being watched with a kind of horrified fascination. Access to reports of developments was enhanced for James and Alice Fisher through their ownership of four provincial newspapers. With wire-reports streaming in daily from an ever-growing number of press bureaux, what had been rumour one day turned into awful truth by the following morning.

Alice was shocked by how swiftly and completely James's prognostications had become a reality. 'Where,' she asked him, 'will it all end?'

James had snorted with derision. 'It certainly won't be all over by Christmas,' he told her. 'As to where, or when, I have no idea. Any more than those so-called experts. Of one thing I am sure, life will never be the same again. Many barriers have been pulled down that will never be rebuilt, much of what we have come to regard as permanent has vanished forever.'

'It won't reach us here, surely?' Alice wanted to know.

'It already has,' James pointed out. 'Australia has already entered the war. When Britain declared war against Germany on 4 August, Australia lent her full support; backing this up by promising to provide a force of 20,000 men to ensure imperial defence. They have also been talking about the Australian Imperial Force, as they call the new unit, combining with the New Zealand Army Corps. Whether there will actually be any fighting on Australian territory I very much doubt, but make no mistake, Alice, we are in this war and only time will tell how deeply.'

* * *

Enlisting was the order of the day. Insidious propaganda, backed by direct appeals encouraged young men to join the swelling throngs at recruiting offices hastily established throughout Britain. Across the whole continent of Europe speeches made by peppery old generals and equally fiery, equally elderly politicians exhorted young men to do their duty. Their King, or Emperor, or President as the case may be, wanted them. They were needed to fight for their country. What they did not say was that they needed to die for their country. Nor did those young men who answered the call to arms pause to enquire why their King, or Emperor, or President suddenly wanted them, suddenly needed them. Why, when for the rest of their existence, those exalted beings had totally ignored them? Duty and honour became the watchwords. Slaughter and wasted lives were not mentioned, except by a few brave, well-intentioned individuals who paid the price, being pilloried as cowards, or worse still tried and executed for treason.

So the cream of a generation donned the khaki, or field grey, or whatever colour of uniform had been chosen by their King, or Emperor, or President. They learned to march, handle a rifle, throw a grenade, load and launch a shell, and how to bayonet a man to death. Many and varied were the techniques instilled into those young men in the arts of killing other young men wearing different coloured uniforms.

Their instructors failed to tell their pupils how to avoid a raining shower of artillery shells that spurted deadly shards of white-hot shrapnel. Nor did they instruct their charges how to jump over, or round, or duck under a withering hail of machine gun fire, nor where to take shelter from a drifting, poisonous cloud of mustard gas. How could they, as the instructors themselves did not know the answers to those atrocious and insoluble riddles.

* * *

In late September of 1914, Mark Cowgill volunteered and was passed fit for duty in the British Army. He was given orders as to where to report for induction and after three days of hectic leave-taking, set off from Byland Crescent to begin training. Within days of joining his regiment he was known to one and all as Sonny. Elsewhere many others were passing through similar procedures. Ephraim Barker, Jesse's twin brother, was accepted into the King's Own Yorkshire Light Infantry, where his quasi-American accent made him the butt of much amicable ribbing.

From Byland Crescent, neighbouring sons all volunteered, two of them in the Royal Navy, the third, into the Royal Marines. Both Firth boys were in the KOYLI's alongside Ephraim Barker, while another joined the artillery. Dr Culleton's son, Steven Junior, was most upset that he was far too young to enlist.

Nor were the women to be left out. Those who could call upon the remotest qualification, plus many who were unqualified, were drafted into the nursing profession. Their role would be to tend the wounded, in itself a tacit acknowledgement by the generals and political representatives of the King, the Emperor or the President, that there would be casualties. Of course there would be, for this was war and you can't have a war without casualties.

Others would work in munitions factories, replacing men who had gone to fight. They would make deadly instruments of war for the men who had gone to fight. With these they would be able to kill and maim other young men wearing different coloured uniforms. As this process was being conducted by both sides it might have been seen as counter-productive, but at least it would keep the nurses busy.

Sister Rachael Graham volunteered. From Sheffield she travelled to Sussex, where she was put in charge of a group of young and inexperienced women whose duty would be to tend the wounded sent back to England for treatment and rehabilitation. This process would have the long-term aim of getting the injured men healed and wherever possible, fit enough to return to the battlefield, where presumably, the enemy could have another go at killing them.

* * *

Ada Cowgill, having vacillated over whether to leave Paris, found herself caught up in the tide of war. She volunteered for nursing duty and was assigned to a field hospital in France, some forty miles behind the front line. Following the first Battle of the Marne the German advance had been halted, thwarting their plans to capture Paris. Along the Western Front both sides adopted defensive position by digging mile upon mile of trenches. As 1914 drew to a close, Christmas Day saw a truce between men facing one another across no man's land. A truce, but no end to the war that would, the experts said, 'be all over by Christmas'.

Christmas celebrations in 1914 ranged from normal, through muted, to non-existent. For countless men, women and children, Christmas 1914 was like no other they had ever seen, or wanted to witness again.

* * *

Charlotte Tunnicliffe spent Christmas alone. Alone that is, unless you count a three-month-old child as company, which

Charlotte certainly did not. There was a bitter irony in the way she spent that Christmas compared to the one that had preceded it. That Christmas had been spent in an orgy of passion with her lover. This year Charlotte waited in vain for Jesse, or for news of him. Charlotte needed little reminder of her lover, or the passion they had exchanged. Their tiny daughter Jessica provided reminder enough.

Three miles away, in a small side street of tiny, through-by-light terraced cottages, Naomi Fleming also spent Christmas alone. Alone, for her child was as yet unborn. She had been lucky so far in obtaining this tiny shelter, her first home in England, then to have obtained casual work sewing for a local dressmaker. Both house and job had been advertised in a local shop window and Naomi, as she now thought of herself, was grateful for them. Like Charlotte she also wanted news of her lover Jesse, father of her unborn child. Unlike Charlotte she had no hope, however faint: he did not know she was in England, let alone Bradford. She knew he would not be knocking on her door that Christmas. Indeed a knock on the door was what she dreaded most. It might be a forerunner to discovery of her identity, which would lead to internment — or worse.

* * *

Elsewhere, Christmas was spent in a variety of ways. In Baildon, Michael and Connie Haigh spent a traditional Yuletide with their eight-year-old daughter Marguerite and their sons Edward, now five years old and George aged two. The only clouds to mar their festivities were concerns over Connie's brother Sonny, away fighting in France, and regret over the continuing feud between Michael and Connie's father.

In Australia, anxious parents bade farewell to reservists called-up to back the war effort. All eyes were trained on the news filtering through from Western Europe as they feared for the safety of their loved ones. James celebrated Christmas with Alice and their growing family. Saul, their eldest son was sixteen now and fervently hoped that the war would not end before he had the chance to fight. He kept this aspiration closely hidden from his mother. Along with Saul were his sister Cissie, now thirteen, Ellen who was nine, Philip aged five and baby Mary, just six months old.

In Byland Crescent the house was empty save for Albert and Hannah Cowgill. The irony of the twists of fate that had led them to eating their Christmas dinner in lonely and uncompanionable silence was not lost on Hannah. Her love for Albert, if not gone, was diminished by all that had occurred since they moved into the house. Hannah was more worried than she would care to admit about Albert. Prior to Sonny's enlisting in the army Albert had recovered from his former habit of heavy drinking, but with Sonny's departure the tendency had returned. For this, as well as the rift between Albert and Michael, Hannah laid the blame fairly and squarely on Clarence Barker whom she suspected of engineering both, to suit his own devious purposes.

Elsewhere in Byland Crescent, Christmas 1914 was a sombre affair as almost every household worried about the fate of loved ones overseas. The residents of Scarborough might have been forgiven for thinking that the war could have little effect on a place as small and insignificant as the Yorkshire seaside resort. After all the town was known only for its small and declining fishing fleet, flat, sandy beaches, spa water and air of genteel holiday entertainment. Eleven days prior to Christmas 1914, these illusions were brutally shattered.

The German battle cruisers Deerflinger and Von Der Tam, accompanied by the light cruiser Kolberg, took station less than a mile offshore, barely outside the town's twin bays. They commenced activities by laying mines and bombarding the ancient and deserted castle. Receiving no retaliatory fire as a result of this aggression, the bold matelots closed in and shelled the town itself. Two hundred and ten buildings were damaged and eighteen people were killed as a result of this unprovoked hostile action. They included eight women and four children. What threat they constituted to the might of the German Navy remained a puzzle to the citizens of the town long after the smoke from the cruisers stacks had dissipated as they retreated into the North Sea.

* * *

In the Manor Row offices of HAC, Clarence Barker spent every spare moment of his time plotting and scheming. His only worry was the persistent rumour that the government was about to introduce compulsory conscription. Clarence did not want to fight; he loathed and feared the thought of going to war. He was afraid. He began talking to men who had been rejected on medical grounds, to attempt to find out what symptoms were needed to avoid being called upon to serve. He even made surreptitious visits to a series of doctors, in an attempt to find any who might be open to a little persuasion. If he could bribe a doctor to give him a certificate of unfitness, the danger of having to fight might be averted.

* * *

In Albania, Jesse Barker was unaware of the two families awaiting him in Bradford. He was unaware of much, save for that which threatened his own survival. On the run for months, he had picked up but a few snippets of information regarding the conflagration that was sweeping the continent of Europe. He had no real idea who was fighting whom, all he knew was that the actions of the Black Hand must have had some part in it. Fear made him a fugitive, even though he knew he was in Albania, he was unsure whether they were friend or foe. Jesse spent that Christmas, as he had the preceding months, hiding in forests and fields by day, living rough, and barely surviving. The money he carried was of no use but he clung to the bag in the hope that when he returned to civilization it would once again have value. As he attempted, with painfully slow progress to make his way southward he scrounged or stole whatever food he could get, from wherever he could get it. When he could get none, he tried to live off berries and nuts but without much success. He sought whatever rude shelter he could get along the way to survive the harsh Albanian winter. No longer was he the dapper, handsome young man who had won his way into the hearts and beds of Charlotte, Hildegard and many others. Jesse was unrecognizable, gaunt in face and figure, his long hair and beard matted and unkempt, his clothes hanging in rags from his skeletal frame.

* * *

In France, thousand upon weary thousand of armed men cowered in trenches and foxholes, slits and shell holes, facing each other across a no man's land pitted with craters and curtained with barbed wire. Winter had ground all offensives to a halt. Along that front line, the only carols to be heard were the blasting timpani of artillery shells, the whining descant of mortars and the chattering, repetitive chorus of machine gun fire. Along that line Sonny nestled into a makeshift shelter in a vain attempt to combat the numbing effects of the bitter weather, the atrocious living conditions, the constant aura of fear and the all-pervading stench of death and decaying corpses.

Also in France, only fifty miles away from her brother, in scarcely better conditions, Ada assisted in operation after operation in the field hospital to which she had been assigned. Her only perfumes were those of the basic antiseptics and disinfectants or the sweet, sickly stench of gangrenous limbs which the surgeons stitched, cut, and in desperation, hacked, in their efforts to stay the appalling loss of life.

The luckiest ones were sent home to England, home to Blighty. Some would go to the outskirts of Chichester, where Rachael Graham and her staff of willing but inexperienced and untrained team of helpers barely noticed Christmas come and go as they attempted to cope with the influx of casualties.

This was the Christmas of 1914. And worse was to come.

CHAPTER TWENTY-TWO

By Christmas of 1916 it was clear the predicted short campaign was going to be a long, bitter, and bloody struggle. 1915 had seen the introduction of several new and sinister forms of warfare. One of these was the concept of Total War. A step away from fighting anyone wearing a different coloured uniform, in Total War anyone carrying a different coloured passport was a legitimate target. This involved such dangerous foes as women, even when pregnant, the elderly, children, and babies in arms. Perhaps this was intended to wipe out potential future threats by eliminating children, who might grow up to become enemies, and erasing the memory of past defeats by slaughtering the aged.

As part of the novel and interesting philosophy of Total War, Germany announced a submarine blockade of Great Britain, declaring that any ship approaching England was to be considered a legitimate target. They sank the liner *Lusitania* killing 1198 civilians including 128 Americans. Presumably the fact that they spoke English was sufficient to condemn them to the status of legitimate targets.

Not wishing to be outdone in this spirit of modern warfare, British commanders authorized the use of poison gas in battle near Loos. The effect was not what they had intended however, for a change in wind direction resulted in the gas being blown back over British lines, resulting in more than 60,000 casualties. The generals had not learned that there was one more powerful than they.

1915 had not been a good year for Allied commanders, which probably accounted for their desperation for success. They had started the year with high confidence launching an invasion against the Turkish held Gallipoli Peninsula. This was to be another short campaign. In fact this one was, to all intents and purposes, 'all over by Christmas'. After nine months of almost non-stop merciless slaughter, Allied commanders began withdrawing their troops. Not the original troops of course. Almost all of them were either dead, wounded, or imprisoned.

Two months after the humiliating end to the Gallipoli campaign, British politicians, no doubt at the behest of their military commanders, showed commendable foresight, and presence of mind, by introducing compulsory conscription. This meant that any young men who had opted for the comfort of their own beds and firesides rather than the cold, muddy, and distinctly dangerous life in the trenches would no longer have any choice in the matter.

The politicians and generals would not have considered taking this step had it not been deemed absolutely necessary. Casualty figures must have shown that they were running dangerously low on volunteers, with insufficient numbers stepping forward of their own accord. How sensible a precaution this proved to be was illustrated during the course of 1916, when the Battle of Verdun resulted in over one million casualties and the Battle of the Somme yielded over one million more. No territory was actually gained as a result of either of these bloody encounters, but neither was any lost, so obviously the exercise, despite the loss of over two million lives, was absolutely necessary and totally worthwhile.

* * *

Albert Cowgill had been forced out of retirement to resume control at Manor Row. HAC had suffered greatly at the hands of Clarence Barker; now, with so many staff absent and government restrictions in place, commercial life was difficult. Clarence Barker had eventually been made to enlist with the advent of conscription. Having received his call-up papers, he went to attend a medical, armed with a letter from a doctor whose cooperation he had bought. The letter listed various ailments that would render Clarence unfit for service. The sergeant supervising the medical session barely glanced at the document. 'So your doctor doesn't think you are fit,' he stated, before crumpling the letter into a tiny ball and tossing it contemptuously into the waste bin. 'Well, you look fit enough to me.' He gave Clarence a wicked grin completely devoid of humour. 'Round here it's my opinion that counts. So you'd better start learning French.'

* * *

The day Clarence Barker sailed for France to join his infantry regiment, news came through from the front line that his younger brother Ephraim, Jesse's twin, had been killed in action. In Byland Crescent too, 1916 proved to be a year of great sadness. Two of the neighbouring boys had been killed, one in the Battle of Jutland, the other on the Somme. Josiah Firth's eldest son had been invalided home, surgeons having removed what remained of his right leg following wounds received during the same battle. There also, Sonny Cowgill had been severely wounded. Sonny, promoted twice due to heavy regimental losses, had received two machine gun rounds in his left shoulder and several pieces of shrapnel in his right leg. He had been sent back to England for operations to remove the offending pieces of metal in time to save both the arm and the leg. If that proved possible, the medics thought, he might just pull through.

As Sonny was delirious during the journey back to England and for some considerable time after the operations he had to undergo, his parents knew nothing of his wounds, his promotion to the rank of Captain, or the Military Cross he had been awarded, until much later. The citation for the medal stated that, to protect the men under his command, he had completed the destruction of the enemy machine gun post despite the severity of the wounds he had already received. The citation failed to mention that Sonny was already unconscious when the grenade he had thrown so accurately exploded in the firing slit of the concrete bunker. Only two of the bunker's occupants had been killed by the grenade itself, the remaining four were victim to the exploding machine gun rounds detonated by the accuracy of Sonny's grenade.

* * *

Rachael Graham studied the manifest handed to her by the ambulance driver with vague interest. Two more casualties were listed on it, whose wounds were so bad that there seemed little hope of their survival. Rachael set about supervising their transfer to her emergency ward.

If Sonny Cowgill owed his survival in the first instance to the skill of the surgeon who removed the bullets and shrapnel, his long-term recovery was wholly due to Rachael. Sister Graham had seen many young men pass through her wards during the two years her temporary hospital had been open, a lot of whom had been saved through her skill and the devotion of her staff. Sadly, still more had succumbed to their wounds. It would have been natural for her to regard Captain Mark Cowgill as just one more, deserving their best attention, but unlikely to survive. Yet, as soon as she saw him, Rachael knew that this was different, this was a young man she had to save. It was virtually unheard of for her to take personal charge of a patient as she did with Sonny, assigning supervisory duties for the rest of the wards to her assistant. Day and night for almost two weeks she tended Sonny, ensuring his comfort, changing his dressings, bathing the wound sites to stave off infection. Eventually Rachael began to think she stood a chance of winning the long, slow, and arduous battle. His delirium eased, he began to have brief periods of semi-consciousness, and the colour started to return to his complexion as the grey pallor faded.

Then, one morning, as suddenly as if he was waking from a good night's sleep, Sonny opened his eyes and looked at her. Rachael had been changing the dressing on his leg and was conscious of being watched. She glanced up at his face and blinked with surprise to see him conscious.

'Hello,' he said his voice barely above a whisper. 'Who are you?'

'Sister Graham,' she replied formally, hiding the pleasure at this small sign of recovery.

Sonny smiled, a weak smile, but a smile nonetheless. 'Graham, that's a bloody silly name for a girl,' he commented, before falling asleep once more.

From that point on, his rate of recovery increased. Despite the fact that he was no longer on the danger list and had been adjudged fit enough to be moved from the emergency ward to the recuperation wards, Rachael continued to care for him personally, fitting this in with her other duties. Recovery proved to be a long, painful process. Each new day presented a challenge in his fight to return to full health and regain the use of the limbs so badly mauled. In all his efforts he was aided by Rachael, from the day he first sat up, to the time when he started, cautiously and gingerly, to exercise his wasted muscles. It was Rachael who brought his crutches and stood by him as he tried his first shuffling and faltering steps.

During all that time they talked at length until they knew more about each other, their lives and ambitions, than most young lovers might do. No longer Captain Cowgill and Sister Graham they had become Mark and Rachael, although if Sonny wished to tease her he would revert to calling her Graham.

Still on crutches, he was granted permission for a gentle walk in the grounds of the hospital. Naturally, he could not be allowed to undertake such an ordeal on his own, Sister Graham would have to accompany him. Together they walked slowly across the lawns of the old Georgian manor house that had been converted for the duration of the war. To one side there was a high brick wall, gated and private. Sonny suggested they try the gate. It was unlocked and when they passed through they discovered a hidden garden within. Years of neglect had taken their toll, but it was still enchanting, a place of secrecy and seclusion. Sonny looked around, pleased at their discovery. 'I feel we're improperly dressed,' he told Rachael. 'I should be wearing frock coat and knee britches and you' — he glanced at her uniform, starched and severe — 'should be wearing a crinoline gown.'

Rachael smiled, content because he was happy. She felt a glow of pride to see him so restored, pride and something more. As if he sensed what she was feeling, Sonny rested one of his crutches against the wall and took her hand in his. 'Dear Rachael,' he said softly, 'I have so much to thank you for. I owe my life to you. Your skill, your care and devotion are what pulled me through.'

He put her hand to his lips and kissed it. She felt the touch of his lips on the back of her hand, warm but dry. She looked up. Sonny was smiling, shyly. Rachael felt her heart beating a little faster. Retaining his hold on her hand, he pulled her gently to him. Then he kissed her.

* * *

The pub was in a small village, no more than a hamlet really, by the name of Westergate. The village lies midway between Chichester and Arundel, about five miles from each. Nearby is the seaside resort of Bognor Regis.

Sonny had learned of the pub from a ward orderly during the latter days of his convalescence. 'If you ever want a secluded, romantic spot, with a landlord who asks no questions and leaves guests to their own devices I know the very place,' he'd told Sonny. Quite why he thought he might need this information Sonny was not sure.

As they travelled in a hansom cab towards the village, Sonny told Rachael, 'I've made arrangements and sent a telegram to the landlord.' He reached for her hand held it tightly. 'I understand it is a very picturesque spot. Besides which I like the pub's name and the story behind it.'

The pub was a tiny, creeper clad building. There was a small bar, a tap room, with just one letting bedroom and a bathroom on the first floor. While Sonny was speaking with the landlord, Rachael examined a document describing the pub's unusual name.

The Labour In Vain, had been named after the exploits of a former owner's wife when the building was a private house. Returning from the Caribbean a year before her husband, this lady had allegedly given birth to a child whose skin tone was decidedly dusky and whose hair, dark and tightly curled, bore no resemblance to that of either parent. On hearing of her husband's imminent return the errant wife had commenced a programme of washing and scrubbing the unfortunate infant in a doomed endeavour to conceal the consequences of her misdemeanour.

Rachael's examination of the document hid her mild panic. Now that the time had come for them to be alone she felt shy, nervous, and apprehensive. When they were alone, she voiced her fears to Sonny.

'Mark, my darling, are we doing the right thing? It seems so irresponsible when all the time men are dying in this dreadful war.'

They were standing next to the four-poster bed. Sonny took her in his arms and kissed her tenderly. 'I don't care. I love you, Rachael. I have done so ever since that morning I opened my eyes and saw you. I love you and I want you, now and for always. Even if there is no always for us after I return to the Front, I cannot face the thought of never having had this moment with you.'

Rachael answered him in the only way she was able, by returning his kiss. As he held her she felt the strength of his ardour, felt also the matching tide of passion rising within. An insidious voice within her seemed to be encouraging her, saying, 'go on, you know it is what you want.' After a short, one-sided struggle, Rachael gave in and listened to the voice.

CHAPTER TWENTY-THREE

Naomi sat playing with her little son Joshua in the tiny room of their cottage. It was Christmas 1916 and she had given up all hope of seeing the boy's father again. Although her heart ached for Jesse, Naomi knew she had been lucky to survive. She still feared detection, but it was no longer with the abiding sense of panic that had been with her in the months following her flight from Vienna. As the tide of battle had swept across Europe involving nation after nation, Naomi had been shocked at the effect their actions had precipitated.

Now, she was in calmer waters. The poverty of her early days in the West Riding had eased following Joshua's birth. Naomi was young and strong, she needed work to earn money. Labour was at a premium with so many working men away fighting. Naomi got a job in a nearby textile mill where they produced uniforms for the British Army. In addition to the wage from the mill, which was sufficient to keep her and Joshua, Naomi had maintained her sewing out-work. This enabled her to save a little money. At some stage she might be forced to move again, this time with her infant son. Naomi realized she needed to be prepared for that eventuality. Finding someone to mind Joshua for her while she was at work had been easy, the money she paid the woman was no great drain on her resources.

* * *

Charlotte was also alone that Christmas, brooding and lonely. No word had come from Jesse, although it had been three years since she had seen him. She was convinced he was dead; another victim of the war that had already claimed so many lives and was claiming more and more each day. Charlotte found her life boring, dull, and grindingly tedious. As much as she loved her daughter Jessica, Charlotte needed more. When they had learned of her pregnancy with an illegitimate baby, Charlotte's friends had deserted en masse. Few of her neighbours gave her the time of day. Her mood varied between repressed, frustration, anger and self-pity. In the past Charlotte would have eased the tedium and loneliness by taking a lover, letting the excitement of the affair take her over. Now there were few eligible or desirable men about, certainly for a woman over the age of forty, with a two-year-old daughter.

* * *

Michael and Connie Haigh spent another joyful Christmas that year. They were awaiting the birth of another baby. Connie had received a letter from her brother James who had written to inform them of the birth of his son Luke, his, and Alice's sixth child. He went on to tell them that Saul, now eighteen years old, had joined the forces and was due to leave for Europe at any time.

* * *

So violent had the German attacks been that casualties were arriving in greater numbers than ever. Rachael had been working non-stop. Her workload had been so hectic she barely had time to pay attention to personal matters. Apart from her anxiety over Mark — unlike his family, she never thought or spoke about him as Sonny — Rachael had been too preoccupied with care for her patients. It was all the greater shock when she was able to confirm what she had suspected for several weeks. She was pregnant.

Rachael sought an interview with the doctor in charge of her unit. 'I wish to step down from duty,' she told him, her tone matter of fact.

The harassed and overworked doctor was on the point of refusing when he noticed that Rachael was close to tears. 'Why?' he asked her gently.

'Because I am going to have a baby,' she replied bluntly.

'Oh dear me,' the doctor said, shocked. 'I don't suppose this has anything to do with that handsome young officer you nursed so devotedly?' he asked shrewdly.

'Yes, as a matter of fact it does,' Rachael admitted.

'Very well, I'll start sorting out a replacement. Have you made any plans?'

'I intend to return home to Sheffield. I am going to write to Mark, to tell him the news.'

Before she had chance to start the letter, before the doctor had chance to organize a replacement, casualty listings from the Somme turned her world upside down, her nightmares into a hellish reality.

* * *

Even delivery of mail was affected by the need for men to feed the hungry cannon's roar. Trenches had to be filled, the front lines manned at all cost. Nobody stopped to ask if the price was too high. To speak out thus would have laid the speaker open to a charge of cowardice. The true cowardice was to remain silent while the slaughter continued.

In spring of 1917 Hannah received a letter from her daughter Ada. There had been no direct communication between the two women for years, the bitterness, anger and recrimination that had accompanied Ada's departure had seen to that. For a moment, on opening the envelope, Hannah had been tempted to destroy the contents unread. Wiser counsels prevailed however, and she sat down in the sitting room to discover what her daughter had to tell her.

Dearest Mama,

I hope you receive this letter. I believe many go astray. Of course that is mere rumour, but we have so little news here that for the most part, rumour must suffice. I say 'here' as I am not allowed to tell you exactly where 'here' is. Suffice to say that I am attached to a field hospital close to the front line. I volunteered for nursing duty at the onset of war and have been here, or other similar places, ever since. I cannot tell you of the horrors I have seen, or the conditions in which I have lived, not for fear of the censor's blue pencil, but because you would think I am exaggerating.

There was a lull in the fighting last week. Perhaps they had run out of shells, or men to fire them. During the break I was able to snatch a few hours away. I went for a walk in the countryside close to the village where we are billeted. It is pretty there and the landscape reminds me of Yorkshire. Away from the carnage I witness daily I was able to think clearly and knew I must write this letter.

There is only one certainty here, that each day will bring more death, more broken and mutilated young men to our make-shift little hospital. Amongst our uncertainties is the course of the war itself, or our own fate, for we have no right to claim exemption because of the work we do. Artillery shells do not recognize friend or foe, cannot distinguish between soldier and nurse.

I feel old, Mama, and that comes from all I have witnessed. Sometimes I wonder what happened to that young girl I once was, the one who was so happy, so fulfilled. Her existence seems a lifetime away, it is hard to comprehend that it is only four years past. Nor is it only I who feel that way. It is plainly writ-ten on the faces of the doctors here, in the eyes of the young men they bring in, often hourly, from the battlefield. Such weariness is in those eyes as you would expect in only the very old.

A part of me feels strange about writing to you. I have been away so long, debarred myself from the company of my family that it is as if I am writing to a distant acquaintance instead of my mother. I know naught of what has happened in the family since my parting from you, yet now I feel this compulsion to tell you all my small news. I do this in the hope that you will come to understand me, even in time to forgive that part of me that guided the choices I made, that signposted the route I had to take.

I will speak a little of my partner in what you will no doubt see as my sinning ways. Neither of us was reluctant, hesitant, nor seduced. We entered our relationship joyfully, lovingly, with no fear or misgiving. That must sound strange to an onlooker. We knew from the beginning that we would be set apart, reviled, feel the disgust, and loathing of others. We knew we would encounter these, yet we cared little. Is that not the truest measure of our feelings? Yet Eleanor too is separated from me now, albeit only by a small strip of ocean, yet I feel a greater separation rooted in my experience here.

I dare not allow myself to think about the future. Life here teaches one that such hopes and dreams are futile. All I would ask, should you receive this letter, is to try for that understanding, even if forgiveness is beyond you. One more request, a selfish one I fear. Should this horror engulf me, please find it in your heart to forgive Eleanor along with me. Please tell her, if you feel able, of this letter, of the deep and abiding love I have for her and how I miss her in my loneliness.

I have spoken no word of the family. It is not because they are out of my thoughts or prayers. It is because I love them so dearly that I worry that even to think of them might prove unlucky. By such superstitions we survive here. Please assure them all, Papa, Connie, dear Sonny and all the rest of my deepest love, as I now tender to you, Mama.

Your erring, but loving daughter,
Ada.

Hannah rose unsteadily and carefully replaced the sheets in their envelope. She crossed to the bureau in the corner of the living room and placed the letter inside. Her movements were slow, her step uncertain, made so by the tears that blurred her vision.

So estranged had Albert and Hannah become that she pondered for several days as to whether to tell him of the letter. Eventually, it was another letter that decided matters for her. This one, obviously delayed in delivery, was from Sonny, in which he reported his continued recovery. On the strength of this, Hannah plucked up courage. 'Albert, I've had another letter. From Ada,' she told him, somewhat hesitantly.

To her surprise, Albert seemed pleased rather than angered. 'Where is she? I have been wondering about her.'

Hannah went over to the bureau and returned with the letter. He read it several times before he eventually laid it aside, his head bowed as he sighed deeply. 'Hannah, my dearest, what is happening to us, why are we being punished in this way?' Hannah put her arms around him and together they wept for their children.

Relations between them began to improve following Ada's communication. Albert's drinking lessened again and Hannah eventually dared to hope that the recovery might prove permanent.

* * *

Jesse's decision to travel south was a wise one, his policy of remaining hidden even wiser. Albania was neutral in 1914, under the auspices of the International Commission and in 1915 central and southern parts were under pro-Serbian control. However Austro-Hungarian forces entered and occupied northern Albania in autumn of 1915. By Christmas of 1916 some parts of the south were under French control, others were occupied by their Italian allies. This was not an easy alliance however, and the country remained a melting pot until the end of the war.

Jesse slipped across the Albanian border into northern Greece during the autumn of 1916, as the weather in that mountainous part of the country began to worsen. He was in a parlous condition by then. Malnutrition and dysentery had taken a heavy toll. His feet were in terrible shape. His shoes had long since worn out. He had managed to obtain a pair of boots by an act of burglary, but they were one size too small. This in turn led to dreadful sores and blisters that hampered his walking pace and made every stride pain-filled. What clothing he possessed was pitifully threadbare and totally unsuited to survival of a winter in the mountains. Lack of washing or basic hygiene facilities had laid him open to more than one type of parasitic infestation. Jesse knew that without help he would stand no chance of surviving until spring. He decided to give himself up. He was, in truth, weary of running, exhausted from the constant fear of discovery, too drained physically and mentally, to care much what fate had in store for him.

* * *

In July of 1917, a major offensive was planned around Ypres, better known to English soldiers as 'Wipers'. The battle for Passchendaele would involve a massive artillery bombardment followed by a large scale infantry advance on German positions.

On the last day of July the bombardment commenced. When the heavy guns finally fell silent it was time for the infantry to attempt their assault. All along the sector as whistles blew to sound the advance, soldiers emerged from trenches, dug-outs, foxholes, and shell craters.

Clarence Barker cowered in a corner of the trench in which he had lain for three days. He had skilfully avoided combat on every occasion, skulking behind his unit. Now he knew he should join his comrades who had gone 'over the top' but his brain would not will his legs to move, or stiffen their jelly-like consistency. An officer appeared at the other end of the trench. Although he was not attached to his regiment, Clarence knew the man. The officer frowned. 'Come on, man, over the top with you,' he snapped, his tone clipped and abrupt in that arrogant and commanding manner peculiar to public schools.

When Clarence failed to move the officer stepped forward, raising his pistol. 'Funking it, eh?' His tone was contemptuous. 'Get out of this trench in the next thirty seconds or we won't bother with a court martial, I shall shoot you on the spot.'

Without realizing that he had moved, Clarence fired his first shot of the war. He raised his rifle and shot the officer dead. Fear, coupled with the realization that he had just murdered a man in cold blood made him vomit instantly. A split second later, he evacuated his bowels.

Unseen by neither Clarence nor the officer, the trench contained another occupant. One of Clarence's regimental comrades had been hit by a stray bullet as the advance commenced. The shot had creased the side of the man's head, just below the rim of his helmet. He had lain in the base of the trench for several minutes before consciousness returned. He watched now as Clarence stumbled blindly from the trench and the memory of the horrific crime he had committed.

CHAPTER TWENTY-FOUR

Klaus Von Buhlen was a Prussian cavalry officer. Centuries of land owning superiority gave him a full measure of arrogance, the bier kellars and taverns added a swaggering bravado. These twin assets rendered the need for military training negligible if not totally superfluous. Along with his deep and abiding love for food and alcohol he had an equally high regard for women. Women, that is, who could be cajoled or, failing that, coerced into allowing this brave hero to have his way. His attitude to life was simple and uncluttered enough to dispense with the need for rational thought. What he wanted, he took. If force was required to help him achieve his ends, then that was what he had been trained for.

Klaus had embraced the coming of war as a chance to indulge his belligerent tendencies. When it became clear that the days of the cavalry were numbered, he switched to the infantry where his natural air of command, plus a bribe helped him achieve rapid promotion.

By 1917, when he was wounded and captured, Klaus had, by one means or another, reached the rank of colonel. The loss of their commanding officer did little to weaken the morale of the troops under his command, for Klaus was not popular. He was detested for his swaggering, bullying attitude. He was the type of leader categorized by British troops in a previous conflict as a 'Go On' rather than a 'Come On'.

The wounds Klaus suffered prior to his capture were more humiliating than life threatening. Shrapnel had hit him in a swathe of tiny fragments that had embedded themselves in his lower lumbar and posterior regions. Klaus, in short, had been shot up the backside. For six days after his capture Klaus lay in a bed in a small ward of a British field hospital. Klaus hated the British for several reasons. First and foremost he hated them because they were the enemy. He wasn't exactly sure why they were the enemy, but refused to allow that complication to cloud his judgement. In addition they had more arrogance than Klaus himself, they had far better military tacticians, equipment, superior numbers and were also lucky in battle. Otherwise, how else would Klaus have been captured? He could have blamed his own stupidity and ineptitude, but such was clearly unthinkable.

As Klaus waited for his wounds to heal he watched all that went on around him, plotting his escape. Late at night offered the best chance, when the weary surgeons left for whatever rest they could get. That gave Klaus a few hours when the hospital was least busy, before the dawn chorus of artillery fire acted as an unwelcome alarm clock summoning surgeons and nurses alike back to their posts. Late at night there were very few people about, merely one or two of the nursing staff, whose main preoccupation was with the more seriously wounded British patients, plus one or two guards, whose main preoccupation seemed to be the nurses.

Six nights after his detention, Klaus saw his opportunity. His wounds would not hamper his plans. He arose, silently and unseen, shortly after midnight, and carefully unfastened the window close to his bed. This was the only exit available to him as the door to the ward, in addition to being locked at night, led to a corridor patrolled by guards. Outside the window was a small, dimly lit courtyard of flagged stone, unfrequented at that time of night.

Klaus effected his exit through the window undetected. So far he had been operating on territory he knew; the next part was unfamiliar to him. He made his way cautiously along the walled side of the courtyard then turned the corner of the building. Further progress was hampered by the wall of a building set at right angles to his ward. Klaus would have to enter that building or admit defeat and retire. He decided to go on.

Halfway along the wall he found a door, which to his relief was unlocked. Inside was a hallway with corridors leading off to left and right. The dim lighting showed Klaus that the passages were of similar length, with doors along each side. He chose a corridor, cautiously trying each door along the way. Most were locked, but one showed him a store cupboard containing dressings and surgical instruments. Klaus needed a weapon. He selected a wickedly sharp scalpel, re-closed the door, and continued down the passage.

He had almost reached the end of the corridor when a door to his left suddenly opened. Klaus found himself face to face with a young nurse, clad only in a dressing gown. The room behind her was wreathed in steam. She had obviously been taking a bath. Time seemed suspended as Klaus and the young girl stared at one another, equally startled. Klaus was the first to recover from his shock. Producing the scalpel he leapt forward and placed it at the girl's throat. He motioned her back into the room she had just left. His brain was working quickly. The girl would have to be silenced, or any chance of escape would be gone. That much was clear. At the same time, his adrenalin pumping from the encounter and the very escapade he was attempting, Klaus could feel his own arousal. The girl was young, pretty and the smell of her clean scented body fresh from the bath was exciting. Klaus had not had a woman for over twelve months. Now he had the opportunity to rectify that. Why not, he thought, he was going to kill her anyway.

He motioned to the woman to remove her robe. Her eyes widened in fear and she made no move to obey. The scalpel made short work of the material as he slashed the front of the gown. The robe hung open revealing her breasts, one bleeding slightly where the scalpel had nicked her skin. Lower down Klaus could see the dark mass of her pubic hair. His excitement mounted. With a skill the resident surgeon might have admired he wielded the scalpel once more to cut away a six inch square of fabric. As the girl opened her mouth to scream, Klaus deftly inserted this strip of cloth into her mouth as a gag. Returning the scalpel to her throat, he motioned her to kneel down. From a kneeling position it took but a slight push with his boot to send the girl sprawling onto her back. The remnants of the robe fell open leaving her all but naked. Klaus knelt before her. He unfastened his trousers, cautiously in view of the scalpel in his right hand. He forced her legs apart and climbed onto her. Then he raped her.

The girl fought him every second of the violation, kicking, gouging, and scratching in a desperate, vain attempt to save herself. When it was over Klaus stared at her impassively as she lay motionless, silenced by the gag, almost choking in her own vomit. Then he slit her throat. He rose to his knees, carefully wiping himself with a corner of the robe he had ripped off in the struggle. When he was satisfied that he had cleaned the semen from himself he rose to his feet and started to fasten his trousers.

A sudden noise made him turn, scalpel at the ready. Two British soldiers stood in the bathroom doorway, one a captain, the other a sergeant. Their rank failed to impress Klaus. The large pistol being pointed at him by the sergeant was another matter altogether. Klaus raised his hands above his head.

The English captain stared at Klaus, hatred and revulsion evident on his face. When he spoke it was with barely controlled anger. 'Oh, so now we want to surrender do we? Sergeant, Fritz here wants to surrender now.'

'Really, sir,' the sergeant's voice was neutral, impassive.

'I don't think we want him to surrender, do you, sergeant?' the captain continued, steel in every syllable.

'No, sir,' the sergeant replied stolidly.

'I think we want him to continue trying to escape, then we can shoot him dead, don't you agree, sergeant?'

'Yes, sir.' There was not a flicker of emotion in the sergeant's voice.

'But before we do that, I think we ought to have a little fun with him. Fritz looks to me like a man who enjoys a bit of fun, what do you think, sergeant?'

'Yes, sir.' Still, the deadly impassivity in the sergeant's voice.

'Let me see . . .' The captain might have been deciding which horse to back at Royal Ascot, except for the additional harshness in his voice. 'Why don't we take that pretty little scalpel that Fritz seems so keen on and slice his balls off? Then, when we've removed that overactive member of his, we can have a little fun cutting off other bits of his anatomy, like his tongue, his ears — oh, anything you can think of, sergeant. I leave it up to your imagination. Does that meet with your approval, sergeant?'

The eager tone of the sergeant's reply was the first indication of any emotion. 'Absolutely, sir, but what about the noise?'

'Ah yes, the noise. I suppose Fritz might squeal a bit. He looks the type.' The captain looked round then strode across the room. He twitched the gag from the dead girl's mouth. 'Here, use this. Fritz seems very fond of exchanging bodily fluids. Let him choke on her vomit.'

Klaus found his voice at last. 'You cannot do that, it is not allowed. It is not proper procedure.' He would have continued had it not been for the pistol barrel the sergeant placed against his temple.

Four hours later, as the distant sound of the first artillery salvos of the day began, like a mullah calling the faithful to prayer; a discerning listener might have heard a single pistol shot intermingled with the heavier howitzers.

The sergeant eyed the motionless body on the ground in front of him. He kicked the corpse savagely, without eliciting

201

any response. Hardly surprising, as Klaus's brains were spilt across the muddy floor of the stable. The sergeant nudged the mutilated corpse once more with his boot.

'That, Fritz,' he said, his voice still as calm as if he was ordering his favourite tobacco, 'is what we consider to be proper procedure around here. So don't try telling me what's allowed and what isn't.'

The captain, his face a weary grey mask of distress, filled in the casualty report form. He paused at one section headed, 'Cause of Death' then wrote, 'Enemy action'.

Nurse Cowgill's relatives would have grief enough, without additional trauma.

CHAPTER TWENTY-FIVE

It was only following his return to France that Sonny realized how close he had come to accepting the senseless savagery of the war, the grim harshness of life on the front line. It had become almost a way of life, unpleasant but nonetheless almost normal. His love for Rachael, the time they had spent together amid the peaceful Sussex countryside sharpened the contrast and underlined the grotesque abnormality of trench warfare.

This unnatural existence, pinned down, night and day, enduring a deafening cacophony of artillery exchanges, loud enough at times to be heard in London, was like being trapped in some obscene parody of a thunderstorm. As with an electric storm, lightning could strike anywhere — luck decided where as much as the skill of the gunners. Survival might turn on a microscopic amount of powder, added or omitted in a munitions factory, or a slight warp in a shell's casing. Detonation of the larger artillery shells, or clusters of them, was so completely destructive that anyone receiving a direct hit would be vaporized. Many of the graves established after the conflict were empty, there being no remains to bury.

There were many more insidious dangers. Gangrenous attacks on the feet and lower limbs such as trench foot and frostbite were caused by constant exposure to mud and water. These usually ended in amputation. If not, they ended in death. That was the peril of the winter months. In summer there were the rats and lice. Large colonies of rats moved into the trenches, eager to feast on the rotting corpses that were impossible to move. The lice came as a result of poor sanitation and the impossibility of maintaining even the most basic levels of hygiene. With them, the lice brought disease in many shapes and forms. Typhoid fever was the worst, although the effects of dysentery were almost as bad.

You could survive the artillery, withstand the diseases, yet still fall victim to other killers. Gas was one, mustard gas in particular. Shellshock and suicide from depression and fear were others. All of them were insidious killers on the Western Front, the true numbers of their victims never to be counted. Shellshock and the side effects brought about curious behaviour in their victims. Some deliberately maimed themselves in an effort to be sent home. Blighty wounding, it was called. A soldier might shoot himself in a place unlikely to prove fatal, but seriously injuring himself in the process. Or he might thrust an arm over the parapet of the trench in the hope that an enemy sniper might do the job for him. Other manifestations of shellshock might involve walking out into no man's land, calmly and serenely accepting the release of a hail of bullets from the enemy guns. Less immediately fatal, but equally debilitating would be the complete mental breakdown of men no longer able to cope with the hell that was trench warfare. Loss of speech and memory, inability to control one's limbs or emotions or merely an all-pervading fear were but a few of the symptoms. The dropping of a metal object such as a knife onto a tiled surface could prove sufficient to send a man diving for cover as if the heaviest German artillery barrage had started up. These effects could last long after the war had ended, some of the victims never recovered.

Men began to lose hope, that basic precept of life. It could be seen in their eyes, devoid of any expression or emotion, like those of their comrades lying in no man's land. Without hope they forgot to care. First they would become forgetful in small matters such as food, or hygiene, or dress. Then, more dangerously, they forgot to be afraid. That was when they became a liability to themselves and to others. Finally they forgot to care about anything. That was when they were close to the end.

Sonny's unit had been ordered back into the front line, to join a combined force of British and Australian troops that had been sent back into the trenches, back towards Amiens, back to the Somme.

* * *

Christmas 1917 had been a time of sorrow in Byland Crescent. Albert and Hannah had dreaded the arrival of any news from France, knowing it would surely have concerned Sonny. It was an even greater shock when they received a letter stating that it was Ada who had been killed. Mercifully the full circumstances of their daughter's death had been kept from them.

If Ada's sacrifice did anything, it healed some of the divisions within the family. Connie and Michael had travelled over from Bradford to be with them, in the hope that by sharing their grief they might in some way lessen it. Although the atmosphere was stilted and uncomfortable at first, by the time they returned to the West Riding, much of the bitterness of the past few years had been dissolved by the tears over Ada's passing.

Albert and Hannah had themselves been drawn closer together in their mourning. Losses in the war were mounting to such horrifying levels that they felt a strange sensation of companionship. Everyone, it seemed was in mourning. No household was unaffected. It was, therefore, with Albert's blessing that Hannah wrote to Eleanor Rhodes in the early days of January 1918, to share the news of their loss with Ada's lover. She ended the letter by inviting Eleanor, should she so desire, to visit them at Byland Crescent.

* * *

Night after night, day after day, Clarence Barker cowered in a trench, unwilling or unable to move from this pitiful shelter. If spoken to he would not reply, neither would he generate a conversation. Occasionally he would be overcome by violent trembling sensations in his limbs, accompanied by violent contortions of his facial muscles.

In March of 1918 when the German army began their five pronged thrust in an attempt to break the stalemate on the Western Front, they preceded it with the heaviest artillery barrage of the war to date. It was particularly heavy throughout Clarence's sector. Hour after hour, day and night, with eager response from the British guns, shells screamed overhead. Survival is all a man can hope for in such desperate circumstances and that survival, in the end, is down to luck. At the beginning of April it seemed as if Clarence's luck had run out. Aided by their observers, the German gunners at last found the range of the British positions and shell after shell homed in on their trench line.

In rapid succession five shells burst around Clarence's trench. When the drifting smoke cleared he stumbled, more dead than alive, from the smoking ruin of his erstwhile shelter. He half walked, half crawled away from the scene of devastation that had decimated his regiment within five minutes. His hair was singed, his face and body interlaced with a network of bleeding scars caused by thousands of tiny pieces of shrapnel, his uniform torn into unrecognizable shreds. He was half blinded and completely deafened by the percussive effects of the explosion.

* * *

It was mid-April when the final phase of the German onslaught hit Sonny's regiment and their Australian colleagues. Sonny had been given close liaison duties that resulted in him spending more time with the ANZAC troops than with his own men. He was there when they arrived at the battlefield, helped them dig into their new position, and gave them a few tips from his own experiences. Sonny's outgoing personality, lack of arrogance and directness of speech, allied to his ready sense of humour made him immensely popular. Australians, then as now, respected a man for what he says, thinks and does, rather than any stripes or pips on his uniform. To Sonny, a hardened veteran by that time, some of the colonial troops seemed mere boys in their youth and vulnerability. The more he got to know them the better he got to like them. Their easy manner and lack of pretension struck an answering chord in his own personality.

One young Australian soldier muttered something to his colleague when Sonny first addressed them. Sonny looked at the man, no more than a boy in fact. 'Would you care to share the thought with the rest of us?' he asked quietly.

The young soldier blushed. 'I told my mate you sound just like my dad.'

There was general laughter at this, but later, as the troops were dispersing the young soldier sought Sonny out. 'I wasn't being cheeky, sir,' he told the Englishman. 'You really do sound like my dad; you look a bit like him too.'

Sonny grinned, much to the young Australian's relief. 'Whereabouts is your dad from?' he asked.

The Australian scratched his head. 'I don't rightly know,' he confessed. 'He and Mom are from the Old Country, right enough; you can tell that by the way they talk. They never speak about England though, but I reckon they must be from round your way, because of the way you speak.'

'I'm not so sure,' Sonny had laughed. 'All you Aussies sound alike to me; maybe it's the same the other way round.'

'No way,' the younger man said. 'You have a different sound to your voice than the other English I've heard. They use a long 'A' sound, soft like, you use a short, hard one, more like we do at home.'

'Well, I'm from the North of England, from Yorkshire if that helps,' Sonny told him. 'What's your name by the way?'

'Fisher, sir. Private Saul Fisher.' The Australian drew himself to attention.

'Okay, Saul, now we know each other.' Sonny dismissed his younger colleague with a nod.

As he walked away following their chat, Sonny was plagued with a vague feeling of familiarity, something about the young Australian that provoked an elusive memory of his own, which, frustratingly, he was unable to identify.

Circumstance, rather than choice, threw the two of them together once more a few days later, when the German offensive was at its height. They were pinned down in a trench that had become more of a prison than a refuge. For three consecutive days and nights the intensity of the bombardment held them captive in the dug-out. Such was the ferocity of the shell fire that even conversation was difficult at times. They settled down to ride out the storm. When reading became difficult, each of them set about writing letters home. Sonny commenced a letter to Rachael, while Saul Fisher continued a letter to his parents he had begun over a week previously. At one point he paused to ask Sonny a question. So deafening was the bombardment at that point that he had to repeat it three times before Sonny could understand him. Sonny's reply sounded unnaturally loud as the barrage ceased for a few seconds.

The German gunners had paused to adjust their range. On a given signal the whole of their battery started firing once more. With deadly accuracy a cluster of shells rained down on the Australians' trench network. Four of these hit the roof and side wall of the dug-out occupied by Sonny Cowgill and Saul Fisher.

* * *

The German advance ground to a halt near Amiens, stopped in its tracks by the fierce opposition of the British and Australian forces. After a brief respite the allies started to draw up plans for a counter offensive. During that lull in proceedings there was time for battlefield casualties to be removed and for the dead to be buried.

The Australian officer looked with horror at what remained of the trench and its occupants. The percussive effect of the shells exploding within that enclosed space had been devastating. He guessed there to have been somewhere close to a dozen men in that part of the trench system when it had been hit. All that remained were body parts strewn hither and thither. Identification would be a nightmare. The officer turned to his adjutant. 'Like a bloody jig-saw puzzle sorting this lot out. Thank God for identification tags.'

The adjutant nodded, gazing in awed fascination at an eyeball that, devoid of its socket, lay staring blindly up at him from the ground. 'Sweep them all together, bury them here and mark the grave for later,' he suggested.

The officer agreed. 'Collect any personal items you can identify, letters, photos and the like and post them back to the relatives,' he ordered.

The work took many hours but eventually it was complete. Eleven identity tags had been recovered. Ten of these were from the ANZAC regiment, including one Private Saul Fisher. The eleventh was that of an English officer, Captain Mark Cowgill.

* * *

Alice was heavily pregnant when the news arrived. Shock brought on labour and their daughter Dorothy was born six weeks premature. James, who had remained with Alice throughout the delivery of their daughter, said afterwards that it was the most beautiful and rewarding experience of his life, apart from meeting Alice.

Grief over the death of their son ruled out any thought of celebration following the birth, besides which Alice had been much weakened by the ordeal. News received from England and France shortly afterwards turned 1918 into a year of sadness that spanned the globe.

* * *

Albert was crossing the hall at Byland Crescent when the telegram arrived. He watched Henry open the door to the messenger, took the proffered envelope and in a daze tore it open.

"... *deep regret* ... *Captain Mark Cowgill MC* ... *believed killed* ..."

The words on the single sheet of paper swam before Albert's eyes. He turned blindly down the hall. Henry, for twenty years Albert's butler and friend, watched his employer take three strides then stop abruptly and stiffen. There was a pause, then, as Henry moved forward, Albert Cowgill slumped to the floor and lay, rigid and sightless from a massive stroke.

Four weeks later Albert suffered a second stroke. This one, coming so hard on the heels of the previous attack, proved fatal. Albert Cowgill, last of the generation that had made HAC market leaders in the textile industry, died in his sleep. He was sixty-three years old. An era had drawn to a close.

CHAPTER TWENTY-SIX

In an asylum based near Lisieux in Normandy, the medical superintendent examined the report from his deputy with interest. Their wards had been filled to overflowing during the past four years, mostly with victims of the terrible events happening to the east. 'What,' the doctor wanted to know, 'of the Silent One? Do you have any idea yet who he might be?'

The deputy shook his head. 'He has been here two months now. He has not uttered a word. In fact we are not sure whether he can speak or not. He has, I believe, some sight in one eye, although the other is still clouded. I cannot be sure if that is permanent or not. He does not, I think, have any hearing. I have tried the usual test, dropping a tray behind him, but with no result. His clothing, what there was of it, was so torn as to be unrecognizable. As to his physical health, once we had managed to remove all the tiny pieces of shrapnel from his body the cuts and bruises seem to have healed very well. Physically I would say he's in very good shape. Mentally, I do not know. I am used to my patients giving me irrational answers; I am not used to getting no answer at all.'

'Refresh my memory. Give me the background to the Silent One's case. Where did he come from, what do we know about him?'

The deputy glanced at the file, although he knew the scant details already. 'He was discovered by a local farmer sleeping in a barn towards the end of August. Despite the fact that the man was obviously malnourished, no attempt had been made to steal any food. The farmer called in the gendarmes, who did not know what to do with him, as he had committed no crime they were aware of, so they brought him to us.'

* * *

True to his word, the Australian adjutant had collected all the personal possessions he could find in the trench. In one parcel he sent a small notecase to Byland Crescent, Scarborough, containing photographs of Albert and Hannah Cowgill, plus a family group comprising Michael, Connie and their family. In addition there was a studio photograph of a strikingly beautiful young woman Hannah did not recognize. Strangely it was the sight of this last photograph that caused Hannah to start weeping.

Several weeks later James and Alice received a similar parcel. Along with the family photographs the adjutant had managed to retrieve Saul's half-finished letter. James, his eyes misting over with tears, read the crumpled, stained letter to Alice.

Dear Mom and Dad,
This is a crazy kind of war, but I'm doing OK so far. I'm with a great bunch of lads, we look after one another true as we can. Things are a bit crook at the minute with Jerry throwing everything but the kitchen sink at us.
The English seem a pretty fair bunch too, apart from one or two of their officers, who carry their noses in the air as if they've trodden in some kangaroo dung (sorry, Mom). But we're lucky the officer they've attached to our mob is a regular sort of bloke, right enough. He and I get along just fine. I told him he sounds just like you when you talk, Dad, so I

reckon you must be from the same part of the outback. He
even looks a bit like you, only younger. He's here with me
now, we're in the dug-out, that's a sort of side trench with a
roof shelter. We're stuck here till Jerry gets tired or runs out
of ammo, so we're both busy writing home. He's writing to
his girl while I'm writing to you.

Now here's something strange that you might understand,
Dad. He's got a funny nickname, which he explained is
because he's the youngest in the family, they call him So . . .

At that point the writing ceased abruptly. James put
down the letter, his hands trembling with shock. 'They call
him Sonny . . .' he said flatly. 'Oh, God, no, not Sonny as
well,' he wailed.

Alice held him close. 'You don't know that for sure.'

James lifted his head from her shoulder. 'Looks like me,
talks like me, the youngest of the family, known to one and
all as So . . . Alice, who else could it be?'

As he wept for his son and brother, Alice attempted to
console him, knowing in her heart that for this grief there
was no real consolation.

* * *

On 24 April 1917, in a small private nursing home in a
select suburb of Sheffield, Rachael had given birth to a son.
She named him Mark Edwin. She resolved that one day she
would take him to Scarborough to meet his grandparents
who were unaware of his existence.

Three days after the Great War, the war to end all wars,
was finally brought to a merciful halt by the signature of an
armistice in November 1918, Rachael descended from the
train at Scarborough with her young son in her arms. She
summoned a taxi cab and asked the driver to take them to
Byland Crescent. Reaching their destination, she looked up
at the tall, proud houses as she made her way towards the
door of Number 1. There was little sign in Byland Crescent

of the celebrations that had filled streets elsewhere with excited, cheering throngs, caused festive streamers, bunting and flags, to appear on many buildings. Byland Crescent had paid too heavy a toll for there to be any rejoicing.

In answer to her vigorous pounding with the knocker an elderly man in morning coat answered the door. 'May I see Mr and Mrs Cowgill please?' Rachael enquired.

A look of pain crossed the butler's face. 'I regret, Madam,' he replied, 'that Mr Cowgill has passed away. I do not believe Mrs Cowgill is expecting any visitors this morning,' he added with a finality he hoped would prove dismissive.

Rachael was made of sterner stuff. 'Please ask Mrs Cowgill to grant me a few minutes of her time?' she asked, smiling sweetly at Henry.

Henry bowed stiffly and formally. 'Please step inside. I will convey your request, Madam, but I cannot guarantee that Mrs Cowgill will see you. May I take your name?'

Rachael took a deep breath. 'Please tell her,' she faltered for a second. 'Please tell her, that Mrs Rachael Cowgill and Master Mark Cowgill are here to see her.'

PART FOUR: 1919–1922

'I went into a public house to get a pint of beer,
The publican 'e up an' sez, 'We serve no redcoats here.'
The girls be'ind the bar they laughed an' giggled fit to die,
I outs into the street again an' to myself says I:
O it's Tommy this, an' Tommy that, an 'Tommy go away';
But it's 'Thank you Mr Atkins', when the band begins to play,
The band begins to play, my boys, the band begins to play
O it's 'Thank you Mr Atkins', when the band begins to play.
Extract from 'Tommy'
Rudyard Kipling (1865–1936)

CHAPTER TWENTY-SEVEN

All over Europe the ravages of war were apparent. Armies were dismantled and borders redrawn, men returned home. Already politicians were calling it 'the war to end all wars' and stating that 'this must never be allowed to happen again'. Those self-same politicians who had confidently predicted that the war would be over by Christmas 1914, now stated with equal confidence, that the continent of Europe would never see such bloodshed again. Even as they were making such solemn pronouncements a number of them sat around a conference table in the Palace of Versailles and set about drawing up terms and conditions on the defeated nations that guaranteed that it would happen once more.

The politicians and generals had leapt into the Great War with zeal and enthusiasm. They had trotted out speeches such as 'doing one's duty' and 'fighting for the honour of one's country'. They were very big on duty and honour, were the politicians and generals. Patriotism was another favourite. Of course they didn't actually have to do the fighting themselves; perhaps if they had they would have been more reluctant to rush into battle, less ready with glib phrases that condemned millions to death, disfigurement, and lifelong physical or mental anguish.

So they sat around and deliberated, possibly exchanging a few of their favourite trite remarks as they drew up a peace treaty that ensured a macabre heredity. Having supervised the death, disfigurement, and anguish of one generation, they carefully condemned the next generation to even more death, disfigurement, and anguish. They planted the seeds of that horrific fate in the reparation terms of that infamous document. Mass unemployment, poverty, recession, and inflation combined to ensure the successful germination of these deadly seeds, fertilized and nurtured the poisonous young plants until the time was right for the harvesting of their grim crop.

* * *

In Byland Crescent the remnants of the Cowgill household attempted to pick up the pieces of an existence decimated by war. During the months following Albert Cowgill's death, staff at Byland Crescent had become concerned over Hannah's welfare. Bereft of almost all she held dear, there seemed little purpose in life, until, to the stunned surprise of everyone, Sonny's widow Rachael arrived, bringing with her Hannah's young grandson Mark. As soon as she entered the sitting room at Byland Crescent, Hannah exclaimed, 'I recognize you.'

Rachael looked startled until Hannah explained. 'Your photograph was in Sonny's wallet. They returned it to me with his Medal Card. It is all I have to remember him by.'

The atmosphere was a little stiff at first as Hannah, reserved and cautious, attempted to come to terms with the shock. Rachael for her part was awkward, shy and in some distress. The infant Mark was responsible for breaking the ice when Rachael was introducing him to Hannah. He toddled across the room, looked up at his grandmother, smiled cherubically, and loudly, and lustily, blew a large raspberry. Rachael looked up in mild alarm and caught her mother-in-law's eye. They both burst out laughing.

'So tell me how you met my son?' Hannah asked.

'It was when he was wounded,' Rachael explained. 'I nursed him and we fell in love. We managed to get married by special licence, in Chichester the day before he returned to his unit. We only had a few days together. When I realized I was expecting I moved back to Sheffield to my family. It was there I read the daily listing in the paper and knew he was missing, presumed dead.'

As Rachael recounted the story of how she had met Sonny, the older woman experienced a variety of emotions. Her sadness over Sonny's death was heightened by her sympathy for Rachael, so clearly and deeply in love, that prospect of a life together so tragically and brutally cut short.

'My dear, I suddenly realize how fortunate I have been. Albert and I had a long and, for the most part, happy marriage, but you, and I suppose many other widows, will be looking back on only a few brief years, sometimes months, or even weeks of happiness.'

Above all, however, Hannah experienced a delight she never thought she would be capable of experiencing again. Her joy stemmed from Mark, the grandson she had obtained when all hope seemed forlorn; whose very existence represented hope for the future.

Hannah insisted that Rachael stay for lunch. Over the meal she questioned her daughter-in-law further about her family, her background, her hopes and plans for the future, including the upbringing of her son.

'My family and yours seemed to have suffered equally,' Rachael told her. 'Perhaps it is the same story in almost every house in the land. I lost two of my brothers on the Somme, the third was gassed in Flanders and is now an invalid. One of my brothers-in-law was also killed in action. As far as the future is concerned, I have made no firm plans. There is family money that would support me but I am loath to take that option. I suppose with my qualifications and experience I could find a nursing post easily enough, but I have to consider Mark and what is best for him.'

Hannah had inherited her father's talent as a quick and accurate judge of character. Rachael, she felt, was an admirable young woman with whom she would get on well. As her daughter-in-law talked, Hannah formulated her plan. After lunch, as they were sitting over cups of tea, she suggested an alternative. 'Why not bring Mark with you to Byland Crescent to live?' She waved Rachael's protestations aside. 'There's room enough and more, it will bring life, light and company into the house again. Byland Crescent has not echoed to the sound of children's laughter for many years. You would be welcome to bring friends to stay whenever you choose and there will also be visits from Mark's cousins and their parents, my daughter Connie and her husband Michael Haigh, along with other family and friends. They will all want to meet you and Mark.'

Her final argument clinched it. She leaned across to Rachael and placed her hand on the younger woman's arm. 'Above all else, I would like to have you here, and I think it would be what Sonny wanted, for Mark to be brought up in the same house as his father.'

When Rachael left to return to Sheffield late that afternoon, agreement in principle had already been reached, only the fine detail remained to be worked out. As soon as she had waved goodbye to her daughter-in-law and grandson, Hannah dashed to the telephone. She could not contain her excitement as she related the thrilling news to Connie.

* * *

The wills left by Albert and Sonny Cowgill, instead of allowing their estates to be wound up satisfactorily, resulted in a legal tangle. On the one hand it seemed fairly clear that Sonny had predeceased his father. On the other, the War Office stubbornly refused to acknowledge the fact. Many soldiers, their officials argued, had been posted missing, only to turn up alive and, in some cases, well. Despite pressure from the family's solicitors the War Office remained obdurate. It began to look as if the Cowgill family and HAC, the business they controlled, would have to wait for seven years before they could apply to have Sonny's death officially confirmed.

Into the void left at HAC by the loss of Albert and Sonny Cowgill stepped Clarence Barker. Returning from war service he slipped into the role of heir apparent by virtue of the terms of his uncle's will. This document had named Clarence as Albert's heir should Sonny predecease him. Although the War Office still had to ratify the fact, Clarence lost no time in asserting his claim to that share of the estate that would give him control of HAC.

Clarence Barker had spent the last months of the war in a military hospital in France, one which dealt with trauma victims, such as those suffering from shellshock. He was released from hospital and discharged from the army several weeks before the armistice was signed on 11 November 1918, when hostilities finally ceased. He returned to Bradford, where his account of his military service bore only slight resemblance to the actual facts.

Others were returning too, some with great distinction, some in positive anonymity. Charlie Binks fell into the latter category. Charlie's services had been in demand from the outbreak of the war, not as a combatant, but as a chemist. His work was conducted in secret, he was known to only a handful of fellow scientists and certain War Office officials. Although he wore a uniform and carried the rank of captain, the only hostile act Charlie witnessed was a pistol shot fired by a marine in Bristol, the result of an outbreak of domestic disharmony rather than international warfare.

Charlie returned to Outlane Chemicals, where he was joined by his eldest son Robert, one of many young men who moved straight out of school uniform into overalls at that time. Their task was to replace skilled workers who had either perished in battle, or whose wounds were such as to render them unfit for work. In addition many were still serving in the forces, for the peace was a fragile one requiring policing, and in certain theatres, war had not ceased. The

Bolshevik revolution in Russia had led to civil war. Each side called for help. The politicians and generals, obviously by no means sated by the recent bloodbath, volunteered that help. Not in person of course, they had troops enough at their disposal, without the politicians and generals becoming involved themselves.

At home, demand was rising for goods and services, the essentials and luxuries that had been unobtainable during the war. As factories were undermanned, they had to get labour from whatever source they could. Women, who had been co-opted to work in factories and mills during the war, had become accustomed to earning a wage, to having money of their own. Finding a continuing demand for their services, many women eagerly seized the opportunity to go on working. No thought was given at the time to the long-term effect when millions of young, fit men were demobilized. Then there would be labour enough, labour to spare. Unemployment on a large scale had not been experienced to any great extent in the past. There would be an overflow of workers not only in Britain, but throughout Europe. Just one of the seeds of disaster was on the point of germinating.

* * *

Baildon was a pretty village, in a rugged sort of way. A village of winding streets, that struggled up the slopes of the crags on which it perched. The hills themselves were an outpost of the moorland that stretched, or more properly straggled, from dale to dale across the western part of the county of Yorkshire. From Swaledale and Wensleydale in the north, through Nidderdale, Wharfedale and Airedale, and ever southward to Calderdale and beyond. Baildon was a stone-built village, soot-blackened from mill chimney and hearth alike. Michael and Connie Haigh settled in Baildon shortly prior to the start of the war. Their house was towards the top of the village, where West Lane meandered its course towards Shipley Glen and onward to Eldwick and Gilstead. Theirs was a detached Victorian house with extensive gardens, a tennis court, orchards, and a kitchen garden. The latter had been very useful during the war, when food rationing threatened shortages. Connie had discovered in herself an aptitude and liking for horticulture, an inheritance possibly from her grandmother, Ellen Ackroyd.

Connie had an able assistant, a villager known to one and all as Barty. His full name was Bartholomew Verity, but he had been Barty from the moment the water had dropped from the vicar's fingers onto his forehead. Barty had been a soldier at one time, but that career had been terminated by the rifle of a skilled Boer. By way of mementos he lacked two fingers on his left hand and had a permanently stiffened left leg.

Unfit for active service and lacking any skill or trade, his disabilities rendered him unable to command any sort of regular employment, so Barty was reduced to any sort of casual or menial labour. After some years Barty had startled the village by producing, much in the style of a conjurer, a bride of quite buxom beauty some fifteen years his junior. Kathleen Verity was of Irish descent, sturdy and wholesome, with a no-nonsense attitude to life and a bawdy sense of humour. Evidence of the latter was produced when she was asked how she and Barty had come to get married. 'Oh,' she remarked casually, 'Barty just climbed into my bed one night and has refused to leave ever since.'

Her devotion to Barty and the grain of truth in her jest was proved by the five children she had borne him. It was to support this brood that Barty needed something more substantial than hand-outs or jobs lasting a week or two. When he heard that Michael and Connie Haigh had moved in, Barty had lost no time in calling to introduce himself and offer his services.

Connie had taken a liking to the old soldier from the beginning. He was attentive and eager to please, quick enough to grasp instructions and trustworthy enough to be left to complete a job unsupervised. He was personable, in a rough and ready, soldierly way, with the added bonus of being fond of children.

Although they privately still mourned the death of their eldest daughter, Michael and Connie had consolation enough in their other daughter Marguerite and sons Edward and George.

The arrival of Rachael and baby Mark in Scarborough provided an excuse for a family outing to the seaside. It was then that Michael met up with Josiah Firth, a neighbour of the Cowgill family in Byland Crescent. Josiah had a flourishing textile engineering business in the West Riding, but was now looking to retire. Josiah had hoped that his eldest son Jonas would follow him into the business, but the loss of his right leg during the third Battle of Ypres had put paid to such plans.

When Josiah told Michael of his intentions, Michael responded by asking him to name a price. WPF&D, the group he controlled, was in a very healthy financial position. Their parent company had an aggressive policy towards acquisitions and diversification. Michael felt sure that the group's head would endorse the planned purchase. He resolved to send a cable to the Group's head office to seek such approval.

* * *

Charlotte Tunnicliffe had been desperate for a new interest in life. She had her daughter Jessica, now five years old, but attending to her needs was far from all consuming. There was a certain irony that, with the cessation of hostilities and many more available men to choose from, Charlotte, possibly from the first time in her adult life, found she was uninterested. Although she was in her mid-forties, she had kept her looks and figure and was still a highly attractive, sensuously good-looking woman. She was also extremely wealthy, for her late husband Isaac Tunnicliffe, had proved to be as shrewd as he was boring. It was a telling insight into

Charlotte's character that she rarely thought about Isaac, or regretted his passing, in the way she worried over the loss of her lover Jesse.

It may have been Charlotte's considerable physical charms, or the equally attractive state of her bank balance that caused her bank manager to become so attentive to her financial affairs. Once probate of Isaac's will had been granted, there were considerable sums of money to invest. Charlotte had no previous experience of investment, but once her bank manager introduced her to the mysterious workings of the stock market, Charlotte found it to be a fascinating and exciting hobby.

She was fortunate in the early days, as several of her investments paid off handsomely. This fired her enthusiasm and she set about learning more of her new recreation. She proved to be shrewd in her choices, bold but prudent in her risk assessment, and with a gift for recognizing the right moment to buy and sell. By the time the Treaty of Versailles was signed in 1919, Charlotte had increased the value of her husband's bequest fivefold.

CHAPTER TWENTY-EIGHT

The superintendent asked his deputy for an update on the Silent One. 'Is he painting again?'

'Yes indeed, Monsieur.'

'Still the same scene?'

'Yes, Monsieur. He paints a beautiful landscape. Always a village, with green fields beyond. In those fields, the centrepiece of the picture, a large ruined abbey, roofless, open to the sky. When the painting is complete he takes a brush and daubs red paint across the canvas. It is most disturbing. The red splashes are reminiscent of bloodstains. Then he gets his rag and spirit and wipes the canvas clean. The next day he begins to paint once more, the same landscape, always the same landscape.'

'Never any variation?' the medical supervisor wanted to know.

'Not in the slightest detail. I tried to intervene once, to stop him destroying the picture. He is quite talented and the landscape is rather good. I thought it might be beneficial for him, if the painting represented a memory, to show him that the memory could be improved.'

'What happened?'

'He became so agitated I was compelled to return the painting to him. Not violent you understand, but very distressed. As soon as I gave the painting back to him he started splashing it with red paint once more. It is as if he is trying to perfect the painting, or it is a memory of something that was beautiful but then got desecrated. God knows there has been enough death and destruction in the last five years.'

The supervisor looked at his assistant, considering all the subordinate had said. 'He still has not spoken?' The question was only partly rhetorical.

'Not a word. He has been in this hospital for nearly a year and he has not uttered a sound during that time. He seems quite content in his own world, except if something upsets him, when he becomes very agitated.'

After further consideration the supervisor nodded. 'You may have a point. It could be that he is living in the past, before the cataclysm that changed it all. The picture may be symbolic of something that was dear to him, something that was destroyed, possibly not literally destroyed, if only in his broken mind. His brain may be unable to cope with the new reality, so he has regressed into his past. There may even be no church, merely a symbolic association. We will just have to continue to be patient.' The medical supervisor sighed and added, 'As we have to be with so many of our inmates whose minds have been shattered by the war.'

* * *

He was never sure why he painted; he only knew that it was important to paint. He felt drawn back to the same scene every time he lifted his brush, but as soon as the picture was completed he realized he had left something out. Something terribly important, the vital component that was the reason for the painting. The problem was, try as he might, he could not remember what it was.

At first there had been silence. It had only been external silence however. He had always been aware of people around him, although he could only see clearly with one eye, the other being clouded. Those people had spoken sometimes, he was sure of that, for their attitude betrayed the fact and he could see their mouths moving. Despite that no sound penetrated his consciousness. That was due to the roar. He knew the roar well, too well. It was the sound of guns; big artillery pieces that thundered constantly through his brain. Occasionally, there would be voices too, voices he remembered from the past. Or was it memory? He could not be sure. Sometimes he thought he had dreamed all those men who marched, rank after rank, file upon file, through his subconscious.

The guns and the men were greedy for his attention, they occupied his mind, to the exclusion of all else. From time to time he felt there should be more; something he was trying to remember, but the guns would not allow him. Even if they did, his men demanded his attention.

There was Crane calling out to him. John Crane, the jovial butcher's boy from Swindon. Crane, who had been blown apart by grenades in 1915, calling out for help. And McKillick, the dry and humorous little Scotsman whose life had been extinguished by a sniper's bullet on Christmas Day of 1916. McKillick was talking loudly, excitedly as ever, although the track of the bullet through his skull was clearly visible. No bigger than a sixpence at the front, where it had entered over his left eye, large as a soup bowl at the back where it had exited. There was Davidson too, calling out to him from no man's land, though he had lain there since 1915 and his corpse was bloated beyond recognition and now represented only a meal for scavenging rats.

Their voices and images, along with countless others, paraded constantly in front of him. Always they were accompanied by the guns. Never ceasing. Day in, day out. Night after night. Pounding, pounding, ceaselessly pounding.

Gradually though, the clamour had eased, until now there were long periods when he heard nothing. Absolutely nothing; neither the external sounds nor the noises inside his own mind. Occasionally this silence was lifted, like a blind being raised to reveal partial daylight. For short periods he heard the sound of voices close to him. Not the spectral internal voices these, rather those of living, breathing individuals. Hearing failed to bring comprehension with it. It was as if the sounds were penetrating but his brain was incapable of decoding them. It did not occur to him that the reason his poor, befuddled, battered mind was unable to decipher the sounds was that they were in a foreign language.

* * *

Among the army of young men seeking work in 1919 was Simon Jones, son of Albert Cowgill's sister Emily. Simon had qualified as an accountant, but his qualification had come only weeks before the outbreak of war. Four and a half years later, having survived with only superficial wounds and with an honourable, if not spectacular service record, the humdrum existence of an accounting practice had lost its appeal.

It was becoming fashionable, indeed prudent, for the larger commercial undertakings to appoint their own internal accountants. With business life becoming ever more complex, the spread of public liability companies meant that board members were accountable to their shareholders. The appointment of a properly qualified company secretary, or accountant, even a finance director, was becoming the vogue.

Simon Jones, being a clear thinking young man, sat down to consider his options. He was twenty-nine years old, single and unattached. This gave him mobility and the capacity to work long, anti-social hours without a clash of interests should the need arise. He was well qualified, via an accountancy practice with a reputation second to none. To weigh against these advantages was the fact that at twenty-nine he was without commercial experience. Simon was aware that most companies warranting an internal accountant would, from choice, prefer someone with a proven track record.

Simon's first call on the hunt for an employer was HAC. He hoped that his late uncle's firm would be open to a little benevolent nepotism. The interview with his cousin

Clarence Barker was not a success. Clarence had more than one reason not to employ anyone capable of conducting too close an examination into HAC's trading records. Neither did Clarence relish the prospect of another family member joining the firm. Additionally there was Simon's war record, which compared favourably with Clarence's own, less than glorious military career.

As Simon later put it, 'It was like being eyed by a wet fish.'

Clarence stared at his cousin coldly. 'You have no experience and there is nothing in your past to make you fit to be in charge of the finances of so prestigious a Group as HAC. All you appear to have achieved in life is to have killed a few Germans, quite how you think that fits you for such a post, I fail to understand. Perhaps if war breaks out in Cheapside you might prove useful, otherwise I have absolutely no reason to want to employ you. Please leave now, you have already wasted enough of my time.'

The interview left a sour taste in Simon's mouth and emboldened him on his next step. He walked from HAC's offices to those of WPF&D, where he asked to see Michael Haigh. Simon was well aware of the divisions between Michael and Clarence, knew also of the rivalry between the two companies.

Michael Haigh knew more about Simon than the young man was aware; what is more, he had been pondering the appointment of a group accountant for some time. WPF&D had a company secretary but the man was ageing, looking to retire and they needed a younger, more energetic successor to help move the group forward. Simon had no reason to hope that Michael would see him without an appointment, so he was pleasantly surprised when, after only a few minutes delay he was ushered into Michael's comfortable and spacious office.

Simon told Michael that he had applied for a job with HAC and been turned down by Clarence Barker. Something in his tone intrigued Michael, who enquired casually how Simon had got on with Barker.

'Not very well, I'm afraid, sir,' Simon answered bluntly. 'To be honest he thought me presumptuous in the extreme, merely for applying to HAC. That was perhaps as well, for I'd already decided I couldn't work for a man I'd taken such a dislike to.'

There was little he could have said to influence Michael Haigh in his favour, than his low opinion of Clarence Barker. Haigh listened with interest as Simon outlined the case for employing him. 'I realize I am at a disadvantage because of my lack of experience, but no sooner had I qualified than the war started. I never will gain that experience unless someone is prepared to risk giving me a job. I was trained at Paige's and that's about as good as you can get. I qualified head of my year in the Association's examinations and I am as keen and energetic as can be.' When he finished he was a little breathless and pink in the face.

Michael Haigh promised to give Simon's application consideration and the two men parted. In the event, Haigh had almost made his mind up in favour of the young man. Two days later he dictated a letter offering Simon Jones the post of assistant group secretary. It was one of the shrewdest decisions of Michael's business career.

* * *

Connie had written to James to tell him of Sonny's and their father's deaths, and the appearance of Rachael and Mark at Byland Crescent. It was fully twelve months before a reply came.

Dear Connie,
I am sorry I have not written before now. We knew of Sonny's death before your letter arrived. We were already grieving, not only for Sonny, but also for our beloved son Saul. Saul died in the same attack as Sonny. Indeed we believe that they were together right at the end. Saul's regimental adjutant collected Saul's personal belongings and sent

*them to us. Amongst them is the fragment of a letter Saul
was writing to us at the time he was killed. From the content
it is clear that he and Sonny had become friends, although
ironically neither knew who the other was, nor how closely
they were related.*

*Alice has been deeply, terribly upset by what happened to
Saul. I do not believe she will ever recover from this; I too
have been in a poor state. I miss the boy so badly that I
cannot bear to think of him sometimes, it hurts so much.*

*I have taken a long rest from the business to be with Alice
and the family, for my own sake as much as theirs. Little
Luke keeps us all going. He seems, in some strange way, to
have inherited Sonny's impish charm. Now we have baby
Dorothy to distract us too, she is a very happy, smiley soul
and is our little joy.*

*I felt a deep sadness when I read of Father's death. Not the
biting grief as over Saul or Sonny, but a quieter, equally
heartfelt emotion. I wish matters could have been different,
for although I could never forgive him his words or actions I
never ceased to love him.*

*Alice and I were greatly cheered by the news of Sonny's
widow and son. It must have been quite a shock for Mother.
What a shame that Father did not survive to see the little
one. From what you wrote, Rachael sounds a very good sort
of a girl and the presence of an infant at Byland Crescent
will be a tonic for Mother, I'm sure.*

*We were pleased to hear that Michael has been so successful;
he seems to go from strength to strength since he left HAC.
I wish I could get rid of the loathsome Clarence, but the
lawyers tell me there is nothing I can do until we get official
confirmation of Sonny's death from the War Office.*

*Our own businesses have flourished in spite of my absence,
or possibly because of it. I have returned now, soon Alice
will be re-joining me, when we have obtained the services of a
governess for the younger children. Alice enjoys being involved
in the business and I think it will help take her mind off
other matters.*

*Your niece Cissie has a boyfriend. She is seventeen now,
so I suppose it is to be expected. They look quite comical
together, as he is about eighteen inches taller than she. He is
thin, beanpole thin into the bargain, which just makes him
look even taller. He is a reporter on our local paper and his
dry slant on local news is most amusing. I think they will
be getting engaged soon, so before too long I expect I shall be
reporting to you as a grandfather!*
Your loving brother,
James.
Ps. I have just been told off for not sending Alice's love also.

The distress felt by Alice, the girl Connie had hardly
met and now a grieving mother, the long parting from her
adored brother, James, and the death of a nephew she felt
she knew though they had never met, all contrived to bring
deep sorrow to Connie.

CHAPTER TWENTY-NINE

Clarence Barker lived alone in a flat in a small cul-de-sac of Victorian houses. He rarely entertained, save for one or two ladies he paid for their services. Clarence did not want the commitment of marriage or relationships, neither was he interested in raising a family. Women entered his life purely for his sexual gratification. Once that had been satisfied his sole object was for them to leave as swiftly as possible.

Clarence had enjoyed a successful week, little of which was down to his own efforts. Figures from the scouring plant were good, the chemical and dyeing division was ever more profitable, and his senior salesman had reported excellent sales figures within the merchanting division. Clarence decided to celebrate. He arranged for his favourite prostitute to be at his flat at 9 p.m. and to be prepared to stay the night.

It was as he was ushering the woman from his door on the Saturday morning that he picked up an envelope from the mat. He glanced at the inscription with only mild curiosity. The wording focused his attention immediately. It read 'Private C.E. Barker', followed by his regiment and service number.

He tore the envelope open and removed the single type-written sheet from within. He started to read but the first few words were enough to make the page swim before his eyes. He felt dizzy and nauseous, breathless as if he had been running a marathon.

After a few moments, when the room had ceased to sway, Clarence groped his way to an armchair in the sitting room. He sat there for a few moments until his equilibrium returned, then started to read once more.

Dear Private Barker,

They tell me that pathologists can distinguish between one bullet and another. I imagine that a bullet from a British rifle will be different to one from a German rifle for example. So, as the bullet you shot Major Ogilvie with remained inside him and as I know exactly where he is buried, I imagine it would be easy to find out that he was shot with a British rifle. I believe that shooting one of your own officers when he has ordered you into battle might be classed as treason as well as murder. Not that it matters, as they would hang you for either crime.

Now, that would seem, to many people, to be justice. To me it seems like a waste of a life. Even if I reported what happened to the authorities, it would not bring Major Ogilvie back to life. I was in the trench that day. I saw everything that happened, heard every word that passed between you and the major. How the major accused you of cowardice and ordered you over the top. I saw you shoot him, then I saw you throw up and shit yourself. I was even part of the burial party that buried the major, that's how I know exactly where his grave is. I see you have a nice prosperous lifestyle. You wouldn't want a little thing like a murder or treason conviction to spoil that would you? So, I think the best you can do is to share some of your wealth and good fortune with some of your gallant comrades in arms. Well, one, to be more precise: me.

Let's say it is on behalf of the memory of all those who failed to return — like Major Ogilvie. An initial donation of £1,000 would be sufficient to prevent me going to the authorities — for the time being. I will give you a few days

to organize it, then I will write to give you details of how and where I want the money delivered.
A Comrade.

* * *

The changes occurred so slowly that it was many months before the Silent One noticed any difference. Recall came first, a negative recall at that. One day he became aware that the guns had ceased. Or, if they had not ceased precisely, it had been a long time since he had heard them. He puzzled over this for some time, then realized it was the same with the voices. They were no longer with him night and day, shouting for help he could not give them; help that never arrived, screaming in unending, incurable agony. After a while, he began to think of the times when the guns and voices returned as his bad days.

In their place came other sounds, other sensations. He heard voices right enough, but human voices, voices of birds and other creatures in the countryside surrounding *The Place*. He never knew its name, thought only of it as *The Place*. When they had brought him here, months, years ago, he was unsure of time as with everything else, it had seemed right. Now he began to wonder why he was here, what he was doing in *The Place*. He began to formulate ideas, seek for explanations. For the first time since *Then*, he felt words forming in his mind. He did not utter them, something within him prohibited that, but he felt sure one day he would speak once more. He had spoken before, he was sure of it, how else could he know the words, but it had been a long time ago. Before *Then*. *Then* had changed everything. He dared not think of *Then*, for merely thinking about it would bring the guns and the voices back, roaring and screaming.

Next came the painting. He began to wonder why he painted. He began to wonder why he always painted the same scene. He began to wonder why he always destroyed it. One day the answers came. They came quite suddenly, startlingly so. He was outside at the time, painting his one and only landscape. It was summer, a warm, sunlit day, the lawns around *The Place* had been cut, the smell of the newly mown grass hung heavy as incense in the clear air. The trees lining the long, winding drive were a mixture of hues. Such a tranquil setting, such a lovely summer's day should have bred contentment. Instead he merely felt a restlessness he could not put a name to.

As he painted, he glanced up from time to time. Other inmates of *The Place* were strolling in the grounds. None spoke to him. Many were buried within their own minds, lost in their own worlds, imprisoned within their own barbed wire, the no man's land of the soul.

One exception was a group of three. They were standing in the middle of the huge undulating lawn, over fifty yards distant from the painter. Although they were out of earshot, their attitude and stance made it clear they were conducting a conversation. The painter studied them for a few moments before returning to the picture, almost complete once more. Suddenly he realized what was missing, he looked up at the three men swiftly, then back to the canvas. Now he knew why he had been compelled to destroy each of his previous efforts. Slowly, with infinite care, he began to paint in the missing element.

Soon it was done, and the painter stepped back from the canvas to study his work. There were the houses, their grey stones contrasting with the weathered sandstone of the abbey beyond. There was the abbey itself, standing proud in its ruinous state, like a defeated yet un-humiliated warrior. The fresh verdant green of the fields was the same as he had always depicted them, but there, in the foreground, was the change. A group of people, deep in conversation. That was what had been missing from the painting all along. People!

'That is it!' the painter said in triumph. 'That is what I wanted.'

This time there was no move towards the red paint, no compulsion to destroy what he had created. This time it was right. He carefully set down his brush and walked away. The painter was totally oblivious of his surroundings, unaware that the medical supervisor, who had been passing at the time of the painter's utterances, was standing, rooted to the spot in shock on hearing the first words the Silent One had uttered since entering the asylum.

Unconscious of the shock he had created, the Silent One walked away. He had a new thought in his mind, spawned from his painting. It was time for him to leave. Time for him to go in search of *The Abbey*. He had always needed to find *The Abbey*, he realized that now. The difference was, now he knew why. If he found *The Abbey*, the people would be there. That was what he really wanted. To find the people. He was not sure why, but he knew he had to go in search of the people within the painting.

The following day they told the supervisor that the Silent One had left, simply vanished during the night. He was not surprised, merely saddened that so many questions would remain unanswered. He was, moreover, unconcerned. He knew that his patient was on the road to some sort of recovery. He had finished the painting without destroying it, he had spoken, if only briefly and he had painted human figures. All these were positive signs. It would have been pleasant to have known more about him though. In almost two years they had learned nothing more than that he was a talented painter. Until the last day, when he had spoken, that was. Then one mystery about him had been revealed. The Silent One was an Englishman.

* * *

By the time a war-weary Britain celebrated Christmas of 1920, Michael Haigh was congratulating himself on the appointment of Simon Jones as Group Secretary for WPF&D. Within a year Simon had reorganized the group's finances, introducing reporting guidelines that ensured each department delivered up-to-the-minute and meaningful financial information. With this Michael and Simon, now his de-facto second in command, were able to introduce new working practices. This in turn achieved substantial economies throughout the group's activities and resulted in vastly improved profits.

Michael, emboldened by the success of Simon's new systems and seeing the resultant rapid growth in the group's resources, looked around for further acquisitions. He had already bought a controlling interest in Josiah Firth's textile engineering business, but to ensure the group continued to make progress he needed more. Michael felt that organic growth, subject to the vicissitudes of trading conditions could scarcely be relied upon. He set out to buy into companies whose activities complemented the group's existing portfolio.

WPF&D was a merchanting operation in origin. The Four Horsemen had themselves bought a worsted spinning company. Now with Simon Jones's assistance, Michael obtained, in quick succession, a wool-combing plant in Bradford, a worsted clothing mill in Huddersfield and a woollen cloth maker's business in Dewsbury. By Christmas of 1920, after a breathless eighteen months of activity, the group had also acquired a hosiery yarn spinning operation, giving it a stake in almost every aspect of the textile industry from the importation of raw materials to the sale of the finished cloth.

If Simon Jones had been the right man for the job, then it was equally true that the job had been the right one for him. The excitement and cut and thrust of business life were more in keeping with his bold, almost audacious personality than the prosaic daily routine of an accountancy practice would ever have been.

In one area of his life however, Simon was far from bold, a world away from audacious. The truncation of his social life by the war had given him little opportunity for contact with women, save those in his immediate family circle. Following his return to civilian life, Simon found himself gauche, shy, and ill at ease with women, unsure and awkward in their presence. It was of little help that he had no circle of friends to draw him out, for those who had survived the war had gone their separate ways.

CHAPTER THIRTY

Simon Jones did not dislike women; on the contrary, he was immensely attracted by them, it was more that he was unable to react to them. He was in this dangerously frustrated frame of mind when his mother demanded that he escorted her while she took his sister Eva shopping. Eva was due to be married in the spring of the following year. She and her mother wanted to ensure the success of her big day and were searching for a wedding dress. As Simon's father was away on business, it fell to Simon to stand in for his parent in the quest.

The day selected for the shopping expedition was the Saturday two weeks prior to Christmas, which would ensure that the shops and Bradford city centre in general were busier than normal. They left the house a little after 10.30 a.m. By 4 p.m. Simon was weary, bored, and hungry. He spent a considerable part of the day marvelling at the ability of his female relations to spend so much time poring over a garment, assessing its quality, trying it on, exclaiming at how good it looked, how much it suited the wearer, how the colour was just right, only to reject it for any number of apparently trivial reasons.

To complicate the issue and prolong their search they had a secret agenda, one they had failed to mention to

Simon. In addition to a wedding dress for Eva, they had also to search for dresses for her three bridesmaids as well as an outfit for their mother. The latter had been achieved early on in the day, raising Simon's expectations that the foray would be a brief one. As time wore on without any further success this false hope was replaced by deepening gloom.

By 3 p.m. however, bridesmaids' dresses had also been selected. About this time Simon was assailed by a fresh wave of panic. This was occasioned by a discussion between Eva and their mother. The gist of this was a plan involving a journey to neighbouring Leeds should they meet with no success in Bradford. Time and opportunity were both running out and Simon was horror-struck at the thought of a further tormented day, when his mother directed him to a dress shop on Manningham Lane. The only consolation for Simon was that these premises were on their way home. He parked the car outside the shop his mother indicated and ambled morosely across the broad pavement in the wake of the two women.

When he entered the shop Simon saw his mother and sister being directed to the first floor by a female assistant. He groaned and said, 'I'll wait down here.'

The assistant turned and smiled at him. Simon gazed at her in awe. She was tall, fair haired, stunningly pretty and with a superb figure. She glanced at him, then, enquiringly at his companions. 'My brother Simon,' Eva told the assistant casually. 'He's here under protest as our chauffeur.'

'And treasurer!' Simon retorted acidly.

The assistant laughed, the sound sending a shiver of excitement down Simon's spine. 'By all means stay down here if you so wish,' she told him. 'If you prefer it, I will escort your sister and mother upstairs.'

'No,' Simon replied a little more cheerfully. 'I've come this far I might as well come the rest of the way.'

It was Simon's good fortune that the shop had a gown that was exactly what Eva and their mother had been looking for. To enhance Simon's good fortune, it took them a long time searching through the long rails of wedding gowns until they found it. After that it had to be tried on, for, as Simon was by then well aware, what can look right on the hanger can be a disaster when worn. He was aware of this because he had heard it so many times that day.

The prolonged wait gave Simon ample opportunity to talk to the assistant, which was the only reason he had agreed to go upstairs. 'I suppose you must get this sort of thing all the time?' he asked her, casting a despairing glance towards his relatives.

The young woman laughed. 'Usually, it is the bride's father I get to meet, rarely her brother. The fathers are usually much more bad-tempered than you.'

'I can't believe anyone would be bad-tempered with you,' Simon said gallantly.

The assistant blushed slightly, but still smiling, replied, 'I think it's the outrageous cost of the gowns that makes them bad-tempered.'

Her warm, slightly husky, indefinably accented voice intrigued him. He glanced at her hands. They were bare of any rings. She would be, he guessed, in her late twenties. He found her extremely attractive. 'You know my name is Simon, my sister Eva told you that, so please tell me your name?'

She had noticed his look at her hands, had guessed correctly the reason for it. Her blush deepened. 'Naomi,' she replied. 'Naomi Fleming.' She paused, then added severely, 'Mrs Naomi Fleming.' His look of dismay was so comical she almost laughed out loud.

'Oh no!' he exclaimed bitterly. 'I hoped you weren't married.' The words burst from him before he could stop himself. In an instant he was as scarlet as she had been only a second earlier.

'I was married, but I no longer am. My husband was killed in the war.'

It was the story she had made up years earlier, to explain the presence of her son Joshua, the absence of the child's father. Instantly Simon was a mass of confused apologies.

The dress was ordered on the spot, although a few minor alterations had to be made. To the surprise of both his mother and sister Simon volunteered to collect and pay for the gown once these had been completed.

He hustled them from the store then drove them rapidly home. He deposited them, jumped back into the car and drove hastily off, leaving the two women staring alternately at the departing vehicle and each other, their eyebrows raised in amused surprise.

When Naomi locked the shop at closing time, she was startled to hear her name called out. She looked round. Simon Jones was leaning against his car. 'I thought you might like a lift home,' he said innocently.

'You drove all the way here just to offer me a lift home?' Naomi asked.

Simon, unused to the ways of women, merely nodded.

'I know I told you I was widowed, but how do you know I am unattached?' she asked him severely.

'I don't,' he confessed frankly. 'I merely hoped so.'

Naomi stared at him for a moment. She liked what she saw. His openness and lack of guile stood him in better stead than many who had tried for a close acquaintance with her. She smiled at him. 'It's only a short distance, hardly worth the effort.'

Simon snorted. His reply made her chuckle. 'After a day spent like mine, don't talk to me about wasted effort.'

A few minutes later he brought the car to a standstill outside her tiny, terraced cottage. By this time Naomi had marshalled her thoughts. She found Simon to be an attractive, an apparently honest and decent young man. Part of her cautioned against involvement. She ignored it. For the first time Naomi realized she was lonely. 'Would you care to come in for a cup of tea?' she asked.

'I'd like nothing better,' he replied, the sincerity in his voice bringing the colour to her cheeks once more. 'Except,' he added, 'you must be hungry after a day's work, I know I am after a day slogging round the shops with my nearest and dearest. Would you not prefer something to eat?'

'Well, what I do on most Saturdays is call at the shop at the end of the next street and collect fish and chips.'

'That sounds a great idea. Shall I go for them?'

Naomi looked at him. It was a make-or-break moment for them. 'Could you make it three portions?' she asked softly.

Simon cast her a sidelong glance.

'I have a son,' Naomi explained. 'His name is Joshua.'

Simon smiled at her. 'Nice name, Joshua. How old is he?'

'Five years old,' Naomi replied, relieved by his reaction.

'Who looks after him when you are at work?'

'A neighbour. Or rather a woman who lives a couple of streets away.'

'In that case,' Simon suggested. 'Why don't we collect Joshua, then he can have a ride in the car, kids like riding in cars. We can pick up the fish and chips en route.'

'That won't give me time to tidy up,' Naomi objected.

Simon put his hand on hers then held it for a moment, thrilled by the touch. 'If you think I've driven all the way back, then brought you home merely to check on the tidiness of your sitting room, you're sadly mistaken,' he told her bluntly.

Her heart beat a little faster. She could not be sure whether this was due to the touch of his hand or the boldness of his remark.

* * *

Clarence Barker was desperate. Worse still, he was frightened. He had been paying the blackmailer for almost eighteen months. The first demand, for £1000, had been followed, two months later, by another for the same amount. This had continued throughout 1919, with payments totalling

£20,000. Then the blackmailer had asked for more to ensure his silence. Clarence's bank account was being drained.

Clarence realized that he could no longer continue to pay the blackmailer from his own funds. The alternative, exposure, was even more terrible to contemplate. Gradually, Clarence began to formulate a plan. It was a two-pronged stratagem. The first part was devised to buy himself time; time to discover the identity of his tormentor. The second, more time to deal with him.

Using his authority as Managing Director of HAC, he authorized the company's purchase of a small blending and willeying plant. This was, on the face of it, a sensible acquisition, as it would allow HAC's salesmen to offer pre-blended wool to potential customers, a useful addition to their sales portfolio. The complementary willeying process, by which extraneous matter was removed from the raw fleece or skin wool, would also enhance sales and assist scouring operations. All in all, it was a shrewd business transaction. Clarence however, had an ulterior motive.

At the same time as he bought the blending company, Clarence, in a series of meetings with his solicitor, authorized the setting up of another company, ambiguously named Phoenix Wools. The company letterhead showed only the registered office, which was that of the solicitor and an address for correspondence, which was a post office box. Quietly, during the early part of 1920, Phoenix Wools began invoicing small lots of wool to HAC Blending Company. Clarence, who had taken personal control of blending operations, authorized the invoices for payment.

Short of a detailed check of delivery notes the system was foolproof, for there is always a weight loss during the blending and willeying processes. The turnover was sufficient to disguise the phantom deliveries, so the fraud was easy to cover up.

Emboldened by the success of the first few invoices, Clarence gradually stepped up the amounts. The invoices continued unchallenged, the payments continued to be made and Phoenix Wool's bank balance continued to grow, until such time as it was emptied. When that took place, the money was filtered through a succession of accounts with various banks, their sole purpose being to disguise the ultimate destination of the funds, which was Clarence Barker's personal account.

The second part of Clarence's scheme was to rid himself of the blackmailer. Clarence had still no more clue as to the man's identity than when the first demand had arrived. The blackmailer was shrewd, of that Clarence was aware, for whenever instructions for delivery of the money arrived, they would differ from all previous ones.

Clarence had once tried waiting in concealment close to the place where the money had been left, but to no avail. The selected sites were always at remote locations, usually on the moors, but even though Clarence had waited almost forty-eight hours, he had caught no sign of the blackmailer. The consequence of Clarence's attempt had arrived in the next demand. The blackmailer made it painfully clear that he knew of Clarence's actions. No repetition of such behaviour would be tolerated, the blackmailer asserted. The veiled threat had left Clarence more terrified than ever. It also settled one outstanding doubt in his mind. When he discovered the man's identity, Clarence knew how he would deal with him.

He began to make his plans with great care. He bought all weather clothing, sturdy boots, and supplies for a long vigil outdoors. In addition, he made a more sinister purchase. Many soldiers had brought home mementos of the war, in the shape of service revolvers and ammunition. Twenty-five pounds secured one of these for Clarence. He had killed once before, in the heat of battle. Now Clarence was planning another murder, this time in cold blood.

CHAPTER THIRTY-ONE

Simon Jones had fallen into the habit of taking Naomi Fleming and her son Joshua on regular car outings. The idea occurred to him on their first evening together, after they had eaten their fish and chips and Naomi had put Joshua to bed. They had spent the greater part of the evening talking, during which time Simon was desperate to think up ways of furthering their relationship.

'Tell me,' he enquired, 'how much do you know about Yorkshire?'

'Very little,' Naomi replied candidly. 'In fact, I have never been out of Bradford since I arrived here.'

'Well, how about this,' Simon suggested diffidently. 'If you and Joshua entrust yourselves to me, I would be happy to act as driver and guide on a series of journeys of discovery around the county. There is much more to Yorkshire than mill towns,' he added. He listed some of the delights that would be in store for them. 'There's the seaside, with places like Scarborough and Whitby, some beautiful countryside in the Dales, sleepy little market towns like Ripon and Thirsk, ancient ruins and monuments such as Rievaulx Abbey, cities like York and Leeds and modern shops.'

Naomi had little hesitation in accepting Simon's offer. Even had the prospect of the treats he had listed held little appeal in themselves, the companionship would have been enough. The time passed rapidly in Simon's company and the evening had been more than pleasant. It had highlighted the loneliness of her life, the emptiness of her existence.

Naomi was a young woman with an unfulfilled capacity for enjoyment and laughter. For the past few years, she had spent all her time working or caring for Joshua. She needed more than that. Simon was offering her the chance of more, broader horizons, new experiences. She had been tempted before. Such were her looks and vivacious personality that it would have been more than a little surprising if they had not, but in the past she had always turned them down.

Her reluctance had stemmed from fear. Companionship led to commitment and commitment in turn would involve explanations to awkward questions. Naomi was aware of the fraudulent life she led, when even the name she bore was a false one and the prospect of the discovery of her past terrified her. Or rather they had done until she met Simon. Oddly enough with Simon she felt a sense of safety and security that had been missing from her life.

Naomi's employment meant that their excursions were limited to Sundays, or, very occasionally, evenings at the theatre. There were few productions suitable for the five-year-old Joshua, apart of course from a visit to Bradford's new Alhambra Theatre, where the management staged some of the country's finest pantomimes.

As the months passed the couple became gradually closer. It was obvious to Naomi that Simon had formed a liking for her young son, equally that Joshua, unused to male company, thought the world of Simon. Less clear to Naomi were Simon's feelings for her, or for that matter, hers for Simon.

Although he enjoyed her company, took delight in her pleasure at each new treat he provided, he had made no effort to force the pace of their relationship. In quiet moments Naomi found herself thinking of Simon more and more. She was deeply fond of him but was puzzled over where the relationship was heading.

Simon was equally confused. He had come so far with Naomi but could not bring himself to risk the next step. He was aware of some mystery surrounding Naomi, some deep disquiet beneath the surface of her extrovert nature. Had Simon been more experienced in the ways of women he might have been bolder, forced the issue sooner. That, had he but known it, would have been a huge tactical error.

It was late spring of 1921 before matters came to a head. Simon explained the position to Naomi. 'It's time for WPF&D to prepare their annual results for the auditors. This means a heavy workload I'm afraid. What's more it has to be done for each group company. We have bought several subsidiaries recently, which merely adds to the workload.' He paused. 'The bulk of the work falls on me as Group Financial Director because I am responsible for the accuracy of all the figures. I'm afraid we will have to forego our outings for a few weeks as I'll be working flat out seven days a week until the job is done.'

Naomi concealed her disappointment. 'I understand, Simon, your career must come first. I wouldn't want you any other way.'

Despite her brave words the following few weeks seemed interminably long, the weekdays flat with nothing to look forward to and the evenings drab and lonely. Sunday, the day of the week she had most enjoyed became intolerable.

She had not seen him for over five weeks and was wondering when she might see him again, when, midway through another long Saturday evening, as she was ironing some blouses for work, there was a knock on her door. She opened it to find Simon standing outside, somewhat nervously holding his hat in one hand. His smile was diffident, apologetic, his face looked tired and strained, and his body drooped with exhaustion.

Naomi invited him in, then sat him down in her tiny sitting room while she made him a cup of tea. When she returned, Simon was asleep in the chair. She studied him for a long moment, then, as if she had made a decision, she roused him to drink his tea. Simon apologized for his lack of manners, but Naomi waved the apology aside. 'One thing for certain,' she told him forthrightly, 'you are in no fit state to drive to Shipley tonight. You can stay here until you have had a good night's sleep.'

Simon stared at her; his mind numb with weariness. He knew he should not accept but was too tired to argue. He meekly acquiesced as she took him by the hand and led him upstairs. The cottage had just two bedrooms, the main room used by Naomi and one, little more than a box room, occupied by Joshua.

Naomi left Simon to undress, then went downstairs to lock up. By the time she returned Simon was fast asleep. Naomi quietly undressed, slipped her nightdress on, and climbed into the double bed alongside him. Simon did not even stir. Naomi lay for a long time watching the sleeping form of the man she now realized she loved. Without conscious thought Naomi slipped an arm around his waist. Simon murmured contentedly in his sleep.

He was dreaming. In his dreams he held Naomi in his arms. They were both naked, silently engrossed in one another to the exclusion of the world about them. Simon was happy, for he now knew for certain that this was what he wanted, what he had wanted from the moment he had met Naomi. He sighed with pure pleasure.

When he awoke it was with a sense of disappointment. It had, after all, been only a dream. A pale sun was filtering through the edges of the curtains. Suddenly, Simon was aware that something was wrong. The morning sun never shone on his bedroom window. Nor was that window in the right place. It should have been to the right of his bed, not the left. Disorientated, in that brief moment between sleep and complete wakefulness, he turned over in the bed, to discover, to his immense shock, the sleeping form alongside him.

What, who, and how, crowded in on him until he suddenly remembered. At the moment of his recall, as if in answer to a signal, Naomi opened her eyes. The vague light was sufficient for him to see her smile, still drowsy from slumber. He realized with mild panic that he was unclothed apart from his underpants, that Naomi was wearing only a flimsy, revealing nightdress, little more than a slip really.

As Simon searched for words Naomi reached across, put her arms round his neck and drew him close to her. Then she kissed him. Simon, his excitement only too evident, tried to apologize, explain, excuse. Naomi slid her hand into his underpants, feeling the heat of his arousal. 'Simon,' she told him, her tone one of plain command. 'Shut up and make love to me.'

CHAPTER THIRTY-TWO

With the comforting presence of her grandson Mark, now a lively three-year-old, added to the companionship of her daughter-in-law Rachael, Hannah Cowgill had become like a new woman. Although she still grieved for her husband Albert, her daughter Ada and Mark's father Sonny, the presence of the little boy and his mother in the large house at Byland Crescent had brought a new light into Hannah's life.

As Henry the butler confided to Mrs Dallas, the maestro of the kitchen, it was not even the old Hannah Cowgill they remembered from ten or twenty years ago, it was a woman who seemed to have regained the youth and vigour of one forty years her junior.

The truth was, that brought up in a Victorian atmosphere of restraint and gentility, where duty and obedience took precedence over fun and laughter, Hannah had thence been plunged into a lifetime of marital service to her husband and growing family, further quelling, if not quashing her capacity for enjoyment.

Rachael and young Mark had released her from the bondage of correctness, released along with it a stream of energy and vivacity that few of her friends and family suspected Hannah possessed.

Byland Crescent echoed to the chatter and laughter of a family once more. In this, the tones of little Mark and the younger Mrs Cowgill were frequently overshadowed, sometimes engulfed by those of Hannah herself. Connie remarked on the transformation to her sister-in-law, asking in her forthright way whether she had been feeding her mother some sort of drug to work the improvement in her health and spirits. For Connie, her husband Michael Haigh and their three children, the visits, made previously out of filial duty, became a positive treat.

Hannah rediscovered the joys of walking with an agreeable companion and an energetic infant. There is no finer place than Scarborough for this and together the two women and their young charge roamed the resort from Oliver's Mount to North Bay, to the Spa and South Bay, through the expanding suburbs and down into the labyrinthine streets and alleys of the Old Town.

As they walked, they talked. They talked of the past, the present, and the future. All three held a separate yet special delight and interest for Hannah. Like a child with a favourite bedtime story, she never wearied of listening to Rachael's account of how she had met and fallen in love with Mark.

'I never called him Sonny, as the rest of the world seems to have done, I always called him Mark,' Rachael remembered. 'It felt special to refer to him by a name no one else used. He was terribly wounded when he arrived at my hospital. He wasn't expected to live. I think the doctors were merely going through the motions. From the beginning something told me he was special, that I had to save him. I'm not sure why, but later I wondered if I was falling in love with him even then. He was unconscious for a long time and maybe that was what he needed, giving his body time to recover from the trauma. Day after day, night after night I sat with him, although I was breaking every regulation by neglecting other patients. I changed his dressings twice a day, bathing the wounds each time. I tried to feed him, although in the early days that was difficult. Sometimes he would take in a little soup, or gruel, even ice cream, although he was unconscious. I think that gave me hope and encouraged me that he might pull through. Eventually he woke up, which was quite a surprise in itself.'

Rachael smiled as she recalled the moment when Sonny regained consciousness. 'I had been changing his dressings. I looked up to see Mark staring at me. I was so thankful I went off into a quiet corner and howled with relief and happiness. If I hadn't realized earlier, that should have told me I was in love with him.

'It wasn't until much later, when he was up and about, although still on crutches, that Mark told me he loved me too. At first, I worried that it might have been from gratitude, but then he kissed me and the passion in that kiss convinced me that he did love me. After that it was inevitable that we should marry, so when he got leave, he suggested we use our time together to get married.'

'Do you ever feel cheated that you had so short a time together?' Hannah asked her.

'Every day,' Rachael told her bluntly, 'every morning when I wake up. Sometimes when I see young couples together, with their whole lives in front of them I think, that should have been Mark and me. Then again, I wonder if they will stay happy or drift apart. That too seems a waste, for I know Mark and I would not have been like that. In another sense, I think a lifetime together would have been insufficient. So, I have to be content with the glorious memory of that fleeting moment that was all we had, to be grateful that I have young Mark, for while he is with me, so is his father also.'

Hannah, her eyes bright with tears, embraced Rachael.

Later, in a calmer, more reflective mood, Hannah asked Rachael if she had given any thought to her own future. 'You cannot spend the rest of your life looking after Mark. As he grows up, he will need you less and less, then eventually he will marry and be away. By that time, I shall be dead and gone. What will you do, for I cannot see you living out the rest of your life alone?'

Rachael confessed that she had given the matter little thought. 'My nursing was not a career, more a calling. I was a sort of missionary, full of zeal and the desire to help people, to cure them if I could. After that it was Mark, briefly, then baby Mark, who needed me, still needs me. If you were meaning would I consider marrying again the answer is a definite, no. I had all I wanted then it was taken from me. Any other man would always rank as second best. Nor would it be fair to him, for my heart will always remain Mark's and no man could endure being second fiddle to a ghost, always suffering by comparison. I suppose if I did anything it might be to return to nursing. That way I can still be of some service.'

* * *

The chairman of the bank looked ill at ease. James Fisher handed him a cup of coffee then strolled back behind his own desk. The office was large, light, and airy. The new headquarters of Fisher Springs Pty. had been completed only a few months previously. James Fisher had supervised the design and construction of the rest of the building but had left the fitting of their private office to Alice. She was seated behind a second, identical desk set at right angles to that of her husband.

Two walls of the office were almost completely of glass, flooding the room with light. To protect the occupants from the full effects of the hot Australian summer, each window was provided with a set of blinds and the windows themselves were hinged to open fully, enabling the restorative breezes that blew even during the hottest spells to cool the room. That breeze, so aptly named the Fremantle Doctor, was gently ruffling the papers on James's desk as the three gathered to discuss the bank's crisis.

James invited the man to begin.

'The problem arises,' the chairman started by saying, 'from our own success. We, the bank, have expanded rapidly, outstripping our investment and now we are becoming exposed. Our vulnerability lies in the fact that we have insufficient reserves to continue lending without causing a cash flow deficit, yet demand is increasing. We need further investment, yet most of our customers are borrowers rather than lenders. If we stop lending, we would spark off a crisis of confidence, which in turn would cause a run on the bank. The irony is that we are highly profitable, yet all our profits go straight back into new advances.' He paused to allow his listeners time to digest the problem.

'I came to you, because you have only a fraction of your banking business with us. Rumour has it that your company is cash rich. If there is anyone in the State capable of providing the resources we need, Fisher Springs would be the one. It would take a big investment, but the returns would be worth it.'

James stared at the banker for a long moment before replying. Patrick Finnegan had only recently joined the bank from a lucrative post in New South Wales. If Finnegan had been in charge when he and Alice had started in business, they might well have been the bank's biggest customer by now. 'What sort of money do you consider necessary to cover your current needs?' James asked.

The reply was instant. 'Around a million,' Finnegan stated bluntly.

Neither James nor Alice so much as blinked. 'What of the future?' Alice asked.

'The future?' Finnegan echoed.

'You've told us what you need to cover current borrowing levels, but that means the bank would be merely marking time. If the policy is right, but merely needs the right level of investment, how much would the bank need to continue its growth and expansion, open new branches, that sort of thing?' Alice wanted to know.

Finnegan stared at her with respect and admiration, amounting almost to awe. 'I must confess, Mrs Fisher,' he admitted. 'That is a question I did not expect to be asked today. However, I reckon it would need at least three million to cover all eventualities.'

Again, there was no discernible emotion, on the face of either of his listeners.

'Anyone putting up that sort of money,' James commented, his tone neutral to the point of disinterest, 'would surely expect to have control of the running of the bank.'

Finnegan's smile was a little twisted. 'Anyone prepared to put up such an amount would certainly have control of the bank,' he replied.

A look, no more than the flicker of a glance, passed between James and Alice before James rose to his feet, his hand extended to signal the end of the interview. 'We will study the paperwork you have supplied' — James nodded to the papers on his desk — 'and we will give you our reply within forty-eight hours.'

A few minutes later, having shaken each of them by the hand, Finnegan left the building. He was still unsure whether the meeting had been a success or failure.

CHAPTER THIRTY-THREE

The letter Clarence Barker had been awaiting arrived towards the end of March 1921. It contained yet another demand. Clarence exhibited every symptom of compliance with the blackmailer's terms. Breaking from his usual routine he visited several banks, drawing out from each a sum of money sufficiently large to be noticed by anyone within the premises, enough to be remembered by the cashier who served him. This time Clarence was taking no chances.

Returning home, he parcelled the money up as instructed, ensuring that the package was completely waterproof as the blackmailer requested. He had already lodged his protective clothing in the boot of the car several weeks earlier, where it was hidden from prying eyes. Under cover of darkness, he added some provisions for the vigil ahead and awaited instructions regarding the venue for delivery of the money.

He did not have long to wait. Much as Clarence had come to expect the place chosen by the blackmailer was in a different location to all previous ones, it had only one aspect in common, its remoteness. Clarence had three days to complete his preparations, three days before the appointed hour for the delivery of the extortion money, three days to visit the site and select a suitable place of concealment. Had Clarence been a better soldier he might have realized that one of the arts of a good general is the capacity to outthink the enemy.

The day after he received directions, two days before he was due to deposit the money, Clarence set off early in his car. Although he was dressed for the office and although he set off towards Bradford, the premises of HAC were not to be graced with the presence of their Managing Director that day. Instead of turning into his normal parking space in Manor Row, Clarence continued down Cheapside into Forster Square and thence out of town. He commenced a zigzag journey deviating through several small towns and villages until at last Clarence was certain that he was not being followed.

On the high moor road, in the triangle formed by Hawkesworth, Menston and Burley-in-Wharfedale, lies an almost unnoticed track. There, army recruits were brought for rifle and small arms practice, at the shooting range situated at the top of the track. At that time the army was not recruiting however, it was reducing in size.

The range and the track leading to it were virtually unused. During the less inclement summer months the locality had a considerable popularity amongst the more ardent courting couples. For them the very remoteness was ideal, for there they could express their regard for one another without fear of being observed in the act. In March however, not even the hardiest or most amorous of these would be in evidence, so the only inhabitants of the terrain were a few dozen expectant ewes and a sprinkling of early lambs grazing hopefully at the sparse moorland grasses.

Clarence had sufficient wit to avoid approaching the lane directly. He drove past it then continued towards the next village. Several hundred yards further along the road he found a suitable place to park inconspicuously and began to walk back towards the track. It was a good half hour's walk before he reached the place he was seeking. The blackmailer's directions had specified a group of stones at the side of the track, arranged in a rough square, with a larger rock on top. This would protect the money, not only from the elements but also from the eyes of all but the most observant passer-by.

Having identified the location, Clarence searched the vicinity until he found a suitable place of concealment. He did not need to look far. Thirty yards from the dropping place was a shallow depression in the hillside, an old water-course in all probability. There, a man could lie down in perfect shelter unless directly approached. Satisfied with his day's work Clarence returned to retrieve his car.

Two days later he was back. This time, with no attempt at concealment he drove his car along the track, stopping at the pile of stones to deliver the parcel of money. Turning the car round proved impossible, so he had a long, nervous return down the lane in reverse gear. Reaching the road, he turned the car as if heading back towards Bradford. Instead, upon reaching the junction he swung left and drove the short distance to Menston. Passing through the village he took the other wing of the moor road that brought him in a long sweep to Burley Woodhead. Another left turn at the top of the village and he was heading back towards the shooting range. Shortly after he had passed the Hermit Inn, he found the hiding place for his car and pulled in. He donned his weatherproof clothing and boots, collected the small parcel of provisions, then casting an anxious glance about him to ensure he was unobserved, checked the revolver and ammunition he had brought.

This time his walk was a more arduous one, for he had to traverse the moor rather than approach it directly. Eventually, after more than an hour's trek he reached the spot. Not only had the walk been physically demanding, his nerves, already stretched as taut as piano wire, were further tested by a couple of encounters with matrons and their offspring, whose bleating alarms had sent Clarence's heartbeat into overdrive.

It was by no means easy to identify the depression in the half-light of an approaching March dusk, so it was with considerable relief that Clarence disposed his belongings about the hollow and lay down to wait. The evening sky was dark and moonless but slowly, as the last traces of reflected daylight vanished, stars became faintly visible. For the waiting Clarence, that was the only good news, for although it signalled a clear, dry night it also meant that it would be a cold one.

If Clarence had expected his vigil to be conducted in a background of silence, such was not the case. Had he been a countryman, or one used to the ways of nature, such sounds as he heard from time to time would not have alarmed him to the point of panic, but Clarence was town born and town bred.

Admittedly the bleat of lambs attempting to locate their parent in the dark, or the answering call of their mother was identifiable enough to do little to upset Clarence's equilibrium, but the sudden, startling call of a hunting owl was a different matter. Then, after several hours waiting, came a totally unnerving scream, almost human in cadence that had Clarence biting his lip as he fought to restrain an answering call of fear. It was the sound, to Clarence's untrained ear, of a creature in the most unimaginable pain and distress. The deception was scarcely Clarence's fault. Many others, hearing the sound of mating foxes for the first time have imagined it to be that of some animal undergoing intense torture.

Clarence regained his composure and waited. And waited. He was numbed by cold, cold and fear, terrified of the outcome when the blackmailer arrived to collect his payoff. He had no idea of the time, but eventually he noticed an imperceptible change in the night. The sky was not as dark as it had been a few minutes earlier, the stars not quite so bright. It was the first sign that the long March night was coming to an end.

It was perhaps twenty minutes later, just as Clarence was convincing himself that the perceived change in the light had not been a trick of his imagination, that his ears caught a new sound. This was a sound that Clarence recognized. It was, although far distant, the unmistakeable hum of an internal combustion engine. Someone somewhere was driving a motor car. As Clarence listened intently it seemed to him as if the sound was growing in volume. Slowly, inexorably the noise of the engine grew louder. The car was definitely coming nearer. From a faint hum it had become a steady, pulsating throb. Clarence, unaware of how far sound carries through a still, silent night, was convinced that the vehicle was close by.

Then, several miles away, across the moor, Clarence saw the gleam of two faint pinpricks of light appear, then, as swiftly vanish once more. He watched, to have his doubt removed when they reappeared. As suddenly as they came back, they were gone again, only to appear once more seconds later. Suddenly Clarence understood. They were the headlights of an approaching car. The moor road along that stretch resembled an elongated switch-back, the repeated vanishing act being caused as the car alternated between crest and hollow.

Without much supporting evidence, Clarence was certain that the approaching vehicle was the blackmailer's car. What law abiding citizen, he reasoned, would travel so lonely a road at such an hour. He checked his revolver and stretched his stiff, cramped limbs, then settled down once more, huddled against the cold, frost-laden grass and waited.

As he watched, the car approached the junction and the headlights swept towards him as the driver opted for the left fork, adding fuel to Clarence's theory. After what seemed an age, the car approached the end of the track. For a brief moment Clarence thought he had been wrong, that the car was continuing along the road. The headlights swung into the track and disappeared; with them went the sound of the engine. The driver had switched off the ignition. He would not be driving up the track as Clarence had expected. Confirmation came via the sound of a car door opening, then closing. No matter, Clarence thought, he had waited so long, a few minutes more would make no difference.

The minutes passed, then, Clarence saw, much nearer, another light. Smaller, fainter, swinging from side to side, this was no headlight. It was, he realized, the beam of a torch, moving in time to the walk of its bearer. Closer and closer it came until Clarence could make out the silhouette of the man carrying it. Then it was opposite him and the beam became fixed. Tracing its path Clarence saw that it was shining on the stones, under which lay the parcel of money. Any last vestige of doubt vanished. The torch bearer was there for one purpose only.

Slowly, with infinite care, Clarence raised himself onto all fours, then onto his feet. His quarry was facing away from him. Step by step, inch by inch Clarence began to move towards the man, who was now bending over the pile of stones. Twenty yards, fifteen yards, slowly the gap between them decreased. Ten yards to go, then Clarence was at the side of the track. He heard the chink of stone against stone as the man lifted the covering rock to one side, then the grunt of satisfaction as he retrieved the parcel.

As he did so, Clarence stepped forward. His foot came down on the loose grit surface of the track and the sound of the impact echoed through the still night air. The torch beam wavered wildly as the man turned, startled, towards Clarence.

Casting caution aside, Clarence took two swift strides forward. He could see the man clearly behind the torch beam.

Clarence lifted the revolver. He saw the vivid spurt of jagged flame and felt the kick of the recoil before the thunderous sound of the shot hit his ears, deafening him. He saw the man stagger back. He stepped a further two paces forward and fired again. As the man slumped to the ground Clarence fired again and again until the chamber was empty. As each bullet struck home the man's body twitched, then lay still.

Silence returned, although Clarence, deafened by the sound of the shots, could not recognize it as such. He stared at the dead man for a second then, fear overtaking him, he snatched up the parcel of money and bolted across the moor, stumbling in his headlong flight, unaware of anything about him, transfixed solely with the need to get away from the scene of his hideous deed.

CHAPTER THIRTY-FOUR

There is very little that can shock a banker, but James and Alice Fisher managed to do so with ease. Patrick Finnegan had been hopeful that Fisher Springs would put up the money needed to see the bank through its crisis. In his wilder, more optimistic moments he had even dreamed that they would provide the full amount needed for the bank to continue its expansion programme. The terms outlined by James left him open-mouthed and speechless.

James and Alice had spent many hours poring over the comprehensive documentation Finnegan had left. During the process neither spoke much, for this was their way, save only to request a fresh document, or seek confirmation on an interpretation of a clause. As they worked each made comprehensive notes, these would form the basis for their decision-making.

When they had completed their appraisal they set aside the paperwork, collected their notes, and began to argue. There was no set format to this process, but usually one or other would bring out the negatives in any proposition. They had adopted the method when they started acquiring other businesses for the expanding group. It was an enjoyable and exciting game and in a way, they found it stimulating. Such was the effect that their son Luke had actually been conceived at the end of one such session, a fact that James often mentioned to Alice in private moments. That, as she had replied austerely, had been in the old days before their new headquarters had been built. James had pointed out that their office, with blinds to each window and a sturdy lock on the door was as private as they could get. He had received a gentle smack, little more than a caress for his temerity. The gleam in his eye warned Alice that she had failed to daunt him.

Their discussion took a long time, for it was the biggest investment of their career by far. Not that it would overstretch Fisher Springs. Only James and Alice knew the full extent of the group's wealth, but in cash terms alone the amount they were considering investing was well within their grasp.

James did not indulge in any preamble but launched straight into the offer. 'We have discussed your problem,' he told Finnegan, 'and our terms are as follows: Fisher Springs is only interested in the bank if we can achieve one hundred per cent ownership. The terms granted to your original investors contain a clause permitting the bank to repurchase the shares at the current market value. By our reckoning that figure is today approximately four million.

'If we buy up all the existing shares and provide the amount required to ensure the bank's expansion, our investment would total eight million initially. The offer is conditional upon us being able to buy every share. It is also conditional on you remaining as chairman and chief executive. If any of the terms of the offer cannot be met, the whole is withdrawn.'

There was a long pause while Finnegan digested the facts and got his breath back. He gulped slightly before stating, 'I can promise you the last one here and now. It would be a pleasure working with you.'

'Selling it to the shareholders should be easy,' James continued. 'The value of their holding is dependent on confidence in the bank. If that disappears, their share certificates will only be useful for lighting fires. After the acquisition goes through you might like to consider another strategy for the bank. Australia is opening up rapidly. Immigration is being actively encouraged, that means more new homes will be needed every year. We know this because we see the figures from our construction division. More houses mean more lending against the property, so that is going to be a major growth area. If the bank comes under the Fisher Springs umbrella we would want it to be market leaders, not followers. Property loans are a specialized form of banking and it would be sensible to either train up or recruit specialists to run the operation. We will ensure sufficient sums are set aside to set up a home loans section. Finally, we are sure there must be other small banks in similar difficulties, either now or in the near future. We would expect you to bring us details of any that you want to acquire. Organic growth is fine, but acquisition is faster. We intend to run the two side by side.'

The terms having been outlined, James and Alice spent some time discussing the finer details with Finnegan. When he left the building an hour later Finnegan was in a delirium of excitement.

* * *

The discussion in the boardroom of Outlane Chemicals was rational, unheated, although the opinions of the two participants could scarcely have been at greater variance. Charlie Binks, whose genius as a designer of chemical dyes was recognized throughout the industry, had been responsible for the creation of the company in the first place. Since its formation under the parentage of HAC Group, Outlane Chemicals had contributed hugely to the group's long-term financial success. Herein, lay part of the discontent that led to the disagreement between Charlie and his son, Robert. Robert was as talented a chemist as his father, but unlike Charlie he felt restricted by the narrow confines of the world of chemical dyes. Robert thought the company was underperforming and failing to achieve its full potential. He wanted them to diversify.

Elsewhere it was an age of discovery in the chemical industry. New products were coming to the market with increasing regularity, products that were either totally innovative or as chemical substitutes for other, traditionally manufactured substances. Robert considered Outlane Chemicals to be significant enough to take part in the new wave of experimental processes. He felt strongly enough to have written a dissertation on the subject to the HAC board. Since there was only one other remaining board member this, in effect, had meant Charlie Binks and Clarence Barker. It was the refusal of HAC to allocate funds for Robert's project that had led to the disagreement.

Charlie had tried to soften the blow. 'It isn't that I don't see the advantages of diversification, Robert,' he explained, 'but you gave no evidence of any long-term benefit. I stated your case as best I could but as I could not cite a product. Clarence refused point blank to even consider the matter.'

Robert grimaced in disgust. 'That argument's a nonstarter. How many times have I heard the tale of how Uncle Albert backed you, when chemical dyeing was in its infancy?'

'At least I had a product in mind,' Charlie pointed out.

'Yes, but it was a huge gamble, with no guarantee of success. For all they knew you could have just been another mad professor. At least with this project we would be working on the back of a company with a guaranteed income to fund our research.'

'Well Clarence won't hear of it and without his sanction we cannot proceed,' Charlie countered.

Robert was not so easily deterred. 'Does he need to know about it, Father?' he enquired, his face expressionless. 'He never comes here and from what you tell me he rarely looks at our figures. If he did see a figure for research, it could be put down to a new generation of chemical dyes.'

Charlie blinked in astonishment at his son's duplicity. There was a lot of truth in the argument, he conceded reluctantly. 'Give me a product, give me the germ of an idea and I might, just might, consider it.'

'Easy,' Robert responded. 'Paint and fertilizer. I reckon they will be the next two big chemical products. Agriculture is changing fast and as the population grows it will need to produce more, become more efficient. That means higher yields from their crops, that in turn means better fertilizers.'

'And paint?' Charlie enquired.

'I've heard there are some interesting experiments being carried out on the Continent and in America to do with the production of paint from artificial sources. One rumour suggests it is something to do with the refining of petrol.'

Despite his initial reluctance Charlie felt that familiar stir of excitement when a new challenge was presented. 'All right, find out more about both, do some costings and let me see them. I'm not promising anything yet, but I will consider it.'

* * *

'Are you going to tell us a little about your girlfriend?'

Simon Jones stared at his mother in amazement. 'How did you know I have a girlfriend?' he asked.

Emily Jones laughed. 'Simon my dear, you have always possessed a special type of naiveté. Apart from the fact that she is called Naomi, works in a dress shop and is one of the prettiest girls I've seen for many a year, I know nothing about her.'

Simon's astonishment manifested itself in a series of incoherent stammering sounds. His mother relented and explained, counting off the facts on her fingers. 'You met her when we bought Eva's wedding gown. You talked to her as I've never heard you talk to any girl before. Those fitting rooms are by no means soundproof. As soon as you could, you dumped Eva and me here and rushed off, obviously intent on meeting her when the shop closed. You were out all evening but didn't want anything to eat when you came in. Since that time you have been missing every Sunday, which argues that whoever your companion might be, she works on a Saturday. You have been moody and irritable for a long time, presumably while matters between you remained unresolved.

'More recently you seem to have forsaken us almost entirely, but on the rare occasions when you have graced us with your presence you seem to have been in a world of your own, a happy one too judging by the idiotic grin you can't get off your face. Do you realize your father told you last week that Bradford City had lost two–nil. That would normally have been the signal for a week of mourning, but all you did was smile and say, "great". Last but not least, the fact that suddenly you seem to have found your own bed uncomfortable, as you rarely sleep in it. Either that or you have found one that is more comfortable. Hers for instance. Then you ask me how I know you have a girlfriend.'

If Simon was shocked by the depth of his mother's knowledge, he soon rallied. 'You don't mind?' he asked, almost timidly.

Emily put her arms round her son. 'Simon my dear, you are a grown man, well on the way to being a successful businessman of some standing. Your father and I have no greater wish for you than to see you as happy as you are now.'

'What does Dad think?'

'As far as I remember it' — Emily laughed — 'his only comment was "lucky young bugger". So come on, tell me all about Naomi.'

* * *

'So that, my darling, is what I did.' Simon kissed Naomi lightly on the forehead and absent-mindedly pulled her closer in his arms. 'It was then that I told her of our plans and she invited me to bring you and Josh for tea on Sunday.'

'You don't think she minds the fact that we are going to live together even if we are not married?' Naomi asked.

'I'm sure she would prefer it so, but she seemed to accept what I said, that we wanted a little more time to ourselves first.' As he spoke Simon was caressing her. Naomi fought against her own arousal for a while, fought, lost, and gave in.

During the afternoon Simon had taken Joshua to Valley Parade football ground and it would have been difficult to judge which of the two had been more excited when the final whistle signalled a Bradford City win. Afterwards they had sauntered along Manningham Lane to collect Naomi from the shop. Following the established ritual of a fish and chip supper the household had retired to bed early. Simon and Naomi, glad of the chance to be together for a whole weekend, were determined to make the most of it.

Later, Simon lay on his back and Naomi sat, her legs across his thighs as they discussed the plans for the flat they were in the process of buying, close to Manningham Park. The discussion was rather one sided as Naomi itemized purchases she considered essential. Simon, for his part, engrossed in exploring her lovely body with his hands, kept his contribution to the debate limited to the occasional 'okay' or 'sounds fine'.

The previous week they had been to see a production of *Oliver Twist* with which Naomi had been much taken. As she felt Simon stirring, she opened her eyes wide and, with an innocent giggle said, in her best interpretation of Mr Bumble, 'More, you want MORE!'

CHAPTER THIRTY-FIVE

The newspapers carried the story of the discovery of the body on the moor far more quickly than Clarence had anticipated given the remote location, the time of year and the less than inviting weather; he had hoped there would have been a few days breathing space. Clarence, however, had reckoned without the sheep and lambs.

The newsvendor's cry pre-empted Clarence's reading of the placards by a split second. 'Body found on moor,' the man declaimed. 'Man gunned down on shooting range.'

The paper seller's sense of the dramatic was matched by the sensational style of the reporter from the local evening paper, the *Argus*. Under the screaming banner headline 'Murder on the Moor', Clarence read:

'Farmer Thomas Heaton made a grim discovery when going to check his flock of young lambs this morning. The peaceful pastoral scene was marred by the presence of the bullet-riddled corpse of a man in his late twenties or early thirties. As yet the police say they have no clue as to the identity of the dead man. A police spokesman stated that, given the remote location on the high moors, the tyre tracks in the lane and the poor weather conditions, they believe both murderer and victim arrived at the scene of the crime by car, possibly even the same car. The spokesman added that a full description of the dead man would be issued once a post-mortem examination had taken place.'

The article went on to describe the locality, facts with which Clarence was only too well aware. He read and re-read the pertinent details again and again. One omission stood out glaringly. There was no mention of a car being found at the scene. Were the police keeping that evidence in reserve until they had identified the corpse? Or, more horrible to dwell on, had the blackmailer been accompanied? Clarence was seized by a fresh wave of panic.

Over the succeeding days and weeks, during which Clarence bought newspapers as he had never bought them before, few new facts came to light. The post-mortem examination yielded little, but for a description of the dead man that would have fitted a million others, and the fact that he had been a soldier as there were scars from old shrapnel wounds on the body. This comforted Clarence slightly, as he knew the blackmailer to have been a soldier. Still no mention was made of a car, nor was there any further clue as to the identity of the dead man. So little in the way of solid evidence emerged that, had it not been for the sensational nature of the crime, the newspapers would probably have dropped the story early.

As it was, the headline writers were having great fun with the few solid facts at their disposal. 'The Murder on the Moor' and 'Slaughter at the Shoot' were amongst the favourites, although 'Death Amongst the Heather' and 'Soldier Gunned Down' was also prominent and one writer even managed 'Lambs to the Slaughter', which achieved limited acclaim.

With the passage of time, Clarence began to relax, for the second time it appeared that he had committed murder and got away with it. At the end of July, when the vast majority of the West Riding textile industry closed down, he even treated himself to a week's holiday in Morecambe. Although the blackmailer's demands had ceased, Clarence continued the practice of sending spurious invoices from Phoenix Wools to HAC Scouring. These, he thought, would help pay for a few of life's luxuries.

There was a considerable amount of mail awaiting his attention on his return home. He picked the pile up and took it through to his study to open. He had almost completed the task when he came across an envelope, the size, shape and colour of which, even the typeface were horribly familiar. His heart lurched, almost stopped, as he read the inscription, 'Private C.E. Barker'.

There could be no doubt, it was from the blackmailer. Feverishly he tore open the envelope and read the contents.

Dear Clarence,

Now that was not a very nice thing to do, was it? Poor Tommy, he didn't have much of a life. A homeless, unemployed soldier; down on his luck and keen to do anything just to earn a couple of quid. Such as collect a parcel from a moor in the middle of the night. I call him Tommy, because he was a soldier, although naturally that isn't his real name. I've come to the conclusion that you are really not a very nice man, Clarence. Your first murder was almost understandable, but to gun poor Tommy down like that was just plain sadistic.

So now I've got you bang to rights for two murders. So, listen carefully. I've been making a few plans and some changes to the way the money gets paid. I'm not going to take any chances after what you did to Tommy. You will receive your new instructions within the next few days.

Oh, I almost forgot. Now that I am being asked to keep silent about two murders, I think my reward should increase. Increase quite a lot in fact. So, make sure you have £10,000 ready within three days.

Clarence wept tears of desperation and self-pity. There were no tears of remorse mixed with them for his slaying of the unfortunate ex-soldier; Clarence was just not made that way.

* * *

Simon and Naomi's occupation of the flat overlooking Manningham Park was preceded by a flurry of activity. Most of this involved shopping, for neither Naomi nor Simon possessed much in the way of household goods. Kitchen utensils, furniture, crockery, cutlery, and linen were all high priorities and with the restrictive hours of her employment, Naomi was forced to entrust the bulk of the shopping to Simon. Recognizing his limitations and inexperience in this field, Simon took the precaution of consulting his mother and sister Eva. Eva had only recently undertaken the same process prior to her marriage and between them the two women were able to prevent several disastrous errors of judgement Simon would otherwise have committed.

A few days before their move, Simon undertook a solo shopping expedition in Bradford. He had but one shop, one purchase in mind. The staff of the celebrated jewellers and silversmiths was obliging and helpful to the young man so obviously unused to making so momentous a purchase, but then they had ample experience of diffident young men, with little clear idea regarding stone or setting, style or size of finger.

The house removal went without hitch and on the last Sunday of September the trio sat down to an evening meal together, their first meal in their first home. As Simon remarked during dinner, they were now just like a proper family.

When the meal was over and Joshua had retired, somewhat excitedly to his new bedroom, a spacious and airy chamber, Simon and Naomi sat close together on their new sofa.

After a while Simon took his courage in both hands and broached the subject he had been waiting all day to bring up. 'I meant what I said, about us being a proper family, but

273

there are a couple of things which will help to make it even more so. First of all, if you and Josh approve, I could start proceedings to adopt him. I think he would like that and I know I would be proud to act as his father. Secondly, even more important' — he reached into his pocket and pulled out the box — 'Naomi, will you marry me?'

The diamonds in the ring flashed and sparkled through her tears. Naomi had expected this, wanted it even, though she knew she could not accept, not without explanation, and explanation meant that she might lose him. If she lacked anything it was certainly not courage. She looked at Simon, strong and steadfast. He made her feel safe. Every day with him made her realize how much she loved him. She knew how much he loved her, but would that love withstand the revelation of her past. Only Naomi knew the full extent of the gamble she was embarking on, of exactly how much she stood to lose.

'Simon, my darling,' she told him, her hands holding his as she looked into his eyes. 'Please believe me when I say there is nothing I want more than to say yes, but there are things I must tell you before I do. Things that might make you hate me, might make you want to reconsider. I have wanted to tell you many times, but my courage always failed me, because I was scared of losing you.'

Before she could say any more, he put his hands on her shoulders and kissed her on the forehead. 'I've known all along there was something. I have always known you would tell me if and when you thought it right. There was your accent for one thing. It is only slight and most people would not even notice it. You told me you were born and raised in Australia, but I met a lot of Australians during the war, none of whom sounded remotely like you. If I had to guess I would opt for somewhere more European in origin. That being the case I think it's pretty clear that you are probably some sort of master spy, like Mata Hari for instance.'

The last sentence made Naomi smile. She knew Simon's light-hearted approach was intended to make things easier for her, and she loved him for his considerate nature. 'Very well,' she said. 'You are not too far wrong. For a start my real name is not Naomi Fleming, but Hildegard Schwartz and I am part Austrian, part Serbian.'

Simon listened in awe as she told him of her past, the harsh upbringing, and the cruelty of her Austrian father towards both her and her mother, the hatred this had imbued in the small child for all things Austrian. She told him how she had been recruited in her teens by the Black Hand and how they had given her the assignment to liaise with an English arms dealer. 'We became lovers, he is Joshua's father. Or rather was, for I believe he must be dead.'

She continued her tale, recalling the hysteria and persecution in Vienna following the Sarajevo assassination and her subsequent flight across Europe as war pursued her. Only at the end of her tale did she succeed in shocking Simon, in a way neither of them suspected.

'My darling, Naomi, or Hildegard, I love you. The past you left behind you has nothing to do with you and me. As I see it, whatever you did was purely through a sense of misguided patriotism, and Lord knows there was enough of that about at the time. So, tell me, when you reached England, what made you come to Bradford of all places?'

Naomi smiled. Her heart rejoiced, for she had told Simon the very worst about herself and it had not repelled him. She knew that everything would be fine now. 'It was the only place I knew. My lover was from Bradford. By the time I arrived in England I was expecting Joshua, so I thought his father would return here if he survived.'

'Who was this mysterious arms dealer?' Simon wanted to know.

'His name was Jesse, Jesse Barker.' Naomi told him.

Simon leapt to his feet as if he had received an electric shock. 'What!' he exclaimed.

'Jesse Barker,' Naomi repeated in some alarm. 'Why, do you know him?'

Simon, much to her relief, began to laugh. 'Know him! Naomi, my darling, Jesse is my cousin.'

'What!' Naomi in turn was thunderstruck.

'My mother Emily and Jesse's mother, Bessie, are sisters. Jesse and his twin brother Ephraim were Bessie's younger sons. Ephraim was killed in France. Jesse disappeared before the war and has not been heard of since. Everyone presumes him to be dead. Only the eldest brother Clarence survived.' Simon's face wrinkled with distaste as he mentioned Clarence Barker.

Despite her preoccupation with Simon's relationship to Jesse, Naomi was intrigued. 'You don't like Clarence, I take it?'

'I loathe him. He is a detestable crawling sneak, a worm of a man. Not at all like Jesse. Jesse may have been a rogue, but he was a lovable rogue. I think, my darling, you would find out if you enquired that you were by no means the only woman to discover how lovable Jesse was. It is safe to assume he is dead, for with all his faults Jesse was not the type to stay out of contact with his family. I know they all think he is dead, although, Jesse being Jesse, he could just as easily be languishing in a prison cell somewhere. So, my dearest, you are stuck with his much less colourful, boring cousin if you still want him.'

Naomi smiled and Simon knew that he had triumphed. 'There is no comparison. I love you, Simon Jones. I think I loved you from the moment I met you. That love just keeps on growing. I want to spend the rest of my life with you. You know the worst about me. Spy, war criminal, impersonator, fraud, mistress of an arms dealer, involved in some most unsavoury events, mother of at least one illegitimate child, yet you still want me. Can you wonder that I love you?'

'How do you mean, at least one illegitimate child?' Simon asked.

'Well, unless we get married that is.' Naomi was studiously matter of fact. 'Did I not tell you I'm pregnant?'

CHAPTER THIRTY-SIX

The reduction in the household at Byland Crescent had led to a comparable reduction in the number of servants. Gone were the housemaids, the laundry maid and the scullery maid, gone too was the general factotum. Hannah's long-term personal maid had retired and gone to live with her widowed sister on the outskirts of Middlesbrough. She had been replaced by Sarah Welham, a housemaid at Byland Crescent in years gone by. Sarah had been widowed early in the war. Her husband, a trawler-man, had been killed when his fishing boat hit a mine.

Gone too was the jewel of the kitchen Mrs Dallas, gone with her the redoubtable Henry. The retirement of both butler and cook had come as a surprise to Hannah. When they announced that they had bought a post office in a small village near Whitby it had raised little comment. Sarah, who had not lost her capacity for gossip over the years, told Hannah, 'Of course they are only bringing into the open what we knew all along.'

Hannah looked puzzled.

'Henry and Olive have been lovers for over twenty years,' Sarah informed her.

'I'm beginning to wonder what the rest of the household has been getting up to over the years. First it was my son James getting Alice the housemaid pregnant, then eloping with her to who knows where, then there was Ada's trouble, now I find that my butler has been secretly bedding my cook for more than twenty years. I'm not sure that I want to hear any more,' Hannah told Rachael wryly.

Before they departed, the two elderly lovers managed to find suitable replacements for both posts. To continue the tradition of fine cuisine at Byland Crescent, Olive Dallas produced a former pupil of hers.

Her name was Joyce Holgate. Joyce was a widow. Like Rachael Cowgill she had been widowed young. She was a good-looking woman of little more than thirty years of age. She had a young daughter, Jennifer, only a few months older than Hannah's grandson Mark. This would undoubtedly have been a stumbling block before Hannah's rejuvenation, but she saw the presence of the little girl as an attraction rather than a disadvantage. Rachael agreed enthusiastically, for Jennifer was a sweet natured little thing, who would be a playmate for Mark and, as they were looking after one child, why not two.

For his part Henry re-introduced another former member of staff. George Mills had been general factotum when the Cowgill family had moved into Byland Crescent, almost twenty-five years earlier. He was a local lad, from a fishing family, but had an aversion to the sea. With the outbreak of the Boer War George had enlisted in the army, where he had remained until 1916. His rise to the rank of Sergeant Major had been merited reward for gallant service, but the loss of three toes on his right foot, sliced off by shrapnel had ended his military career. Although he still limped slightly, George professed himself fully recovered and eager to resume working at Byland Crescent.

It was in early summer of 1921 that George, with the gravitas he considered appropriate for his new position of authority and responsibility, but which occasionally reduced

Hannah and Rachael to fits of giggles, informed the elder Mrs Cowgill that during her absence there had been a telephone call for her. Hannah saw Rachael's lips beginning to twitch at George's mode of delivery and hastily turned her gaze towards the butler. She raised an eyebrow enquiringly and George added, 'From a Miss Rhodes, Madam.'

Hannah had been on the point of saying that she did not know of a Miss Rhodes when George amplified his earlier statement, 'A Miss Eleanor Rhodes, Madam. She stated that she would call again at a later time.'

Rachael saw Hannah's face cloud over, as if at a painful memory. She glanced enquiringly at her mother-in-law.

'Eleanor Rhodes,' Hannah explained carefully, 'is a painter. I cannot remember if I told you the story of my daughter Ada, or if Sonny talked of her to you?'

Rachael shook her head. 'Apart from the fact that she died in the war, I know nothing about her. To be honest I did not like to enquire for fear of causing pain.'

If Hannah thought that the younger woman might have been shocked by the revelation of Ada's sexuality, she was wrong. Rachael's sole reaction was to comment that in her opinion lesbian relationships were probably more common than people realized. Two of the nurses in her own unit had been suspected of conducting such an affair during the time they were serving together during the war. There was also, she added, ample evidence in history to suggest similar precedents.

Later that evening George announced that Miss Rhodes was on the telephone once more. The gist of the call, as Hannah reported to Rachael, was that Eleanor had an exhibition of her work on display in York and while she was in the vicinity, she wished to call upon Mrs Cowgill. 'I hope you don't mind?' Hannah enquired. 'I feel it is important, both for Eleanor herself and for Ada's memory. Eleanor came to stay with us several times when they were at school together, before we discovered the nature of their relationship. After that, there was so much anger, so much bitterness, and Ada became an outcast just as James and Alice had been. It is only with hindsight that I realize the futility of all that destructive anger. Fortunately, I was reconciled with Ada before her death, but in a way that merely adds to the grief.'

Rachael hastened to reassure Hannah that she would have no problems meeting and talking with Eleanor Rhodes.

* * *

James and Alice were studying a newspaper article when Patrick Finnegan entered their office. Although he was still the new boy within the Fisher Springs organization, Finnegan had already proved his worth many times over. Outside the banking hall, his genial, easy-going attitude to life had made him a firm favourite.

James glanced up from the paper. 'Good morning, Patrick,' he greeted the newcomer. 'Alice and I were just reading this.' He held up the broadsheet.

'It's about the work of an organization called the Imperial War Graves Commission. Apparently, they are trying to create some sort of order from the chaos in France and Belgium, giving the dead a proper burial place, documenting locations and creating decent cemeteries and so forth. With all the casualties, that's going to be a mountain of a job.'

Finnegan knew of James and Alice's loss, knew also about the work of the Commission, and was able to offer some constructive advice. 'My brother-in-law is involved with the Commission, so I have a bit of influence there, so to speak.' He eyed the couple speculatively. 'If you want me to find out anything specific, I could give my sister a call and get her to work on him. He's an idle bastard most of the time, but if she kicks him, he'll get moving.'

Alice in particular appreciated the delicate way Finnegan had approached the painful subject of Saul's death. She smiled at him. 'You're such a kind, thoughtful man, Patrick, you really should be married, you would make such a good husband.'

Finnegan grinned and winked at James. 'But you are already spoken for, Mrs Fisher,' he told her. 'Besides, I enjoy myself too much as a bachelor.'

'What he actually means,' James interpreted for Alice, 'is they won't tempt him into marriage until he can become a Mormon, then he can have as many wives as he wants.'

Finnegan shook his head sadly, his whole demeanour that of a man woefully misjudged. 'No fear,' he said. 'Think of all the mothers-in-law.'

Returning to the newspaper article, James told Finnegan a little of their plans. 'We came out here in 1898 and we have neither of us taken a holiday since. If we can locate Saul's grave we intend to go to France, see some of the country and visit our son's resting place.'

Finnegan's eyes darkened with sympathy. 'Leave it to me. I'll get some action for you.'

Finnegan was as good as his word. Within a month he was able to tell them, that Saul's grave had been located. Armed with this information, James and Alice were left with only one problem to overcome before proceeding with their scheme. They needed someone they could entrust the safety and wellbeing of their children to during their absence.

* * *

If Rachael carried any pre-conceived notion regarding Eleanor Rhodes, the appearance of the young woman dispelled them. Eleanor, she discovered, much as Hannah had predicted, was a gentle girl, pretty in a pale, blonde way. She was shy and obviously nervous of visiting Ada's mother. Hannah, with the active cooperation of Rachael, strived to put their visitor at her ease.

'I've brought a couple of paintings,' Eleanor told Hannah, 'which I would like you to have. I don't usually do portraits, but I felt compelled to paint these.'

Although she was renowned for her landscapes, the paintings demonstrated that Eleanor was equally talented in her portrayal of living subjects. The first was a portrait of Ada. It showed her seated at a table on a pavement outside a Parisian café. She was reading, a lock of hair had fallen across her forehead on which there was a frown of concentration. The genius of the portrayal was in Ada's left hand, which Eleanor had captured as Ada had gone to push her hair back. So lifelike was the depiction that the viewer could have been forgiven for expecting the hand to begin moving as they looked at the painting. 'It is the last thing I did before I left Paris,' Eleanor explained. 'Actually, I only did the sketch in Paris; I completed the painting after I returned to England to look after my mother.'

Eleanor caught Rachael's enquiring glance. 'My mother became ill just as the war started, in the spring of 1914 to be precise. I had lost my father some years earlier. My mother's nerves have always been poor and I think losing my father pushed her over the edge. Although her mind wandered, she had long periods of lucidity at the beginning. That actually made caring for her more difficult, as one never knew when she would become irrational. Gradually though, her condition worsened and she lapsed into her own, strange world. The odd thing was that throughout all this her body remained strong, right up to her first stroke, a couple of years ago. She died in the early part of last year and to be brutally honest I believe it was a release for both of us. That might sound callous but in cases like that, one grieves beforehand if you understand me.'

Before she unwrapped the second canvas, Eleanor turned to Hannah, apologetically. 'I had intended this for you alone, but that was before I learned about Rachael and little Mark. So, if I may, I will give it to Rachael, although I am sure you will all share it.'

With that, Eleanor slid the brown paper from around the painting and held it up for her audience to inspect. The background was a rural scene, the subject a young boy of twelve, possibly thirteen years of age. Dressed in white flannels, white shirt and sweater, the only colour was the bands at the neck and cuffs of the sweater and the vivid blue of the boy's eyes. Eleanor had caught the exact pigment of his suntanned complexion, the confident, easy manner, and the hint of athletic energy. He was smiling at the artist, laughter in his eyes and at his mouth. 'Sonny,' Hannah whispered, her eyes filled with tears.

Although both she and Rachael were initially upset by the paintings, they rallied to express their appreciation to the artist for the considerate nature of her gift. Eleanor's visit had only been planned for the day, but Hannah suggested she stay overnight before returning to York. Eleanor accepted the invitation gladly and over the evening meal she revealed some of her plans.

'I feel as if I have wasted so much time. Until Mother died, I had not touched a brush for three years. I feel I owe it to myself to make up for that lost time. There is one thing I have promised to do, however. I have set enquiries in motion to try to find Ada's grave. If and when I succeed, I plan to visit France and go there. I thought it would be good to have a proper stone for her, something personal. I believe she would like that and I wanted to consult you first, to get your approval of the scheme.'

Both Hannah and Rachael were deeply moved by Eleanor's plans and before she left Byland Crescent the following morning Hannah promised to write when she had given the matter due thought. It was, she assured Eleanor, only the wording itself she was debating.

After her departure, Hannah and Rachael were of one mind over the young artist. As Hannah remarked, there was one point in Eleanor's favour. 'She and Ada were so obviously happy together. It seems a strange thing to say, given the nature of the relationship, but if she made Ada happy, that makes me content. It also convinces me, despite the conventional way of looking at things, that they were absolutely right for one another.'

* * *

Simon Jones married Naomi Fleming in January of 1922. The wedding was a civil ceremony, the reasons being, as Simon told his mother, that neither he nor Naomi were churchgoers and that Naomi had been married previously, albeit widowed.

Neither of these was the real reason for restricting the ceremony to a civil one. When the couple were putting plans together for the wedding, Naomi suddenly came up with a stumbling block. Apart from the dubious passport with which she had entered the country in 1914, she had none of the paperwork required to confirm her identity. This was hardly surprising, as that identity was a totally fictitious one.

On mentioning this major hurdle to her fiancé, Naomi had been surprised how calmly he had taken the blow, which to her seemed an insurmountable obstacle. 'Don't worry about that, darling.' Simon had told her. 'I'll see what I can do.'

Whatever his plans were they were obviously bearing fruit with some speed, for he came home from work one day the following week to demand her date of birth. She supplied the information, a trifle mystified, his only comment that it would be as well if some of the facts were accurate doing nothing to enlighten her as to what he was up to.

She was more than a little startled ten days later when Simon entered the flat brandishing an envelope. He thrust it into her hands, demanding that she examine the contents and memorize them. She obeyed the instruction, to find inside, to her astonishment, a marriage certificate making the outrageous claim that Harold Fleming, a bachelor domiciled in Ruislip, had married Naomi Fleming (nee Crawley). Naomi Crawley's father Richard, a lithographic printer, had been one of the witnesses to the ceremony, Harold Fleming's father Brian, a sheet metal worker had been the other.

Also inside the envelope, Naomi found a birth certificate for the aforesaid Naomi Crawley. Her mother, Suzanne Crawley, she was intrigued to learn, had, before her marriage to Richard, rejoiced in the name of Suzanne Batty.

Bewildered, Naomi looked up from the papers. 'Who are these people?' she asked.

Simon grinned. 'No idea, I made them up.'

'But I've never been to Ruislip in my life. I don't even know where Ruislip is.'

Simon's grin, if possible, widened. 'It's in Surrey, but don't worry about it.' He pointed to the certificates. 'None of them has ever been to Ruislip either.'

Naomi was still bewildered. 'But Simon, where did you get these from?'

Simon's face took on an expression of extreme gravity and he glanced around as if in fear of eavesdroppers before he leaned forward and whispered confidentially, 'I broke into the Registry Office last night while you were asleep, I was disturbed as I was stealing the certificates and had to shoot my way out. This morning I filled in the details.'

Naomi clipped him on the head for this nonsense and a wrestling match ensued. Eventually Naomi forced the truth from him by methods he later claimed to be underhand. These involved tickling him until he was forced to tell her the exact version of how he came by the documents. 'The printing orders for the group are quite large. Before I took over each company within the group did its own ordering, but I argued we could get a better deal, both on price and service if we channelled it through one printer. I've got to know the boss of the company we use pretty well, so I simply asked him to do me a favour. I explained what I needed and he did the rest. The certificates are very convincing. I checked them against some genuine ones and I could not tell the difference. Despite that I think we ought to limit the number of times we use them. So if that means we only have a civil ceremony I hope you don't mind.'

Naomi was overjoyed, touched also by the forethought Simon had shown, for, producing a second envelope from his pocket, he showed her a birth certificate he had obtained for Joshua. With these details, he told Naomi, he thought he would be able to instigate adoption proceedings.

Their wedding, at the end of January, was Simon's first visit to the Registry Office. He thought it was the happiest day of his life, until he returned there at the end of April to register the birth of his daughter Daisy.

CHAPTER THIRTY-SEVEN

Robert Binks's career at Outlane Chemicals came to an inglorious end, the result of an unfortunate chain of coincidences, none of which he could have done anything to prevent. His father's decision to take a holiday earlier than usual was the first of these. In the absence of the family, Robert was left in charge of the house as well as being in temporary control of the business.

The second coincidence was a burst water pipe. It happened on Sunday night, at the end of the first week of his parents' holiday. As he was unable to arrange for a plumber, Robert took the sensible course of switching the water off at the main and going to bed. The following morning the plumber duly repaired the leak, but by the time he had finished it was almost midday.

On the Saturday prior to this, Clarence Barker had received another demand. Invoices from Phoenix Wools to HAC Scouring were failing to keep pace with the price of the blackmailer's silence. Clarence, searching for other avenues through which to divert funds, decided after a weekend of deep and troubled thought, that it was high time he took a closer interest in the activities of Outlane Chemicals. He rearranged his diary and embarked upon a surprise visit that Monday morning.

When Robert Binks walked into his office a little after midday, Clarence Barker was seated behind the desk studying a file that lay open on it. Although most of the contents were unintelligible to him, as they consisted of complicated scientific formulae, the title on the cover *Chemical Fertilizer Research Notes. Volume 3, Cereals*, and a page of figures detailing research expenditure, were only too clear.

Clarence glanced at the clock on the mantelpiece. The time was 12.27 p.m. Before Robert had chance to explain the reasons for his late arrival, Clarence Barker launched into a virulent attack. 'I'm not exactly certain why you seem to believe that company rules exist only for the obedience of other employees and do not apply to you. I have been waiting almost three hours for you to arrive, three hours might I remind you that I am paying you to work. Not only have you been absent all that time, quite without authority, but you have failed to inform anyone that you intended to arrive late. I appreciate that the telephone is a comparatively recent invention, but I would have thought that you would have mastered its intricacies by now.'

Robert winced at Barker's sarcasm, but before he had chance to explain, Clarence continued. 'Although your appalling timekeeping is in itself an offence, during your absence I have been doing a little research of my own. As a result of which I find, to my utter amazement that you have been engaged in expenditure of large amounts of money in areas that were strictly forbidden. Outlane Chemicals was set up to manufacture chemical dyes for the textile industry. Just that, nothing more. It was never invented to be used as a vehicle for you to indulge in such wild, hare-brained ideas as this.' Clarence gestured contemptuously at the open file.

'That is why I refused your father's request for funds. May I remind you of that, for it took place several months ago, but now I find you have continued with it. Your persistence in following this research is a flagrant defiance of that

288

refusal. As such it classes as a direct disobedience of my orders which I cannot and will not tolerate. Your actions leave me with no alternative but to dismiss you from the company's employment. Furthermore, should you be successful in obtaining another position, which I permit myself to doubt, you will have to do so without the benefit of a reference, as I would be unable, if requested, to vouch for your honesty, integrity or discipline.'

Less than ten minutes after he had entered the building, Robert Binks left it. During that time he had not spoken a word. However, his final act of disobedience left him grinning with pleasure. That pleasure was one of the memory of sight and sound. The sound of breaking bone as his fist landed squarely on Barker's nose, followed by the sight of the Managing Director of HAC sprawled, cowering on the office carpet, his eyes fearful in a distorted, bloodstained countenance, the snow white of his shirt liberally splashed with a bright crimson any dyer would have been proud to achieve.

* * *

The care and safety of their six children during their absence was a thorny problem for James and Alice Fisher. In the end the solution came from two sources, both close to home. James had mentioned their dilemma to Patrick Finnegan, by now a close confidante. The head of their banking division had been sympathetic, his practical suggestion going some way towards providing a solution.

'If you can get someone to look after the kids, I'll take care of the practical side of things. I can sort out household bills, clothing, pocket money and all the other domestic expenditure.'

It was a generous offer, for Finnegan was a busy man and with James and Alice away for six months, the extra responsibility would prove no sinecure. The second component to their solution came via an equally casual conversation, this one between Alice and the head of their newspapers division. Randolph Charles was an astute editor whom James had head-hunted to control their chain of regional newspapers. He was a colourful character, Australian born and bred, who delighted in recounting the gory and larcenous activities of his ancestors, who had arrived in the colony via the convict ships in the previous century.

On hearing of Alice's problem, Randolph had suggested she should speak to his sister and brother-in-law. Their daughter, he told Alice, had been a primary school teacher during the war. She had given up this work after her fiancé had been killed in France and was now at a loose end, having spent several years as governess to a family in Melbourne, until the children had grown old enough to go to school. She was twenty-six years old and, in Charles's opinion, more than capable of handling the Fisher's children.

Within a quarter of an hour of meeting her, James and Alice realized she was exactly what they had been searching for. Louise Bean was tall, athletically built, and strikingly handsome. Her spun-gold hair and vivid blue eyes betrayed her Nordic ancestry. She was softly spoken, yet her voice contained strength and character. Laughter was never far from her eyes or mouth. Old enough to act as a substitute mother to the younger children, she was young enough for Cissie and Ellen to regard her in the light of an elder sister. Philip, who at thirteen was developing a keen interest in girls, naturally fell in love with her on the spot.

The organization for the trip had been completed. Louise moved into the large house and commenced her duties, while at Fisher Springs, Patrick Finnegan was deputed to control their business empire while they were away.

'It's all quite straightforward,' James told the banker. 'You act like a board chairman. You preside over a meeting each month. The department heads report their figures to you in turn, then you kick their arse for not performing better. It works a treat.'

Finnegan grinned. He knew he was going to enjoy this. He had already been introduced to Louise Bean, his counterpart in the Fisher household. His eyes had sparkled in appreciation of her blonde good looks, but if his handshake had been fractionally firmer than strictly necessary or had lasted a second or so longer than might have been expected, only she was aware of it.

One precaution suggested by Finnegan came as a shock to both James and Alice. 'You ought to make a will each before you set off, if you haven't already done so. You've got a mighty big business here, one worth millions. Boats do sink, even in these less troubled times.'

James and Alice had looked at one another in astonishment. Neither of them had ever given a moment's thought to the idea of making a will. They rectified this omission prior to their departure, appointing Finnegan and Randolph Charles as executors together with their London solicitor Simon French. Once they had signed the documents, they forgot all about them.

* * *

The Silent One had been walking for so long it seemed like second nature to him. There had been breaks of course, periods of time when he had stopped walking for one reason or another. He needed money, mostly for food, or clothing. He refused to beg, as he had seen others do. He had watched them and the very act of asking for money seemed demeaning. So, he found work, often on a farm, whatever he could do to earn enough money to buy a coat, a shirt, a pair of boots, or a meal, according to his particular need. Once he had achieved his objective he set off once more, always walking, always heading for his destination, the goal he had set himself that spring morning so long ago. Two further springs had passed since then. He knew where he was heading but was unsure where that knowledge came from. He thought it might be from that locked part of his memory, the past that was still in darkness.

Ever since he had reached England he had been heading north. Even crossing the Channel had been difficult, for he had no papers or identification. He had managed it eventually when a crew member from one of the ferry boats had been injured while handling cargo at the French port. He had volunteered to take the injured man's place and once the voyage was over and the ship unloaded, he had simply walked ashore with the other members of the crew, straight past the Customs officials, who, busy with the passengers, had not spared them even a glance.

Perhaps when he reached *The Abbey* all would become clear. He had relied on this for so long that 'when I reach *The Abbey*' had become a sort of silent mantra that he repeated to himself. *The Abbey* would unlock those darkened recesses in his mind, the places he could no longer reach alone. Either *The Abbey*, or the people. Significant though *The Abbey* was, he knew that it was the people who really mattered. That knowledge was only part of the equation. He had been unable to fathom why those particular people were so important, more so than any others.

He was close now, that proximity raising his expectations and with it his sense of excitement. He had slept the previous night in a barn, courtesy of a farmer who had eyed the tramp with gruff sympathy. Something in his bearing had marked him out as trustworthy, overcoming the farmer's natural caution. In the morning the farmer had watched with interest as the tramp had washed meticulously at the pump in the yard, before carefully combing his long hair and beard. Minutes later, having replaced his soap, towel and comb in the dilapidated canvas bag he carried, the tramp knocked at the farmhouse door to bid the farmer farewell and express his gratitude for the shelter. To his surprise he was bidden to enter and invited into the kitchen, where a mug of steaming tea and a plate of bacon and eggs prepared by the farmer's wife awaited him.

When he departed, his canvas bag was slightly heavier, due to the loaf of bread and chunks of cheese that the couple had insisted on giving him. Two hours of brisk walking followed, then, as he mounted a long, shallow rise, he knew, beyond all doubt that round the next bend he would be greeted by his first sight of the abbey.

He strode forward, his pace quickening as the distance to the bend shortened. Then he was round it and there it was, exactly as he remembered it, exactly as he had painted it, time after time. He continued along the road, getting ever closer. Eventually he stopped, in the middle of the cluster of grey stone cottages, no more than half a dozen of them, barely enough to warrant the term hamlet, let alone village.

How long he remained there he could not be sure. He stationed himself directly in front of the ruined wall of the abbey. It was there he had positioned the people in the painting. He waited and waited, expecting what, he was uncertain. Enlightenment? Or perhaps at least an understanding of why he was there? Neither came to him. Everything was right, the abbey, the fields, the houses, yet nothing raised a flicker of memory. Then, with a dreadfully saddening sense of disappointment he realized why. Just as there had been in all of his destroyed paintings, the people were absent. Occasionally a villager would wander past, eying the tramp with mild curiosity. Once, a van wheezed asthmatically up the long hill into the village, its wake a cloud of dust from the un-metalled road. It was mid-summer and the heat caused vehicle and road to shimmer slightly in the haze. The van continued out of the village, but no one had alighted. These were not the people. The people, like his life, like the van, had moved on.

He turned away at last, his heart heavy with an indefinable grief. He had counted so much on what he would find at the abbey, so many questions he thought would have been answered. Now he felt rootless; rootless and alone. Alone and lost, for he had no idea where he would go now, what he would do now. Now was all he had however, for he had already lost the past and it seemed the future was also being closed to him.

He walked for several miles in blind uncertainty. On the hillside above him, etched into the earth, he saw the outline of a large white horse. He stared at it, wondering who had gone to the trouble of digging out such a figure and why it should seem vaguely familiar, but recognition would not come. He continued walking and wandered into a village, looking about it without interest. He was tired and needed time to recover from the bitterness of the morning's failure. Only a few yards down the long, straight village street he noticed an unlikely building for so rural a setting. It bore all the appearance of a blacksmith's but from the building alongside came the muted hum of machinery. The tramp looked at the sign bolted to the wall of the building. It indicated the workshop housed a craftsman, manufacturing furniture. Alongside the sign was a small, half-glazed door. In one of the panels a rough and ready sign had been fixed, the letters scrawled in an uneven hand on a piece of brown cardboard. 'Casual Labour Wanted. Apply Within.'

CHAPTER THIRTY-EIGHT

No major crises rocked the Fisher household during the absence of James and Alice. In the first weeks after their boat sailed, the younger children found it in themselves to indulge in a little self-pity at their desertion, but Louise soon noticed the symptoms of such attacks, whereupon the sufferer was given little leisure for such outbursts. Cissie, Ellen, and Philip took their parents departure far more stoically. Cissie had her reporter boyfriend to console her should she have felt lonely. Ellen, less worldly and more studious than her elder sister, relied on her books for solace, if any was needed. Philip, his emotions already in uproar as puberty beckoned insistently, found himself far too preoccupied to worry about James and Alice. A girl from his school, two years older than he, was making clear and unmistakeable signals that she wished to further their acquaintance. Philip however, who imagined himself in love with Louise, was torn between the two.

Louise had done nothing to encourage such feelings, but, recognizing the signs, was at pains to quash her young admirer's ardour without trampling too hard on his feelings. The running of such a large house and the attention needed by the children left Louise with little time for relaxation. She came to regard the frequent visits paid by Patrick Finnegan, who was taking his duties as administrative head of the household seriously, as her only chance to unwind.

Louise found the company of the young banker stimulating, in a way she had not experienced since the death of her beloved fiancé. Finnegan's attitude, that of a friend and colleague, was exactly what Louise needed. In their lively, enjoyable debates, Finnegan managed to convey, without expressing as much, that he found Louise extremely attractive. At one time she would have regarded such an attitude as mildly offensive, but such was not the case now. Finnegan, experienced in the ways of women, knew just how far to go and no further.

Soon Mr Finnegan and Miss Bean became Patrick and Louise, before much longer Louise was arranging the family's evening meal around Patrick's visits. This helped Patrick enjoy the children's company and check on their welfare without the need to curtail his visit by dashing back to town to dine. In pursuance of his promise of diligent watchfulness on behalf of James and Alice, Patrick was soon volunteering to accompany Louise and the family on their weekend outings.

Even the most expensive, well-maintained cars develop faults. Patrick and Louise had taken the children on a shopping expedition. It was evening when they returned, tired and hungry, to the house. Patrick stayed for dinner, during which the family was entertained to a pyrotechnic display, courtesy of a violent and sudden thunderstorm approaching from the west. All except for Louise, that is, for she feared and detested thunder and lightning. Heavy rains accompanied it and when Patrick attempted to start his car to return to town the vehicle refused to cooperate. It was Saturday night, and the nearest town was ten miles away and there would have been absolutely no chance of raising a mechanic. There was no other option. Patrick, drenched to the skin from his futile attempts to start the car with the starting handle, would have to stay the night.

Louise took control of the situation, in the way that only a schoolteacher could. 'Upstairs with you,' she ordered.

'Turn right, the second room along is a guest room. Strip off that wet clothing and get into a hot bath. You will find a bath robe hanging behind the door in that room and towels in the bathroom. Bring your wet clothes downstairs. I will be waiting in the kitchen with a hot drink. I'll set your clothes to dry while you're drinking it.'

Feeling somewhat like a naughty schoolboy, Patrick meekly agreed. The thunderstorm returned in the early hours of Sunday morning. Despite her brave face in front of the children earlier, Louise was petrified. As the storm grew nearer, she was unable to sleep, restless and afraid. Her fear turned into terror as the storm positioned itself almost directly over the house, each jagged flash of lightning, each reverberating crash of thunder increasing her sense of panic. Time after time, the lightning illuminated the night sky and the thunder rolled menacingly. A vivid flash and a sharp crack were Louise's breaking point. A scream of terror broke loose as she could stand it no longer.

Seconds later there was a knock on her door. Patrick was standing in the doorway, wearing the robe she had supplied. His hair was dishevelled, as one newly awoken from sleep. 'I heard you call out,' he explained apologetically. 'Are you okay? Can I get you anything?'

A fresh roll of thunder intensified her alarm. She took Patrick's hand and pulled him inside the room. 'Please, I hate thunder, please don't leave me?' she begged him.

He lay beside her on the bed. Her head was buried in his chest as she sobbed her terror away, her arms wrapped tightly about him for comfort. He could smell the clean, fresh scent of her hair, feel every contour of her athletic body pressed trembling against his own. Despite his noblest intentions he could feel his awakening arousal.

Louise became aware of it also. She opened her eyes wide and gazed at him for a long moment, then, as if she had come to a decision, she slid her hand inside his robe. They stared at one another briefly then her nightdress joined his robe on the bedroom floor. It was almost dawn when they finally slept, exhausted, in each other's arms. By that time the storm had long since ceased. It had abated before the storm of their passion.

* * *

The dismissal of Robert Binks had given Clarence Barker an idea. All he needed was to engineer the resignation of Robert's father, Charlie Binks. As he waited for Charlie to return from holiday, Clarence began preparatory work. Research, as Robert had so clearly demonstrated, could mean anything, so Clarence instructed his solicitor to form another company, using the same format that had worked so well at Phoenix Wools, the phantom supplier he already owned. The new company would be able to invoice Outlane Chemicals for fictitious research work in the same way as Phoenix Wools invoiced non-existent bales of wool to HAC Scouring. All Clarence needed to do was to free himself of Charlie Binks.

In the event it proved easier than Clarence had imagined. Only a few minutes after 9 a.m. on the morning Charlie was scheduled to return to work at Outlane Chemicals, he marched instead, unannounced, into Clarence Barker's office at Manor Row. The door slammed against the wall as Charlie, quivering with rage, stood in front of Clarence's desk.

'You stupid, ignorant bastard,' Charlie began. 'You couldn't manage your way out of a paper bag. I go away for a few days and you have the nerve to interfere with my business. Why couldn't you keep your nose out? Robert was late because of circumstances at home, the research he was doing would have led to some very lucrative contracts, but you had to intervene, show you were boss, didn't you. The truth of the matter is, it is you who are not fit to be in control of this business. No wonder Michael Haigh left. I was prepared to give you the benefit of the doubt while you left Outlane Chemicals alone. But I see now that Michael was right all along. You can't be trusted. Without that trust there can be no future for me with HAC. So, you can take this as my resignation.' Charlie strode towards the door, paused and delivered one last broadside. 'You are going to regret your stupid arrogance, far sooner than you realize. I'll make you pay for it. None of this would have happened if Sonny had been here. You haven't heard the last of it, though. You will live to regret the day you crossed swords with Robert and me.'

Most of the HAC staff heard the monologue through the open door. Not only did they hear it, but they enjoyed it into the bargain. Clarence's unsightly appearance, sporting a nose that was clearly broken and two black eyes that were now tinged with most of the colours of the rainbow, had caused much speculation in the office following the departure of Robert Binks a week earlier. Their enjoyment now was a consequence of their liking for the Binks family and their loathing of Clarence.

Clarence sat for a few minutes after Charlie Binks had stormed out. He puzzled for a little while over Charlie's closing remarks then dismissed them as the ravings of a bitter and angry man. It had obviously been pure bluster. He, Clarence, was now in sole charge of the whole of the HAC Group and could do whatever he wanted with it.

Less than three hours later, Charlie Binks took part in another meeting only a few streets away. At this one however, the atmosphere was relaxed and cordial. All four participants had one thing in common. A dislike, amounting to hatred, of Clarence Barker, coupled with a wish to do him as much harm as possible.

The other parties to the meeting were Charlie's son Robert, Michael Haigh and Simon Jones. Robert had set the meeting up during the latter part of his father's holiday, after a telephone call to Charlie's hotel in Morecambe.

Charlie began by outlining the reasons behind their departure from Outlane Chemicals. Robert told them frankly of his interview with Barker, culminating in the punch with which he had floored Clarence. Simon reached across and shook Robert by the hand at this point, while Michael commented dryly that Robert had made them jealous, as they had all wanted to do that for years.

If there had been any doubt about either Michael or Simon's willingness to fund a new company, as Charlie and Robert suggested, Charlie dispelled this when he displayed his trump card. He invited them to inspect a document he had brought with them. He passed it across the desk. Michael scanned it closely before passing it to Simon who read it through, and raised his eyebrows, before returning it to Michael with a nod of his head. Haigh fingered the document then looked directly at Charlie. 'Let me get this straight. If I interpret the wording correctly, this agreement was made between Philip Ackroyd and Albert Cowgill, acting as directors of HAC and your father, Harry, acting on your behalf. It states, again if I am reading it correctly, that in the event that you leave Outlane Chemicals, all patent rights in respect of any compounds registered during your term of employment there, revert to you?'

Charlie nodded cheerfully, a smile twitched at the edges of his lips.

'Furthermore,' Haigh continued, 'none of those compounds can be produced without your written approval and payment of royalties to you?'

Charlie nodded once more. 'So that means,' Haigh summarized, 'that if you revoke your permission, Outlane Chemicals ceases trading and, in effect, is out of business?'

Charlie Binks's expression became momentarily grotesque as he attempted to combine a vigorous nod with an ear-to-ear grin.

* * *

The decision to enter the chemical industry was almost the last executive act Michael Haigh conducted for WPF&D for some time. Michael was dampened by a brisk shower while working in the garden with Connie, he thought no more of it, but continued working until the task was complete. He developed a slight temperature overnight but ignored it and went to work as usual. By lunchtime he was feeling definitely off-colour and in the middle of the afternoon told Simon he was going home early, a most unusual event. It was the last the office would see of him for several months.

Connie phoned the doctor later that evening as Michael's temperature continued to rise. The following morning, she phoned the office. She warned Simon Jones to be prepared for a prolonged absence. The diagnosis, as yet unconfirmed, was suspected bronchial pneumonia. In his absence, control of WPF&D fell upon Simon. His first task was to report Michael's illness to Fisher Springs via telegram. The reply conferred parental blessing on Simon, who reported the fact to Connie Haigh, adding that instructions from Fisher Springs were that, "Unless Mr Haigh is fully recovered when he returns to work; kick him out again."

It was Simon Jones, therefore, who supervised the setting up of the new chemicals division, which, in tribute to their parent company, he named Springs Chemical Company Ltd. Charlie and Robert were appointed to the board of the new company, with Michael Haigh as Chairman and Simon as Secretary and Finance Director. The first board decision was to instruct solicitors to write to Outlane Chemicals, with a copy to the Manor Row offices of HAC, withdrawing permission to produce any dyes covered by the patents taken out by Charlie Binks.

Once that had been set in motion, Simon set out the terms of reference for the new company's trading activities. Charlie, he suggested, should devote his time and energies to setting up production of dyes based on his existing patents. At the same time Robert should visit all Outlane's customers to inform them of the changed situation and to offer Springs Chemical services. After that, his time would be free to develop other products. A budget for research would be agreed once specific products had been identified and costed. Simon's brief to Charlie and Robert was succinct. 'We want you to identify potential growth areas and concentrate on them. This company will get off to a flying start by virtue of Charlie's dyes. However, that is only a start. We want to keep the momentum going, increase it all the time. That means diversifying away from textile products.'

The look of anticipatory delight on Robert's face was reminiscent of a cat left alone with a bowl of cream.

* * *

James and Alice enjoyed the long sea voyage but felt confined on board ship. It was only in the latter part of the crossing, as they were nearing the continent of Europe, that they began to relax. They had become so accustomed to the regime of work and home that the pursuit of leisure was an art they had to learn. France afforded them the opportunity to do this and they grasped it eagerly. They spent a week exploring Paris before heading south. They stopped for a long time in the Loire valley. James had read a considerable amount about the wine growing regions of France and was struck by the similarity of the climate to that of parts of Australia. When he mentioned this to Alice, she teased him, suggesting that the trip was a cover-up for him exploring the development of another industry. James denied this, but nevertheless made copious notes of all he saw and was told. He determined to do a little research on his return home.

They continued south and east, a meandering holiday that gave them ample scope for the relaxation they sought. Eventually however it was time for their final mission, the pilgrimage that had brought them thousands of miles to visit the battlefields where Saul had fought. The countryside, still pitted with the unmistakeable scars of war, was beginning to become clothed in a merciful camouflage of green.

Eventually they came to the spot itself. They stood; each mumbled a message for their son, assuring him of their undying love for him, that he was remembered, remembered and cherished, and that they would carry him in their hearts forever. Alice placed a simple wreath on the grave, her eyes blinded by tears. James laid a hand on the simple cross, as if it were his son's shoulder. 'Farewell, Saul, my dear boy,' he told him. 'Sleep in peace.'

Together, hand in hand as they had been all their lives, James and Alice Fisher walked slowly away. They left behind, not only their son, but the memory of their youth.

* * *

In a cemetery, eighty miles away, a fair-haired woman inspected a recently erected headstone, its inscription sharp and new. A gentle autumn rain began to fall as she read once more the words she had agreed with Hannah Cowgill.

> *Nurse Ada Cowgill*
> *aged 31 years*
> *Who gave her life, saving lives*
> *Rest in the Arms of the Lord*

Softly, Eleanor Rhodes began to weep.

CHAPTER THIRTY-NINE

The Silent One was disappointed when he had to leave. The job had been a temporary one, as cover for a permanent employee who had injured his back in a fall. They had been glad to hire him, for their business was exacting and labour intensive. He had stayed in an outhouse connected to the village pub, two doors away from the workshop. The landlord had been uncertain at first, but reasoned that if they trusted him at the workshop he must be honest enough. Besides which, there was nothing worth stealing in the outhouse.

The tramp stayed for two weeks, until the employee returned, his back injury recovered. The tramp collected his wages, looked around the small workshop for the last time, drinking in the fresh, clean smell of newly cut oak, remembering fondly the satin-like finish of the newly planed timber. His sense of sadness as he left the building was almost as keen as that he had felt at the abbey.

He collected his meagre possessions and attempted to pay the landlord for his lodging. The innkeeper waved away the fee, arguing that the tramp had not used any of the pub's facilities, except for a couple of straw bales to sleep on and some water from the pump to wash in. Each meal he had taken at the inn had been paid for at the time, so no money was owed. Strangely, this heightened the tramp's reluctance to leave.

The landlord watched the departing figure with sympathy. Whatever the cause of the tramp's problems, it was certainly not drink, for in the time he had spent there he had drunk nothing but water, or the occasional glass of ginger beer.

It was late in the afternoon when the tramp arrived in the sleepy little market town of Thirsk. Summer was turning rapidly to autumn, as evidence of which a steady downpour added to his misery. Seeking shelter from the rain, he stood for a while in a shop doorway on the north side of the marketplace. The shop had no window display as such, merely a selection of advertising posters. He was still undecided what to do next and, as the rain showed no sign of abating, he turned to read them.

They were advertising holidays. As he moved to one side to allow a customer access to the shop, another poster came into his line of sight. The name of the town caught his eye at once. He stared, transfixed by the name. It stirred something in his memory, but exactly what that something was, he was unsure.

He knew from experience he would have to walk. The rain had eased at last, so he made his way out of the town. A signpost informed him that his destination lay a little more than forty miles away. By his reckoning he should reach it in three days, given good walking weather.

* * *

Patrick Finnegan sat in the boardroom of Fisher Springs, presiding over his final monthly departmental meeting before James and Alice returned. The figures from all sectors of the business, including those cabled through from their international division, were excellent. As the meeting came to a close the various delegates left, with parting words of thanks for his help over the preceding months. Eventually only Randolph Charles remained.

Aware that many still regarded him as a newcomer within the Group, Patrick had made Randolph his sounding board for many policy decisions. The newspaperman's advice had been astringent but helpful. It was not about business, however, that Charles spoke. 'Now, young Patrick,' he began with a grin, 'What's all this I've been hearing about you and that niece of mine?'

'What do you mean?' Patrick asked, with an air of innocence that would have fooled no one.

'I mean that when she visited her folks last week her mum and dad reckoned she had a sparkle in her eye and a spring in her step she hasn't had for many years. They didn't need to ask the reason, for all she said was "Patrick this" or "Patrick that" or "Patrick says" or "Patrick thinks". Anyway, that's only the half of it. I bumped into Cissie Fisher in town yesterday and she told me you've become a regular house guest over there. She told me there was a lot of movement during the night and that you've developed the ability to sleep in a bed without disturbing the sheets. So come on. What do you have to say about that?'

The final part was pure invention on Charles's part, but it was convincing enough to fool Finnegan and reduce his conversational skills to virtually zero. 'I . . . er . . . I . . .' he mumbled.

'I hope you're going to make an honest woman of her?' Charles persisted.

'I . . . er . . . yes, if she'll have me,' Finnegan replied weakly.

'Oh, she'll have you all right, I'll bet my boots on that,' Charles asserted confidently.

'I hope to goodness you're right,' Finnegan breathed.

He had made the decision over a week ago but was delaying popping the question until James and Alice returned. The realization had been growing on him steadily over the weeks and months. Never, for all his experience with women had Patrick met one whose attitude to life matched his own as Louise did. For the first time he was with a girl whose passionate nature was as strong as his own and who was not afraid to express her urges. Her robust, earthy sense of humour equalled, indeed surpassed his own at times, but that was by no means all. She was as caring as she was passionate, as tender as she was strong. For the first time in his life, Patrick Finnegan was truly, deeply in love. If he needed anything to reinforce that view, it was the reluctance with which he parted from her and the keenness with which he looked forward to their next meeting.

* * *

For several weeks Connie had been uncertain as to whether Michael would survive the devastating attack of pneumonia. He had pulled through eventually, but the illness had left him extremely debilitated. Now he was in the convalescent stage and their doctor had advised a change of scene. 'Take him away from this damp West Riding air and the smoke from all those mill chimneys,' he had suggested. 'Not too far, the effects of a long journey would be very bad for him. Take him to the coast and let him get some clean fresh, sea air into his lungs. You have relatives at the coast do you not?'

'My mother lives in Scarborough,' Connie had replied.

'Ideal,' the doctor enthused. 'It has a bracing climate, not too cold, exactly right for him. Add some good home cooking to build him up. Just what the doctor ordered,' he grinned.

Their arrival in the resort was welcomed by one and all. Rachael and Hannah loved to see the Haigh family descend, for the big house at Byland Crescent echoed to the laughter and games of children once more. Mark and his new playmate Jennifer were in their seventh heaven and even the servants enjoyed the liveliness of company.

True to the doctor's prediction the sea air and the plentiful, wholesome food supplied at Byland Crescent began to work a gradual improvement in Michael. As August slipped into September, he began to talk of a return to work in the near future. Connie, however, soon put a dampener on any such wild ideas.

* * *

There is a crossroads outside Bradford, on the high moors above Queensbury, close to the Raggalds Inn. There, when the wind blows, it howls across the open moorland, while the valleys on either side might be suffering no more than a stiff breeze. When it is accompanied by wet weather, the rain falls horizontally, driven on the wind, as if reluctant to hit the ground. It is a dangerous road on which to drive, even if one has not partaken of the hospitality on offer in the inn.

In the early hours of the morning a reveller emerged from the inn. This was far later than the licensing laws permitted the inn should be open, but in so remote a place the law relating to such matters was interpreted liberally. He had been inside the hostelry since early the previous evening, by all accounts. He climbed into his car with the intention of driving back to Bradford. He was in no fit condition to drive a motor car, but it was raining heavily and he was in no condition to walk either.

The rain swept across the moor as he emerged from the car park onto the road, far too hard for the single, short bladed windscreen wiper to cope with. The car, a powerful one for its day, had reached a speed of approximately forty-five miles per hour when it reached the crossroads, where it came to an abrupt halt. It came to a halt because the bonnet of the car was buried in one of the dry-stone walls that are a feature of the countryside in that region. The driver, unchecked by any safety device, was thrown against the windscreen by the collision. The unyielding stone of the wall had driven the engine block back towards the passenger compartment, where the steering column had pinioned the driver's chest, causing massive internal injuries. Whether or not these would have proved fatal was immaterial, for the jagged glass from the broken windscreen had severed the carotid artery in the driver's neck.

Two hours passed before the alarm was raised, too late for the driver, who had been dead since the impact.

News of the accident featured heavily in the local paper the following evening. Clarence Barker read the report with only passing interest. The identity of the dead man had not yet been made public, obviously to give the police chance to inform the next of kin. Clarence moved on to read other news items; he had enough worries of his own.

No sooner had Charlie Binks departed from Outlane Chemicals than Clarence had received a solicitor's letter. The gist of it was to withdraw permission for the production of dyes covered by patents in Charlie Binks's name. The letter listed the relevant products and upon enquiry, Clarence discovered to his fury that they represented the whole range of Outlane Chemicals' dyes. The company existed in name alone.

HAC's salesmen had been placed in an invidious position by this event. Almost all their customers had been in the habit of buying their dyes from Outlane Chemicals. When stocks ran out, as they did very swiftly, those customers had been forced to turn to other suppliers. Many had gone to Springs Chemicals, the newly formed subsidiary of WPF&D. Some of them, angry at being so badly let down, had gone to the extreme lengths of cancelling substantial orders for wool. Others, while not going so far, had made it plain that in future, WPF&D would be their first port of call.

Clarence was angry, angry and afraid. All he had worked for, schemed for, plotted and connived for, seemed to be slipping from his grasp even as he achieved it and he could see no way to remedy the situation. Without the profits from Outlane Chemicals the Group results would soon look extremely shaky. HAC Scouring figures had already been adversely affected by Clarence's need to siphon off funds to pay the blackmailer. In desperation, he had been forced to write himself a cheque to meet the latest demand. There had been no other solution, but in his innermost heart Clarence realized it was the beginning of the end and without some miraculous intervention, all would soon be lost.

* * *

Dr Richard Miller studied Rachael as she moved amongst her patients. He had been working at the hospital over a year when he was introduced to Sister Cowgill. She had taken over the duties of a colleague who had retired to raise a family. That had been ten months ago. Miller had been extremely taken with the new Sister and time had merely intensified that feeling. Sadly, he felt he was getting nowhere with her. She was polite enough, friendly, cheerful and efficient, but purely professional. Whenever Richard tried to move their conversation onto a personal level, she quietly but firmly returned it to medical matters. The rebuff was gently delivered, which did nothing to soften the impact.

Hospital gossip being what it was, Richard knew that Rachael had been widowed by the war and that she had a young son. Neither fact deterred him, any more than the equally strong rumour that she was the heiress to a considerable fortune. Richard sighed, for he knew he would have to let fate take its course. He was a great believer in fate. Fate had enabled him to survive the war when many around him had been killed.

CHAPTER FORTY

The tide had receded to low water level, leaving the sand flat, firm and even. The little boy marched confidently to the middle of the beach and pitched his set of wickets, bought for his birthday. The two women watched indulgently as he carefully paced out his own interpretation of twenty-two yards. He handed the ball to his mother and requested that his grandmother keep wicket. 'Is my bowling not good enough for you, Mark?' the boy's grandmother laughed.

'You spin it too much,' Mark replied with all the seriousness of a five-year-old.

The game commenced to the mutual enjoyment of the players and the few spectators. The majority of these were seagulls, it was October and the south beach was deserted apart from a few hardy souls, it was a chilly day.

It must have been uncomfortably cold for the tramp, but the man, his eyes gathered in a frown of concentration, showed no inclination to move as he watched from a distance. He was a man of indeterminate age. It was difficult to tell beneath a long shaggy mop of unkempt brown hair, sprinkled, as was his equally untidy beard, with occasional strands of silver. What was it about what they were doing? It seemed familiar. The tramp knew that he ought to recall it.

He gave up the attempt. He didn't like remembering things. He had tried it before but when he did remember it brought the nightmares on. He didn't want the nightmares back.

The ball had rolled to the tramp's feet after a particularly fine hit to leg. The tramp stooped stiffly and picked it up, then handed it to the small boy, who had run to retrieve the outcome of his fine stroke. As he passed it over, the tramp muttered a few words of encouragement. The minute he did so he wished he had kept silent. That was his rule. Stay silent, stay clear of trouble. The thought disturbed him and he got up from his bench and moved off.

The small boy walked back across the beach, puzzling over what he'd heard the funny man say. 'Grandmama,' he said to the wicketkeeper, 'that man said something strange.'

'What man?' his grandmother asked in mild alarm.

'That one on the bench.' He pointed across towards the promenade. 'Oh, he's gone now. He was sitting there, on that bench. He had long hair and a beard. He gave me the ball back then said something odd.'

'What was that?' Mark's grandmother was definitely uneasy.

'He said, "Good shot, Sonny, but watch out for the leg breaks". What does that mean?'

Hannah almost reeled with shock. 'He said Sonny! Mark are you sure he said Sonny, you couldn't have mistaken it?'

'No, Grandmama, he definitely said Sonny. Why, what does it mean?' Some of his grandmother's alarm had transferred to the boy.

'I don't know, Mark, I really don't know.' Hannah's brow was furrowed as in thought, or possibly pain.

As they walked back to Byland Crescent, Hannah and Rachael discussed Mark's strange encounter. 'It must be pure coincidence, Mother.' Rachael had fallen into the habit of addressing Hannah thus, which pleased both ladies.

'It may well be,' Hannah conceded, 'but for the reference to leg breaks. My father used to torment Sonny when he was Mark's age, by bowling him leg breaks that he couldn't hit. I remember Sonny getting so frustrated by it, but determined to master them in the end, which he did.'

'What is a leg break?' Rachael asked.

'I have absolutely no idea. The point is, it is quite normal to refer to a small boy as "Sonny", but why would a complete stranger talk to young Mark of all people about leg breaks?'

* * *

The boy and *The Abbey*, how were they connected? He tried to think, but he didn't understand. The few passers-by on the promenade that late autumn afternoon saw only a tramp, roughly dressed, muttering away to himself as he shambled along the sea front towards the castle.

He wanted to remember but he was scared. The boy had not been before *Then*, of that he was certain. So how was he connected to *The Abbey*? *Then* still scared him too much to dwell on it, even though the nightmares had receded. He sometimes felt he would never unravel the mystery of *Then*, what came before it and what had happened after it. He remembered *The Place*; that was easy for it held no terrors. He remembered the journey, the long trek from leaving *The Place*, but much of what had gone before was still locked in a part of his brain he could not, dared not reach. Memory was patchy and confused. He had found *The Abbey*, but it had not been what he wanted. He did remember that, the small village, the ruined cloister exactly as he had painted it. He remembered also, the disappointment when he had realized that this was not what he had been searching for. Then the expectation when he had reached the town of Thirsk and seen the poster.

He had no clear idea why, but when he had seen the poster he had known he had to come to Scarborough. This had not worried him. He had not known why he had ended up in that small town, why he had been compelled to visit *The Abbey*, why he had painted it time after time.

It was almost as if his mind was making connections. But were they the right connections, or was some short circuit

313

sending him on fruitless journeys to meaningless places? To the Abbey; to Scarborough. When he reached them, nothing triggered more than a flicker of memory.

Now he had reached the seaside resort and the confusion and disappointment were just as great. Parts of the town seemed familiar, in some hazy, undefined way, but there was no startling revelation, nothing to convince him that Scarborough had been any less of a wild goose chase. He clung to the hope that whatever had drawn him to this coastal town was still to be discovered.

He gave up the struggle and concentrated on finding a refuge for the night. Scarborough was a cold, inhospitable place for a vagrant at that time of the year. Tomorrow he would try to fathom the mystery of what had brought him here. Tonight he must concentrate on keeping warm and safe.

Ironically, it was the warning of impending danger that proved to be his undoing. The eastern coasts of Britain are prone to sudden, unpredictable banks of fog, dense and impenetrable, that can form, even on the brightest of sunny days. Scarborough is particularly susceptible to these. Locally they are known as sea frets.

As the tramp climbed the narrow, winding path towards the castle, a bank of low cloud began forming over the headland at the extremity of the south bay. The castle stands sentinel between the resort's twin bays. A monument to the town's ancient importance as a defensive outpost and trading port, the castle had long been abandoned as a fortification and was merely an added attraction for summer visitors.

Directly below the castle, in his office alongside the quay, the harbour master watched the bank of fog rolling inexorably across the bay. Soon, he knew, he would need to activate the fog warnings.

On the hilltop above, the late afternoon became suddenly darker, colder, and clammier. Before the tramp realized his peril, visibility dropped to zero as the fog enveloped him, obliterating the narrow path. He had been walking briskly until that moment, heading for the castle itself. There, he thought he might find some shelter from the chill of the autumn night. Although Scarborough welcomed visitors, the comfort and warmth of its many hotels and boarding houses were reserved for those prepared to pay. Cautiously he inched his way forward, uncertain whether he was keeping to the path or straying from it.

The mournful booming of a fog-horn is a disturbing sound even at a distance, close to, reflected and amplified by the fog, it was terrifying. His nerve broken by the sudden cacophony of sound; the tramp turned away from the noise. He had only taken one step when his foot, instead of landing on the grit of the path, came in contact with the damp, slippery grass of the hillside. He stumbled two paces then slipped once more, this time, unable to regain his balance, he tumbled, headfirst down the face of the cliff.

He felt a sharp pain in his arm as it made contact with a rock, before consciousness left him as his head came in contact with another, larger boulder. He had no way of knowing that the stone had saved him from far more grievous injury. He lay unconscious against it. Below him the cliff plunged three hundred feet towards the sea and the rocks below. He lay there until early the following morning when an elderly but sharp-eyed local resident walked his dog along the path by the side of the castle. The dog, a Jack Russell terrier, barked loudly at something lying further down the hillside. The old man peered cautiously over the edge. The sea fret had vanished as quickly as it had arrived. He saw the body lying sprawled on the cliff face and hurried to raise the alarm.

CHAPTER FORTY-ONE

In Bradford, the solicitor fingered the envelope on his desk. He looked at the covering letter and read the instruction his client had left once more.

"In the event of my sudden death, in violent or unexplained circumstances, this letter is to be delivered to the criminal investigation department of Bradford Police, for the attention of a senior officer."

On the face of it the instructions were clear enough, but the solicitor still hesitated. His client had died suddenly, that was certainly true. The cause of death however was not apparently mysterious. A car crash while under the influence of alcohol could hardly be classed as mysterious. It was certainly a violent end, but hardly in the way his client had meant. That being the case, his dilemma was whether to take the envelope to the police or not.

By virtue of their profession, most solicitors are cautious souls. In deciding that it was better to be safe than sorry, he was merely conforming to type. He called his clerk and instructed him to make an appointment for him with a senior CID officer.

* * *

Samuel Clayton was twenty-eight years old, relatively young for the rank of Detective Inspector. Casualties amongst the police force had been heavy during the war, more so than most other professions. In addition to the many who failed to return from the trenches, there was a rush to retirement by elderly officers who had stayed on beyond their allotted term owing to the desperate shortage of men.

Sam Clayton had survived almost unscathed and had benefited from the gaps in police ranks. His promotions had been little short of spectacular and many of his colleagues had predicted he would reach the very top of their profession. He was ambitious enough, confident of his own ability to tackle the most difficult of cases.

Sam eyed the solicitor with interest. The man's clerk had merely stated that the solicitor had a letter to deliver. His opening remark, that it was a 'communication from beyond the grave' had intrigued him. The solicitor passed the envelope and covering letter across the desk.

Sam read the covering letter with growing curiosity. When he had finished, he tapped the unopened envelope on the desk. 'Do you have any idea what is in this?' he asked.

The solicitor shook his head. 'My client had written and sealed it before he brought it to me. All I know is what is in the instructions.'

'Well, let's find out, shall we?' Sam slit open the envelope and removed the contents, which proved to consist of two, closely typewritten sheets. The second sheet had been signed and witnessed at the foot of the page, with the seal of a firm of London solicitors affixed. Sam began to read.

This is the sworn statement and confession of me, Arthur Bilton, resident at Flat 1, No. 4 Ashburton Road, Bradford, in the County of West Yorkshire.

I confess that since the year 1919 I have been guilty of the crime of blackmail. As such; being in fear of my life I confess these facts in the knowledge that if my identity becomes known to my victim he will seek to destroy me, therefore, should this letter come into the possession of the police, I have taken this step to identify and seek to have my killer brought to justice, not merely for my murder, but for the other crimes I herewith accuse him of having committed.

First, the circumstances leading to my crime.

In the service of my country, I served throughout the war as a private in the King's Own Yorkshire Light Infantry. During July 1917, while fighting near Passchendaele, I witnessed the murder of an English officer, one Major Ogilvie, in cold blood by an English soldier.'

The statement went on to give further details about the dead officer, including the location of his grave. Sam Clayton looked up for a moment, an expression of distaste on his face, before he resumed reading.

I turn now to the death of James Watson. As far as I am aware when writing this, no identification of his body has been made, probably because Jimmy had no relatives. I refer to the Murder on the Moors case, featured so luridly in the press. Jimmy was also in my regiment but was invalided out with shellshock. He was unable to find work and down on his luck when I bumped into him, quite by chance. I gave him a job as a handyman and errand boy and used him to collect the blackmail money on my behalf. He was doing that when he was murdered.

I was able to keep a careful and discreet watch over my victim because I took the flat below him for that very purpose. He murdered Major Ogilvie and also murdered Jimmy Watson. He lives at Flat 2, No.4 Ashburton Road, Bradford, his name is Clarence Barker and he is Managing Director of HAC Group, the big textile firm.

I examined the body of Major Ogilvie. I was able to do this because I was one of the burial detail that day. You will find the bullet still inside him, which should prove he was shot with a British rifle. Added to which Barker probably still has in his possession the British Service revolver he used to shoot Jimmy.

Barker has killed twice and will not hesitate to kill again. I realize I have been wicked and wrong in my actions, which have brought about the death of my friend and comrade Jimmy Watson, but Barker is a contemptible worm and a coward who deserved all he got.

Sam raised his eyes from the document. The solicitor was watching him, a look of expectation on his face. Sam smiled apologetically. 'I'm afraid I cannot show you this document. It contains allegations concerning two murders. It identifies the person who allegedly committed the crimes and, if these allegations are correct, that person will face capital charges.'

* * *

When James and Alice Fisher returned home, they received a few surprises, none of them unpleasant. The first of these came as their children rushed from the house to greet them, in various degrees of excitement. Alice looked up at the veranda. Louise was standing there watching with quiet approval. Alice nudged James and gestured towards the house. Standing alongside Louise, his arm about her waist, was Patrick Finnegan.

'I was going to ask her after you got back, but I couldn't wait.' Finnegan confessed to James. 'If you still need Louise to take care of the kids, we thought she could continue, even after we got married. Now you two are back you don't need her to live in.'

'I'll talk to Alice about it,' James promised. 'Naturally, we're both delighted for the pair of you. It's time you settled down anyway, if only so the mothers of young girls in the area can get some sleep. How are things at the office?'

'Couldn't be better,' Finnegan replied. 'Every section is reporting good figures. Randolph's bought another newspaper business and he's working on a new project, which he's being very mysterious about. The MD in England,

Michael Haigh has been very ill, but last I heard he's on the mend and should make a full recovery. From what the boys at International tell me, his deputy Simon Jones has been doing really well in Haigh's absence. Oh, by the way, they've opened a chemical plant over there as well. All the details are on your desk.'

When James and Alice reached the office, they spent a day poring over the mass of information and paperwork that had accumulated during their absence. They were shocked by the serious nature of Michael Haigh's illness but heartened that he was on the road to recovery. They were impressed by the reports submitted by Simon Jones, and James was particularly gleeful on reading about the demise of Outlane Chemicals at the expense of Springs Chemical Co.

* * *

It was a few weeks later as Clarence Barker was finishing his meal when there was a knock on the door. Two tall, heavily set men stood there. 'Clarence Barker?' the elder of them enquired.

Clarence nodded, instantly fearful.

'Clarence Barker,' the man's voice took on an official tone, 'we have a warrant for your arrest in connection with the murder of one James Watson. I must caution you that you are not obliged to say anything, but that anything you do say will be taken down and may be used in evidence against you.'

The following morning, when staff at all the HAC group companies arrived for work, they were shocked to find their offices already open, while a team of detectives was at work examining the books of each department.

CHAPTER FORTY-TWO

'Three new patients for you this morning, Rachael,' the night Sister, Rachael's counterpart, reported the changes as she handed over at the end of her shift.

'There's an Edward Jackson; suspected heart attack. Old Mr Pearson is back with his appendix.'

'Not again!' Rachael exclaimed. Old Mr Pearson and his grumbling appendix were regular visitors to the ward.

'I'm afraid so. The third one is an unidentified tramp, brought in a couple of hours ago. He fell off the cliffs close to the castle and has a broken arm, a few cuts, bruises to the head, and suspected concussion. We bathed him and tidied him up a bit with a pair of scissors, but he hasn't said a word. Those are the new cases, the rest are pretty much as you left them yesterday. Doctor Miller said he would pop in about 10 a.m., probably just to drink tea and look into your eyes.'

Richard Miller arrived much earlier than that, while Rachael was still checking her patients. He waited for her to finish, whiling away the time reading, with some fascination, the case notes of Mr Pearson and his grumbling appendix.

Rachael had almost finished her tour of inspection when she reached the bed occupied by the tramp. She glanced at the sleeping man, of whom little was visible with his untidy mop of hair and beard. She let him sleep, concentrating on the charts hanging on the foot of the bed. She looked up from them, to see the man had turned and opened his eyes and was watching her, frowning slightly, staring.

Rachael looked at the man, his tanned skin bruised, his appearance drawn and unkempt, despite the efforts of the nursing staff. She smiled at him, but before she had time to ask how he was feeling, the tramp spoke.

In a firm, clear voice he stated, 'Graham, that's a bloody silly name for a girl.'

Rachael Cowgill collapsed to the floor in a dead faint.

'Sister Cowgill, Rachael, Rachael, are you all right?' Miller hurried down the ward as soon as he heard the falling clip board and had seen Rachael slumped on the floor.

Rachael sat up a little way, her head swimming; her senses reeling with shock.

'What happened?' Miller demanded.

Rachael opened her mouth to reply, but although her lips moved, no words came out. Her eyes were wide, like a startled rabbit. She shook her head then tried again. 'That man . . .' She turned to the bed, where the tramp was watching her with mild curiosity.

Miller was angry. 'Did he upset you? What did he say? What did he do?'

'Nothing,' Rachael snapped impatiently — why didn't Miller go away?

'You say he did nothing, said nothing. So, what has upset you? Do you know him or something?' Miller persisted.

Rachael turned to the bed once more, her face transfigured by joy and wonder as she scrambled to her feet. She nodded in answer to Miller's question, while watching the tramp, whose puzzled face wore an expression of dawning recognition. The tramp lifted his free hand and held it out towards her. Rachael reached forward and grasped it in hers as tears began coursing down her cheeks.

'Who is this tramp?' Miller asked with an element of disdain in his tone.

Without even sparing the doctor a glance, Rachael replied witheringly, 'He is not a tramp! He is Captain Mark Albert Cowgill MC. He is a hero.' She glared at Miller and stated firmly, — 'But above all else: he is my husband.'

* * *

When Rachael had recovered sufficiently from the shock, Mark was moved to a private room. She tended his injuries, remembering as she saw the old scars, how she had nursed him back from the point of death, so long ago. Now she was faced with a different challenge, a new set of wounds, both physical and mental. She sent for the hospital barber who cut his hair and removed the remaining years of growth from his face.

Before she could consider taking him to Byland Crescent, she had to make sure that he was fit to leave hospital and make him presentable enough not to shock his mother, his sister and brother-in-law and, most important of all, his son. She did not know if her letters had reached him. Was he aware he even had a child?

There were many arrangements to be made, much sorting out to be done, but for the present these could wait. In the euphoria of Mark's return, Rachael was concerned only with getting him well, home, and keeping him safe. So much time had been lost to them that she wanted nothing to delay their being together.

Rachael decided against telling the family of her findings until she was sure Mark could cope, each day feeding him a little information about his past. For five days she fought to keep her precious secret until, having been reassured by the doctor that it was safe for him to be discharged, they left the hospital. The clothing she had managed to smuggle out of the house was far too big after his years of deprivation, so they set off to buy him some more suitable attire. She held his hand tightly all the way across town. She had only just found him again and Rachael was taking no chances.

For the tramp, a tramp no longer, the mists within his mind were beginning to lift. They did not roll back with the speed that the sea fret had dissipated, this was a gentler evaporation. As they were about to cross Castle Road he stopped quite suddenly and turned to her. 'Rachael.'

She was unsure from the way he said it whether it was a statement or a question. 'Yes, Mark?' she replied, with equal neutrality.

'You have another name.' This time it was definitely a statement.

'Graham? Cowgill?' she queried.

He shook his head, a frown of concentration on his face, which cleared to a smile of triumph as he remembered. 'Wife, that is it, wife,' he said. He pondered a little longer. 'My wife. Yes, of course, you're my wife.'

Rachael's smile broadened. 'That's right, my darling, and you are my husband.'

He blinked a little at this suggestion, thought the idea over for a second or two, then agreed. 'Yes, I suppose I must be.'

They discovered the joys of shopping together courtesy of an exclusive outfitter in the town. The sales assistant, a young man with a rather superior air, had grave reservations about serving the man of downbeat appearance, but Rachael's uniform and her positive, no-nonsense attitude swayed him. Once Mark had been dressed from head to foot, the assistant had eyed the discarded clothing with some contempt. 'What,' he enquired, 'would sir like me to do with these?' As he spoke, he gestured to the pile of clothes.

During the long dark time when Sonny had been on the road, he had suffered many humiliations, many indignities. Now he knew he did not have to put up with them any longer but was unsure what to do.

Rachael wasn't. She turned on the assistant, her eyes flashing with rage. 'It isn't *sir*, it's Captain to you. Captain Mark Cowgill MC, if you don't mind, or even if you do mind. Now, I suggest you take them and do what you will

324

or throw them away.' With that, she took Mark's arm and they turned to leave.

She was still reluctant to take him home, wanting him to herself a little longer. They found a small café and ordered tea. The waitress eyed the couple as she prepared their order. The tall, distinguished looking man was really something, she thought, some girls had all the luck. She saw Rachael reach across the table and take Mark's hand in hers. The waitress sighed, romantically.

'Mark, my darling, I promise I will take you home soon to see Mother and Connie and Michael, but first, I must ask, did you receive my letters?'

Mark shook his head. 'I don't know,' he replied.

Rachael smiled. 'Then I must tell you there is someone else at home for you to meet, someone you have never seen before. Mark, my darling Mark, we have a son. He is five years old.'

Mark stared at her. 'I, we, have a son?'

Rachael sat in silence watching his expression change as minutes passed while he struggled to understand.

Great chunks of memory came back to him. 'Chichester — and that pub with the funny name,' he murmured, remembering the inn where they had spent their honeymoon.

Rachael squealed with excitement. 'That's right, my love.'

He nodded. 'He was on the beach. I spoke to him,' he stated with conviction.

'He told us, and said you warned him to beware of the leg breaks. When he said that you'd called him Sonny it really got your mother spooked.'

'My mother was there?'

'Yes, and what made it worse for her was that when she looked round and you had vanished, she was convinced he had seen a ghost, the ghost of her father.'

'They used to call me Sonny, and my grandfather used to tease me with leg breaks,' he remarked.

'Yes, my dearest, but you have been missing for over four years.' She squeezed his hand.

'I didn't know where to go, who I was, I couldn't remember anything.'

'Darling' — Rachael leaned forward, and Mark knew she was going to ask him something terribly important — 'now that you are back with us, safe at last, please answer me one question. Just exactly what is a leg break?'

It was perhaps fortunate that they were the only customers in the café, for Mark's great guffaw of laughter would have terrified any of a nervous disposition. 'Ah, but you are a woman,' he told her condescendingly. 'You wouldn't understand.'

The words, the humour were so much the old Mark that at last, Rachael was finally convinced that despite all he had suffered, everything was going to be fine.

* * *

Later, much later that afternoon, the couple headed for the house. Rachael could feel the tension in Mark's grip as they walked, arm in arm across the town. They turned the last corner and Mark stopped suddenly.

'Of course, that explains it.'

Rachael followed his pointing finger as he indicated the sign for Byland Crescent.

'I don't understand. What do you mean?'

'I was looking for the people. The people who had been there in my memory. That was why I went to the abbey.'

'The abbey? What abbey?'

'This one!' He laughed and pointed at the sign again. 'This one, Byland Abbey.'

* * *

Rachael entered the sitting room where the rest of the family was gathered. 'Mother,' she began, 'Mother, Connie, Michael, I have a surprise for you, a wonderful, wonderful surprise. Please, don't be shocked. I've brought someone

326

home,' her voice quavered as she fought to hold back the tears.

Hannah rose to her feet, unsteadily. She knew in her heart something momentous was about to happen. Rachael opened the door wide and drew her husband into the room.

'Mother, I have brought Sonny home.'

Rachael turned to her son, standing motionless at his grandmother's side, clutching her skirts, as he stared wide-eyed at the stranger. She reached out her hand, calling him forward, and lowered herself to face him. 'Mark,' she said gently. 'This is your daddy.'

EPILOGUE

'This is a war to end all wars'
US President Woodrow Wilson

'We were preparing, not Peace only, but Eternal Peace'
**Harold Nicholson,
British delegate to the Paris Peace Conference, 1919**

'Yet when we achieved, and the new world dawned,
The old men came out again and took our victory
To remake it in the likeness of the former world they knew.
Youth could win, but had not learned to keep:
And was pitiably weak against age. We stammered
That we had worked for a new heaven and a new earth,
And they thanked us kindly and made their peace.'
**T. E. Lawrence
(Lawrence of Arabia) 1888–1935**

THE END

ACKNOWLEDGEMENTS

In any work of fiction there are many people who unknow-ingly contribute by a chance remark or, in this instance, knowing an historical fact. I especially want to thank Robin Coulthard and the North Eastern Railway Association, for searching their archives to enable me to portray the train journeys accurately.

My thanks to my reader, Wendy Warrington.

Thank you also to the real Patrick Finnegan and Steve Culleton, whose generous charitable donations gave me the opportunity to take theirs, and their families' names in vain.

To Val, for countless hours of hard work, trying to keep me in line, and all the brilliant team at Joffe Books

And to Mary Crocco, reviewer, and finally to all the Indie Brag team.

Thank you for reading this book.

If you enjoyed it please leave feedback on Amazon or Goodreads, and if there is anything we missed or you have a question about, then please get in touch. We appreciate you choosing our book.

Founded in 2014 in Shoreditch, London, we at Joffe Books pride ourselves on our history of innovative publishing. We were thrilled to be shortlisted for Independent Publisher of the Year at the British Book Awards.

www.joffebooks.com

We're very grateful to eagle-eyed readers who take the time to contact us. Please send any errors you find to corrections@joffebooks.com. We'll get them fixed ASAP.

Made in the USA
Coppell, TX
15 August 2022